THE GARDEN OF STONE HOUSES

Anya Pavelle

Chandra Press

ISBN-13: 9781949964370

Published by: Chandra Press
Cover design by: Anya Pavellle

CONTENTS

PROLOGUE: THE INITIATE

The Initiate card signals the beginning of a spiritual journey. Those who seek wisdom may be inexperienced, but they should still take a leap of faith. Such things require courage and trust in the universe, an admittedly difficult thing when initiates are still too innocent to learn the full measure of the world's savagery.

Selene

October 31, 1848, Faubourg Marigny, New Orleans

T he first time the spirits visited me at our little yellow Creole cottage was on an early autumn evening when the air was just beginning to crisp after a long, humid summer. Huddled in a dark corner of my room between my bed and the wall, I loomed over my cards and gazed upon the people painted on them. I was hosting a tea party for my doll, who was named Babette, and the illustrated guests on the cards.

Because my room was next to Maman's at the back of the house, I always settled myself far enough away from her room so I wouldn't hear the noises coming from within. Those disgusting grunts sounded exactly like the pigs over at the stockyard Maman and I passed on the way to the market. I also wanted to

1

be far away from the rancid smell of Monsieur Le Jaune's sweat as it mixed with my mother's lemon verbena perfume.

I was six, and Babette and the cards were my only friends aside from Tante Jeanne, who gave me lessons in reading, mathematics, and proper comportment some days. Not on days like when the spirits first appeared, though, because Maman wouldn't permit any visitors when M. Le Jaune was here. She confined me to my room on those days.

I was about to ask Babette if she wanted any tea when I saw two spirits saunter in through my closed window. My child's mind instantly understood they weren't human because the red evening sun shone right through them, almost giving them a pallor of translucent blood. The taller of the two wore a dapper black suit and matching top hat. My eyes fell to his bony hand, which clutched the ivory skull knob that sat atop his sleek walking stick. This spirit looked like walking death, but that didn't scare me. Half of his face was deep brown, and the other was bone white. Dark glasses concealed his eyes. If he had eyes at all, that was.

His skull-face broke into a teeth-and-mandible smile when I looked up at him and his shorter companion, a beautiful lady spirit who'd linked arms with him as if they were on a Sunday promenade. Elegantly arranged red, curly hair like Maman's towered atop her brown face. Her dress, a deep purple silky garment, wrapped around her body and flounced out just like Maman's. I stared at the dress covetously because Tante Jeanne said I was much too young for dresses fit for a queen. The lady spirit had accessorized her gown with a skull necklace and fingerbone barrettes that she'd laced through her hair. I could tell she was friendly, too, because of her sparkling green eyes. Peering back and forth between them and Babette, I quickly decided these visitors were far more interesting than Babette and the frozen smile someone had painted on her dainty, porcelain face.

Not wanting to offend these dignified entities, I stood and straightened my dress. "It's a pleasure to meet you. My name is Selene O'Neil," I said as I curtsied, something Tante Jeanne had taught me to do when introducing myself. "Could I offer you some tea?" I gestured to the two cups of pretend tea Babette and I had previously shared with the people on the cards. The poor vessels had cracks in them, which was the reason I was allowed to play with them at all, and I worried my meager offerings would offend these distinguished guests.

The male spirit laughed. "Oh, thank you, but we prefer rum or coffee."

"Baron!" The lady swatted her companion playfully on the arm. "Be polite to the young thing. You'll frighten her."

The man looked chagrined and removed his top hat, giving me a deep bow. "Je suis désolé."

"You don't need to apologize. I'm not afraid," I said. Indeed, this whole affair was curious and exciting. I longed for visitors on days when Maman confined me to my room. "I'm sorry I can't offer you some coffee or rum. My maman drinks those, but I have to stay here right now."

"Never mind the rum. I'm Maman Brigitte, and you can call me Brigitte," the lady replied. She then pointed to her companion. "And this is Baron Samedi, or simply Baron."

"I'm happy to make your acquaintance," I said.

Brigitte gave me a warm smile. "We know your papa. He's told us all about you."

"Papa!" I gasped.

Only faint images of him danced on the edges of my memory since his death years ago. When I caught the aroma of wood and lemons, memories of him would immediately transport me to him. His hazel eyes had matched my own, and I also inherited his tan skin, a relic of his Spanish heritage.

In addition to his blood, I'd inherited Papa's deck of cards. My mother had ordered me to protect this precious gift with my life, so I kept them in the drawer of my nightstand, a beautifully carved piece of furniture I also cherished because my father had made it long ago. The cards and nightstand were the only tangible things I had left of him.

Now, Maman had Monsieur Le Jaune instead. He'd edged into

Maman's life and taken care of her after Papa died. *Hate* is a strong word, but it sure fit how I felt about "*Oncle* Maurice," as he'd commanded me to call him. Even though he'd given me Babette, I couldn't muster up any gratitude in my cautious, spiteful heart. For not only was Oncle Maurice not my papa, but he also loathed me.

Maman didn't see the poison darting from Oncle Maurice's eyes when he handed me little presents. I suppose she felt indebted to him because, in addition to letting us live in this cottage, he gave us money for food, clothing, and my lessons. I didn't know how she tolerated Oncle's presence. She used to look at Papa with such love, something she never did with Oncle. After all, from the unpleasant noises that emerged from her bedroom during Oncle's visits, I knew she paid a price for all of his *gifts*. I once asked her why we stayed in New Orleans. She said we had no support system in the country, and Maman's family in Ireland was dead. In sum, she stayed with Monsieur Le Jaune simply because he kept us alive.

"Don't be alarmed," Baron said kindly.

"But I'm *not*," I insisted, giving him a curious look. "I just don't understand. How do you know him? He's dead! Is it because you're ghosts?"

"We work with your papa," Brigitte explained. "And we're not ghosts. We're *loas*. Spirits. We help people when they ask."

"That's true, my beautiful Brigitte! But you're not telling her all of it." Baron laughed and slapped his knee before bowing again to me. "Selene, your papa also worked with us before he died. As can you, if you wish."

"Yes! Please! Can you help me talk to Papa, too?" I blurted out, sounding like the impulsive child Oncle Maurice said I was. *Don't be improper,* I chastised myself. *Be polite to your guests, and remember what Tante Jeanne told you about minding your manners.* Blushing, I curtsied and let my eyes fall to the floor. "Please forgive my outburst, but I would like to work with you very much. And could you please tell me how I can talk to my papa?"

"Why do you think we're here?" As Brigitte twisted her

necklace, I realized she and Baron had become more solid since they'd materialized. More *real.* So much so, they even cast shadows on the floor now.

"How can I talk to him? Can I see him, too?" My voice came much louder than I'd intended.

"Shh, child, shh. Whisper, or *he'll* hear you," Baron cautioned, bringing his bony fingers, quite literally speaking, to the side of his face that had lips of flesh. "I'm not talking about your papa, but the man next door."

"Oncle Maurice?" I asked in a hushed voice. I certainly didn't want him to come in here.

"Yes, him," Baron said, giving me a knowing look.

I nodded and lowered my voice to a whisper. "How can I see my father?"

"You can see him when you're older. When you can visit him on your own." The beautiful lady pointed to my cards. "Until then, use those to talk to him."

Perplexed, I knelt and skimmed through the pile of cards, scrutinizing them for clues on how they could help me speak to Papa. Someone had painted a lush carpet of gold stars and crosses atop a purple background on one side. Not seeing a way to communicate with the dead, I flipped the pile over and studied the cards featuring people. I usually spoke to them, of course, when offering them tea, but they'd never said a word back. Finally, I turned to the cards with varying numbers of swords, cups, sticks, or star-covered disks on them. I used these cards to practice my arithmetic. I didn't understand how I could use them to contact my dead father, though. I let out a frustrated breath and looked at Brigitte. "How does it work?"

The beautiful spirit let go of Baron's arm and sashayed over to me. She drew her skirt under her and sat down. "It's simple," she explained. "Before you try, spend time with every card until you know all their meanings. Trust your instincts. After you understand the significance of each, organize the cards in a deck. The purple background side stays up. Then, ask your papa a question out loud, shuffle the cards, and turn them over one at a time until you have your answer, be it one card or ten."

I stared in wonder and doubt. "That'll work? They've never spoken to me before."

"So you think," said Baron, twirling his walking stick. "But your connection to those cards is what summoned us here in the first place. And with practice, you'll become stronger."

I stood and clapped my hands in delight. "So *that's* how you got here."

Baron nodded. "Well, that, and your papa asked us to come. We said we would if we felt invited by you."

Smiling down at the cards, I absorbed this news. "And I can see Papa when I'm older?"

"Yes," Brigitte assured me. "Until then, we'll keep you company. If you need us at a specific moment, call us with a glass of water and maybe a bit of Oncle Maurice's tobacco. But only if you can take some without being seen. You should also first leave something small for Papa Alegba. Like chocolate or a shiny penny, for example. Ask him to open the door, and then call us through. We can come without him, of course, but it's more polite to ask his permission."

"Who's Papa Alegba?" I asked, wondering where I'd get gifts for him and these spirits. Maman didn't give me chocolate too often because she said it would ruin my teeth, and I was too young to carry money. I also didn't dare steal tobacco from M. Le Jaune.

"The Gatekeeper," Baron said. Probably sensing my limited access to gifts, he added, "If you can't find chocolate or a penny for him, find a discarded gift on the street or sing him a song. He'll take any gift that comes from your heart."

I beamed at this news. To my six-year-old mind, this made sense. Places like houses, gardens, or courtyards had gates and doors, and sometimes you needed certain keys to get them open. I could find the proper keys I needed if I used my heart and wits. "Where do you live?" I asked, curious about their home. "Behind Papa Alegba's gate?"

"Yes, behind a gate of sorts. The gate to the garden of stone houses," Brigitte replied. "It is a lively place with many parties. Your papa often comes."

The garden of stone houses. The only gardens with stone houses were the many gated cities for the dead that dotted New Orleans. This information confused me, though. Maman had told me Papa lived in Heaven. "He doesn't live in Heaven?" I asked.

Maman Brigitte came over and touched my arm, which felt like a butterfly's kiss. "He does, of course. We all do. But when we come to visit Earth, we stay in our garden."

I nodded slowly. These spirits and my papa went on holiday together, it seemed. "Which garden?"

Baron stroked the skull knob of his walking stick. "We are in all of them, child. Every single one."

As my eyes absorbed every detail of these lively spirits, a deep longing filled my lonely little heart. Their holiday home sounded much better than my small, dark bedroom that smelled of mold and the pungent roses from the walled garden outside.

"Can I come with you?" I pleaded.

Baron sighed and moved to Brigitte's side. "Not yet, child. There'll be plenty of time for that when you're older."

Older. When, exactly, was older? It seemed too far away for my taste, but I wasn't about to be rude to my guests and demand to come with them now. "I understand. And thank you." I curtseyed again. "I promise to keep your visit a secret."

Brigitte smiled at Baron. "See? She's a smart one. Just like her father said." She then turned to me. "You must be brave until you can visit your papa in the garden of stone houses. He also wants you to promise you won't get angry at your maman."

At six years old, I didn't feel brave. I couldn't protect Maman from M. Le Jaune and, sometimes, didn't have the will to endure my endless days in this moldy house. Oncle Maurice made me and Maman suffer in silence, and as a result, my frustration often manifested as anger toward Maman for not fighting him. Because these spirits requested I behave, though, I promised to obey them and, if needed, bury my anger and sadness deep in a place where it couldn't hurt me. "I promise," I said.

"Then it's time for us to go," Baron said, craning his neck to look outside the window. "Stay in this room until that dreadful man leaves."

"I always do," I replied. They needn't have told me. Although my mother rarely spanked me, she would certainly do it if I left my room before Oncle Maurice departed.

I wanted to be a good girl, not because Maman or Tante Jeanne told me to, but because I sensed these spirits expected it of me. So, I spent the rest of that evening studying the cards and arriving at my own interpretations of each until Maman's bedroom door creaked open and Oncle's heavy footsteps thumped across the parlor floor. I loved how his steps got quieter and quieter until he reached the door that led from the parlor to the street. He wouldn't return for the evening once he left.

Knowing Maman would fetch me as soon as she scrubbed all traces of Monsieur away in a bath, I picked up the cards and returned them to their home in the nightstand.

At first, I worried I'd never see the spirits again. My childhood echoed with loneliness, and their company had shined a bright light into my solitary world. Thankfully, though, they appeared again three nights later. We spoke of my progress in understanding the cards during that visit. I welcomed the spirits in through my window again nine nights after that. I grew to trust them, especially after I made contact with my father through the cards.

Throughout my childhood, the spirits came every three or nine days, numbers Baron Samedi and Maman Brigitte liked. They also came when I summoned them for advice or solace. When I felt assured the spirits would stay with me forever, I surrendered Babette to a little street urchin.

CHAPTER ONE:
THE MAGE

When the Mage appears in a tarot reading, you have the strength to begin your journey. Seek the Dagda if you need wisdom for navigating the world of magic. He's Father God and one of the kings of the Tuatha De Danaan, a godly race of folk who lived in Ireland before the arrival of humans. He is a powerful Druid who uses the magic of the trees for his ends. Although the Tuatha De Danaan now live in the hidden cairns and barrows of the earth, sometimes they call to the children of Eire, who now make that sacred land their home.

Selene

*October 20, 1860, Faubourg
Marigny, New Orleans*

Since the spirits first arrived, I judged the benevolence of each year by the amount of death it brought the city in the form of yellow fever. The year 1853 was especially horrible with over seven thousand succumbing to the disease. In 1858, too, nearly five thousand perished. Like the boat pilots on the Mississippi who marked the river's depth with their sticks, I gauged my luck based on the purported dangers that lurked beneath the surface of things.

Little of our alleged fortunes had changed since the spirits visited me. Maman and I still resided in the same cottage with its four small rooms and deceptively quaint facade. Behind the twin French doors that met the sidewalk, death, rather than love, shrouded us in its beautiful gloom.

In the soft, dulcet voice she used when fantasizing about death, my mother often told me the story of Tristan and Isolde, a popular tale from her native Ireland. Isolde was the beautiful daughter of an Irish king who promised her hand in marriage to King Mark of Cornwall. King Mark sent his nephew, Tristan, across the sea to collect Isolde and bring her to her new home. On the way, Tristan and Isolde fell in love. And like so many other tales of star-crossed lovers, they died in the end. Maman insisted the tale contained a lesson, though, a beautiful kernel of truth that sustained those anxious to join their loved ones in the great beyond. She told me that a briar sprung up from Tristan's grave, and a rosebush grew from Isolde's. Over time, these plants intertwined their limbs, even growing back when King Mark ordered them destroyed.

Maman reverently concluded this tale with the old adage: *Love endures death, and an early death is a blessing if your loved one lives on the other side.* I couldn't argue away that truth. Papa had told me from the spirit world that he yearned for Maman with every particle of his ghostly body, and I knew, deep in my heart, Maman's love for him blazed as brightly as Isolde's did for Tristan. Why else would she whisper this story to me nearly every night before bed? Still, I sometimes wondered how Maman tolerated Oncle Maurice touching her if she missed Papa so much. Survival? There had to be something else.

"Selene, take a deep breath," Tante Jeanne commanded, pulling me back to my minute bedroom, which had dingy walls and small windows that creaked in protest when I opened them on stuffy New Orleans days when the air weighed as much as a bucket of water.

We stood in front of my battered full-length mirror, where I saw Tante poised like a gargoyle behind me. Protective, stoic, and grim, she looked just like the stone guardians that hovered over Paris from their perches on Notre Dame de Paris. I'd never traveled there, of course, but Oncle Maurice once showed us Paris's famous monuments, including that cathedral, through his stereoscope. Maman had gasped in surprise as Oncle's expensive machine unfurled the distant city before her eyes, but I remained wary, peeking through his deception but not immersing myself in it. The loas had warned me to avoid Monsieur Le Jaune whenever I could. Maman didn't question this arrangement so long as I acted superficially polite to him.

My otherworldly friends also told me that the law of reciprocity ruled both the physical and spiritual worlds. No one should expect something for nothing, for that expectation always leads to ruin. In return for the spirits' council and protection, I gave them respect, my devotion, and small gifts—a fair exchange that mirrored the material world's dynamic. *Take comfort. The universe will balance itself*, they whispered to me from the ether. Those words alleviated some worries, for they assured me Maman would one day find joy for all she endured at Oncle's hand.

Because I cared for Tante Jeanne, and to give myself some much-needed air, I obeyed her by taking a breath and straightening my spine. I usually helped Maman into her corset, so I knew how the blasted contraptions stole a woman's breath. Accordingly, my poor ribs constricted as Tante drew together the strings of my new corset as tightly as her diminutive arms could.

Ace of Pentacles, I thought. *It's important to keep an open mind and take one step at a time, cautiously, into whatever new venture comes your way. Good things will come, but don't be foolhardy by jumping into an unfamiliar situation. Instead, build a solid foundation slowly and surely.*

Papa had instructed me to think about building such a foundation that morning through the cards, and he hadn't steered me wrong yet. Every morning before my chores, I asked him for advice through a beautiful ritual requiring a small glass of water for Alegba, a bit of seed for Maman Brigitte's birds, and a dash of tobacco for Baron, all of which I placed beneath the live oak tree in our garden. Then, I called my father through the gate and selected a card to guide me through the day. He whispered to me when the wind rustled through the oak's Spanish moss.

Maman knew of my covert exploits, of course. She told me to make sure the gifts were hidden behind the tree or covered with dirt or leaves lest Monsieur Le Jaune find them. She, too, left little bowls of milk for the fairies just as she'd done back in Ireland, as well as offerings for her own saints. In that habit, at least, Maman and I mirrored each other.

Tante studied her handiwork in the mirror and frowned, an expression that had etched itself on her face ever since my body began to sprout and bloom. "Tiny waists are en vogue, and you certainly have one," she said in her melodious French accent.

For some reason, she sounded sad, as if she disapproved of what she saw. Looking into the mirror, I couldn't see anything displeasing. I'd inherited my heart-shaped face from Maman, and Papa gave me his hazel eyes, dark curly hair, and olive skin.

Still, I didn't know the reason behind Tante's efforts. Maman had never suggested that young men would come courting. Why would they court a girl with no social standing or money of her own? Not that I wanted or needed such a thing. Thanks to Tante Jeanne's thorough educational agenda, I could read and write in English, French, Spanish, Latin, and Greek. I also excelled in mathematics. Even though she'd adeptly prepared me for work as a teacher or governess, respectable occupations that would allow me to support myself and Maman, Tante Jeanne found increasingly arcane subjects to teach during our lessons. I didn't mind my teacher's continued visits. I welcomed any company to the cottage save for M. Le Jaune's.

Tante Jeanne next helped me step into my crinoline and a petticoat before she slipped a violet silk dress over my head. As she buttoned the back, I arranged the dress over the hoop-shaped petticoat so it hung evenly. Then, and only then, did I notice the bodice hung low on my décolletage and left my collar bone and the top of my shoulders fully exposed. Perhaps *that* rather grown-up aspect of the dress had prompted Tante's grimace of disapproval.

"Why did Oncle get me a new dress? And a silk one at that?" I asked, tracing my fingers over its unfamiliar cuts and becoming increasingly uncomfortable with the way I looked in it. I loved the color because purple was Maman Brigitte's favorite color. She said wearing it made her feel like an empress of the dead, which was true enough. But the silk fabric was far too grand for me when it came from the man who tormented my mother. Usually, I alternated between my three simple calico day dresses, only purchasing a new one when I outgrew the others or they frayed beyond repair. I couldn't imagine wearing something this fancy to conduct mundane errands, visit the cemetery, or call on my bosom friend, Patrice, who'd admittedly loved this costume. M. Le Jaune purchased Maman new clothes, an act entirely for his benefit, of course, and spent money on me begrudgingly at best. So, why this exquisite dress?

Tante tutted and kissed me on the head carefully so she wouldn't disturb the soft curls she'd artfully arranged. "You're going to accompany your maman and Monsieur Le Jaune to Etoile for tea today. He thought you should have something special for the occasion."

"What?" I pulled away from Tante Jeanne and gaped at her. Her answer made no sense. Etoile was Oncle Maurice's proper home. He came here to see Maman because of Madame Le Jaune, his wife. "So, Madame is gone?"

"No, Selene," Tante replied, guiding me to the bed. She sat me down across from her and nestled my hands in her trembling ones. "Madame will be there. She's asked for you and your maman to come."

"Why in heaven did she do that?" I asked, incredulous. Although Maman and Tante sheltered me from many sordid details, I knew the reality of our situation. Maman wasn't married to Oncle Maurice, but she behaved with him as a married woman would. Tante's news that Madame Le Jaune expected us at her home puzzled me, for it meant Oncle Maurice's wife not only knew about Maman, but also me. Wealthy men with social capital conducted their private business with discretion. Only stupid men flaunted their indiscretions in their wives' faces. For that reason, I couldn't imagine why Mme. Le Jaune would invite us into her home unless she wished to berate us. *No one* bought someone a new silk dress to berate them.

"Mon petite, you'll need to ask your maman." Tante gently brushed tears from her eyes.

Nothing about this day made any sense, and the Ace of Pentacles was usually such an auspicious card. "A new venture on the horizon," I said my father's words out loud.

Tante blanched. "A new venture of sorts. I'll fetch your maman for you," she said, before dashing through the door that led to Maman's room and shutting it behind her.

Although Tante Jeanne hadn't meant to, she'd left me alone with my uncertainty and a rising sense of panic. Something was wrong. Very wrong. Dumbfounded, I gazed out my window and into the walled garden with the beautiful live oak tree that gave me a shady reading spot and sheltered my spirit friends' gifts. I needed to speak with Papa at the garden of stone houses, a place where he could materialize right in front of me. For some reason, I could only speak to him at the cottage, not see him. As soon as I grew old enough to attend to errands on my own, I began scavenging gifts from the streets of the French section of the city, sometimes with Patrice. I brought these little tokens for my spirit friends to their garden and talked to Papa among the beautiful crumbling tombs.

How I loved that secluded, peaceful city for those in eternal slumber, with its high walls and snaking vegetation. I loved scampering down the narrow avenues and admiring the polished marble facades of the wealthier tombs as the silent legions of angels stood guard. However, nothing lasts forever. Eventually, these stately homes decayed, exposing their humble brick cores to the world. In the oldest of tombs, I sometimes caught a glimpse of ancient bones, almost as if I were peeking at something forbidden, like a shy lady's face beneath her mourning veil. The houses of the dead also had gifts deposited at their doorsteps by ladies wearing lace gloves or, other times, by gentlemen whose many duels had earned them gunpowder-tinged hands. Of course, I also saw the customary cigars, coins, and offerings of rum for the Ghede, the rowdy bunch of spirits that lived with Baron and Maman Brigitte. People from all walks of life bargained with the dead in the cemetery, perhaps one of the most egalitarian places in New Orleans.

Suddenly, Tante Jeanne let out a cry in Maman's room, so I stood up awkwardly in my new ensemble and put my ear to the thin door. I didn't regret eavesdropping—not when some horrible matter plagued Tante Jeanne. The spirits had also taught me the concept of necessity compels. In matters of great importance, we must do what we must even if it violates a social norm.

"Quelle horreur, Colleen," Tante Jeanne whispered fiercely. "Are you considering this proposition for her? It's hardly in her best interest!"

Tante always has been my resourceful defender. Although Oncle did compensate Tante Jeanne for all she did, I knew she considered me and Maman to be her family. Still, my tante was an enigma. She lived in a convent as a laywoman, working as a beekeeper and teacher at the convent school. Her only friends were Maman, me, and her bees, who spoke to her as my spirits did to me. When I asked why she practically sequestered herself away in the convent, she said she wanted peace from the world and its evils.

Her response puzzled me, for women with her countenance often married well. Although in her late thirties, she was still a beautiful woman, what with her silken blonde hair and large green eyes. But just like on Maman's, the specter of sadness always haunted her face. Both women looked as if they couldn't bear that their happy memories were but only memories. Maman's look of eternal mourning told me how much she truly missed Papa, even if she buried this sadness in her heart when around Oncle Maurice.

"Selene just has to say yes for today," Maman replied in her lilting Irish brogue, a feature that came out when she was alone with me or Tante Jeanne. "It's only temporary."

I drew in a sharp breath. I had, inexplicably, some important role in today's visit to Etoile, but not enough information to understand the implications of *saying yes*. I pressed my ear closer to the door and heard Tante Jeanne's next words, which rang both plaintive and angry. "To go back there will be torture for you. How will you bear it? With another bottle?"

"Yes, another bottle if I wa—," Maman's voice broke. "If I *need*. If I don't bring Selene, you know what that bastard threatens to do."

Another bottle. Lately, I'd been finding far too many empty bottles of *Dr. Prinson's Curative Elixir* hidden under her bed. When she finished one, her face glowed from the elixir's main ingredient, laudanum. *That* part of this mysterious conversation made sense, but not the others. How would a visit to Etoile torture Maman? I couldn't imagine she'd ever been there, not with Madame Le Jaune in residence. Most alarmingly, someone had threatened Maman if she didn't bring me to Etoile. That alone boiled my blood.

"Colleen, you have choices," Tante insisted. "You were once a lady's maid."

"I'm ruined as a lady's maid. That old toad won't give me a reference," Maman replied.

"Well, then, Selene is old enough to work as a teacher or governess. Both of you must leave. Go North. You know I can arrange that," Tante said. "Find Selene a husband far from here. No one will find out her secret."

Tante's words only confused me all the more. We couldn't leave New Orleans. Far from the garden of stone houses, I didn't know if I'd be able to communicate with Papa and the spirits. I also couldn't abandon Patrice. And... find me a husband? That prospect made me shudder so hard my skeleton shook. Unlike most girls my age, I had absolutely no interest in men.

The room started spinning, so I quietly slid to the floor in a puddle of silk. As the daughter of a dead man and a kept woman, I had no marriage prospects in polite society. This mysterious trip to Etoile couldn't be that type of social call. I didn't want to leave the city, but if this venture was heinous enough to make Tante cry, then perhaps I should entertain the thought. I'd brave anything to secure Maman's freedom if Patrice could accompany us. But, most alarmingly, what secret did Tante Jeanne know that I didn't? I softly rested my ear back against the door and prayed to hear an answer to that ominous question.

Maman stayed silent for a second that dragged on and on. Finally, she spoke. "No, Selene wouldn't be inclined to marry. And what about when she has children? The *risk* of it."

"Colleen, every path has its risks," Tante warned. "But you've chosen the hardest path of them all."

Soon, Maman began crying. Tante joined in, both of them forming a dissonant chorus of sorrow. The muffled sobs sounded like those of a wife who knew her husband visited women like my very own Maman. Or, more appropriately for my mother's circumstances, the tears were from someone with her heart in the grave and a secret too horrible to bear alone.

Maman sniffed. "Be that as it may, I need to fulfill my promise to my saint. Until then, we have to stay here."

"Even at Selene's expense?" Jeanne asked.

"Certainly not." Maman cleared her throat. "Maurice only *thinks* he controls me with Selene's secret. I'll send her away with you if need be. I promised David I'd keep her safe."

David was Papa's name. Maman promised she'd keep me safe? From what, exactly? More perplexing still, what was this secret she withheld from me? Was it something Oncle Maurice knew? Inside my new dress, I boiled and seethed, and not from the weather. M. Le Jaune had no right to my secrets, especially ones my mother concealed from me.

"David would be against this," Tante replied.

"Not necessarily. Remember, he said he understood me accepting M. Le Jaune's offer in the letter I found after his death," Maman said, her voice hollow.

"We do need more time to execute our plan," Tante Jeanne admitted with defeat. "But we shouldn't sacrifice Selene for our plans."

Maman began quietly crying again. "Of course not! I'll tell Selene she must accept the offer for today just to buy us time. Time to get our justice."

"It might be revenge, not justice, that you truly seek," Tante suggested gently.

Justice. That was a lofty concept I didn't often see materialize in the world. In a just world, Maman wouldn't surrender her body to M. Le Jaune, and this country wouldn't condone slavery. No, New Orleans lacked the type of justice I thought fair. What brand of justice did my mother seek? What type of vengeance, for that matter? Only the buzz and hum of insects outside filled Maman's long silence. Eventually, she sighed. "For me, revenge and justice are the same thing. We must have faith, Jeanne. My reward for all this sacrifice isn't far away. I'm sure of that."

Little of this exchange made any sense to me. I knew Maman hated Oncle Maurice at the heart of things, that she tolerated him because he supported us. Somehow, too, I had a pivotal role in Tante Jeanne and Maman's plans. Me, the girl whom Oncle Maurice hated enough to buy a new purple dress for a mysterious social call to his mansion, where his wife and mistress would have to meet face to face. Papa said to not rush into new ventures without creating a foundation, but my mother had thrust me into this venture without giving me the information I needed. Although I wanted to ask Papa for more advice, I heard Maman and Tante Jeanne resume their conversation through the door.

"You need to prepare Selene for today," Tante said. "She deserves as much."

"I'll tell her to accept the young Monsieur's offer today alone," Maman vowed again. "The rest, I'll explain tonight. There's not enough time for it all now."

"Oui, oui, I know. You should go see if she's ready. The carriage will be here soon," Tante Jeanne replied. Her words rang ominously in my ears.

Who in the world was this *young monsieur* I'd be meeting? I didn't want Maman to know I'd been listening, so I crept slowly across my room to my bed, hoping the creaky wooden floor wouldn't give me away. Then again, did it matter if Maman heard me? I had no reason to feel guilty—not when she harbored secrets I had every right to know.

***

The streets of New Orleans looked much different when viewed from the elevated vantage point of a carriage, especially the fancy one Oncle Maurice sent to ferry us from our home on Elysian Fields Avenue to Etoile, his estate on the outskirts of the city. Living away from the city center gave him a respite from the congestion and noxious smells New Orleans had to offer. It was autumn, but the unseasonably hot sun steamed the moist horse shit that littered the ground, permeating the air with its putridity.

We sped past the brick and plaster homes of the French section with their intricately carved wire gates, balconies, and galleries, and my nervous heart beat in time with the pace set by the horse's hooves as they struck the cobblestone-paved street.

Maman fanned herself with a decaying lace fan. That particular day, the heat flushed her cheeks with color, an eerie accompaniment to her intoxicated smile. Another bottle of magical elixir indeed. "Selene, please make sure your bonnet is covering your face. The sun is strong today." She said *today* in a formal tone, sans the remnants of the brogue she adopted when in M. Le Jaune's company.

Oncle Maurice nodded. He had light gray eyes, the color of a newly minted corpse. "We don't want you getting dark. You might as well use that bonnet. It cost me a pretty penny."

He and Maman sat huddled together, quite disgustingly I might add, across from me in the carriage. If he was so worried about my skin, he should have brought his covered carriage rather than this open-air contraption. Gritting my teeth,

I reached up and yanked the purple lace veil over my forehead, grateful that it at least obscured some of him. And Maman... at least the lace curtain between me and the world partially hid her drugged smile, courtesy of the laudanum, and simpering manner when she spoke to Oncle or endured his caresses. At least she'd kept her promise to Tante and assured me that I just had to accept any offer for today. And no matter how unsavory the offer, I needn't follow through. Maman's assurance on that front had abated my worry enough to get me into the cursed buggy. To my consternation, however, she hadn't explained her reasoning. Nor had she even given me a hint.

"Even girls in my circumstances?" I asked with a smile fixed on my partially obscured face. Left with no other option, I'd goad Maman into telling me the secrets she hid.

She froze in horror as a happy smile erupted on Oncle's face. "So, you've finally told her?" he asked. "I anticipate she'll be much more receptive to today's offer. As she ought to be."

Maman's fan dropped to the carriage's floor, and she quickly worked to regain her composure. "Selene and I haven't had the chance to talk. All she knows is that we're going to Etoile to accept a generous offer."

"A pity you weren't more explicit about where she comes from. She thinks much too highly of herself. I might have bought her a dress fit for an empress, but that doesn't mean she's not as common as a street urchin," he said to Maman while giving me a scornful look.

Although Monsieur's slights about my parentage should have offended me, I barely registered his contempt. In fact, my heart warmed at the mention of an empress. Maman Brigitte felt like an empress in a purple dress, so I knew my spirit friends were with me in that carriage thanks to M. Le Jaune's use of words. They made their presence known through signs and enjoyed doing little things to influence Monsieur. For example, he sometimes purchased Baron Samedi's favorite tobacco instead of his preferred brand and left it at the cottage after imposing himself upon Maman. I then gifted Baron with this tobacco.

More to the point, little did Oncle Maurice know that sometimes common women ended up as true empresses. Empress Theodora of Constantinople, wife to the Emperor Justinian, came to mind. She began life as a circus dancer who disrobed for money and became a woman of great prestige thanks to her intellect and beauty. I certainly didn't have the political clout of a queen, but I did have loas at my side. I let out a breath and reminded myself they would protect me.

With my narrowed eyes, I sent Monsieur Le Jaune all my loathing through the pinprick holes of my veil. He was a proud man, perhaps fifty years old, and he had light brown hair. He wore a top hat, suit, brocade vest, and elegant cravat, but his florid cheeks contrasted horribly with his otherwise wan complexion. His face, consequently, bore the look of permanent anger.

The difference between Oncle and Maman struck me hard. Maman wore her emerald green dress, a color that accented her copper hair and green eyes. I thought her achingly beautiful but in a fragile, ethereal way. Even though her face had turned paler and more drawn these past few months, Maman glowed from within like a fairy, not like someone who belonged to this Earth. Perhaps her sheer rarity compelled M. Le Jaune to keep her dressed in cheap finery and under his alleged control. He saw Maman's superficial parts, but my eyes probed deeper.

Fatigue, resignation, and menace leaked through the chinks in her armor, something apparent to those who looked closely enough to see it. Maman exuded anguish, and I certainly didn't want her to sacrifice herself for justice or vengeance.

By eavesdropping on Maman's and Tante's conversation, I'd learned their plans involved a promise to one of Maman's saints. Perhaps I should trust that Maman had divine protection, too. "Please tell me what this is about," I begged.

Maman shifted her gaze from me to the gutter detritus that passed in a blur. "After refreshments with Madame Le Jaune, you'll meet her and Monsieur's son, Raoul. He'll make you an offer," she announced in a monotone voice. "He's a gentleman, so I expect you to act like the lady Tante Jeanne taught you to be."

Oncle grabbed Maman's arm tighter to him. "I should hope so. Her lessons certainly cost me enough."

An offer? The only type of offer young men such as Raoul made to girls like me was for plaçage, but I couldn't imagine my mother would ask me to accept such conditions, not even to help her in her mission. No, she had likely arranged for me to tutor their son. Monsieur and Madame Le Jaune had probably spoiled the boy instead of instilling in him a solid work ethic. They likely expected me to fix their mistakes and have him magically absorb the heap of knowledge every young gentleman should possess. Before I could inquire further about this mysterious offer, the driver wretched the carriage sharply to the right and halted it. M. Le Jaune spun around to face the driver. "You almost killed us!" he yelled.

Maman and I shrunk back in our seats, frozen. So much hate echoed through the streets of this otherwise beautiful city, corrupting every nook and cranny. As much as I loved being close to my spirit friends and Patrice, this city ran on the blood and sweat of the abused.

"I'm sorry; there was a dog in the road," the man said quickly.

"I don't care!" Monsieur shouted back. His enraged expression intensified with the volume of his voice. "Ridiculous!"

Maman quickly regained her composure. She stroked M. Le Jaune's arm and forced a tight smile to her face. "Maurice, please. There's no harm done."

M. Le Jaune snapped back around and grabbed Maman's wrist. "Don't you interfere in my affairs. Remember what happens when you take initiative."

Maman's eyes widened, and for a split second, I got a glimpse of the hate that burned within them. She fluttered her lashes, which immediately set her mask back in place. "Maurice, please, let it be."

"I'll deal with my slaves how I see fit. It's not a woman's business." He pushed her hands away and turned to the driver. "Carry on. It's hot today, and we're expected at Etoile."

The reins cracked near the horse's back. As the carriage lurched forward, Maman and I dared not even move. Stillness can be beautiful, even stoic, because women have learned to forge inaction into a powerful weapon, sometimes the only refuge we have. With this depressing worldview in mind, I thought back to my Ace of Pentacles. It generally forecasted something auspicious for the patient among us, but all I felt then was unadulterated dread. Maman was hiding some important secret, making it impossible for me to lay a solid foundation for this seemingly inauspicious venture.

CHAPTER TWO: THE HIGH PRIESTESS

Ayizan, a very old loa, was the first mambo, or priestess, of Voodoo. You may honor her with palm fronds, holy water, or holy oil. She'll initiate you into the world of mysteries and is a helpful loa. Draw the High Priestess card, and you'll enter a world of mystery, inner wisdom, and spiritual enlightenment.

Selene

October 20, 1860, Etoile,
New Orleans

F or the remainder of the trip to Etoile, the lace gloves Oncle Maurice had demanded I wear hid my clenched hands and the callouses I had earned scrubbing floors. Maman slept most afternoons as of late, so I did the cleaning.

As we sped through New Orleans' streets toward the city's edge, the smell of rotting vegetables and baking excrement gradually lessened. The streets also widened, and live oaks stretched their tangles of spidery arms over the road in a shady, protective canopy away from the bustle of New Orleans. I loved how, as we became closer to nature, the air turned sweet, laden with the aroma of the fresh grass and the wildflowers that dotted the roadside. I closed my eyes and summoned the sound of my father's voice, which resonated as deeply as those of the day laborers who soothed themselves with their songs.

Thinking of him gave me the strength I needed for this unknown venture. The sharp movement of the carriage turning woke me from my meditation. When I opened my eyes, I saw the driver had turned onto a semicircular avenue that had an entrance and an exit onto the street. A large house sat at the exact center point of the avenue. A skull-jarring gaudiness assaulted my senses when Oncle's unfortunate driver screeched the carriage to a halt in front of Etoile's front door. A riotous explosion of azaleas formed a blockade around the mansion's entrance. The white Greek Revival house was two stories tall and accented with dark green shutters and monolithic white columns like those on the most ostentatious of tombs. When I gazed up at the mansion, the entire facade pressed down upon me, a feeling augmented by the whimsical flotilla of Spanish moss that hovered in the noon sky.

"Splendid, is it not, Selene?" M. Le Jaune asked as he helped Maman out of the carriage. He did the same for me, and I held in my revulsion as my hand touched his disgustingly moist one.

"It's a formidable structure," I managed.

Releasing my hand, he looked at me in surprise. "An accurate observation. One couldn't accuse you of being obtuse. I suppose your lessons were worth the investment."

Flatter him, Selene, a spirit whispered. *Flatter him and his son for now. It will serve a greater purpose.* I couldn't tell if the voice was Papa's, Baron's, or Brigitte's. Not that it mattered. The message came through strongly in my heart, so I heeded that advice and gave Oncle Maurice a little bow. "Tante Jeanne is a wonderful teacher."

"We're very grateful for Selene's education," Maman added.

Oncle Maurice rested a hand on the small of her back. "As you should be."

To my delight, Maman visibly cringed at his touch. "You should go first," she suggested. "Followed by Selene and me."

M. Le Jaune laughed and thrust himself ahead of us. "How

25

right you are. Otherwise, Madame might throw the refreshments she's so laboriously had the slave prepare right in your pretty face."

I trailed behind him into the foyer, which had marble flooring and boasted an elaborately carved banister that ran the length of the grand staircase. We continued into the parlor, a room with pink and gold brocade wallpaper, matching drapes, gold-accented furniture, and an armada of ornate knickknacks covering the side tables and the mantel of the fireplace. A woman with golden hair and bedecked in a pink dress sat on a green settee, a fixture that offered my eyes a blessed reprieve from the room's damnable amount of pink. This woman, probably none other than Madame Le Jaune, rested her book on the coffee table and patted the empty seat cushion. "Selene, join me," she commanded as she avoided looking at my mother. "And remove your veil so I can see your face."

A pity. I had so enjoyed having a shield, even a lace one, between me and this world. I pushed back the veil, and my eyes flitted back and forth between Maman and Madame. I drew in a breath, praying neither woman would explode. Something told me the slightest deviation from today's agenda would propel Mme. Le Jaune into a hysterical state, so I obeyed her. Part of me wanted to see the woman's fragile exterior crumble into dust. How delicious it would be. And how awkward for the rest of us in the stuffy parlor. My more practical side didn't want to expend the energy soothing a woman who probably kept a vial of smelling salts tucked firmly in her cleavage for the emergency du jour. I had more important things to spend my mental energy on.

Although the settee had little room to spare courtesy of her enormous hoop skirt, I somehow negotiated my body, which moved in direct opposition to the crinoline, into a seated position without too much fuss. "Thank you," I said with pursed lips.

Through the spectacles perched on her nose, Madame appraised me as one does a colt. Her golden eyes narrowed as she studied me. "Please help yourself to some café au lait and a beignet," she said, gesturing to some fluffy pastries and cups of coffee on the table in front of the settee.

Even though I didn't want to take anything from this woman, for it would obligate me to her, I smiled as sweetly as the sugar she'd just forced upon me. "I'd be delighted to have just one."

"Quite wise," Mme. Le Jaune agreed with a satisfied nod. "You mustn't let too much sugar ruin your teeth or figure."

Ruin my teeth or figure? Those were words my maman or Tante Jeanne would say. Not this... *stranger*. My eyebrows raised, I looked to Maman for help. She and Oncle Maurice had positioned themselves as far from one another as they could, on chairs at opposite ends of the room. Quite rightly, they didn't want to flaunt their relationship right in front of Madame Le Jaune. But despite Maman and Oncle's efforts, Mme. Le Jaune's displeasure lingered around us like a waft of magnolia blooms slamming into my face with hurricane force. To distract myself, I gingerly nibbled the beignet and sipped the nauseatingly sweet coffee. "How delicious," I said between bites of beignet that clung to my teeth.

"Amelie, where is Raoul?" M. Le Jaune asked. The tail end of his question held the hint of a groan.

"I told him to wait in the library while I had a word with Selene." Madame straightened on the settee and pivoted her head toward Maman, the first time she'd acknowledged her presence. "Why does the poor dear look so confused?"

"Selene knows she's here to meet Raoul," Maman replied, ignoring Madame's accusatory tone.

Madame Le Jaune shot Maman a withering look. "*Meet* Raoul? That's all you said? Will she be amenable? I won't have her reject my son's offer. As if it were even her place to do so."

Tired of this endless speculation, I rested my coffee cup in its saucer, sending the sound of porcelain striking porcelain ringing through the air. "I'd like to know the purpose of this visit, please. You'll find I'm able to speak for myself."

"It's quite simple," Madame said, her lips curling into a patronizing smile. "Raoul needs a companion. My *husband* believes you'll do." As a slight to Maman, she emphasized the word husband with particular gravitas.

Companion. A terrible word for women in Maman's position, for the company she kept was unwelcome at best. I held a sliver of hope M. Le Jaune the younger simply needed a scholarly companion, and although I dreaded learning the truth, I kept my voice as pleasant as a spring zephyr. "Companion?"

"Raoul will be married next month." The glow of contempt in her eyes, Mme. Le Jaune glanced at her husband. "However, it's a business arrangement as these things so often are. You'll be a pleasant diversion for our son. He only feels a forced congeniality for his fiancée."

Pleasant diversion my foot! Batting my eyelashes, I sipped more coffee, careful not to let it drip from my trembling lips and onto my new dress. I needed more time to formulate an answer to the day's contemptible business. Maman had said to accept the offer for today, and the spirits wanted me to flatter the Le Jaunes for some reason. I ignored the flood of terror that set my heart galloping and met Madame's gaze. "Me? But why? I'm hardly anyone special."

Madame's pinched expression eased. "I'm happy you understand how fortunate you are, considering the circumstances of your birth."

"Because I'm poor and my dead father was Spanish instead of French?" I asked before taking another bite of pastry. As the fluffy beignet dissolved in my mouth, I prayed Madame wouldn't remind me that my mother's status of *whore* also tainted my prospects in polite society. Not that I cared about what the stuffy people who ruled this city would deign to grant me.

"Spanish?" Madame let out a dainty gasp and stared at Maman. "I can't believe you've been so secretive."

Maman avoided Madame's gaze by studying the marble fireplace with great intensity. "Well, in essence, she's correct."

Mme. Le Jaune's brows knit together. "Colleen, you've always had a problem with the truth, and it made you a disaster of a lady's maid."

Lady's maid. I knew Maman had worked as a domestic back in Ireland, but I hadn't known she worked in service here in America, too. My mother always deflected my questions about her early life in this country, and I hadn't prodded further out of fear she'd drown her painful memories in an extra bottle of laudanum.

Madame Le Jaune had just, oddly enough, given me a precious fragment of knowledge about my mother's past. Madame's harsh condemnation of my mother's domestic skills meant only one thing. Maman had worked in service under Mme. Le Jaune, perhaps here at Etoile, which made Oncle Maurice's wife the mysterious "Old Toad" who had refused to give Maman a reference. That revelation led to only more questions, such as how my father figured into the Le Jaunes's world. My mind spun out of control, but I kept my eyes firmly anchored on Maman. She had subtle tics that betrayed her moods. Now, her jaw clenched in such a way that I knew she'd soon erupt. All the laudanum in the world couldn't keep her anger at bay when it boiled over.

"Amelie, please retract your fangs," Oncle Maurice said as he jumped up from his seat and rested his hand on his wife's shoulder. He narrowed his eyes at me. "You're amenable to meeting Raoul, are you not, Selene?"

Flatter him, the spirits repeated. Because I trusted their counsel, I contrived some ladylike nonsense perfect for Monsieur's ears. "My mother and I are grateful for your patronage," I said. "I would very much like to meet your son."

"Very good. I should go find Raoul," Oncle Maurice volunteered.

"Do," Madame Le Jaune said. As her husband all but sprinted from the room, Madame sighed deeply and gave me a conspiratorial grin. "Men can be silly creatures. *Impractical.* My husband was determined to formalize this arrangement at your mother's home, and while that's how these things are conventionally done, I wanted to meet you first."

I returned Madame's insult with a tight smile. In that parlor, we three ladies formed an awkward triumvirate to rival that of Julius Caesar, Pompey, and Crassus. The little sounds of Madame's crinoline scratching against her skirt as she constantly adjusted it and Maman's teeth grinding echoed throughout the parlor. I, meanwhile, finished my beignet and was tempted to have another to make Madame fear for my teeth. Before I could indulge in that impulse, though, Oncle returned with a man of perhaps twenty in tow. This young man had light brown hair and ruddy cheeks like his father, but he stood taller and had a more dignified bearing than the elder Le Jaune. Although he wasn't unpleasant looking, he leached apathy and arrogance.

Raoul's gray eyes lit up as he approached the settee. "Selene! Enchante."

Channeling Brigitte's coquettish humor, I forced a blush to my cheeks, stood, and held out my right hand. "The pleasure is all mine, Monsieur."

"Please accompany me outside," he said, kissing my hand. "I'll show you our beautiful gardens."

With all of New Orleans's parks, gardens, and cemeteries, I didn't suffer for want of a stroll, but I stood and linked my arm in his. "As long as there's shade, I'll be delighted," I replied. Little did this pompous fool know, I'd storm right past Cerberus simply to escape the parlor. M. Le Jaune joined his wife on the settee and lit a cigar. He blew out a puff of smoke that curled around his and Madame's heads, much like the wispy hand of a ghost reaching out from the grave. Soon, the parlor would have the stink of a dank gambling palace, so I gladly left Raoul's parents in that little hell. I didn't even care that Maman had to stay with them. She'd brought me here, sacrificing me on the altar of her mission, so she could very well endure the Le Jaunes' company while I fended off Raoul's ambitions.

With a solid grip on my arm, Raoul whisked me out the house's back entrance. A garden that spanned my entire field of vision greeted us in all its blooming glory. The sickly sweet ambrosia of flowers hung like fog around me. Unfortunately, beauty usually works best in controlled doses, not as a military-sized gathering of avant-garde soldiers.

My eyes skipped across myriad beds of bloodred roses and scarlet amaryllis until they settled on an old woman who tilled the soil with a small spade. This woman was crouched so that her feet partially blocked our path through the garden. "Excuse me, ma'am," I said, not wanting to startle the lady as I walked around her.

"I'm sor—," she sputtered out before she locked eyes with me and broke into a wide smile. "Are you Selene?"

I'd never met this woman, yet she knew my name. Her face, too, looked eerily familiar. She was around fifty years old. Her brown eyes sparkled with recognition, and what I suspected were unshed tears. I knelt so I could study her face more closely. "I am," I replied. "Have we met?"

"Why the devil are you kneeling in the dirt?" Raoul asked, snarling. He hoisted me up by the wrist and clenched me with enough force to leave a bruise. Rage contorted his formerly gen-teel features, reminding me of Monsieur Le Jaune's anger against his driver. Raoul had his father's temperament burning in his heart. He also believed his given entitlements to be as natural as the setting sun.

"So sorry. I wasn't thinking clearly." I relaxed my arm, afraid to shake it out of his grasp. As much as I wanted to challenge Raoul, I had to keep my wits. I'd find out who the older woman was later. Giving the lady a wink, I fanned my face with my un-encumbered hand and faced Raoul. "Could we perhaps find some shade?"

At these words, the fury on Raoul's face melted away. "Of course. How inconsiderate of me," he said as he maneuvered me down the garden path to a shady bench that rested under an oak tree. "Please, sit."

"Thank you," I said. Raoul finally released my hand, so I sat down and smoothed my skirt, which he had wrinkled when yanking me up.

Raoul slid onto the bench. "You've been told of my family's offer?"

"Yes, and I'm amenable to it," I said. I cast my eyes to the ground, where a swarm of fire ants was devouring a dead caterpillar.

"Of course, you're amenable," he said, tittering as if I'd made a witty joke. His eyes roamed over my body before anchoring on my décolletage. "I'll find you a new home—a little nest. After all, you can't continue living with your mother."

Privacy with Raoul. Maman had ordered me to accept this offer just for today— something I'd do. But even the knowledge I wouldn't have to meet with Raoul didn't ease the nausea building inside me. I cringed as I pictured his hot body dripping sweat onto my skin. If he had his way, he'd trap me under him in a humid, musty room without a cross-breeze to offer relief. I'd have only the sounds of his grunting to occupy me, pure misery unless my spirit friends released me. My mind easily conjured this vision, for I had listened to my mother live through that nightmare every week of my life.

My throat tightened. "Why *me*?" I asked, careful not to let my voice crack. That question vexed me. I couldn't see my mother offering me up even to help further her mysterious plans, and because Oncle Maurice hated me, it made no sense to pair me with his son. And as for Raoul or Madame, how did they even know I existed? I was missing something important. I frowned and met Raoul's eyes. "Pardon me for saying this, but surely you have many other women you could choose."

"Of course I do," Raoul admitted with a chuckle. "But you were bred for this, non?"

Too often, society forces the sins of parents onto their children. I didn't approve of my mother's means of supporting us, but never before today had her *occupation*... for lack of a better word, impacted my future so directly. It made sense to Raoul that the daughter of a whore would become one likewise. If we followed that logic, Raoul was predestined to become a horrible person, a badge of honor his father had pinned to his silk vest. I slid the hand closest to Raoul under my skirt so it wouldn't fly up and slap him across his face. Determined to steer the conversation to one less precarious, I asked, "And you find your fiancée displeasing?"

Raoul slouched back on the bench with a dramatic sigh, drumming his fingers on his knee. "She's plain and inspires no passion."

"Then why marry her?" I asked.

"Because of her large dowry," Raoul said. His jaw tightened. "You mustn't tell my father I told you, but he needs Vivienne's dowry to pay off his debts and shore up our reserves. He's fond of the roulette table."

I'd wondered what dirty family business had forced Raoul to accept an arranged marriage. So—Monsieur Le Jaune, the cocky bastard who flaunted his alleged wealth every chance he got, was a degenerate gambler. I kept that little morsel of knowledge close to my heart, protected by my silk bodice and confining corset. Perhaps I'd find a use for the information one day. Secrets such as that lay waiting to be exploited. "Does Vivienne's family know?" I asked. Something told me they didn't. Wealthy people worked to preserve their wealth, not throw it into the gambling den.

"I won't worry about that," Raoul said. "They're being compensated. My father's mother's family comes from a line of counts, you see. Vivienne's parents want their daughter to marry someone with an aristocratic pedigree. She was engaged before me, but her father insisted she marry me instead."

"I see," I replied. At a loss for what to say next, I stared at the three buildings across from the garden. The smallest one was a stable. As an exporter of fine furniture, M. Le Jaune also had a workshop and a storage building for items awaiting export. Unlike the mansion, those structures didn't have the luxury of shade. The day's waves of heat undulated toward the buildings, cresting and smashing into them. On warm days, the Le Jaunes took refuge in breezy, shady spaces and sipped drinks. Their poor slaves, however, had no escape from the sweltering heat. I couldn't see the furniture carvers, but the pounding of their hammers and the swishing sound of their saws echoed off the Mississippi River. Those sounds pierced through me, triggering a stab of agony that flooded my eyes.

As I wiped away tears, my eyes flitted back to the stable. Something horrible had happened in that building. I had enough contact with the spirit world to sense the stable was haunted, but I didn't know *what* had attached itself to the structure. This entire estate had insidious roots, ones deftly concealed by layers of finery. The beautiful red flowers grew in soil tilled by slaves, their bones likely unceremoniously plopped in the dirt not too far away upon death. Madame's pink parlor and its many accoutrements belied the family's debts, too. If anyone scraped away the surface of this place, they'd find a ton of rot waiting for them.

"You needn't worry about Vivienne," Raoul said, probably interpreting my silence as worry over his fiancée. "If she found out, though, she'd bear it. These arrangements are to be expected."

I felt a rush of pity for Raoul's fiancée. Not only had her father broken her first engagement, but he'd also yoked her to Raoul, someone who actively worked to betray her before the wedding. "I understand," I said, my eyes still scaling Etoile's grounds.

Raoul grabbed my hand and stroked it. "You should smile."

Because he expected it, I forced the corners of my lips nearly up to my ears. I didn't want Raoul to see the distaste in my eyes, so I focused on the tree above us and silently asked my spirit friends for guidance. A beautiful glass prism the size of a peach pit hung on one of the low branches. I hadn't seen it at first because the tree's voluminous Spanish moss sheltered the crystal from the late afternoon sun. At another time of day, it would cast fragments of rainbows at my feet. Rainbows were usually little slices of joy and merriment, but not today.

I didn't understand why I had to subject myself to this man. What greater purpose could it possibly serve?

This is your chance to free her, the tree whispered. I stiffened, turning to Raoul, who, by all appearances, hadn't heard the live oak speak. The spirit world had answers for people willing to listen and think. Some people ignored blatant signs from the other side, and others assigned meaning to every tweet of a bird or sway of a tree branch in a strong wind. I certainly understood this tree's message. The spirits were telling me that by enduring Raoul's company, I'd have the opportunity to free Maman from Oncle Maurice's clutches. Perhaps I had a role in her plans, too.

"Maman had the prism put there for a garden party," Raoul said. He reached into his jacket pocket and pulled out a small purse. "Buy yourself one. And some books to keep you occupied while waiting for me. In the meantime, I'll begin looking for your new home. The French section would be best. It's close to my favorite gambling palaces—not that I gamble like my father, mind you."

Raoul's face hardened with those last words. Monsieur Le Jaune expected Maman to lift his bad mood du jour, and I searched my mind for how to do likewise for Raoul. He didn't want my real opinion, just my praise for his gentlemanly benevolence. A compliment about his offer should satisfy him. The French section of New Orleans had its benefits. Namely, its proximity to both Maman and Faubourg Treme, where Patrice lived. "That sounds wonderful, Raoul," I said.

He leaned closer to me. "May I kiss you?"

Maman hadn't told me to expect a kiss today, but I nodded and shut my eyes, hoping he'd mistake my aversion for him as shyness. His lips were somehow cool and lizard-like in the day's heat. Unable to control myself, I jerked back when Raoul's lips hit mine.

"What's the matter with you?" he demanded.

"I've never kissed a man," I said, praying he'd accept my excuse. It was true, after all. Fighting nausea, I held my breath.

Raoul inched closer to me and stroked my cheek. At first, he kept his eyes locked on mine, but then he broke into a wide grin. "Don't be afraid. We'll progress slowly." And before I could thank him profusely for that blessing, he stood and held out his hand. "Let's rejoin the others in the parlor. Best we get back before my mother kills yours."

"It would be a pity to have your mother's parlor stained with blood," I said.

Raoul laughed. "Reupholstering the settee would be a frightful expense."

I almost uttered the words *an impossibility courtesy of your father's gambling debts* but stopped myself. I doubted Raoul's wit at the expense of his family extended that far.

He escorted me back inside, where, as I had predicted, cigar smoke blanketed the room in a thick fog. Monsieur and Madame Le Jaune were sitting together on the settee, and poor Maman still studied the marble fireplace with such concentration one would think she planned to carve a replica.

"You've settled upon things?" M. Le Jaune asked. Never in my life had I seen tension so clearly etched on someone's face.

"Selene will make an agreeable companion," Raoul said as he deposited me next to Maman.

Madame Le Jaune gave her husband a sidelong glance. "At least our son will have *some* pleasure."

Thanks to Raoul's confession, I understood the true scope of Madame's anger. She loathed her husband not only for his unfaithfulness but also for his gambling habits. Madame had hinted her own marriage was one of convenience, and although she didn't want to see Raoul unhappy with Vivienne, she sanctioned the marriage because it would help her maintain her lifestyle. I still didn't know why she thought I was the best plaything for her son, though. Little did she know, I had no intention of fulfilling that role. Weary from the day's events, I caught my mother's attention and motioned to the door with my eyes.

"As grateful as we are for your hospitality, Selene looks piqued," Maman said as she stood. "I think we should go home to rest."

"It's this unseasonable weather," I added, grateful for that blessing. Women could blame all sorts of flighty behavior on the weather.

"Indeed," Oncle Maurice said. He sprung up from the settee with the vigor of a much younger man. "I'll have the driver take you home."

After Raoul gave me a parting kiss on the cheek, M. Le Jaune escorted me and Maman to the carriage. To my great relief, he didn't get in with us. Maman owed me an explanation for the day's events, and I didn't want to wait until we got home to pry it out of her stingy heart. The driver had no reason to report our secrets back to the cruel M. Le Jaune. The only problem was that Maman ignored me, staring at the world as it sped by with a laudanum-induced vacant look on her face.

I nudged her leg with my shoe. "Why'd I just promise that fool I'd become his mistress? And what are these plans you and Tante Jeanne have?"

Despite my caustic tone, Maman smirked. "So, you *were* listening."

"Of course I was. None of this makes sense." I yanked off my bonnet and threw it on the carriage floor, an action that collapsed the veil into a beautiful pile of crushed lace. "Papa would hate that you brought me here just like he hates that you're with Monsieur."

Maman flinched and picked up the bonnet. She smoothed the lace, pressing it as if her actions could remove every crease. "Don't be silly. You know nothing about your father."

"I do," I argued back. "He smelled like lemons and wood. He also loves you more than anything."

Maman stopped her hopeless ministrations of the veil and glared at me. "Those are things I've told you. You can't know anything about him. Not when he died before you were born."

The grand edifices and twisted iron balconies of New Orleans spun around me, so I leaned back against the carriage seat. Papa died before I was born? Maman had always said he died when I was young, and that was that. When I pressed for details, she ignored me or repeated the story of Tristan and Isolde.

I never prodded further; asking questions would send her

straight to another laudanum bottle. I knew that truth from experience. Children with volatile parents learn quickly when to ask questions and when to tread on eggshells. I had memories of him and Maman together, so either she was lying, or my connection with the spirit world had given me visions of their time together in life—ones I'd mistaken for memories. Those potential explanations competed for the title of *truth*. But my mind couldn't settle on the truth. Not when I didn't trust Maman. To compound my misery, Raoul's coins clinked together in my purse in time with the horse's canter. His family earned its money on the backs of slaves. Unless I bought gifts for my spirit friends or Papa, anything I purchased with his money would be tainted. I vowed to extract the truth, the mysterious circumstances of my birth that no one dared to mention, from someone living in the spirit world.

Maman couldn't stop me. As the carriage slowed in front of our house, I leaped out and stomped through the cottage until I reached my bedroom. I couldn't wait to rip the purple dress off and, if needed, shred it into ribbons.

Maman trailed behind me, her green dress fluttering like an exotic species of butterfly. "Calm yourself," she said.

"Calm myself?" I asked, spinning around to confront her. "Not until I'm out of this dress! I'll rip it off if necessary."

Maman shook her head and motioned for me to turn around. She fumbled with the buttons, eventually managing to free me from the dress and damned corset. With a gleeful smile, I kicked the heap of silk and strings across the room. Maman sighed and picked it up while I slid on a calico day dress. As I stared at my reflection in the cracked mirror, I fully realized that blood tainted everything in this house except for the cards and nightstand I'd inherited from Papa. My face, which had burned crimson with righteous anger since I fled the carriage, drained of color. "Everything in this house is poison," I said.

"Bringing you to Etoile was a mistake." Maman came closer and gently folded me into her arms. "You and Jeanne should leave tomorrow. I'll stay and finish what I need to do."

I pulled back and desperately searched Maman's face for clues. "What are you planning? Please, just tell me."

"I can't," Maman whispered. She sat on my bed, rested her elbows on her knees, and covered her face with her hands. "I'm afraid you'll be ashamed."

"Of you?" I asked, taking a tentative step toward her.

"No, not of me," Maman replied. "I don't want you to be ashamed of your father."

Her admission confused me all the more. "Ashamed of *him*? Why would you ever think that? Are *you* ashamed of him?"

"Never in my life have I been ashamed of him." Maman threw down her hands and held my gaze, her eyes flashing with a rare passion. "I lost almost everything when he died. You're the only thing left."

With her words, I had confirmation of how much she still loved Papa. But why put on such a grand charade to hide her secrets, ones she couldn't reveal even to me for some godforsaken reason? "Maman, please tell me what's wrong," I begged.

"I can't. I don't know where to start," she said.

I straightened my spine and held my head high. I'd ask the spirits for the truth in her stead. "Fine. Then I'll find out myself. I need to speak with Patrice."

CHAPTER THREE:
THE EMPRESS

When the Empress appears, maternal energies surround you. Erzulie Dantor is a loa who defends mothers and children with the tenacity of a tiger and the precision of a spear. She also offers help in new business ventures. You may honor her with garments of red, Florida water, herb-infused red wine, and roasted pork. A sister to Erzulie Freda, Erzulie Dantor bears the scars of her fights. Don't doubt her capabilities in this arena.

Selene

October 20, 1860, Faubourg
Treme, New Orleans

J ust like Maman, I kept my precious secrets hidden. Only one living person aside from my mother knew of my conversations with the dead. That person was my bosom friend, Patrice, who resided in a place infused with the scents of cinnamon and sage.

Through the front window of a small mercantile on Treme Street that belonged to Patrice's family, I saw my friend standing behind the counter and straightening the creases on a bolt of cloth. My heart beat faster at the sight of her. Patrice's light blue dress hugged her slim form, and the matching kerchief arranged

THE GARDEN OF STONE HOUSES

artfully on her head balanced the ensemble beautifully. Her ebony skin glowed with hints of burnished copper in the store's light. My eyes traced over her high cheekbones, which were as beautiful as a grand cathedral's vaults.

It wasn't just Patrice's beauty I found enchanting. She had the most bewitching mind. Patrice studied the heavens with her telescope and mathematics, filling notebooks with equations I'd never seen in my studies with Tante Jeanne. Patrice especially loved infinitesimal calculus and owned books by Sir Isaac Newton and Gottfried Leibniz. Although the writings of these great thinkers flummoxed me, I could sit for hours and watch Patrice write, her eyes aglow with passion. It took all my strength to cross the store's threshold, knowing I'd have to tell Patrice about the day's events.

When I stepped inside, my friend's eyes darted up from her work. A delighted smile spread across her face. "Chérie," she said. "To what do I owe the honor of this visit?"

Honor? No, I'd seen none of that today. The empty store offered us privacy, but I wasn't brave enough to tell the person I held dearest the truth. I wanted to bury the day's ghastly events in the past and forget them. "Maman had me meet her patron's son for an arrangement, and she's keeping secrets from me," I confessed, wincing.

Patrice slowly, and with great care, rested a bolt of silk on the counter. "Did this man take your rejection well?" Her question challenged me to answer otherwise, daring me to even *suggest* I'd become like my mother, mistress to a loathsome man.

The grandfather clock chimed seven, and each ding thundered through the store. When the last bell's ring faded, I stepped forward and embraced my friend, a gesture she returned heartily. She soon pulled back and held me at arm's length. With her penetrating gaze, she searched my face for an explanation. "Surely, you refused," she said.

My tears blurred Patrice's face, a blessing because I couldn't bear to see an ounce of condemnation in her eyes. "Maman made me accept just for the day. She said someone threatened to do something terrible if I didn't," I rambled. "But then she said she'd send me up North with Tante Jeanne. She insists on staying here to complete some secret. I only pretended to accept Raoul's offer because the spirits told me to flatter him."

My words sprung from me in a torrent, and a messy one at that. I preferred to keep my life tidy, but Maman always managed to spin my days with chaos. My heart raced as I awaited Patrice's response. As someone who knew of my conversations with the dead, she understood the world of spirits. Would my otherworldly friends' apparent endorsement of Maman's mad plan soothe Patrice's ire? Her bosom rose as she took a long sip of air. I held my breath, simply waiting. Then Patrice grabbed my wrist and held it fast. "You belong to me, not this Raoul. M. Le Jaune essentially killed your maman. I won't let that bastard's son hurt you. If you can help your maman without letting that happen, I'll allow it."

"I promise." I exhaled in relief and met her dark eyes, drowning in their beauty. They glowed fiercely in contrast to her stony expression.

Patrice released my wrist. "Then, I'll tolerate this for now. What in heaven are your maman's plans?"

"She wouldn't say, so I'll just have to ask the spirits and Papa." I held up my purse and jingled it. "I'm going to use the young monsieur's blood money to finance a party. Perhaps some chocolate, fine rum, and Cuban cigars."

Patrice's family, unfortunately, understood blood money well enough. Her father had been a slave here in New Orleans until he'd earned enough money from extra carpentry work to purchase his freedom. He then married Patrice's mother, a woman of Wampanoag and English heritage. Madame Du Bois's family had a small store, and she and her husband had purchased it from her parents and renamed it Du Bois Mercantile.

Patrice arrived soon after. Like me, she moved in concert with the spirits. Just like my maman, she also had an ancestor who had been persecuted as a witch. Patrice's ancestor, a woman named Bess, came from a village in Massachusetts called Salem. Bess fled the village when the leaders launched a reign of terror called the witch trials. Bess found refuge with the Wampanoag, and her descendants hid their powers under the night's shadow until they moved to New Orleans. This city was steeped in centuries' worth of magic, so people batted not an eye at otherworldly phenomena. Patrice studied with Marie Laveau and walked with pure magic sparkling around her in a cloud. I'd known it ever since I stumbled into her family's store five years ago with a shopping list and a pocket full of M. Le Jaune's blood money. An immediate kinship formed between us.

Patrice laughed. "I can think of no better use for that money."

Relieved that the tension between us had dissolved, I pulled Patrice into the back storeroom, where only the sacks of oats and barrels of wine would witness what I had planned. "It's you I should be feasting with," I said, before smashing my lips against hers.

She returned my kiss with relish, and I savored simply being with her for a minute. Her moist breath caressed my cheek as she gently drew back. "Another time, mon amour. You have important business tonight."

My all-consuming love for Patrice fastened my feet to the mercantile floor. My true relationship with her was my most cherished of secrets, one neither Maman nor Tante Jeanne knew. I feared they'd be horrified. The world, too, would condemn me and Patrice on many counts. Only the spirits and the dead knew about our love, and they were perfect secret-keepers. I kissed Patrice once more. "You're right."

"Remember your promise," she said as she released me. "Ask the spirits for their help."

Patrice's simultaneous counsel and warning rang in my ears as I blew her a kiss and shifted my attention back to the outside world—that dirty and corrupt place. Despite her grudging acceptance of my situation, Patrice's worries lingered in my mind. All her life, she had seen women crushed by powerful men, their eyes deadened just like Maman's. Patrice had developed a strong armor as protection against the world. Her protective shell, as well as her natural tendency to avoid trouble, kept my love safe.

By the time I left the mercantile, daylight's pulse had slowed, and lamplighters sparked the street's gas lamps one by one like firefly soldiers welded to their stations. Early evening was apace. As I headed toward my favorite cemetery in the old French section, I perceived an uptick in night business. Ladies of the night stood on the street corners while their pimps hid in the shadowy alleyways. The quickening dark also provided a cover for more benign activities, such as lovers meeting in secret, wives dashing to sewing circles, and the faithful preparing for ceremonies with the spirits.

In that beautiful darkness, which blanketed the city in a soft cocoon, it took me but twenty minutes to walk to the nearest garden of stone houses. I passed through the gate and continued down the city of the dead's narrow lanes. So far, the place was absent of the living. The soft scent of lichens and a hint of decaying plant matter waltzed on the soft breeze. Little pieces of brick, mortar fragments, and other detritus from crumbling tombs crunched beneath my feet. When I reached an intersection, I gently placed a piece of chocolate for Alegba at the crossroad and asked him to please open the gate for the Ghede to pass through.

Before long, I sensed the universe cracking open. A subtle shift in air pressure and a buzzing about my ears told me so. My spirit friends awaited their gifts. I found the closest tomb with a cross perched upon it and lit the cigar for Baron before spilling some rum on the ground for Maman Brigitte.

As the spirits entered this world of bones and blood, the air around me crackled with energy. Soon, the moonlight reflected off Baron's ghostly glasses, and Brigitte's skirt flounced along with the moths that danced on the air. These loas usually materialized in front of me, but tonight, they watched from the shadows. They knew I wanted to speak with Papa first and foremost.

Next, the night air whispered on my skin, the most accurate

words to describe the feeling of a beloved family member returning from the dead. Some people fear cemeteries and ghosts, but I felt absolute peace as the symphony of the night's insects enveloped me, much like a lullaby. Then, as the moon rose higher, the mist gathered in front of me, gradually coalescing into a humanoid form. Papa's form, though at first hazy, slowly became more concrete as it emerged from the night. Although he didn't have flesh, the fire of his spirit burned as brightly as a living human's heart. Seeing him after that day's foul events made me dissolve into frustrated tears. In response, he reached out to touch my face with his ghostly fingers, which felt like a butterfly wing's caress. "Mon petit, you shouldn't yell at your maman," he chided gently. "She's doing what she must."

Of course, he knew I'd fought with Maman. He knew everything about me, including Patrice's and my relationship. I wiped my eyes with my sleeve and inhaled a few deep breaths of that humid night's soothing cemetery air. "I'll do my best," I said. "I'm assuming you know she made me meet M. Le Jaune's little despot of a son?"

He laughed at my slur for Raoul for a second before turning serious. "I do."

"You'd condemn me to that fate for the sake of Maman's plans?" I asked.

"No. I'd prefer that you leave with Tante Jeanne and Patrice," Papa replied. "But *if* you decide to help your maman, I promise you'll both succeed before you have to do anything unsavory with that *little despot.* He has an important role, you know."

I doubted Raoul could help me, but satisfied for the moment, I nodded. "I see. Please tell me what I need to know, though."

Papa gestured for me to sit at the base of the tomb. "To understand your maman's plans, you need to see her story. From the beginning."

All I knew of Maman's early life was that she immigrated to New Orleans, met my father, and most of her family had died in the terrible famine that followed the potato blight. Thanks to today's fiasco at Etoile, too, I now knew she'd once worked as a lady's maid for Mme. Le Jaune. Papa offered me that which I coveted—the chance to know my mother as anything other than M. Le Jaune's mistress. Sweeping aside some graveyard rubble, I adjusted my skirt under me and leaned back against a cool marble tombstone that glowed blue in the moonlight. "I'd like that very much."

Papa's eyes grew sad as he took his place next to me. Ghosts didn't need to sit, of course, but he likely mimicked the living to keep me at ease. "Very well," he said. "But remember to have sympathy for your dear Maman. I'm the one who failed her. Not the other way around as she thinks."

***

Colleen

June 30, 1841, Port of New Orleans

It was the sea, not the seed, nineteen-year-old Colleen O'Neil thought with profound relief as her nausea abated. Mercifully, the boat had stopped lurching as soon as it entered the Mississippi River and left the Gulf of Mexico behind. Colleen fought against that unrelenting queasiness for weeks. Her misery robbed her of sleep and the desire to eat. Only St. Brigid, a fierce lady with bright red hair who visited Colleen in her dreams, had offered consolation when she managed to drift off to sleep in her dark, stifling bunk in the bowels of the ship.

However, that stomach-lurching sickness beleaguered her no longer, a great relief because it meant she didn't have Lord Ashington's bastard anchored in her womb. Colleen leaned over the side of the ship and gazed at the muddy expanse before her. Ribbons of water moved in sinuous bands thanks to the strong current, and Colleen was grateful she could see land on both sides of the river. After the endless weeks at sea, she welcomed dry land even if it meant beginning her work as an indentured servant.

This flat, hot, new world didn't have her beloved County

Mayo's emerald hills stretching across the horizon. Unfortunately, too, the humid air glued her dress right to her skin, drenching her as if she'd just emerged from a bath. The odor heaving through the air was odd, too. This place smelled faintly of the swamp, like something just beginning to decay.

Colleen had often fantasized about such a smell wafting off Lord Ashington. That would make him dead, and she, vanquished for what he'd done to her. Only, her former employer wasn't *really* dead. Just thousands of blessed miles away. Colleen also appreciated how this country didn't have English lords who ruled with an iron fist. America had done away with all that during the Revolution. Hoping for a new beginning, Colleen mentally recited the advertisement that had brought her here. *Elegant Lady in New Orleans, Louisiana seeks lady's maid of the highest caliber. Knowledge of fashion and etiquette essential. French not immediately required but must be learned. Must provide references. Passage to be paid in exchange for four years of service.*

"We should be arriving soon, Señorita," said a man behind her.

Startled, Colleen whipped around and smiled politely when she saw the familiar raven-haired deckhand she'd spoken with a few times on the journey. She loved his Spanish accent, which sounded much more melodious than her Irish one. He was also handsome, but Colleen had certainly had enough of all that. "Do I have time to make myself presentable?" she asked.

"Si," he replied, giving her a small bow. "Although not much is needed on that count."

A compliment as grand as that would've made Colleen giddy under most circumstances, but not after what she'd endured under Lord Ashington. In her employer's presence, Colleen's porcelain skin, curly red hair, and bright emerald eyes became a curse instead of the blessing most people assumed. She smiled politely. "How kind. I should get ready for disembarkation."

Before the Spaniard could protest, Colleen strode across the deck and through the dank corridors of the packet ship's underbelly. She inched through the inky darkness, toward the steerage compartment she shared with nearly thirty people. In steerage, captains usually crammed as many people as possible into a single room filled with tiny bunks and filth, but Colleen and the other passengers had gotten lucky on this voyage. The captain had filled half of the steerage bunks with sacks of letters and missives instead of impoverished passengers. Some of the mail had been offloaded in Cuba and replaced with cigars and casks of potent rum that made Colleen's quarters smell like a spicy distillery. Not that she could complain. Steerage usually smelled foul enough to kill a stallion.

By the time Colleen reached her compartment, her eyes had adjusted enough to see ten people queued up for their turn at the makeshift bathing station near the cookstove. The packet ship's captain insisted that everyone on the ship wash once a week in seawater to help keep away disease. To that end, he equipped each passenger with their own bucket and kept a ready supply of seawater in steerage. Colleen smiled when she saw that Ulrika, the German woman she'd befriended on the voyage, had strung up an old sheet from a beam on the ceiling to offer bathers a measure of privacy.

Colleen welcomed the chance to freshen up. She believed in cleanliness and looking polished whenever possible, especially since as soon as she disembarked, she'd have to transform herself from an Irish slut to a lady's maid fit for Madame Le Jaune, the wife of her bondsman. Hoping to make a respectable impression, Colleen retrieved her bucket and the dress she'd stowed in her threadbare carpetbag before joining the end of the queue. She didn't have to wait long for her chance to make herself presentable. After Colleen stepped behind the curtain, she let her worn clothes slide to the floor and scooped a bucket of seawater from the large barrel. She wanted to linger at the bathing station, to drag the wet rag across her bare skin again and again until she erased her tainted past, but other passengers deserved their turn.

Colleen finished quickly and slipped into the new dress, a well-darned pair of stockings, and her scuffed boots. New on the outside, tattered on the inside. That was how she'd present herself to her new employers.

As Colleen emerged from the bathing area, Ulrika appraised her new clothes. "You look lovely. So fine!"

Colleen gave Ulrika a shy smile. She'd always loved reading about the dresses created by Paris's most prestigious fashion houses. Her old mistress, Lady Ashington, had hired Colleen to research the latest fashions. When in a benevolent mood, Lady Ash even gave Colleen her castoff dresses. Colleen had certainly taken advantage of that offer, dressing as finely as she dared. That was, until Lady Ash had taken all the dresses back and cast them into her hearth, screaming, *"You've betrayed me!"*

In her soul, Colleen knew she hadn't betrayed Lady Ashington. No, *Lady Ash* had betrayed Colleen by not protecting her. But Colleen still often searched her memories for evidence she hadn't mistakenly encouraged Lord Ashington's advances. The nuns at school had always warned her she'd eventually suffer because of her vanity and impetuousness. But to her credit, Colleen had tried to fight him off. He'd slapped her for it. The whole debacle was his fault, and Lady Ash's dress was the very least that horrible couple could offer as paltry compensation for all Colleen had endured.

Colleen's lips curled into a satisfied smile as she looked down at her purloined loot, the dress she wore. She'd left her post in disgrace, true enough, but not without stealing one of Lady Ash's dresses. Colleen's former employer probably hadn't even noticed the missing gown. She rarely wore green because emerald yellowed her complexion. Deep green, however, suited Colleen perfectly as did the cut of the dress, with its tight bodice, tapered waist, and fitted sleeves. Although the stolen dress wasn't fancy enough for a ball, it was perfect for a lady to lounge in at home. Or, more to the point, an ideal dress for a lady's maid, even one decked in shame. "Thank you," Colleen replied. "A lady's maid should complement her mistress, but not outshine her."

As soon as she uttered those words, Colleen's heart clenched.

She'd just parroted off Ma's advice—probably the last bit of wisdom she'd ever get from her in person. This far from home, Colleen had only letters to look forward to. They were cold comfort even if they had some minuscule scent of home left for her to savor.

No. This isn't the time for sadness, Colleen scolded herself. She grabbed her carpetbag and returned to the ship's deck. As they approached the port, the next hour sped by. Many years later, Colleen would remember every sensory detail of the new city emerging before her. Tall ships clustered around the long docks, and the scent of swamp and spices infused the humid air. And, most overwhelmingly, Colleen noticed how the blinding white light of the Louisiana sun was hot enough to bake a pie if she so chose. Those impressions all seared themselves into her brain.

The ship finally slowed, banging against the dock as the din of the port's activities surrounded Colleen. Hundreds of people speaking French, English, and Spanish thronged about the harbor and went about their business as if there wasn't a young Irish girl who'd barely avoided scandal and infamy about to join their ranks. That anonymity enticed Colleen.

She scanned the chaos of the harbor, her heart giddy until her eyes rested on a train of loosely-clothed men, women, and children, who someone had gnarled together with chains and shackles.

A man with a whip and menacing countenance prodded the people onto the ship next to Colleen's. She couldn't pry her eyes away from that procession of the damned. They had a far worse lot in life than that of the poorest Irish farmers under the most merciless of landlords. At least in Ireland, landlords couldn't separate children from parents or sell people, body and soul, for a bag of silver coins like Judas Iscariot. And even though the Le Jaunes owned Colleen's labor for four years, she had more rights as an indentured servant than she would have as a slave. Colleen had known this country had slaves, of course, but nothing prepared her for seeing the horrors of the institution firsthand.

People. People just as worthy of respect and dignity as she were bound in chains.

Colleen's hand shot up to cover her heart, to shelter it from the pain of the world. It didn't work. Every breath formed a lump in her throat. Slavery tarnished the promise of this place. Not that Colleen had another viable choice. Lady Ash had banished her from the house without a letter of reference, which Colleen needed to find work in a respectable house. Until she came across Madame Le Jaune's advertisement, Colleen had all but given up. She'd returned to Ashington Manor and begged her former mistress for a letter of reference for the New Orleans posting. Lady Ash, to Colleen's amazement, had agreed. "You'll be there as an indentured servant—almost a slave," she'd told Colleen. "I'll happily damn you to that swampy backwater."

New Orleans might be swampy, but certainly not "backwater" unless one compared it to London. New Orleans was the third-largest city in America. Colleen could, perhaps, do worse. She'd exchanged four years of her life for steerage passage and a place to live. With no prospects in Ireland, Colleen had made that bargain for better or worse.

Her family didn't have the best of reputations. Their small circle of friends in the village regarded them well enough, but most villagers avoided her family on account of an ancestor who'd gotten herself hanged as a witch centuries ago. Colleen had no marriage prospects in the village and didn't want to move elsewhere just to yoke herself to a man she didn't know. Marriage afar or service. She and her six siblings had only those options. As the second oldest, Colleen couldn't sit idly by while even the youngest worked to bring the family its bread. Whatever her future in this swamp, she had to make the best of things.

She drew in a deep breath and followed Ulrika off the gangplank, her boots thumping on the wood and adding to the collective noise around her. The letter of indenture from Monsieur Le Jaune instructed her to find people named Day and Celeste, the ones he'd sent to collect her at the dock. To her great misfortune, though, Colleen had no idea what they looked like or *how* she'd manage to find them in the harbor's mayhem. She craned her neck and scanned the crowd for a sign.

Then, as if to answer her prayers, a bee flew right up to her face, hovering, as if waiting for her. Bees were reliable guides, so Colleen followed the humming creature instead of meandering aimlessly through the harbor. It danced on the wan breeze, paying no mind to the people pouring off ships great and small, until it paused over a man who wore a wide-brimmed hat. Why had the bee favored him? Well, he held a sign that read *Colleen O'Neil*. She burst into laughter. The bee had been her lucky charm after all! With a purposeful stride, she wove through the crowd to the man. "Hello, are you Day? I'm Colleen," she said, holding out her hand. "Thank you for coming to meet me."

The man hesitated for a second as if wondering what to do with her hand, but then smiled and shook it heartily. Only at that moment did Colleen notice his deep tan skin contrasted with her pale tone. Was he a slave? She didn't know, but it didn't matter to Colleen. She met his gaze. Although Day's massive hat shaded the contours of his face, Colleen still saw his eyes glow with mischief and his lips break into a friendly smile. "I am Day. It's a pleasure to meet you, Colleen," he replied. "Celeste would be here, too, but she's been confined to Etoile. Our mistress needed her. As is often the case."

Day's final words had a bite to them, and Colleen hoped her new mistress wasn't as ornery as Lady Ash. "She's a demanding mistress?" When Day nodded, she continued. "I've a task ahead of me, then."

"That's true enough, Madame," Day said, tipping his hat.

Colleen held her ragged carpetbag up. "Madame? Oh, no. I'm merely an indentured servant."

"As am I, unfortunately. For life," he said quickly before turning away. "Please follow me."

Oh, hell. I've offended the poor man, Colleen cursed. She had no right to complain about her lot in life. Colleen followed Day through the harbor, the deep crimson blush on her cheeks growing fiercer with every step. He was quiet as he scooped up her carpetbag and set it gently in the cargo section, next to an assortment of dry goods and what looked like fertilizer. She wanted to shrink back from her mortification, and avoid speaking to him, if possible, by hiding under the damned sacks of food if necessary. However, the cargo section was filled to the brim with goods. Colleen climbed into the wagon and sat on the single wooden seat. "Is it always so hot here?" she asked. "How do you bear it?"

"It's hot from May until October, usually," Day said as he leaped nimbly into the driver's seat. "You'll get used to it."

Colleen fanned herself with her hand. "Until then, I might have to go for a swim. There's water everywhere, it seems."

Day raised his eyebrow. "Water and gators."

"Gators?" she asked, hoping she'd misheard him. She'd read about alligators in a book at school. The accompanying drawing had looked frightful enough.

"Man-eating reptiles," Day replied.

Suddenly, the heat didn't seem so unbearable after all. Better to endure it than get eaten alive! "Holy Mother Mary," she said. "Do they come into the house at night?"

"Not commonly," Day said, working to stifle his laughter as he nudged the horse forward. "They're animals, not thieves after Madame's remaining jewelry."

Thieving alligators indeed, Colleen thought, blushing beet red yet again. How was she to know the habits of every creature in God's creation? Colleen had left school to enter service as a wisp of a girl at thirteen. Her family had needed the money, so she'd tucked into her fate and risen from lowly chambermaid to lady's maid by age seventeen, quite a feat for someone so young. She'd forged a successful path—at least initially. Because of that English bastard, she had to start over, this time as an indentured servant.

Day stopped laughing and cleared his throat. "I understand you were a lady's maid in Ireland. Why come here as an indentured servant?"

Colleen had grown accustomed to providing a vague answer

by way of explanation, but something made her trust this near stranger. She stole a glance at him and stared at the road ahead, her face set into a grim expression. "My former employer, Lord Ashington, took too many liberties."

"That's unfortunate," Day said. He hesitated before continuing. "May I be frank?"

Colleen let out a sharp breath. His question didn't sound judgmental, meaning he likely had worse news—perhaps a warning about her bondholder. Did she want to know? She could start her new post in a cloud of blissful ignorance. But the ignorant gave their enemies the element of surprise. Some knowledge was better than none, as her da used to say, so Colleen nodded. "I'd prefer it."

"Monsieur Le Jaune causes trouble with young women," Day cautioned. "Madame sold off the last two who tended to her because she found out what he'd been doing to them. The only women left at Etoile—that's the name of the estate—are the cook, housekeeper, and the child's nurse."

Colleen collapsed against the seat. She'd escaped one horrible situation and landed in another one. "And these women are older than Monsieur prefers, I take it?" she asked.

"Yep," Day said, his lips pulling into a grimace.

"It's not fair!" Colleen slammed her fist against the seat of the wagon so hard that Day jumped. Pain radiated through her knuckles, so she cradled her injured hand in her dress. That little outburst would likely cost her a bruise. Colleen gave Day an apologetic smile. "I don't mean to punish your wagon."

"It's not my wagon. You can hit it all you want," Day said as he steadied the horse, who Colleen had also, apparently, frightened. "Sorry for upsetting you."

Colleen straightened up and stretched, cracking her back. "Better upset than ignorant. I suppose a demanding mistress is lucky under these circumstances."

"She'll keep you occupied," Day said. "And don't worry. Monsieur won't press the matter. He doesn't want to cross her now."

"She's *that* formidable?" Colleen asked. She'd begrudgingly admit she admired strong women, even if they annoyed her with their prattling on and yelling. Lady Ash had been weak, never confronting her husband or his faults.

Day nudged the horse around a corner. "More like her husband lost more of her dowry at his favorite gambling palace. Monsieur Le Jaune needs to keep Madame happy enough, or her brother won't give her more money."

"Ah, so that's the way of it," Colleen mused. She knew that type of situation well enough. Only, the villagers in Ireland who'd succumbed to the lure of dice or cards had done so in the local pub, not an entire palace devoted to gambling.

"And that's why you're here. You are a gift to appease Madame," Day added. He paused and tilted his chin. "She wanted a genuine lady's maid, all the way from Europe, to impress her friends."

Colleen giggled at his haughty, affected tone. "So, they're a wastrel and a foul-tempered banshee. A perfect pair if God ever made one. I suppose she'll parade me around like a new dress, then?"

"An *exquisite* new dress." Day flashed her a brief smile. "And yes, she'll parade you around and crow with all her might. Around here, some people are nervous to hire foreigners. They're not acclimated. But the mistress? She doesn't care."

Colleen quickly turned away from Day so he wouldn't see her mild blush. She took a deep breath and noticed how he smelled of fresh wood and lemons. By the saints, he was an attractive man. What had gotten into her? She cleared her throat and focused her attention back on her companion, a safe topic on the tip of her tongue. "Acclimated to the climate?" she asked. "Is Madame afraid this swampy heat will make me laze about?"

Day shook his head. "I mean acclimated to *yellow fever*. Foreigners get it easier, which makes it hard for them to get hired."

Yellow fever. That didn't sound pleasant at all. She'd suffered scarlet fever as a child and didn't want any more fevers named after colors, or any other fevers, really. "Is it deadly?"

"It depends on the year," he admitted. "Some years, only a

few die. Others, that number is into the hundreds."

"So, not only do I have to mind Monsieur's eager hands, this heat, and *alligators*, but also yellow fever? God in Heaven," Colleen said. For emphasis, she crossed herself.

Day smiled. "I wouldn't worry. You seem to have a strong constitution."

"I take that as a compliment." Colleen sat back and fanned herself. "Well, I've rambled on to kingdom come. Please tell me more about yourself. Only if you're of a mind to, though. I don't want to pry."

Day let out a bitter laugh. "Are you sure you want to know? It's a sorry tale."

"I come from a long line of sad tales, too. Might as well have some company," Colleen said. For good measure, she tapped the rattiest section of her carpetbag with her foot.

"All right," Day said. "Well, I'm a slave. That's the sum of it. My father was a wealthy Spanish planter, and my mother was my father's slave. So, that's what I am, too."

"He didn't free you?" Colleen asked, gasping. She stared at the man beside her. How could someone keep their own child in chains? He drove forward in stony silence, and in a few seconds, Colleen understood. She closed her eyes as she remembered the way of things for people with money and power. Kings like Henry VIII might set their bastards up with titles and lands, but others took no responsibility for their such offspring. A rare person acknowledged children born out of wedlock as bona fide kin. She resisted the urge to take Day's elbow. "Saints preserve me, I understand. How did you end up with Monsieur Le Jaune?"

Day gently urged the horse around another cart. "All because of a card game," he said. "When I was four years old, my father lost me and my mother to M. Le Jaune playing poker. It wasn't long before my father lost everything else and had to go back to Spain to live on his brother's charity."

Day relayed the story in such a matter-of-fact way that it took Colleen aback. She had troubles and limited choices, true enough, but her worries over her battered carpetbag and the loss of Lady Ash's castoff dresses now seemed silly. To have one's ownership settled based on a card game between drunken "gentlemen?" How fickle. And cruel. "That's horrible," she muttered. "How do you endure it?"

"By finding little morsels of joy in my otherwise bleak reality. They'll tide me over until I have the power to change things." Day snapped the reins so the horse would canter along faster. "Look around. There's still beauty in this city despite its faults."

Little morsels of joy in an otherwise bleak reality. How poetic of him. Day had, seemingly, a rare ability to put things into proper perspective.

As instructed, she soaked in the sights and sounds of the city as it sped by. Colleen would find beautiful things in this world. She didn't have to look far. New Orleans's homes were enchanting, what with their tall windows and delicate wrought-iron balconies. Some of the pastel houses looked like they belonged perched atop a cake for a fairy princess instead of on top of the mountains of horse manure that collected on the street.

As he drove through the French section of the city, Day explained that the architecture was Spanish, for Spain had controlled the city until 1803. During that time, and after a series of fires, the city had been rebuilt with more fireproof materials. Everything was so different from the imposing gray edifices of Ashington Hall. At least New Orleans had a warm dampness instead of one that chilled to the bone. The streets bustled with activity unlike Colleen had seen in her home village or the one ruled by Ashington Manor.

Day somehow managed to skillfully navigate the wagon through the traffic that moved upstream and downstream, usually without rhyme or reason. Then, before he finished telling Colleen about the Louisiana Purchase, Day's voice died in his throat just as the wagon passed a wooden pen filled with men, women, and even children who were waiting for a slave seller to usher them up to the auction block. A bolt of revulsion shot through Colleen. "What a cruel fate," she said.

"And an unpredictable one," Day added. He clutched the reins so tightly Colleen thought his knuckles might snap. "All of Monsieur's slaves work in the workshop, on the grounds, or in the house. Some people would say that's better than the back-breaking work on a plantation. But any one of us could end up on that auction block at any time. That's a special kind of torture."

"Do you ever think about a different kind of life?" she asked, hoping he understood what she really wanted to know. Colleen couldn't ask him directly if he ever felt like running away. The risk to Day for admitting any such thing to a stranger could be fatal.

Day gave her a half-smile. "Every single day."

"I have my daydreams, too," she replied. "Until then, I suppose it's little morsels of joy in an otherwise bleak reality for both of us."

CHAPTER FOUR:
THE EMPEROR

The Emperor card represents paternal energy as well as a time of stability, discipline, and leadership. For help in this arena, call upon Damballa, the Father God in the sky. He's the husband of Ayida Wedo, the rainbow serpent. Damballa appears as a snake and is also known as the Gran Bwa. If you wish to honor him, leave an offering of white rum.

Colleen

August 30, 1841, Etoile, New Orleans

"**M**aureen," Madame Le Jaune crowed from her chaise lounge across the room. "Bring me my smelling salts!"

"Right away, Mum, and it's Colleen. My ma's name is Maureen," Colleen replied in her most saccharine voice, all the while thinking, *You're a stupid creature, you are.*

"Colleen, Maureen. Irish names are too similar," Madame whined.

Because she faced away from Madame, Colleen rolled her eyes clear up to the moon. That small act of defiance made her heart glow with satisfaction. She reached into Madame's vanity and retrieved the pink glass bottle of smelling salts, something the lady required after visits with her three-year-old son, Raoul.

Madame Le Jaune only spent a few minutes a day with the child, who otherwise was supervised by his governess, a woman named Rachel. Though spirited, Raoul didn't warrant anything as dramatic as a daily regimen of smelling salts. What would Madame Le Jaune do when her new babe arrived in six months? Colleen reckoned her mistress would snort an entire ammonia mine's worth of salts when that child arrived. Such *fuss*. Colleen's own ma had birthed seven children and had managed to look after them without a dramatic production to rival Shakespeare.

Ma. Oh, Saint Brigid, help me, Colleen thought. She took a deep breath and steadied her trembling body against the vanity, hoping to forget her troubles until she could properly wallow in them later that night.

Burying her feelings was almost impossible, though. Only a few days ago, she'd received a letter from home. Ma was ill. Quite likely terminally, if the village doctor had it right. Colleen had no reason to doubt Doc Mulaney. Her grandmother, her ma's own ma, had died at forty from a tumor on the breast. The doc suspected Colleen's mother had the same, and that meant Maureen O'Neil had mere months to live. *The family curse strikes again*, Colleen thought with a bitterness that pierced straight through her heart. God struck down most of the women in her mother's family after their prime childbearing years. Life teetered on a cruel edge.

For the moment, though, Colleen did the only thing she could—lose herself in her present duties and get Madame her salts before the dramatic caterwauling resumed. Colleen slowly traversed Madame's pink and gold boudoir so she wouldn't trip in the room's semidarkness. "Right here, Mum," Colleen said through a tight smile as she stood over Madame, who lay splayed on her chaise lounge as if drunk out of her wits.

Not that Mme. Le Jaune could see Colleen's cheerful efforts with her eyes shut as tight as a nun's chastity, that was. "Where, Maureen?" she asked, her limp arm flailing for the bottle. "The light is making me dizzy!"

And you're making me *dizzy*, Colleen thought. On Madame's explicit orders, the curtains remained closed tightly so only a smidgen of daylight snuck through the perimeter of the window. Colleen gritted her teeth and thrust the bottle into Madame's hand. "Here you go, Mum."

As Mme. Le Jaune yanked the bottle open and took a long, noisy drag of the vapors, Colleen bit her cheek to stifle a fit of giggles. How did Monsieur Le Jaune endure his wife's theatrics? Colleen had to admit that Amelie Le Jaune was pretty, with hair that flowed like honey and wide golden eyes to match. Mme. Le Jaune's facial features were also symmetrical. Yet the woman's constant whining ruined her otherwise pleasant countenance. The recent pregnancy was proof Monsieur managed to perform his conjugal duties, maybe with a great deal of whiskey, or whatever men in New Orleans preferred as liquid courage.

At least Madame's constant demands allowed Colleen to avoid Monsieur Le Jaune most of the time. Colleen planned Madame's attire, dressed her, and arranged all her social calls. Colleen also wrote Mme. Le Jaune's correspondences and fetched whatever struck her fancy from the stores in the city center. Mother in heaven forbid that rich women shop for themselves or leave the house unchaperoned. What a depraved notion that was. But a lowly servant, one with a tattered reputation extending clear across the Atlantic Ocean, could leave the house on any mission, savory or otherwise.

It seemed Madame had abdicated all duties of running the household. She gave Colleen, Day, the cook, and the housekeeper a small amount of money each week to make purchases for the household. The weekly allotment was a pittance, certainly not enough to finance an escape from Etoile. Not that Colleen had reason to complain.

Doing Madame's shopping gave Colleen her only morsels of joy, also known as her rides with Day. Monsieur Le Jaune had tasked him to drive Colleen to the hat store, to the seamstress, or to any other place Madame Le Jaune required.

Colleen's pleasant traveling companion advised her on a manner of things, including the best ways to avoid colliding with Monsieur. Colleen succeeded for the most part, but her bondsman still found excuses to lurk about. The brazen fool left French sweets inside her bedroom door, which meant he went inside her tiny quarters while she was tending Madame. He also stared at Colleen when his wife was in the room. The *britches* on him! Simply thinking of that man's leer made Colleen cringe. She often regretted leaving Ireland, especially when she learned Monsieur Le Jaune could sell her bond to someone else. Better the devil she knew.

"Amelie?" called a voice from behind the door.

Oh, speak of the devil, Colleen thought as she held in a groan. Monsieur had come for one of his unannounced visits.

Madame sighed. "Colleen, let Maurice in."

Thankful that Madame had used her proper name this time around, Colleen pulled the door open and jumped back from Monsieur's path in one quick motion. "Monsieur," she said, curt-seying from the shadows.

Monsieur gave Colleen a covert wink and hurried to his wife's side. "Mon amour," he crooned, caressing her forehead. "How are you feeling?"

"Exhausted." Madame's features contorted with pain, and she thrust the pink bottle toward him. "Put my salts away."

"Of course, my dear, of course." M. Le Jaune plucked the bottle from her hand and secured it in the vanity drawer.

Colleen held her breath as Monsieur crept across the room and back to his wife's side. When he passed Colleen, though, he brushed his hand against her posterior and gave it a hard pinch. Jumping back, Colleen drew in a sharp breath to hide her gasp. He'd never grabbed her before. His bad behavior would only escalate, just like Lord Ashington's had. Only this time, Colleen couldn't leave service. What should she do? She couldn't swat him away or tell Madame. Both actions bore terrible consequences for Colleen. With his hand gently resting on his wife's shoulder, Monsieur Le Jaune looked Colleen's body up and down. She needed to escape. *Immediately*. She used the best excuse she could think of in a fragment of a second. "I'll get you some tea, Mum," Colleen said. "For the dizziness."

"Something to settle my nerves," Madame commanded. And with a flick of her wrist, she dismissed Colleen.

Before she lost her chance, Colleen sprinted through the house and to the outbuilding that served as the *summer kitchen*. She had first laughed at the notion of a special kitchen for the summer, believing the Le Jaunes built it to put on airs. But once Colleen felt the full measure of a Louisiana summer, she understood the need for a dedicated summer kitchen. Cooking outside kept the heat of the cookstove out of the main house. Celeste, the cook, could also open more windows in the detached building, which gave her some relief from the sweltering stove.

Some relief.

In the kitchen, Colleen found Celeste, who was Day's mother as well as Madame's cook, preparing the evening meal. The room felt like a Turkish bath that Colleen had once read about in a collection of fantastic stories about the Orient. Celeste wiped away her sweat without complaint.

Colleen marveled at how the cook moved through the kitchen with such surety. The woman radiated strength and grace. Her former master, Day's father, had stationed her in the kitchen at a young age because of her comely face and body. As Colleen knew from her experience with Lord Ashington, beauty was a curse when its owner was at the mercy of a powerful man. Thankfully, by the time Monsieur Le Jaune won Celeste and Day in that fateful card game, Celeste had matured beyond Monsieur's preferences. The cook had witnessed the man harass Madame's former lady's maids, so she advised Colleen as best as she could. Colleen thus felt bonded to the older woman.

"What's the mistress want now—the Queen of England to visit?" Celeste asked, her voice dripping in sarcasm.

"Queen Victoria? Oh, no. An English queen, especially such a young and unestablished one, isn't posh enough for her *ladyship*," Colleen bantered. She joined the cook at the stove and inhaled the fragrant spiced shrimp dish that Mme. Le Jaune craved during her pregnancy. "Madame would prefer the Queen of France—that Marie Antoinette who lost her head."

Celeste's eyes danced with glee. "A shame it's not Madame, but her husband, who has the *noble blood*. He likes his games of chance just like that poor French queen. It'll be the ruin of him, too."

Colleen's lips curled into a triumphant smile as Celeste reminded her of Monsieur's catastrophic gambling luck. Madame Le Jaune often complained that her husband lost money "as frequently as a drunken Irishman spent his coins on whiskey." Colleen hated the barbed insult against her countrymen, but she let the knowledge about Monsieur empower her. His lack of control over his finances weakened the looming impression she had of him as a monster.

Colleen almost felt bad for Madame, albeit fleetingly. Amelie Le Jaune's father, a planter named Monsieur Heureux, had forced his daughter to marry Maurice Le Jaune solely because his mother had aristocratic blood. The Le Jaunes had had power before the French Revolution stripped them of their lands and titles, of course. Colleen found all this obsession with aristocracy odd and ludicrous. .

The English worshipped those with blue blood and title, but M. Heureux, too? Why in heaven yoke his daughter to M. Le Jaune? M. Heureux had boatloads of money at the ready, so his daughter came into the marriage with a dowry.

Colleen failed to see what M. Heureux, or for that matter, Amelie, earned from the bargain. A duke or baronet in the family tree didn't imbue someone with magical powers.

Unfortunately for Amelie, when forging the marriage alliance, M. Heureux hadn't taken into account Maurice's complete lack of financial discipline. Also, Amelie Le Jaune had no one left to rely on after her father passed. Her brother, who she'd never gotten along with, had inherited the family estate. He'd been supplementing Amelie's lifestyle since she married but had recently cut her off because Monsieur Le Jaune kept losing money at the gambling tables. In other words, when Amelie's dowry was spent, she couldn't rely on support from her brother.

The marriage hadn't turned out well for Madame Le Jaune, that was as plain as day. Yet she still trumpeted her husband's heritage at every turn. She extracted *something*, at least, from her father's bargain.

"Qué quiere ella?" Celeste asked, switching to a serious tone.

Colleen worked to unfurl the jumble of Spanish that Celeste spoke with such ease. Colleen was having a difficult time learning French, but she knew she had to learn as much as she could. Celeste received her command of Spanish from the master who'd lost her and Day to M. Le Jaune in the card game. Colleen *thought* Celeste had asked what Madame wanted. "Some tea to calm her damn nerves," Colleen replied. "Although not even the Lord's strongest holy water could accomplish that feat."

The cook giggled. "She's got the temperament of a terrier that's gotten into its owner's coffee. I can't get you the holy water, but I've got some chamomile drying in my son's workshop."

"Does it smell like horses, the chamomile?" Colleen's nose wrinkled at the thought. Day's personal workshop was in the stable building. It was walled away from the horses, true enough, but still in the same building. Since the summer kitchen was far too humid a place to dry herbs, Day's workshop served as the best alternative. "Not that I'd mind giving Madame horse tea."

The cook smiled as she wiped away the perspiration that had collected on her brow. "It'll smell a bit like fresh wood. You'd best fetch some so I can brew her a tea. We don't want Madame getting even more irate."

"Mother Mary, save me," Colleen said, crossing herself. Colleen gave Celeste an amused smile and headed to the stable, a white building across from the main house's beautiful flower gardens, with a skip to her step. She had an excuse to see Day.

In addition to chauffeur, he was Monsieur Le Jaune's most skilled carver. Celeste had told Colleen that Day's artistry earned Monsieur most of his money. Colleen's heart had filled with sorrow when she'd fully realized that M. Le Jaune stole the fruits of Day's labor. As paltry compensation for this theft, M. Le Jaune gave Day his own space for working and sleeping in the stable building. M. Le Jaune's other slaves, meanwhile, worked in the main workshop.

Day's workshop had a separate entrance, so the pleasant smells of chamomile and sage, not horse filth, greeted Colleen. She looked up and saw the bundles of herbs Celeste had mentioned hanging from the ceiling. At first, she didn't see Day, but then she heard rustling coming from outside the shop near the exit door along the opposite wall. Colleen followed the noises and found Day hunched over a small bureau. He wore his trademark wide-brimmed hat to shield his eyes from the sun and was inscribing an intricate scroll pattern into the gleaming wood. He was a true artist.

Day straightened up to greet her. "Colleen. What can I do for you?"

Colleen could think of plenty that Day could do, but she worked to keep her face impassive. Wanting to keep her attraction for him secret, she cleared her throat and hoped a blush hadn't spread across her cheeks. "Your mother wants me to fetch some chamomile tea. It's for Madame."

"Madame has a touch of the vapors?" Day asked, resting his tools on the dresser.

"A storm of vapors is more like it," Colleen muttered.

Her remark earned her a laugh from Day. "In that case, I'll get you enough chamomile to sedate a herd of elephants," he said. "Please follow me."

"Gladly," Colleen said as she followed him inside the workshop.

Day removed his hat, fetched a ladder, and nimbly climbed atop it, reaching up to one of the chamomile flower clusters. Because he was turned away from her, Colleen allowed herself to admire Day's body. That indulgence distracted her from the other reason she'd charged out of Madame Le Jaune's bedroom. Day jumped off the ladder and handed her the bouquet of chamomile. "You have more on your mind than a demanding mistress," he observed.

Colleen's eyes darted to the floor. She hesitated before saying anything about Monsieur's latest overtures or her worries about what she'd do in the future. This was her battle to fight, not Day's. She, at least, had an end date to her servitude. Then again, Day had also been the one to caution her about M. Le Jaune's nasty habit of bothering the women in his service. Why not be honest with the furniture carver? "It's Monsieur," she admitted, securing the flowers in her dress pocket. "He hasn't prevailed in his attempts to bed me, though. That I promise you."

Day opened his mouth but shut it quickly, as if weighing his next words carefully. What he said next was the last thing she expected to hear in his workshop, an ideal place to stow secrets away. "The red-headed woman in your dreams—you think of her as St. Brigid—she can help you," Day said.

Goosebumps raised on Colleen's arms. She took a step closer to Day, wanting to reach out and take his hand. Find out how he knew about the woman in her dreams. She'd never told anyone about the saint's nocturnal visits. But then again, David had intuitive powers. Colleen only hoped the man didn't know how she all but lusted after him with the intensity of a harlot. "I pray to her, and it's a balm to my soul," Colleen said, keeping her tone neutral.

"Praying helps, but you could also try summoning her for help directly," Day said.

Colleen frowned. Praying was direct communication with a saint, but perhaps Day meant a more formal approach. "By lighting a candle at church?" she asked.

"Or by making offerings on your own," Day replied, his voice calm and reverent. "My St. Brigid, who I call Maman Brigitte, appears to me in front of my eyes. Not *just* in dreams. I do it through magic."

Colleen's breath caught in her throat. Day's saint appeared to him? Right before his very eyes? Colleen took a few moments to process this news. How would she react to the sudden appearance of a saint? If St. Brigid manifested right in front of her, Colleen doubted she'd shirk the opportunity.

Day spoke of communing with spirits, which she knew wasn't evil magic. Her ancestor that'd been hanged as a witch hadn't worshipped the Devil, either. People feared mysterious forces, even when the unseen world was etched into the fabric of tradition.

Growing up, she'd heard stories of banshees and fairy folk roaming the green hills of Ireland. Although she'd never seen any evidence of those creatures, Colleen still left out the occasional bowl of milk for the fairies. The way Day confessed to summoning his saint was so natural Colleen not only believed the truth of his words but also in the purity of his actions. His admission about his saint opened Colleen's eyes to how she'd always interacted with the unseen world. She just needed someone to pull back the veil to this hidden reality. What a precious gift!

In her mind, Colleen saw a new future take shape, a kinship forged from their combined experiences. The humid heat and scorching sun of New Orleans mixed with Ireland's cool gray skies to form a temperate climate. Her beloved emerald mountains and craggy cliffs of County Mayo transformed into gently rolling hills when fused with the vast breadth of the Mississippi River. Colleen imagined Spanish moss interlacing with the decorative knots her people had crafted from metal countless centuries ago. She didn't want to let go of the friendship she'd found with Day. "Can you show me how to make the spirits appear?" she asked.

"I can. I feel the magic running through you." Day stepped into the ray of sunlight that streamed in through the window. It was then Colleen noticed how his hazel eyes glowed like a precious stone in the light. "And please call me David. Monsieur insists on calling me Day because it has fewer syllables, but my real name is David. That's also what my friends and dear ones call me."

CHAPTER FIVE: THE HIEROPHANT

When you draw the Hierophant, seek counsel from a teacher. Houngons, mambos, and your met tet, the loa who rules your head, will guide you properly. If your met tet is Maman Brigitte, you can gift her coffee, rum, or perfume. She also loves birds, so you may serve her by feeding these treasured creatures. Maman Brigitte is elegant, sensual, protective, and strong. She'll help you evoke these qualities in yourself. This powerful loa originally hails from Ireland and sometimes appears as a woman with red hair. Saint Brigid, or Brydie, came to the New World with Irish immigrants and syncretized with African spirits to form Maman Brigitte. She's married to Baron Samedi, and they rule the Ghede, a rowdy bunch of spirits who live in the cemetery. They help with all matters of justice.

Selene

October 20, 1860, French Section of New Orleans

Suddenly, the drama before me ceased, pulling my consciousness back into my body. I'd felt my mother's raw and unfiltered emotions in that vision. When she saw my father's face illuminated in the sunbeam, I knew both that she thought him incredibly handsome, and that she'd cared for him greatly. She'd felt alive and fully present around him, but now, Maman was a shadow of her former self, a shadow that walked through the world with one foot in the grave. Although they didn't know it at the point I'd just seen in the vision, Papa and Maman would grow to love one another profoundly. Their love had a calamitous end with Papa's death, though, which drowned my heart with sadness.

As the dank cemetery air threatened to choke me, I leaned back against the tomb and concentrated on the beautiful things in my midst, such as how the moonlight turned the marble stone houses for the dead into glowing opals. I breathed in and out, in and out. Breathing, I could do. My heart soon slowed, and I found the strength to look at my father's ghostly form.

David.

My father hadn't been a Spaniard, but instead a slave named David, with a nickname of Day. He'd met my mother when she worked at Etoile as a lady's maid. I had his eyes and skin color, along with the shape of Maman's face and lips. And that wasn't all. I had a grandmother. An actual, *living and breathing* grandparent named Celeste. The same lady I'd briefly met on Etoile's flower-lined path.

Papa observed me quietly as I digested these revelations. "Are you ashamed?" he eventually asked, his voice soft.

Shame is a word that implies regret and the compulsion to bury the truth. I felt none of those inclinations. "*No,*" I swore with all my heart and soul. "I'm confused. That vision explains so many things but brings up even more questions."

He rested an ethereal hand on my shoulder. "Such as?"

Tears moistened my cheeks, and my questions rambled forth like the Mississippi River itself. "How could Maman be with Monsieur Le Jaune? What happened? *How did you die?*"

I glared at him as I posed that final question. I used to plead relentlessly with him to tell me how he died. And despite my bribes of chocolate, alcoholic drinks, and the finest cigars, Papa only revealed that he'd died in a tragic event he wasn't able to avert. The hungry Ghede usually tore into the gifts and devoured their essence, but Papa never touched my bribes. He remained immovable in his stubbornness. I eventually gave up asking because I didn't want to poison the time we had together with my bitterness.

"My death had a purpose," he replied, ignoring my question as he usually did. "You have to accept that."

Mist curled around my feet, covering the boots Maman had purchased with M. Le Jaune's money. Blood money. What purpose did Maman have for enduring Monsieur? She wouldn't tell me her plans, and now my father insisted the universe had ordained his death for some stupid "greater good." I jumped up and stared down at Papa, who remained seated at the base of the tomb. "Your stupid *purpose* took you from Maman. From *me*," I seethed. "You owe me the truth."

As soon as that demand escaped from my ungrateful lips, I collapsed back onto the ground. I'd just issued a dictate to my father, who had come back from the dead to speak with me. To be sure, I deserved the truth, but I had no right to issue demands like a spoiled child. Papa didn't deserve my rage. No, whoever caused his death did. So did M. Le Jaune for how he treated Maman. Papa refused to tell me how he had died, but I suspected Monsieur had played a role. At the very least, the horrible man had exploited and abused both my parents. I vowed never to call that creature *Oncle Maurice* again. I offered my father an apologetic smile. "I'm sorry. That was uncalled for."

My father had every right to yell at me for my outburst, but he did the last thing I expected. He burst into laughter, his eyes gleaming. "You look like your mother when you shout, mon petit!"

"I do?" I asked. He couldn't mean it. Maman's anger manifested as shattered, empty laudanum bottles and curses that echoed off the walls of our miserable cottage. More often than not, though, I preferred Maman's anger to her usual mood, that of resignation and death.

"Your maman was strong when she was younger. That's how you resemble her," Papa said. He stared quietly into the edge of darkness, the place in the cemetery where the tombstones first became invisible under night's cloak.

He could leave the garden of stone houses and travel wherever he wanted, but he couldn't interact with me outside of these walls. The first time I visited him here and saw him take ghostly form, Papa had told me that he spent most of his time with me and Maman as a silent visitor. He sat with us at the table and lay next to her at night even though she didn't know it. I sensed he had more to say, so I stayed quiet and listened to the hum of cicadas, the whispers of ghosts, and the distant sounds of revelers leaving the French section's gambling palaces. He let out a sigh and met my eyes. "I can't save her from her fate, but you might be able to."

Even on that warm, humid night, my skin prickled at Papa's words. *I can't save her from her fate*, he'd said with such finality and sadness. "What fate?" I asked. "Her and M. Le Jaune's arrangement?"

"That fate, to be sure. And others," Papa replied. "She has noble goals in mind, but she's bent on revenge."

I took his wispy hand. I couldn't feel much with such gestures, certainly not the flesh and blood being I needed, but the trace contact was enough for the moment. "And how do I help her, exactly?"

"Marie Laveau will teach you what you need to know," my father replied.

I sat up straight at the mention of New Orleans's famous Voodoo queen, staring at my father in disbelief. "Marie Laveau? She'll teach me?"

Papa nodded. "She will. Patrice will show you where to find her if you need."

My heart always warmed when Papa mentioned Patrice. He knew she and I loved one another, and I only hoped Maman would be just as accepting of the relationship if she ever found out. I wondered how my father knew Marie Laveau. Then again, my father lived with the loa and had sent them to visit me when I was a child. Perhaps he'd had some connection to the famous woman in life. Through Papa's blood, the spirits pulsed through my veins, too. And instead of being ashamed of him, as he and Maman had feared, I felt a deep connection and the presence of an extended family, something I'd never had before. "Can you tell me more?" I asked.

"When you can control your emotions. Else, you and your maman's efforts will be for naught," my father cautioned.

Although I loathed the glacial pace with which Papa doled out information, I had to admit his words held wisdom, especially in light of my recent tantrum. I studied him, trying to absorb details about the man I'd never met in the flesh. My father was a proper sphinx with his many riddles and vague answers. His face, which was etched with regret, convinced me not to press him further. Instead, I asked another question. Something on much more neutral ground. "Did Maman love you just as much as you do her?"

"Of course she does," he replied, his smile radiating more warmth than a ghost ought to be capable of. The oppressiveness of his secrets vanished under the face of such love. "Your maman also hates Monsieur Le Jaune with a passion. I don't blame her for her choices."

Papa's use of *does* instead of *did* when referring to my mother's love for him cut through the night and demolished any remaining doubts I had about Maman's relationship with M. Le Jaune. I didn't fully understand why Maman did what she did. My father didn't blame her, though, and his love absolved all the sins I'd condemned her of.

In the spirit of exercising patience, I rested my head back against the tombstone, weighed down by the gravity of the tasks ahead of me. Marie would help, but I needed to find out why Maman feared M. Le Jaune so much.

In the periphery of my vision, Baron's dark glasses reflected the night's splendid moon, making them shine as if ice-blue embers glowed brightly in his skull. Then, the rustle of Brigitte's skirts brushed my ears. The loas had arrived to escort my father back to the afterlife. I wanted to stay in the graveyard forever, but it wasn't my time to die yet. A horrible task lay before me —saying goodbye to my father. I leaned forward and rested my head on his shoulder for a moment, inhaling the scent of swamp instead of lemons and wood. "Thank you, Papa," I said as I slowly stood and brushed the graveyard dust from my skirt.

Papa stood up and bowed. "Of course, mon petit." He then dissolved and assimilated with the evening's mist as if he'd never been there. I was alone, save for the dead, who slept soundly on that momentous night when I discovered my father's true identity.

Ace of Pentacles, indeed. The day had certainly brought with it a new venture, as predicted, namely the opportunity to learn magic from Marie Laveau. My father had also assured me earlier that I wouldn't have to be Raoul's mistress in the true definition of the word, thank heavens.

Empowered by my new knowledge, I left the garden of stone houses around ten o'clock and strolled down the street toward Faubourg Marigny. I didn't fear the night and its denizens. Not when it brought me beautiful things. The glint of Baron's sunglasses in the moonlight also confirmed that I walked with protection.

I reached the prison M. Le Jaune housed us in before too long. Like many other small cottages in Marigny, this home had four rooms; there were two bedrooms in the back of the house and a parlor and dining room facing the street. These cottages had no hallways, so each room had doors opening to the outside and to adjacent rooms. At first glance, Maman's cottage appeared cozy despite its shabby furnishings and fading paint. As I knew, however, all facades can deceive, including the ones Maman and I both erected simply to survive.

Through the dining room window, I saw Maman sitting at the table where we partook of our meals. Glowing candlelight illuminated her face, almost as if she were a saint bedecked in a shining halo. Others would call her a fallen woman, but she deserved canonization for all she endured.

I walked in the dining room door. Maman's little teacup rested on the table, which had three chairs set around it even though only the two of us lived there. M. Le Jaune, to be sure, believed Maman reserved the extra chair for him. She and I hid that chair's true meaning so well. We kept it for Papa. That ruse was another facade, a hastily erected Potemkin village. When Monsieur wasn't present, Maman and I set a place for Papa at the head of the table so he could join us from the afterlife. He never physically consumed the food, of course. He simply enjoyed its essence. And after the meal, I placed his portion under the tree in the garden for the spirits or animals to consume as they saw fit. I'd never seen Papa manifest before my eyes in this house, but I could sense him. I knew Maman did, too. Her face sometimes became dreamy as we ate with him.

That night when I returned from the cemetery, in addition to warming her wan complexion, the candle flame flickered off the familiar glass bottle she'd cushioned against her teacup. Maman had dumped laudanum into her tea—*again.*

When my mother heard my boots scuff against the floor, she jumped up from her chair and grabbed me. I returned her embrace and felt her bones poking through her dress. "Where the devil were you?" She released me and all but pushed me into my customary chair. Her voice held worry, but also a thin vein of condemnation. She plopped back down in her seat at the table and poured another generous dose of laudanum into the tea.

Did she deserve the truth from me after keeping a mountain of information hidden all these years? Papa would say she did. And if I wanted to break down the wall of secrets we'd erected between us, I had to offer up something in kind. "I went to the mercantile shop to visit Patrice," I said. "And then to the cemetery."

Maman took a long sip of tea. "The *cemetery?* Why?"

"To see Papa," I replied, leaning forward slightly and holding my breath.

As soon as his name escaped my lips, Maman's hand shook, so much so she spilled at least half of her tea on the stained wooden table. She shot me an accusatory look as she grabbed a towel. She blotted up the mess, her ravenous eyes locked onto the laudanum-soaked towel. Finally, she sat back down and sipped more tea. "That's impossible."

"It *is* possible," I insisted. Maman needed evidence, proof from beyond the grave in the form of information only Papa would know. "I'm not ashamed he was a slave."

Maman slowly set her teacup on the saucer, her emerald eyes boring holes into mine. Excitement, pride, and pain flitted across her face. Those conflicting emotions crackled in the air around us like the sky before a lightning storm. I fidgeted in my chair, awaiting her reply. I wanted—no, *needed*, for her to tell me *everything* and to promise she'd quit drinking laudanum as others did water. Instead, Maman picked up the bottle of poison and stroked one of her fingers along its contours as if she could absorb its amnesiac effects through the glass. To my horror, she then took a long sip before setting the laudanum aside. "Have you actually *seen* him?"

"Yes," I said, hoping my words brought her comfort instead of grief. "He also showed me a vision of when you first met."

"Have you seen the *other spirits*, too?" Maman asked.

At first, I didn't know who she meant by "other spirits," but then I remembered my father's vision. He'd told Maman that her St. Brigid and his Maman Brigitte were the same, or closely related, depending on one's perspective. She also knew about the gifts I placed beneath the tree. I reached across the table and took her quaking hand in mine. "Since I was six," I said. "Why didn't you just tell me the truth?"

"To protect you." Maman took a deep breath and looked away.

"From what?" I prodded, my voice rising in frustration.

Maman glanced nervously at the floor. "When you were conceived, your papa was a slave, and I was indentured. Monsieur Le Jaune owns you. *That's* what I was protecting you from."

Robbed of my speech, I leaned back against my chair. I'd welcomed the revelations about my father's heritage, but not the news M. Le Jaune owned me. Sometimes, when storm clouds roll in on an otherwise balmy day, little hints of fear creep in as the air pressure drops. *Will the storm come here? How damaging will those winds and rains be?* Those thoughts rumble through the mind as people rush to shelter, hoping they'd prepared enough for what was to come. I worried when the great storm of 1856 sent torrents of water down the street. The memory of such events, even those from generations past, imprints itself in the earth's fabric and the blood of survivors.

In that instant, I learned exactly what power Monsieur had over Maman. Although I believed her, something gave me pause. My mind ran the permutations that would prove Maman wrong. What legal calculus classified someone as a free person or a slave? Usually, children gained their mother's legal status, but perhaps my parents' unique circumstance had determined otherwise. And what other explanation did I have for every odd circumstance in my life, including Monsieur's hatred for me and Raoul's comment that I'd been bred to be his companion? Monsieur had probably only educated me so I wouldn't bore Raoul to death.

Tante Jeanne's desire to take me away from New Orleans also made sense in light of Maman's revelation. I exhaled a sharp breath. *"He threatened to sell me if I didn't meet with Raoul!"*

"Which is why I think you should leave with Jeanne," Maman replied. She got up and walked to the window, gazing out at the night and its ghosts. "I always intended that you'd leave long before this point."

The idea of fleeing this city and the horrible Le Jaunes tempted me, but what about Patrice? Or Maman? She'd made no mention of leaving with us, which meant she intended to stay until she completed her plans. Papa had told me to help free her. "Please tell me what you're planning to do."

Maman turned around and looked at me through her glassy-eyed stupor. The laudanum had taken effect, and dreams of Papa likely hovered on the horizon. "To free you and the rest of Monsieur Le Jaune's slaves," she said, yawning.

I shook my head. Maman was suffering under M. Le Jaune to help me, Celeste, and Monsieur's other slaves. Her admission scented the humid night air with revenge, an enticing perfume under the circumstances. Surely, her plans were impossible. Maman relied on laudanum to function and Monsieur for money. "How?" I asked.

"St. Brigid and your father told me you'd learn that when you're ready," Maman said. I opened my mouth to protest, and she held up her hand and silenced me with a strength I didn't know she possessed. "I see them every night in my dreams. That's how I know. Please be patient."

I wouldn't question her methods when her spirits supported her. "Papa told me the same. And that Marie Laveau would help me," I said. "If you can't reveal more about your plans, can you at least tell me more about how you and Papa fell in love, then?"

Maman's lips relaxed into a languid smile. "In the morning."

I nodded. She'd offered a fair exchange. My limbs hung, leaden from the day's taxing events. We'd each revealed some closely guarded secrets. I only hoped I could bear the rest of what Maman kept hidden in her heart.

CHAPTER SIX:
THE LOVERS

The Lovers card signifies a loving relationship based on trust and harmony. For an example, look to La Sirene and Agwe, the husband and wife of the sea. She appears as a mermaid or a human-looking siren and lives in a beautiful palace beneath the ocean's surface. If you need help finding riches or gaining discipline, offer her desserts, white gin, and melons. The same gifts will show your devotion to Agwe, the admiral of the sea. Call upon this couple, and revel in their close ties. This card also symbolizes a profound choice in the future. To decide the best course of action, let go of insignificant things and seize what is important.

Selene

*October 21, 1860, Faubourg
Marigny, New Orleans*

The crisp morning air danced on my skin as Maman and I enjoyed our chicory coffee under the oak tree in our garden. We sat at the small table Maman had once dragged outside so we could escape the house and enjoy a taste of nature. I reserved hope for a true autumn day, one where our dresses wouldn't become glued to our bodies in the steamy afternoon heat. I took a bite of the quiche Maman had prepared, and the sharp cheese and Andouille sausage tingled on my tongue. "Delicious," I said.

"Thank you," Maman replied. As she rested the coffee cup on its saucer, her hand trembled slightly, a sign her body craved more laudanum. At least her mind seemed clear, and the glimmer in her eye brightened up her wan pallor. She'd promised to tell me about her and Papa's happy moments. Those precious slices of information would, hopefully, give me enough strength to handle the end of their story—Papa's death.

"I'm ready to hear more about how you and Papa fell in love," I said.

Maman absently stroked the tattered lace tablecloth I'd spread over the table before breakfast. When she smiled, a younger version of Colleen O'Neil peeked out from behind her mourning veil. "Oh, he set my heart to racing like a horse through the hills of Ireland under a sky full of rainbows," Maman began. "I found out about his feelings for me when he showed me one of his prized possessions. Your deck of cards."

***

Colleen

September 23, 1841, Etoile, New Orleans

During Colleen's brief free moments, she loved watching the Mississippi River from the docks of Etoile, where M. Le Jaune's slaves loaded furniture onto boats that would ferry the elegant creations to markets worldwide. Colleen's world was limited to Etoile, however. She often longed for Keem Bay, the bewitching stretch of shore near her family's village on Achill Island. On sun-soaked summer days, the water shone blue-green. If she built a raft, would the river carry her all the way back to Ireland? She'd lay down and simply stare at the sky as the river and oceans did their work. As much as that fantasy tempted Colleen, though, she had one reason to stay at Etoile—David.

A slight change in air pressure snapped Colleen's attention from the sinuous river. She smiled, and a rush of warmth flooded her heart.

"Daydreaming? Or are you contemplating a swim?" David asked from behind her.

Colleen turned around and worked to keep her face impassive, which was a difficult task under the circumstances. His simple gray slacks and white shirt clung to his body in a way that conjured indecent thoughts.

"Not a swim on account of the alligators," Colleen said. "I'm missing Ireland. A beach on Keem Bay, at the moment."

David drew a step closer, the dock creaking under his feet. "Tell me about this beach."

"Sometimes, the water's the color of the sky on a fair day. Other times, it's as gray and sad as an Irish winter," Colleen replied. So little space separated them, yet she didn't dare come closer. Instead, she shifted her weight.

The creak of the dock ricocheted through the air like a gunshot. She'd behaved and kept her feelings for David secret. Somehow, the attraction and kinship Colleen had felt for this man had morphed into something else—love. Or at least the closest approximation to romantic love Colleen had ever felt. Colleen had sacrificed her desires on the altar of prudence for far too long. But no more. Colleen decided to shove the nuns' lessons about controlling impulsive behavior into one of this city's marble tombs. Her heart hammering in her ears, Colleen locked eyes with David's and prayed she was making the right choice. "But the beach is lonely without the right company," she said, swallowing the lump in her throat.

She held her breath. It wasn't until sparks rose in David's eyes

81

that the vice around her heart unclenched. "It would be lonely indeed," he agreed, letting out a long breath that whistled at the end.

"I'll convince Madame to give me leave for a trip back to Ireland," Colleen replied before realizing the impossibility of those words.

Lost in its lazy brown waters, David stared out at the river. Colleen wanted to drift away from Etoile with David beside her. "I don't think Madame will grant you that much time off, but Monsieur ordered me to pick up some dry goods from the mercantile in town today," David eventually said. "Does Madame perhaps need some medicinal herbs?"

"I'm sure she does," Colleen said. She winked at David. "I'll ask her now."

David inclined his head in a slight bow. "And I'll be waiting in the stables."

Bless that handsome man, Colleen thought as she sprinted toward the mansion. He'd contrived a way for them to spend time together. To what practical end, though? The world had set up so many barriers between them. But Colleen and David had the spirits to help them, something Colleen kept in mind as she went into Madame's boudoir to get permission to leave Etoile for some herbs.

The trip seemed predestined, for as soon as Colleen suggested medicine for her dyspepsia, Mme. Le Jaune had happily ordered Colleen to go to the city. Buoyed by her luck, Colleen quickly gathered the money Madame gave her for expenses from her room. She then jumped into the wagon and took a seat only inches apart from David. She couldn't touch him, so she imagined the breeze between them could do it for her. That delicious, agonizing lack of contact forced a blush to Colleen's cheeks.

Just as the anticipation was about to drive her mad, David drove over a rut in the road, which pushed Colleen up against his shoulder. She shivered when her arm touched his. Alone with David, Colleen would have melted into his touch, but they were driving on the street in plain view of *witnesses*. Colleen jerked upright and scooted as far away from David as the seat would allow.

"Afraid of getting too close to the *slave*?" David asked, his voice low and bitter.

"When there are people around, I certainly am," Colleen shot back. What did he think? That she was ashamed of being seen with him? She hoped not. The words fumbled about in Colleen's brain as she struggled to clarify her intentions. She inched a tad closer to David but left a safe amount of space between them. "It's dangerous for you."

David slowed the horse's pace because of the lumbering wagon ahead of them. "What do you desire in life?"

That question stumped Colleen. Women of her social standing were never asked about their deepest desires. Growing up, Colleen's options in life included marriage to some poor villager who'd overlook her family's witchcraft-tainted history, a post as a maid, or a life sequestered away in a nunnery. Colleen had never felt a religious calling, and no villager sought her hand, so Colleen left Achill Island for the mainland of County Mayo and became a maid just like her older sister, Mary.

Colleen's post at Ashington Manor paid a salary and guaranteed her a bed and sufficient food. She'd done well at the estate. Until she'd caught Lord Ashington's eye, that was. Mary hadn't warned Colleen about that danger. "I want to make fine dresses, not that I ever had the choice," Colleen said, remembering how she used to pore over Lady Ash's fashion books.

"You can't choose the outcome, but you can always choose your next action," David said. He pulled around the slow wagon that blocked his progress through the street.

Colleen scoffed. David sounded too much like an optimistic philosopher right then. *No one* ever offered her a choice. Her family and life circumstances had steered her toward a life in service because they needed to survive. And as for David's own life, he didn't have any choices as a slave. But somehow, David still had faith that he lived a life worth living. Colleen slumped back against the wagon seat.

"You're correct," she said. She'd chosen to come to New Orleans after the debacle at Ashington Manor, truth be told, just as she'd chosen to enter into service in the first place. Perhaps she could have found an apprenticeship with a seamstress if she'd believed in the possibility. Not that Colleen wanted to be bent over a sewing needle somewhere in a dank Newport shop (without present company, that was). She turned to face David. "And what do you want?"

"To be free and have my own furniture store," David said. "Somewhere North, like Canada."

"Are these impossible dreams?" she asked, watching his skillful hands control the horses. She took a breath for courage. "Or could we actually stand *together* on a Canadian beach?"

"I want to make the choice and try," David said. He caught her gaze before quickly shifting his attention back to the chaotic road. Still, in that instant, Colleen's heart flooded with joy. He felt the same as she did.

"I want the same," Colleen replied. She closed her eyes, and her mind conjured a vision of a distant beach, a horseshoe-shaped one like Keem Bay. She and David skipped along the shoreline, a flurry of snowflakes dancing around them. Colleen wondered if this vision was a glimpse of her future or a figment of her desperate imagination. She prayed to her saint for the former.

Although Colleen left bowls of milk for the fairies and spirits, she hadn't truly believed magic could manifest something in the physical world. That was, until she met David. She indulged in her fantasy a few more seconds and then opened her eyes, frowning when she saw David's face had settled into a grim expression. His eyes were fixed on a crow perched on the top of the carriage ahead of them. "What's wrong?" she asked.

"Crows can mean violent storms ahead," David replied. "Are you prepared for that?"

"Of course. Ireland has violent storms, as well," Colleen said, irritation creeping into her voice. She remembered the feeling of wind-driven sleet biting her skin. During strong storms, the ocean churned with the anger of Manannan-mac-Lir, the Irish god of the sea. The gray waves crashed on Keem Beach and cast white froth over the rain-soaked sand. And the cold of Ireland in winter? David knew nothing of it.

"I meant we have a hard path ahead of us," David said. He snapped the reins. "And while Irish winds might be violent, the storms here can flatten a house."

Colleen blanched. She was being cocky again, assuming she knew everything there was to know about a situation. Colleen took a deep breath and worked to fight her rising sense of helplessness. David was right. They had plenty of obstacles ahead of them, namely M. Le Jaune. He owned both of them and could do what he pleased. David was simply trying to warn Colleen about the dangers ahead. He didn't deserve her frustration. "The nuns always told me I was quick to anger," she said. "I apologize."

The hint of a smile softened David's features. "I don't mind. You're *enchanting* when you're upset."

"Oh, you flatterer!" Colleen turned away so he wouldn't see her furious blush. The wagon kicked up all manner of dust and filth, but she would have walked through muck up to her waist with David at her side. "Violent storms or not, I'd rather take the hard path with you than another without."

"Then we'll have to leave New Orleans. Monsieur won't manumit me even if I pay him, and you can't live in that house for the rest of your indenture," David said from the safety of the moving wagon. For all the people on the street knew, he and Colleen were simply planning the day's shopping.

"We must take your mother, too," Colleen added. She couldn't imagine leaving the poor woman.

David slid the reins into one hand and used the other to brush against Colleen's hip, a part of her body the spectators on the street couldn't see. The touch was so light, so quick it looked like an accident, but it sent a cascade of joy straight to her core. The simplest of gestures were capable of holding within them the most profound of human emotions. In the space of that ordinary wagon trip into town, Colleen and David had confirmed their feelings for one another *and* decided to run away from their tyrannical owner. Colleen rested her hand on the rough wooden seat of the wagon and brushed it lightly against David's cotton shirt, all the contact she dared out in public. "Now, how do we execute this great folly of ours?" she asked.

"I like the word *quest* better than folly," he said. "But we'll consult my deck of cards."

Colleen turned to him, her eyebrows raised clear up to the sky. The only person Colleen knew who talked to cards was the old woman who traveled with an itinerant fair that visited her home village once per year. Colleen had spent a good bit of coin just to learn that she had a handsome stranger and a good bit of grief in her future. Not that the reading was wrong, considering who sat next to Colleen in the wagon. But the carnival woman's answer could hold true for half the population of Ireland. David, on the other hand, had a real connection to the spirit world. "How interesting," she said. "Are the cards reliable?"

David paused. "They are, which can be difficult to accept if you don't like their message. Sometimes you can use the knowledge to change the future, but other times, you can't do a damned thing. You have to use the guidance from above as best as you can."

Colleen considered the truth of David's words. Guidance from above had, after all, ushered her on the path to New Orleans. Becoming an indentured servant had been a gamble, but Colleen couldn't stay in Ireland after the bone-chilling nightmare the red-haired woman, St. Brigid, had sent her.

In that eerie vision, Colleen had seen her parents, sister, and cousins huddled around the family's hearth, which didn't even have a lump of smoldering coal. They all had rail-thin limbs and skeletal faces. They were starving. When she woke up, drenched in sweat and gasping for air, Colleen took more than a few swigs of her da's whiskey stash to steady her nerves.

She didn't believe her family would starve to death, of

course. Instead, Colleen believed the dream meant that staying in Ireland would be the death of her. The dream, and Mme. Le Jaune's advertisement, had driven Colleen to sea with naught but a churning stomach and a stolen cast-off dress. "We need to know what's ahead," Colleen replied as she and David watched the crow fly off the carriage ahead.

"I'm glad you're not afraid. Some people believe card reading and talking with spirits are unholy," David said.

Colleen shrugged. "*Some people* also hanged my ancestor for witchcraft hundreds of years back just for having a cunning. We'll be more careful than poor Siobhan was with her herbs."

"Especially around Monsieur Le Jaune," David cautioned. "He lurks around corners."

David's warning sent her heart pounding. Surely, the spirits would protect them from Monsieur because their cause was just. Perish the thought of the alternative.

She yearned to stay seated right next to David in the carriage forever, where they had freedom from M. Le Jaune. David's presence comforted Colleen because it was tangible and immediate, not a great cloud of unknowing that could turn benevolent or monstrous on a whim.

As the wagon passed a walled cemetery, though, Colleen acknowledged, with chilly acceptance, the futility of her wish. The only certainties of life were death and uncertainty itself.

A few minutes later, David stopped the wagon in front of a store called *Du Bois Mercantile*. The proprietors of the store, Monsieur and Madame Du Bois, reinvigorated Colleen's spirits. M. Du Bois had once been a slave, but he'd gotten himself manumitted by paying for his freedom with money earned from extra work. Monsieur Du Bois then married Madame, and they had taken over her parents' little store. Colleen saw M. and Mme. Du Bois's little gestures of open affection and wanted the same with David. *Running away is the only way to have that,* she reckoned as she climbed back into the buckboard with the herbs she'd purchased for Madame's stomach ailments secured in her pocket.

When they returned to Etoile, David and Colleen dropped off the items they'd purchased in town and then sought privacy in David's workshop. The late afternoon sun, a beautiful golden light tinged with copper hues, shone in through the window and illuminated the beautifully painted cards and David's face. "Where did you get them?" Colleen asked, her mouth hanging open as she gawked at the cards.

"From my mentor, Marie Laveau," David replied. He shuffled the deck and rested it on his worktable. "Are you ready to see what they say?"

Colleen gripped the edge of the table. "For the truth and all that comes with it. I'm ready."

His face cast with reverence, David pulled a shiny penny from his pocket and offered it to Alegba, who Colleen supposed was a spirit. He then left a few coffee beans and a small pile of tobacco for spirits called Baron Samedi and Maman Brigitte, the equivalent of her own St. Brigid. Colleen felt honored to witness that simple yet momentous ceremony. Although she didn't see a spirit manifest after David called them, Colleen felt the air become simultaneously more alive and serene. It was almost as if a storm, a benevolent rain shower instead of a tempest, had gathered around them. With his eyes closed, David clasped the cards in his hands and said he wanted to know the best path forward. He then shuffled the deck again and drew the top three cards. As he turned over the first two, his eyes lit up. When he flipped over the last, however, Colleen saw her fear reflected on David's face.

"What is it?" she asked in a whisper, praying all the while his answer wouldn't crush her dreams into dust.

"The first is Temperance, which means biding our time, if needed, as we plan. Next, the Six of Swords suggests travel by water," David said, giving her a reassuring smile. "The Two of Swords, the one that worries me, points to a difficult choice. It's not necessarily bad news. Simply complicated."

Biding their time and a trip by water. Colleen thought of the lazy river that ran the length of Etoile. The Mississippi had seemed like her salvation earlier that day at the dock, and also now, based upon David's reading. Perhaps that notion would prove true. "So, we simply bide our time until we can escape by water and destroy any obstacles in our way," she said.

"That we will," David agreed. "I'll begin thinking about the water path in the meantime."

"We'll just have to avoid swimming with the gators," Colleen joked. She didn't think, then, that the most dangerous reptiles are often more figurative than actual, something she'd soon come to learn in full force.

CHAPTER SEVEN:
THE CHARIOT

The Chariot card indicates you should push forward despite any barriers in your way. Ogoun is the loa most associated with war, and he comes in various manifestations, such as Ogoun Badagris and Ogoun Ferraille. If you need the strength of a consummate warrior, Ogoun will guide your battle chariot. To summon him, offer him rum and objects of metal. Life is a series of battles that we must fight. Of course, we hope to win these various skirmishes. Remember, though, that success takes work on your part.

Selene

*October 22, 1860, Faubourg
Marigny, New Orleans*

As she finished her story, Maman's face was at peace. Our empty breakfast plates and the sun's passage over the garden wall signaled that we'd passed the majority of our morning in pleasant remembrances. The temptation to ask her what happened next overwhelmed me, but I couldn't justify ruining her pleasant mood. Her story didn't end happily. If it had, then she, Papa, and I would all be living happily in Canada. I still didn't understand how she became M. Le Jaune's mistress, but I took her hand and smiled. "Thank you for telling me."

Maman squeezed my hand, and her grip was stronger than it had been in weeks. "I enjoyed basking in my happy memories of your father," she said. "You should go see Marie. I'll clean up from breakfast."

My eyes drifted down to the dirty dishes, perfect symbols of the drudgery of Maman's life. Had Maman ever had a *proper* adventure? Sailing from Ireland counted as one, as did meeting Papa, but the remaining stretch of her existence was pure misery. Maman deserved to live the rest of her days in happiness. As I stood and straightened my purple calico dress, I made a silent promise to give Maman just that—some measure of joy. Until then, I could help with the dishes. "Let me help you clean up before I go ask Patrice for Marie's address," I said.

"I'm capable of cleaning," Maman replied. She shooed me away with her hand. "Also, Marie lives at 152 Rue St. Ann."

I frowned. "How do you know where she lives?"

"She's quite famous, Selene," Maman said, a ghost of a smile on her lips.

Maman said not a word more as she picked up the breakfast plates. She was adept at hiding secrets from everyone, save for Tante Jeanne. That skill allowed my mother to deceive M. Le Jaune, but it also kept her from receiving comfort from others.

Of course, she flung herself into laudanum's warm embrace. She'd drink another bottle later, but for now, she glowed with genuine contentment. I mumbled a word of thanks, gave her a peck on the head, and dashed to my bedroom.

What to wear for a meeting with a famous Voodoo queen? The loathsome dress from M. Le Jaune hung in my wardrobe, but my intuition told me finery wouldn't impress Marie one bit. People easily crafted beautiful illusions with lace, satin, silk, pearls, and jewels. Mme. Le Jaune had all of those things, for example, but her place in society depended upon her ability to conceal her husband's gambling troubles. These efforts likely exhausted her and didn't fool people who bothered to look through Madame's flimsy silk veil.

If Marie agreed to teach me, she'd expect authenticity. The

simple garment I'd put on that morning would serve that purpose well. Purple was both my, and Brigitte's, favorite color. Before I left the cottage, I also secured more of Raoul's coins in my pocket in case Marie charged for her lessons.

At my nervous pace, my walk to Marie's house on Rue St. Ann took but half an hour. I hadn't known her exact address before Maman told me, but I did know her beautiful cottage sat at the back of the French section of the city. Rumor had it a wealthy gentleman gifted her that home after she saved a family member of his from a prison sentence. As I rounded the corner of Bourbon Street and stepped onto Rue St. Ann, the faint sound of a heartbeat echoed softly in my ears. The closer I got to Marie's house, located near an open-air market and gathering place called Congo Square, the louder my heart became. I wondered if a gathering was underway in the square. Every Sunday, slaves and former slaves alike congregated for commerce, drumming, and dancing. But it was a Monday.

I stopped and tried to shake off the heartbeat. Strangely, though, none of the people around me seemed bothered by the loud percussive sound. The horses didn't whinny, and people kept up their conversations, making me suspect the beat existed only in my head.

I'd heard similar music at a party of Baron and Brigitte's, where the top hat clad Ghede danced to the rhythm of the drums. At those parties, I danced and let those jolly skeletons lift away all my earthly worries. Parties hosted by the dead were the most exciting of social events.

With the cemetery festivities in mind, I surrendered control of my feet and let the heartbeat propel me along until I reached a small adobe cottage. The home had a metal placard that boasted Marie's address. A sudden flurry of nervousness settled on my heart and kept me planted in front of the door. What if Marie thought me unworthy of her lessons? She was a famous Voodoo queen, after all.

Before I obeyed my instinct to flee, a beautiful lady with glowing skin and wise eyes opened the front door. For the first few moments, she simply stared into my eyes. "Selene, your father said you were coming," she said, breaking into a warm smile. "I'm Marie Laveau. Please come in."

Ah, so this was the famous Voodoo queen. Her friendly smile melted away my fear. I followed her inside, curious to see how she decorated her home. Marie's front room was an elegant parlor with plush furniture, brocade drapes, and whitewashed walls. Lace doilies covered the side tables and gave the room a touch of delicateness. Then, as we approached a door leading to a back room, I stopped. A powerful force, something far beyond my understanding, radiated from that room.

"Don't be afraid," Marie said as she twisted the doorknob.

I trusted her. More importantly, my father had endorsed Marie, so I didn't hesitate to walk through that door. The air shifted when I entered the back room. There, I discovered Marie's pièce de résistance, a well-equipped altar with flags and banners mounted on the wall behind it. Candles, small glasses of rum, coins, plates of food, dolls, and cigars crowded the altar's surface. The offerings on the altar were Marie's gifts for the loas. Once I pulled my eyes away from the impressive altar, I noticed the room's cozy hearth as well as a table covered in bundles of herbs and jars. "This is the center of your home," I said.

"Yes, it is." Marie sat down at the table and gestured for me to do the same. "Your father tells me you've come to learn how to serve the spirits."

I held up my bag with Raoul's coins. "I can pay."

Marie shook her head. "That's not necessary. As compensation for your lessons, you can help me make gris-gris, potions, and charms for my clients. This is an apprenticeship."

Potions and charms I understood, but not the first word she'd mentioned. "*Gris-gris?*" I asked.

Marie pointed to the ceiling, where a large collection of herbs and flowers had been hung out to dry. "Little bags, filled with herbs and other ingredients, that we craft with specific purposes in mind."

As I inhaled the beautiful aroma of the herbs, the room spun.

"But I've never made anything like that," I said.

"I'll teach you," Marie assured me.

"And tell me what I need to know?" I asked. As much as I appreciated Marie offering me an apprenticeship, I couldn't pretend to be Raoul's mistress forever. I leaned forward. "My parents refuse to."

"You'll learn everything when you can control your emotions. You can't act rashly with magic," Marie replied, a look of amusement crossing her face.

I looked to the source of the room's magic—Marie's splendid altar. A strong power emanated from it in waves that hit my skin like bursts of air from a storm. I was in the presence of this power, yet I possessed none of it. I was a young woman without much experience in the way of spirits, someone owned by a beastly man who also controlled my maman. I didn't even know how Papa had died. Despite my shortcomings, I needed to harness magic to enact justice on my parents' behalf. As soon as I thought the word *justice*, a sharp pain bolted through my head, causing me to gasp and shift my focus from the altar to Marie. "What just happened?" I asked, stroking my forehead.

Marie's intense gaze pierced through me. "You want *revenge*, not justice," she said.

"That's not—" I protested before Marie raised her hand to quiet me. "You want revenge just like your maman. But anger like that inspires revenge *and* keeps people trapped, whereas balancing the universe inspires justice," she explained. "Restoring balance is how you'll avenge your father's death and help free your mother."

I wanted to deny Marie's accusations that I had my maman's temperament, but I remembered my outburst against my father in the cemetery. Rage had taken hold of my better judgment. Papa even warned me that the need for revenge drove Maman, something Tante Jeanne had echoed. I didn't understand how anger could trap her as Monsieur Le Jaune had. And yet, I couldn't deny that my heart burned with anger for how he treated my mother. Freeing her from him would restore balance, Marie had implied.

As for my father's death, however, I had no evidence to assign blame even though I suspected Monsieur had played some role. I knew in my bones I'd become enraged when I discovered who had contributed to his death. Drawing in a deep reserve of air, I worked to calm the impetuous child-self that lived in my heart. "Very well. When should we start?"

Marie stood and clasped her hands together. "Why, right now, of course."

Marie next instructed me on how to interact with the spirit world more formally. I already knew how to ask Alegba to open the gate and how to properly offer my familiar spirits food and drink, but I hadn't realized just how many spirits existed. In addition to demonstrating how to conduct proper rituals that day, Marie also showed me how to prepare gifts to the spirits' liking. The Ghede, for example, enjoyed rum infused with the hottest of peppers, so we sliced dried peppers and slid the pieces right into a rum bottle. In every task, Marie Laveau's movements were quite fluid, almost as if she were conducting a symphony in the world beyond. She tolerated abuse from no one, not even the wealthiest, most powerful white man in New Orleans. I envied her poise and confident bearing.

"You'll become strong if you work hard," she said as she dropped her collection of pepper bits into a bottle of rum.

I almost dropped the knife I'd been using to chop the pepper, for she could also, apparently, read minds. *Quite* the handy skill. "I only hope it's strong enough to do what needs to be done," I said, setting the knife on the table.

"Strength is also about trusting the spirit world," Marie said. "Trust requires surrender."

Trust requires surrender. I finished collecting my pieces of pepper and placed them carefully in the bottle as Marie had done. This task complete, I stared at the knife I'd just set down and saw the light from the fireplace reflected in its blade. Elemental fire and sharp tools were traditionally such lethal, menacing things. However, with Marie, the fire-enlivened object seemed warm and nourishing. Surrendering *here* didn't bother me. On the other hand, surrendering in the context of Raoul frightened what little wits I had right out of me. "How long must I pretend with Raoul?" I asked. Although I hadn't mentioned him to Marie, she probably already knew.

"Not long. And I promise, you won't have to do anything unsavory with him," Marie said. She gave me a motherly smile and pointed to the chair. "Let me show you a useful skill. Close your eyes, and focus on the object of your inquiry. In this case, Raoul Le Jaune. Let your inner senses guide you."

With the chair as my ersatz spine, I relaxed my body and closed my eyes. At first, my thoughts refused to settle. I remained steadfast, though, focusing on my breaths and the lights dancing in the dark. I then thought of Raoul. I soon envisioned him walking the streets of the French section of the city. He stopped in front of a brick town house with iron balconies on the second and third floors. The first floor had window boxes stuffed with red zinnias. Raoul tapped the front door with the door knocker, and an older woman opened the door. She greeted him with a smile before quickly ushering him inside.

The house. Raoul was searching for a place he *assumed* we'd commit our contracted indiscretions. My eyes shot open. "He's here," I said, spinning around to look at Marie. "In this area of the city."

"Very good," Marie said. She picked up a mortar and pestle. "Now, go find him."

"Intentionally? Why?" I asked as I stood and pushed in my chair, which squeaked against the floor.

Marie gave me a cryptic smile. The soft drag of stone against stone filled the air as she ground some herbs. "Trust in the spirits and your instincts," was all she offered.

I doubted my instincts could fend off an amorous Raoul, but I'd surrender and trust Marie's advice nonetheless. She had given me comfort when needed. Only Maman, Tante Jeanne, and Patrice numbered the living souls who showed me kindness. As important as the dead were to me, there was something wonderfully comforting about a warm body who cared. "Thank you," I said, curtseying.

"You are welcome. Please return tomorrow for your next lesson," Marie said as she escorted me back outside.

Although Earth has much to offer the living, the spirit world has its enticements. Papa assured me that Heaven and the garden of stone houses were pleasant places to be as he waited for Maman to join him. He told me the dead can travel through the ether without the constraints of a physical body. They meet spirits, saints, and beings as diverse as the souls on Earth. The dead can taste the essence of food and drink, and they still feel the emotions of the living, including love and longing for their beloved living ones.

Papa told me time is different in the spirit world, but that I would not be able to understand how, so he never elaborated on that dizzying concept. All I had to do now, though, was find Raoul. Not comprehend the mysterious workings of the universe.

I stood outside Marie's house, scanning left and right for clues. I hadn't thought to look for a street address in the vision, so I looked up to the sky. Maman Brigitte loved birds. If she were inclined to help me, she might just do so through those dear creatures. A particular flock of birds caught my attention. They flew in their typical "v" arrangement, which was reminiscent of an arrow.

With no other potential sign from the great beyond, I followed the birds' path, and after two blocks, the brick town house from my vision, flower boxes and all, emerged when I turned a corner. The house was just as pretty as in my vision. Under different circumstances, I would have loved to live in such a place with Patrice and Maman. So long as Monsieur didn't own the house, of course.

Just then, Raoul exited the front door. He stopped to stare at me, his eyes narrowing. "Selene. Are you out conducting errands?" he asked through his tight smile, making his question sound like a poorly disguised demand.

For some reason, Raoul suspected me of something. I swallowed to moisten my dry mouth. Why did it bother him to see me walking around the city? Did he fear he had competition for my affections? As I knew from observing Maman's interactions with M. Le Jaune, men who kept mistresses were a possessive lot.

I was about to say I was searching for a prism, but then I took a breath and listened to the world as Marie had just taught me. The refrain *Tell him the truth! Tell him the truth… tell him the truth…* echoed through my skull. Why the spirits wanted me to tell Raoul about Marie I didn't know, especially considering that M. Le Jaune was suspicious of the spirit world. But I had to trust that the spirits wanted me to tell Raoul about my visit to Marie's. I forced my lips into an innocent smile. "I was visiting a lady in the area. Marie Laveau."

"The Voodoo queen? Whatever for?" he asked, the suspicion on his face settling into amusement.

"For information about my heritage. I just discovered that my father was your father's slave," I replied. It struck me I could use this half-truth to my advantage to make Raoul feel guilty about keeping such a large secret from me. When people feel guilt, they are more likely to humble themselves and less likely to exploit you. I cocked my head. "Did you know?"

Raoul fidgeted in his tight suit and adjusted his gold brocade cravat. "I did. But be that as it may, I've found your new home," he said, gesturing to the second floor of the town house. "You'll see it soon."

"Thank you so much," I said. I donned the mask of an enamored young woman in the company of a pleasant suitor. "You're such a gentleman."

Raoul gave me a half bow and held out his arm. "May I escort you home?"

I held in my revulsion as I intertwined my arm with his. "I'd be delighted."

As Raoul shepherded me back to Marigny, I finally realized that just as some people can sense the beauty in art or the complex characteristics of a song, I perceived the whispers of the dead wherever I walked. That was my precious gift in this life. The dead would, ironically, be my salvation.

CHAPTER EIGHT: STRENGTH

The Strength card suggests you've recently triumphed over adversity and have the skill to defeat future challengers. In addition to calling on Ogoun for his warlike prowess, you can summon the loa of strength, Sobo, when you need security and perseverance. He dresses as a general does for battle, so show him the respect he deserves. To honor him, provide him with goat meat or mutton depending on your resources. With both Ogoun and Sobo in your spiritual arsenal, you can accomplish much and defeat all manner of foes.

Colleen

*October 30, 1841, Etoile,
New Orleans*

Huddled beneath her quilt, Colleen stilled her breathing and attempted to calm her racing heart. The doorknob to her tiny bedroom rattled. Next, the door squeaked as the person outside pressed his weight against it. Even the shadows cast by the moonlight streaming in through her window froze in anticipation. Would he dare break the lock? Colleen wondered. He can't do that without causing a ruckus.

Colleen shivered. Her cramped attic bedroom, equipped with a small cot, dresser, and rough-hewn table didn't even have a fireplace. Colleen still preferred New Orleans's autumn to Ireland's. A Louisiana autumn brought the smell of woodsmoke, cooler temperatures, and fire-colored trees, which carpeted the grass with bright yellow, orange, and crimson leaves. In Ireland, autumn was gray and barren despite what colors the leaves boasted. No matter how much wood or peat her family cast upon the hearth, Colleen never felt warm enough in Ireland's bitter dampness. She pictured her parents huddled by the fire. Her da would use his last cinder of body heat to keep his wife warm.

Except, Colleen's vision was no longer accurate. She'd recently received word that her ma was dead. Colleen couldn't bear to picture her mother as an ice-cold cadaver stuffed into a flimsy wooden coffin.

The doorknob rattled again, and the door creaked under Monsieur's pronounced weight. His moist breath rasped against the thin wooden door. *Would he press harder?* Colleen soon became light-headed from holding her breath, so she inhaled the tiniest bit of air through her nose. She flinched suddenly when he cleared his throat.

"You can't keep me out forever, my dear," M. Le Jaune's voice pierced through the thin wooden barrier that separated them.

Colleen froze. To her blessed relief, his footsteps got softer as they trailed down the stairs. Finally, when the hallway was quiet, Colleen permitted herself to breathe normally. She pulled the quilt tightly around her and nestled into the fabric. She'd won for the night but had the whole war ahead.

Colleen cracked a yawn. At least Madame was sleeping alone in her room nowadays, giving Colleen a respite at night from her demands. She tried to relax her mind, but every few minutes, the thought of M. Le Jaune breaking down her door jolted her wide awake. The vicious cycle repeated for a few hours, until Colleen, blessedly, passed out from sheer exhaustion. Without fail, night passed into morning far too quickly. The set patterns of the sky's celestial bodies paid no heed to Colleen's plight. The morning sun woke her as it crept through her tiny gabled window. She threw off the quilt and changed from her nightgown into a day dress and wrap.

With her body hidden under layers of clothing, Colleen slowly opened her bedroom door and peeked out into the attic hallway, sighing in relief that no one huddled in the morning shadows. She crept downstairs and followed the smell of sweet corn and woodsmoke out to the kitchen building, where she found Celeste preparing a breakfast of porridge, biscuits, and coffee.

The kitchen had a cozy atmosphere thanks to the exposed beams, bricks, and cooking bric-a-brac that lined the walls. Early mornings were a convivial time, for everyone had the opportunity to gather around a long table and enjoy one another's company before Monsieur and Madame arose.

Wanting to keep her feelings for David secret, Colleen discreetly caught his eye as she chose the seat directly across from him. David reciprocated with a polite smile. "Good morning," he said. She bristled at David's formality. Before she could mumble good morning in return, Celeste planted herself next to Colleen. The cook frowned as she studied the dark circles under Colleen's eyes. "How was your night?"

"I fell asleep eventually," Colleen admitted under her breath. She took a bite of the fragrant porridge that steamed in her bowl, praying her answer would satisfy Celeste, yet not provoke David's worry. Colleen glanced at him and saw he'd frozen, his coffee cup suspended in the air. She didn't want David to imagine the worst, so she shrugged. "Oh, don't worry. I locked the door as you advised," Colleen whispered. "Monsieur can't bust in without the missus hearing. He's not *that* daft."

Celeste humphed. "Oh, he's certainly *daft*. Cowardly, too. That's the real reason he won't break down the door. He's afraid to make Madame even more irate."

"At least she's a bit less hysterical in this cooler weather," Colleen added in a louder voice. "And unless she gestates as long as an elephant, the baby will be born before the heat returns, praise the saints."

Previous to Colleen's joke, everyone around the table had been talking among themselves, politely ignoring Colleen and Celeste's hushed discussion of Monsieur's advances. They knew about Monsieur's habits, of course. After the elephant comment, though, the woodsmoke-scented kitchen became so silent any one of them could've heard a mosquito's drone clearly from a mile away. A searing rush of blood burned on Colleen's cheeks. Had she gone too far by comparing her mistress to an elephant? It was a dangerous comment if it reached the wrong ears. She surveyed the people sitting around the table, who studiously ate and avoided meeting her gaze.

When a bird's call broke the silence, David cleared his throat, concern etched on his face. "We should take care," he said. "Not from anyone in this room, but perhaps someone right around the corner."

Colleen knew he was right, but comparing Madame to an elephant, insulting her to that degree, had been empowering, an emotion she missed so much it hurt her to her core. Colleen didn't want to give up that feeling of being in control when Madame dominated almost every facet of her life. Determined to launch one final barb at Mme. Le Jaune, Colleen locked her eyes with David's. "Very well. I'll take your advice. But you must admit, she's just as *immovable*."

David sighed. But when he traded amused looks with Colleen, she knew the conversation had meandered into less treacherous waters. Better he caution her than worry about what Monsieur was up to. Colleen was about to continue with her breakfast, but Rachel ran into the kitchen.

"Colleen, Madame needs you right away," Rachel said, sounding more apologetic than alarmed in the face of that morning's emergency. "I heard her yelling from the nursery."

Colleen plopped her spoon into her bowl. She didn't wish ill upon Madame or the unborn babe, but Colleen didn't need to consult David's cards to know this crisis was likely the product of Mme. Le Jaune's histrionics. "Of course. What's wrong?" Colleen asked.

In the safety of the kitchen, Rachel rolled her eyes. "Lord only knows. She just said to get you."

Colleen glanced longingly at her unfinished, delicious breakfast, but she didn't want to antagonize Madame. "Right away."

"Eat. You'll need your strength," Celeste ordered.

Rachel nodded. "You *should* eat. If she's as ornery as Raoul today, you'll need all of God's strength."

"You should also bring her breakfast," Celeste said, standing up. "Eat while I plate Madame's food."

"I need to get back to that child before he destroys the nursery," Rachel said. Raoul's governess then ran from the kitchen.

Colleen shoveled her porridge and biscuit into her mouth as quickly as she dared without choking on them. It was a real shame not to be able to savor Celeste's delicious food, but at least Colleen would get lunch in a few hours. That was, unless Mme. Le Jaune made some outrageous demand. The elephant comment seemed all the more relevant in the face of her mistress's fickle request.

Right as Colleen finished her food, Celeste deposited a plate of delicate pancakes in front of her. "For Madame," the cook said.

Pancakes in hand, Colleen flashed David another smile before leaving the warm kitchen for the chilly autumn morning. She gave the fire-tinged leaves that dappled the ground with their splendor a cursory look before she marched into the main house and directly to the boudoir, the place Madame had apparently sequestered herself. As usual, the drawn curtains cast the room in gloom. Madame never allowed the housekeeper to air out the boudoir, so the scents of musty air and Mme. Le Jaune's expensive perfume meshed together into an unpleasant cloud. It took all of Colleen's strength not to gag. Monsieur hadn't visited the boudoir in quite a while, a great relief to Madame, who'd once confessed to Colleen that she found her marital duties tiresome.

Colleen felt a smidgen of pity for the woman. Mme. Le Jaune not only suffered from the pregnancy but also endured a husband she hadn't even wanted to marry—an unfaithful one at that. Celeste had said Monsieur had access to a cottage where he could bring his loose women. He didn't own this secret love nest but had won the rights to its use in a poker game. In other words, although he couldn't sell the cottage, Monsieur had it at his disposal. Gentlemen wagered the strangest of things for sport.

When her eyes adjusted to the dim light, Colleen saw that Madame was reclined on the chaise. "I've brought your breakfast, Mum," Colleen said as she set the plate of pancakes on a nearby table.

"Breakfast?" Mme. Le Jaune asked.

"Yes, some of Celeste's pancakes," Colleen replied.

Madame cracked one eye open and twisted to see Colleen, a movement that also exposed her swollen ankles from under her pink brocade dressing gown. Groaning, Madame propped herself up on the chaise. She then sent Colleen a glare to rival Satan himself. "I can't eat pancakes without lavender honey," Mme. Le Jaune snapped. "And you're standing there like an imbecile. Get it *now*."

Colleen's sympathy for her mistress evaporated in an instant. Colleen knew from seeing her own ma's shifting moods that pregnancy made some women irritable. Irritable, yes, but vicious, no. "I'll just go to the pantry, then," Colleen said.

"Don't be stupid. It's not here," Madame all but shouted as she flopped back onto the chaise like a limp rag. "It's at the convent. Have Day take you to buy some."

Colleen froze. As much as she loved the chance to leave Etoile with David, she'd spent the last of her weekly household allowance on the new hat Madame had demanded Colleen purchase. Monsieur controlled how much money his wife spent even though it was mostly her dowry that kept Etoile running. She barely left the house anymore. Why waste whatever money her husband gave her on a hat? "I'll need more funds on account of the hat," Colleen said, keeping her voice low.

"Get it from Celeste," Mme. Le Jaune spat out.

"Yes, Mum," Colleen said as she ran from the room, grateful

she no longer had to abide the smells of perfume and mustiness or Madame's bitter mood. She focused on the bit of joy that had just entered her day. She had an excuse to spend time with David. Colleen skipped over the colorful leaves and sent the bright blue sky a grateful nod. By the time she returned to the kitchen, only Celeste and David remained, the others having started their workday.

"Back so soon?" David asked as he gathered bowls into a stack.

"Madame wants you to drive me to a convent to get some lavender honey," Colleen replied, working to keep her voice neutral. "I hope you know where she means."

"That I do," David said. "I'll ready the wagon. Meet me in the stable in a few minutes."

"Certainly," Colleen replied. Her eyes followed him out the door before settling on the ground, where birds pecked for worms. In an absent voice, she said to Celeste, "Madame told me to ask you for money. I spent my last coin on her new hat."

"It appears Madame has a craving," Celeste said as she pulled the money Madame had given her for expenses from a ceramic jar.

"She does, indeed," Colleen agreed. Only the slight curl of her lip betrayed her thoughts of David and the cravings he rose in her.

"Be *careful*," the cook muttered, yanking Colleen close and staring into her eyes. Celeste smashed the money into Colleen's hand. "Your feelings are painted on your face as plain as day."

Colleen pushed away Celeste's hands and gazed at the older woman in horror. *She knew!* It was either because she was uncanny or because Colleen hadn't been hiding her emotions as well as she thought. Unable to find her voice, she nodded and secured the money in her dress pocket.

The coins clinked together like church bells before an invasion. Although the action would likely prove futile, medieval monks had yanked on church bell ropes with all their might when they saw disaster on the horizon. Colleen had a talent for recalling useless trivia. From school and the books she read to Lady Ash, Colleen remembered how the Vikings invaded Ireland centuries ago and how long elephants carried their young.

Neither of those facts helped Colleen when she wanted to deny Celeste's accusations. Colleen couldn't abandon David. They were each human beings and entitled to love. David's mother, understandably, wanted them to be careful. "I'll take care," Colleen promised. Protecting David was a sacred vow she'd keep.

"Good," the cook said with a curt nod. "You have enough money for three jars." Celeste next slammed the breakfast dishes into the washing tub and started scrubbing, her shoulders tight.

Bearing Celeste's warning in mind, Colleen joined David in the stable. She climbed into the wagon and sat as far apart as she could from him. As David eased the wagon forward, she kept quiet about the conversation she'd had with Celeste in the kitchen. "Your mother knows," Colleen said when they were safely beyond Etoile's grounds. "She warned me to be careful."

"We'll be careful in public," David said. As he shuffled a mere inch closer to Colleen, she imagined her body twisted and melded to his as they did things that would earn Colleen a slap from the nuns. Colleen stole a glance at him and saw the blush on his cheeks. David snapped the reins, bringing the horse to a canter. "I think we need a distraction," he said. "I'll tell you about this convent."

As David drove, Colleen learned that Madame's coveted lavender honey came from a Benedictine abbey. Nearly one hundred years ago, a wealthy French widow had bequeathed her fortune to the church under the condition they establish an abbey and convent school dedicated to educating young women. The convent school was a successful endeavor, and its graduates emerged refined, proper, and genuinely educated. Between tuition and revenues from its honey, the convent was self-sufficient, which was a good thing considering the sporadic arrival of large endowments.

Colleen enjoyed learning this history. She only wished she'd been educated at a similar institution. The lesson ended too soon for Colleen's tastes when David stopped the buckboard in front of a three-story brick building. A large-cloistered garden was attached to one of the convent walls.

"Oh, by the saints, nuns frighten me," Colleen said as she stared up at the convent's edifice. The nuns who'd taught her at the parish school had been old, mean creatures.

"You probably won't have to talk to any nuns," David said, laughing gently. He pointed to a red door on the cloister wall that faced the street. "Knock on that door and ask for Jeanne."

"Jeanne's a kind nun?" Colleen asked.

David shook his head. "She's a laywoman who lives here in exchange for taking care of the bees. I've driven my mother here many times to buy lavender honey. Jeanne does business with women, preferably. But in any case, Jeanne is very nice. I promise."

"I'll hold you to that promise," Colleen mumbled as she jumped out of the buckboard.

Shoulders squared and spine straight, Colleen rapped lightly on the red door, hoping all the while that Jeanne, instead of a nun like the dragons back in Ireland, would greet her. For a few seconds, all she heard was the faint drone of bees coming from within. Then, the door swung open, and a beautiful young woman in a simple dress and kerchief emerged from behind it. "Oui?"

"My name is Colleen O'Neil, and I'm here to buy some lavender honey from Jeanne," Colleen replied. She enunciated her words in case the woman spoke limited English.

"I am Jeanne. Please, come inside," the woman said in a warm voice. And in English, to Colleen's relief, since her command of French was still rudimentary at best.

Colleen followed Jeanne into a heavenly world. A series of covered arcades formed a perimeter around three sides of the beautiful garden, isolating it from the city. A row of fig trees offered a respite from the sun. Bunches of lavender perfumed the breeze around them. As Colleen inhaled the scent of lavender, a wave of tranquility washed over her. Then, in the center of the courtyard, water danced and splashed in a stone fountain. "How beautiful!" Colleen exclaimed.

"Yes," Jeanne agreed. "It's a hidden oasis in this city."

Despite the pleasant drone of the bees and the sound of the day's gentle wind rustling through the fig trees, Colleen couldn't fully escape the city. The faint clippity-clop of horses' hooves on the street intruded into the peaceful space. She pushed away those sounds as Jeanne led her to the shady arcade, where jars of honey sat on a table. "How many jars would you like?" Jeanne asked. "They're twenty cents apiece."

The honey shone like liquid gold from the traces of sunlight that beamed in under the tiled eaves of the arcade roof. "Three, please," Colleen replied, rummaging through her pocket for the proper coinage. She thrust the coins at Jeanne. "Hopefully, that will satisfy *Madame* Le Jaune and keep me from going mad."

Sometimes, shouting out the truth gave Colleen satisfaction. Holding her tongue gave her indigestion. For a moment, she feared Jeanne would report Colleen's comment to Madame Le Jaune. But then Jeanne's eyes lit up with delight. "You poor creature," the laywoman said. She covered her mouth to hide a giggle. "All of New Orleans believes she's très terrible. My maman included."

"Monsieur is worse," Colleen added. She didn't bother hiding the bitterness of her voice. Colleen felt safe confessing her feelings to Jeanne, who she suspected came from the same class as the Le Jaunes. How else would Jeanne know the family socially? Colleen wondered what had made Jeanne leave her world for the convent. Certainly not a religious commitment. Jeanne hadn't taken vows to become a nun.

Jeanne rested the jar of honey she'd been holding on the table. It made a hollow thud as it hit the wood. "I know," she said.

"I left my post in Ireland because of a man just like him. Through no encouragement on my part, I promise you." Colleen sank onto a bench that faced the garden. "I don't know what to do."

"Why not find another position?" the laywoman asked, sitting next to Colleen.

"I'm indentured," Colleen replied. She watched the bees scatter over the plants in the garden. She left it unsaid that she was trapped until David found a way out of New Orleans for them and Celeste.

Jeanne rested her hand on Colleen's shoulder. "Perhaps I can ask the church to purchase your indenture. You can work with me to fulfill a contract."

The heady scent of lavender tempted Colleen, but a horse's whinny from somewhere outside the cloister broke that spell. She couldn't abandon David. Her gaze settled on the door, in her lover's direction. "I would if my heart didn't want what it wants."

Jeanne frowned and looked to the beehives. After a few moments, she turned to Colleen, her eyes wide. "Mon dieu! You are in love with Celeste's son?"

"Please don't tell anyone," Colleen begged, her heart sinking. She cursed herself for her recklessness. Despite Celeste's warning about being careful, Colleen had failed. Jeanne had discovered her secret. From Colleen's face? Because she had looked in David's direction? Colleen's mind twisted with panic. No, Jeanne had been staring at the beehive when she'd discovered Colleen's secret. In Ireland, some people believed bees carried messages from the spirit world. Could Jeanne be a diviner of insects like David was with his cards?

"Do not worry," Jeanne assured her. She crossed herself. "I will not tell a soul, dead or alive, mon ami."

Colleen knew enough French to understand Jeanne's last words. Mon ami. My friend. "Why would you keep my secret?" Colleen asked. She scrutinized Jeanne's face, searching for a sign the beekeeper would betray her.

"Because we're all equal in God's eyes." Jeanne relaxed back against the bench and stared at the garden. "And I understand your predicament."

Colleen wanted to prod further and find out how Jeanne understood her situation, but the beekeeper deserved to tell her story in her own time, if at all. Colleen took a deep breath and savored the serenity of the place, which soothed her nerves like a powerful tonic. "Thank you, Jeanne. Mo chara."

"Chara," Jeanne repeated, a wistful look on her face. "It has been a while since I've heard that word. My mother, who is half Irish, knows some Gaelic. She and I no longer speak."

"Have you been to Ireland?" Colleen asked. She wanted to know what had caused a rift between Jeanne and her family, but again, Jeanne would talk when she was ready.

Jeanne shook her head. "Alas, no. I have traveled to Philadelphia, Charleston, Savannah, and Natchez with my family, but we never went to Europe." She paused for a moment, her eyes drifting from the garden to Colleen. "What is Ireland like?"

Colleen's face relaxed into a smile. "Emerald green hills and craggy mountains, rocky shores, and a few gentle waterfalls," she said, focusing on her home's natural beauty instead of the English overlords. "It's a place of uncanny power, too. There's the fairy folk, I mean. They live in fairy rings, cairns, and mountains."

"It sounds beautiful," Jeanne said.

"It is," Colleen agreed. Just then, the caw of a crow reminded her of danger, of obstacles in her and David's path. She stood and smoothed her skirt. "As much as I'm enjoying your company, I'm afraid I must be going. I've enough to contend with and don't need to add an irate Madame to my list of problems."

"Indeed, you do not." Jeanne went to the honey table. She picked up one jar and paused. She turned to Colleen, her eyes gleaming with mischief. "Tell your horrid Madame I only had one jar of honey ready to sell. You must come back to buy more when it runs out."

Colleen burst into laughter. "For good measure, I'll tell Madame you're giving me French lessons."

"Oui, oui," Jeanne quipped.

Colleen took the single jar of honey from Jeanne, who folded Colleen into a quick embrace. Part of Colleen was reluctant to leave the beautiful cloister garden, but the other half of her couldn't wait to see David again. As Jeanne latched the red door, Colleen stepped back out into the streets of New Orleans, with all of its urban sights, sounds, and smells. When her eyes rested on David, who sat patiently in the wagon, her heart warmed.

David offered her a hand into the wagon. "Only one jar?" he asked.

"Jeanne had more, but she suggested I just get one so you can bring me here more often. A subterfuge on her part," Colleen said as she slid onto the seat. She pursed her lips, fidgeting with the honey jar and wondering if she ought to tell David that the beekeeper knew the full measure of Colleen and David's relationship.

"And the reason for the subterfuge?" David asked. He nickered softly to the horse, and the carriage moved forward.

"Jeanne knows my feelings for you. I didn't tell her. She guessed," Colleen blurted out. She held her breath and braced herself for David's reaction. To her surprise, he kept his eyes on the road ahead and the reins steady. Only his clenched jaw told Colleen he'd heard her. "Please say something," she begged.

David remained quiet for a few agonizing seconds. "Then the spirits had some reason for telling her," he concluded, giving Colleen a resigned sigh. "I think we can trust Jeanne based on what my mother says about her, but we need to be careful."

Colleen stared at David, relieved he wasn't angry. The day had warmed a bit, and he'd unbuttoned his shirt enough to reveal the top of his chest. His muscles flexed as he gripped the reins tightly. The damned nuns at school had always taught her to be virtuous, to snuff out any unholy impulses. But what did those old dragons know? Wasn't love a gift from God? And yes, Colleen knew she felt love and not simple lust.

Colleen stared at the jar of honey that she cradled in her hands like an infant. An urge to throw the jar into the street seized Colleen. She could always buy another jar. Colleen loosened her grip on the honey and held it over the street. "I'm tired of being *careful*," she said. "We're human beings entitled to the same rights as the Le Jaunes in God's eyes. I don't care what the law says."

"We are," David said. He briefly caught her eye before concentrating back on the road. "The prudent thing would be to wait until we escape."

"I don't care about being prudent. I need to do something *I* have control over," Colleen insisted, tears of frustration gathering in her eyes. Maybe she was putting them on a reckless path, but at least she could act like a free person for a spell.

"All right, then," David said. "If you're sure this is what you want, I know a safe place."

The memory of what Colleen said next remained chiseled on her brain until her dying breath, for it was the moment she both liberated and condemned herself. "I'm *damned* sure," she replied as she set the honey safely down on the wagon floor.

With their mutual consent declared, David drove them to a walled cemetery in a quiet neighborhood at the perimeter of the French section. At first, the strange setting baffled Colleen, and she worried about disrespecting the dead or being discovered by visitors. David then explained this graveyard was his secret place and that when he asked the spirits for privacy, they made sure people avoided passing through the cemetery gates.

Colleen and David stretched out in the back of the buckboard, and any lingering regrets Colleen had about the unusual setting for such activities disappeared. She would later remember that day as one of the best of her life. It was also the beginning of a brief spree of happy days—a feeling she wished she could freeze in ice before everything descended into hell.

CHAPTER NINE:
THE HERMIT

Become contemplative rather than war-like when the Hermit card appears. If you need a quiet place to plan the next stage of your journey, consider spending time in the forest or bathing in a sacred spring. The Celtic god and goddess of healing, Grannus and Sirona, respectively, reside there. Heed the call for quiet and become a hermit if it serves your greater goal. Submitting to your calmer instincts is sometimes the best course of action, especially in the midst of uncertainty.

Selene

October 24, 1860, Bourbon Street, New Orleans

My first night in my new home, the wind howled through the trees in the courtyard, rustling the dead autumn leaves. I hardly minded, though, because the wind obscured the din from the streets. Drunk raconteurs yelled profanities after losing their fortunes at the gambling tables, and tired horses hauled their human burdens back to homes with fireless hearths. All that bedlam combined with the chatter of people who paraded through the streets in search of amusements, their faces illuminated by flickering gas lanterns.

Suspicions that M. Le Jaune had a role in my father's death spun in my head. I didn't need ruckus from the street in the pit of my insomnia. I shoved my pillow over my head and turned away from the noise, only to see Patrice's beautiful face. Deep in sleep, she lay prone on her back, begging for me to climb atop her and kiss her soft lips. But it wasn't the time to indulge in wants of the flesh. If I couldn't sleep, I might as well talk with the dead.

I loathed to leave the quilt's warmth, but I gently pushed it aside and crept out of bed. I then rested my foot on the floor, causing the old wooden boards to creak. Patrice shifted at the disturbance, so I froze until she quieted. After tightening my robe to protect me from Autumn's frosty fingers, I tiptoed out of the bedroom and stepped into the main room. I sank onto the settee and stared at the smoldering coals in the hearth.

Earlier in the evening, Raoul had installed me on the second floor of the brick town house. The small apartment had a bedroom, a larger main room, and a minute dressing room. Although many homes featured elaborate wallpaper and bric-a-brac, this apartment boasted simple dark woodwork and white-washed walls. The main room came equipped with a settee, a small table surrounded by four chairs, a smattering of small tables and oil lamps, and an empty bookcase. The large room also had a small fireplace to guard against the chill and French doors that opened onto a second-floor balcony overlooking the street. The bedroom had a view of the courtyard at the back of the house, however. My landlady, a widow named Mrs. Shelley, had furnished this room with a mahogany bed, wardrobe, and vanity.

I'd welcomed Patrice in bed, of course. I didn't worry about Raoul discovering us because sisters and friends of the same sex slept together for warmth and companionship. In fact, Raoul thought my best friend's presence would help protect me against drunk gamblers who might roam the street. My patron would never conceive of the truth of Patrice's and my relationship unless we were careless. And carelessness I would avoid. I needed Patrice with me to keep me sane.

I cringed whenever I thought of Raoul lying under the blankets. Both Papa and Marie had assured me I wouldn't have to fulfill Raoul's expectations of me, thank the loas. I still couldn't wait to leave this city. To make my situation more tolerable in the meantime, I fantasized that I lived in the apartment with Patrice and would soon decorate it with objects that honored the Ghede. Little accents of dark purple, a delicate snake skeleton on the mantel above the fireplace, and trims of black lace were very apropos accoutrements. Why not, when some of my dearest friends were dead, and I was likely conceived in a cemetery?

I stared at the hearth, and my mind drifted to the events of earlier in the evening. After Raoul settled me into the house, we sat at a table on the balcony and ate a fruit compote cooked by Mrs. Shelley. Or more accurately, I nibbled at the thick, sweet dessert so it wouldn't choke me as I swallowed. With the hint of a smirk on his lips, Raoul gobbled his compote as he watched the pedestrian and equine traffic bustling below us. He confessed that he chose this apartment because of its proximity to his favorite gambling establishments. In this, my patron favored his father.

"Don't you like your new home?" Raoul asked with an expectant look on his face. He twirled his red silk cravat through his long fingers, which belonged to a violinist instead of Raoul, who fondled cards or dice.

"Of course," I said, the lie gliding off my tongue. I craned my neck and looked onto the street to avoid meeting Raoul's eyes. The sunset painted the sky gold and bloody crimson.

Below me, a little ragamuffin girl was selling roses on the street corner. The poor thing looked like she hadn't eaten in a month. Desperation burned in her eyes like a lighthouse's beacon. Just then, a well-dressed lady walked by the little girl and threw an apple her way. The apple ricocheted off the cobblestones, accumulating more and more filth with each bounce. The girl lunged after it and devoured the fruit in two bites.

What an act of desperation!

I'd never known hunger great enough to drive me mad. Maman's family in Ireland had experienced that type of hunger, though, when famine swept the island only a few years after she arrived in New Orleans. Most of her relatives had died, which is why Maman never mentioned returning to Ireland despite the tragedies she suffered in America.

Would she have been better off trying to find a new life in Ireland with me instead of staying in New Orleans? I didn't know. Some choices we make are calculated, especially if we have valuable information at our disposal. But other choices are no more strategic than a drunk gambler's throw of the dice. I hoped I was making the right choice by helping Maman instead of leaving with Tante Jeanne. My eyes trailed behind the poor little girl, who was walking down the street in search of more filth-covered apples. Although I had enough food to eat, did I have a better lot in life than that little girl?

Raoul reached across the table and rested his hand on my shoulder, jolting me out of my mental wandering. "Then why do you look so sad?" he asked.

Raoul hadn't implied he'd sell me for displeasing him. But I knew that threat lingered somewhere in his mind as an unformed idea. He probably didn't know he'd resort to such an action if he didn't get his way. I studied his face, which reminded me of a pensive schoolboy and confident aristocrat. A troubling and contradictory combination if there ever was one. "Forgive me. I've never lived alone before," I said. For good measure, I forced a grateful smile to my face. "What do I do when you're not here? I'm accustomed to having my maman, Tante Jeanne, and best friend, Patrice, for company."

"Is that all?" Raoul asked. His tense expression eased as he removed his hand from my shoulder. He took another hearty bite of compote. "You should visit them and invite them here, of course. I wouldn't want you to get bored or into trouble. I'll give Mrs. Shelley my schedule each week so you can arrange your visits around those times."

"How kind of you. I won't feel so alone, then," I said, fluttering my eyelashes and looking at the floor. He'd just permitted me to host Maman, Tante Jeanne, and, most importantly, Patrice, in this apartment. My heart also longed to see someone else, though. My grandmother, Celeste. The visions my father sent showed me little slivers of the woman she was, but I needed to spend time with her in the flesh. Perhaps I could convince Raoul with a dose of spun sugar. I reached out and touched his hand, which grasped the compote glass. "May I invite Celeste, too?"

At my question, Raoul started laughing with food in his mouth. He shook my hand away and slammed down the glass, coughing and nearly choking on his dessert. His face flushed. Part of me hoped he'd choke, but then I shook away that thought. If Raoul died, M. Le Jaune would control me, which would be an even worse situation indeed. At least Raoul thought he liked me. "Are you all right?" I asked. "Do you need some water?"

Raoul shook his head and took a few moments to regain his composure. "Why would you want Celeste? Mrs. Shelley's slaves will take care of whatever you need. Food, cleaning, dressing. You'll lack for nothing."

I'd lack for nothing, including privacy. Raoul had also tasked Mrs. Shelley with spying on me. She'd certainly report my comings and goings to Raoul. He paid the rent, and in exchange, he received discretion and a sharp set of eyes to mind his investment. My landlady hid her intentions well, though. She treated me politely even though she thought I was Raoul's whore.

I shoved aside my irritation and searched my mind for another reason that Celeste should visit. Perhaps the truth would make him understand how precious any living kin was to me. "I don't need her to serve me," I said. "I've just learned she's my *grandmother*, and I want to know her."

"She is?" Raoul asked. I nodded, and he placed the compote glass on the table with an air of finality. "Well, she has work to do at Etoile. You'll have plenty of company without her."

I clenched my hands on the arms of my chair, hoping the smooth feel of the wood could soothe my rising anger. It didn't work. The injustice of everything that happened to my father and Celeste boiled in the pit of my stomach, threatening to explode.

Right as I opened my mouth to launch a torrent of curses Raoul's way, an icy wind swept across the balcony, smacking our faces and rattling the table. Raoul bolted up and ushered me inside, latching the French doors behind him. "I'll have Mrs. Shelley build you a fire," he said, his voice soothing.

"Yes, please." I shivered. The wind had distracted me from my outburst at precisely the right moment. But what if the wind hadn't been the wind at all? As Marie had taught me, the dead possessed amazing abilities. They could manipulate the atmosphere to create cold spots in otherwise warm houses as well as hot patches on blisteringly cold winter days. Cool and heat, air and fire, water and moist soil. The residents of the spiritual world could harness any element they wished. *Something* had aided me that night. I knew it in my bones. I had been careless, and my fate and Maman's plans depended on my ability to play the part Raoul had written for me in his drama. For *now*.

Raoul enveloped my hand in his. "I know what else will ward off the proverbial chill. Some new books and dresses."

"Thank you, Raoul," I said. Books would warm my spirits. I channeled that truth and hoped Selene the actress could convince Raoul of her sincerity.

"And if you're lonely tonight, you should send for Patrice. Mrs. Shelley will arrange it," Raoul said, beaming. He released my hand and dropped some coins in my palm. "Should you have any expenses, please use this."

"What a wonderful idea," I replied. I then rubbed my hands together vigorously as if desperate to warm myself. The sooner Raoul left the apartment and asked Mrs. Shelley to have the fire made, the sooner he'd leave for the night. After all, I had no reason to believe Raoul would spend the night.

Because of my *innocence* in carnal matters, he'd promised me that I could settle into the apartment on my own and take time to grow comfortable with him. Raoul could have taken what he wanted, but he clung to the illusion that he was a gentleman above all else. I prayed his urge to act the gentleman would tide him over until I could help Maman free M. Le Jaune's slaves.

Raoul delivered a chaste kiss to my cheek. "We'll be together soon."

"Indeed." That was the only word I could manage as I blushed, hoping he'd interpret my red cheeks as shyness rather than anger. Raoul wanted me to embody an odd combination of innocent virgin and willing whore, I supposed. He desired a woman happy to paint her lips red in the shadow of night, but not one who'd ever have carnal thoughts of her own save for ones fixated on him. If I acted too innocent, he'd find me cold. But if I appeared too eager to submit to him, he'd worry I'd done so with other men, quite likely.

I'd seen Maman do a similar dance between opposites—in her case, seething hatred and passive acceptance, as she negotiated M. Le Jaune's moods over the years.

"I'll tell Mrs. Shelley to get the fire," Raoul said, before departing into the crimson-tinged remnants of sunset.

With him gone, I took deep, regular breaths and felt the tension in my shoulders melt. As I waited for my landlady to appear, I unpacked my steamer trunk, which, thanks to how little I owned, looked like the gaping, dark mouth of a whale. I hung my few dresses in the wardrobe. After that, I secured Papa's cards in the vanity drawer and set up my combs on top of the vanity. The apartment would never feel homey, but at least it was better than the decaying cottage Maman lived in.

Soon, Mrs. Shelley's chauffeur and handyman, a kind slave named Samuel, appeared with a hot meal and some logs. I learned he lived atop the carriage house behind the courtyard with his wife, Abigail. Abigail was Mrs. Shelley's other slave, and she cooked and kept house for my landlady. I gave him Raoul's money and asked him to bring Patrice here if she were willing.

By the time I finished my dinner, my beloved arrived with

the spark of love in her eyes. Patrice was mine, and she had permission to be here thanks to Raoul. He'd never surmise the truth of Patrice's and my relationship. Such a thing was beyond his limited understanding of what constituted love.

The events of my first evening in the apartment led to Patrice in my bed and me still awake at three o'clock in the morning with burning questions for my dead father. I rested another log in the hearth and stoked the embers until they sputtered to life. The infant flames gave the polished sandstone fireplace an otherworldly glow.

Because of my work with Marie, I'd developed the ability to summon Papa wherever I wanted. I no longer had to travel to the cemetery to see him manifest before me. Thankfully, Raoul believed I visited the Voodoo queen for beauty suggestions and as a way to connect with my father's heritage. He didn't suspect I was learning how to work against him. I next retrieved the gifts for the loas I'd stashed in my trunk and set them up on the dining room table. After Alegba opened the door, I saw Baron's glasses and Brigitte's skull necklace reflecting the firelight from the hearth.

Baron looked at the bedroom and smiled. "You've been busy, my girl."

"That I have," I agreed. People usually envision spirits as wholly pure entities. And although the loas and Catholic saints have much in common, Voodoo spirits also embodied the virtues of seduction, pleasure, and humor. The Ghede, especially, loved the seductive and indulgent side of life.

Brigitte brushed her hips against Baron. "Patrice is good for you, Selene. She puts that imbécile Raoul to shame."

"Imbécile. How appropriate!" I said, laughing softly.

Baron removed his hat and bowed. "Well, I think it's time we left you to talk with your papa."

Although I didn't need Baron and Brigitte's help to bring my father to the apartment, I thoroughly enjoyed seeing them. Papa began to materialize next to Brigitte within a few seconds, and we had our customary embrace when his form became as solid as it could. I then took a seat at the table, ready for information about his death. I was more convinced than ever that M. Le Jaune had played some role.

"How did you die?" I asked, tracing my fingers along the wood grain of the table. During a natural history lesson, Tante Jeanne had once explained that a tree's rings told the story of its life. From a tree's rings, people could learn when the tree was born, about its struggle to thrive, and when a lumberjack ultimately felled it. The small dining table in the apartment had a tree's complete life etched into it, yet I had little sense of my own father's life or death.

Papa took a seat across from me, putting him almost at my eye level. "Are you sure you're ready to know more?"

"Yes. I've been learning to control my anger." I rested back in my chair. Of course, I neglected to mention how a spirit wind had saved me from lashing out at Raoul earlier.

"If you're sure," Papa said. He hesitated and studied me. "But be aware that the line between justice and revenge is a fine one."

I nodded, perhaps a bit too eagerly. Papa closed his ghostly eyes and projected a vision before me, yanking me from the warm candlelit room to a dark place that smelled of copper and grass. At first, I couldn't see anything in the inky darkness. Then, as seconds passed, shadows and colors began to emerge. Someone lay on a floor that was covered with what looked like hay. As the vision became sharper, I saw large swaths of red covering this straw. It was then that my zeal for the truth morphed into dread, which crept into my veins and froze the blood within them.

Yes, *blood.* The coppery smell. The field of red. It was all blood. When the vision finally sharpened to crystal clarity, I saw the face belonging to that broken body on that morbid canvas. There Papa lie, splayed on his back. His eyes were wide open with the terror and sadness he'd experienced during his final moments on Earth. My father had shown me his death portrait.

The actual image was so much worse than the abstract conception I'd had. It's strange how trauma first invokes a sense of shock, an emotionless state that allows one to deny an un-fathomable truth. But denial doesn't last forever. Life isn't *that* merciful. The vision before me forced me to confront the awful truth, triggering a cascade of emotions I wasn't equipped to handle. My throat tightened with an agony powerful enough to choke my lungs. After that horrible pain, I burned with white-hot rage and the need for vengeance. I sprung up from the chair. "Who did it?" I demanded in a harsh whisper. "I'll kill them."

With steely-eyed determination, my father pointed back to my chair. "Sit," he said. "I *forbid* you from killing anyone."

"You forbid me?" I asked. Resentment burned in my eyes. He couldn't stop me from avenging him. He was merely a ghost, after all.

"I don't need to forbid you to do anything," Papa said. His intense gaze slowly melted into an almost beatific one, breaking our stalemate of wills. "You know nothing productive comes from acting rashly."

As much as I hated to admit it, he'd made a fair point. My anger stewed beneath my skin, threatening to erupt like that famous volcano, Mount Vesuvius, that buried the great ancient cities of Pompeii and Herculaneum. Such fury destroys things indiscriminately, and I didn't want myself or my loved ones to be collateral damage. I sank back into the chair. "I won't kill anyone, but I *will* bring you justice."

"I wouldn't blame you if you left New Orleans with Patrice and Jeanne. I wanted your mother to leave long ago," Papa said, his eyes growing sad. "Staying in New Orleans and helping her will be painful. You'll help free her and bring me justice, but the knowledge that comes with all of that will hurt you."

I took a few moments to consider what such a commitment entailed, as well as its potential cost. As Papa once said, we all have to make choices—critical ones that determine our fate and that of those we love. Sometimes these choices require great sacrifice.

What would enacting justice for Papa cost *me*? I'd already promised Patrice I wouldn't end up like Maman, broken and hell-bent on her destructive course of action. *Her* motives, perhaps, straddled the line between justice and revenge, and she paid for that every day. Her plan kept her within M. Le Jaune's reach.

Just then, an image of Maman drinking a bottle of laudanum and bathed in M. Le Jaune's sweat popped into my head. She believed that freeing Monsieur's slaves was worth the cost, and I couldn't behave selfishly in the face of her example. Hopefully, the vow I was about to make to Papa wouldn't conflict with my promise to Patrice. I took a deep breath and made a commitment I'd hold sacred. "I'll help Maman find justice," I said.

"All right," Papa replied. "I'll show you what comes next in your maman's and my story."

CHAPTER TEN: THE WHEEL OF FORTUNE

When Lady Fortuna appears, be aware that she's both fair and capricious. Some events remain fixed by fate, but others can be averted depending on how the wheel turns. If you're the victim of negative circumstances, first remedy what you can in your own life if you bear any responsibility for your adversities. However, if others have wronged you, you may seek justice. Baron Samedi and Maman Brigitte are particularly helpful in this regard. Remember, though, you cannot ask for more justice than you're entitled to.

Colleen

*December 15, 1841, Etoile,
New Orleans*

As autumn progressed to winter, most trees and plants lost the last traces of their color. Colleen didn't find all that barrenness ugly, though. The bare tree branches crisscrossed the azure sky on sunny days and provided a splendid contrast to the lush live oaks and palmettos, which still looked tropical even in the middle of winter. This disparity was another feature that made this place so foreign, and yet, so hauntingly beautiful.

Colleen looked to the world around her for strength when

she missed Ireland. Back home, this time of year, she'd have been helping Ma clean the house for Christmas. Now that Ma was dead, her childhood home would be about as warm as a sparkless lump of coal. However, Colleen's memories of home and the green mountains of Achill Island sometimes appeared in her mind so vividly that she could see the light in her mother's eyes. Colleen also remembered the smells of an Ireland Christmas with its notes of cinnamon, pine, and apple tarts.

To find comfort, Colleen conjured up those familiar scents, such as when the smell of escargot crackling in the pan caused her stomach to lurch. The snails themselves didn't offend her senses. Instead, it was the addition of white wine and grape preserves to the snails, a concoction Madame had ordered Celeste to prepare, that polluted the air. For the second time that year, nausea set Colleen's nerves on edge. Only now, she couldn't dismiss the malady as seasickness. Not when she hadn't been on a boat since the voyage from Ireland. Coupled with her late monthly, Colleen deduced she was with child.

She mentally cursed Madame Le Jaune, who had sent her to the winter kitchen to make some chamomile tea. Unlike the outdoor kitchen used in summer, the winter kitchen was in the main house and didn't have much air circulation to dilute the smell of food.

That day, Celeste was sizzling the snail concoction in an iron frying pan. Poised over the kitchen counter, Colleen stared into the steeping cup of tea. She prayed to all the saints above that the tea would reach Madame's preferred concentration immediately. Unfortunately, Colleen estimated the chamomile flowers needed another five minutes of sitting in the water. Five minutes *exactly.* Any more or less, and Mme. Le Jaune would screech her throat raw because she'd find the tea either too strong or too weak.

Colleen's entire body stiffened as pressure built up inside her throat. The prudent thing would be to get some fresh air, but there'd be the devil to pay if she left without Madame's perfectly prepared tea. Then, a fresh miasma of dissonant smells hit

Colleen again. The contents of her stomach cascaded onto the floor in successive waves as she heaved and heaved.

After securing the frying pan onto the stove, Celeste hauled Colleen's trembling body to the sink and brought up water with the pump. Colleen splashed cool water over her face, bringing instant relief. She took a few moments to rinse the foul-tasting water from her mouth.

"Sit down," Celeste commanded as she guided Colleen to a chair. "I know a thing or two about illnesses."

Colleen wanted to flee by any means necessary, but Celeste had pulled up a chair close to Colleen's, blocking all escape routes. The cook next touched Colleen's forehead, pried open her mouth, and poked and prodded for what seemed like an eternity. Colleen's pulse raced under Celeste's scrutiny. When the cook placed a finger on Colleen's wrist to count her pulse, Colleen wriggled her hand away.

"Stop that! What's wrong with you?" Celeste asked, frowning.

Colleen opened her mouth to explain that she'd just accidentally eaten some spoiled food, but instead of that lie, a choked sob emerged. As tears of shame poured down her cheeks, Colleen understood the futility of hiding her condition from Celeste, who'd find out the truth soon enough. Delaying that inevitable moment wouldn't stop the comeuppance Colleen deserved. *She'd* demanded that David take her right in the buckboard. She'd been impetuous, and her lack of good sense had now put them both in danger. The burden of Colleen's actions weighed heavily on her shoulders, so much so she couldn't breathe. "It's all my fault," she confessed. "I'm so sorry."

At that life-changing revelation, Celeste flinched. She slowly relaxed back in the chair, her mouth hanging open like the whale in the Jonah story from the Bible. Colleen was about to apologize again, but Celeste shook her head and quickly drew a finger to her lips. *Ah, she wants me to keep my damn mouth shut,* Colleen realized, nodding in confirmation. Celeste then went to the kitchen's two doors, which opened into a hallway and outside, and searched for potential eavesdroppers. When she confirmed they were alone, the cook sat back down and glared at Colleen. "I suppose it's David's? You would've told me if the master had violated you."

Colleen dried her eyes with her wrinkled apron. "Yes. I'm to blame." Unable to bear looking at the cook any longer, Colleen traced her eyes along the ceiling's timber beam, bracing herself for Celeste's inevitable string of curses. But the only sound was the crackling of the fire in the cookstove. That unnerved Colleen, who wanted Celeste's condemnation just so she wouldn't have to live in suspense anymore.

"Come, now. It takes two to make a baby," Celeste eventually said, sighing. "At least tell me you really love him. That it wasn't a moment of lust."

"I love him with everything I am," Colleen replied quickly. She locked eyes with Celeste and hoped the older woman could see the truth. Colleen hadn't the words to communicate the depth of her feelings. She envied those poets who conveyed their emotions with just the right phrases and metaphors.

Colleen thought of David, and her heart warmed. He had a handsome face, a strong body, and warm hazel eyes. Not that Colleen forgot the best parts of David as she tallied the reasons why she loved him. She admired his kindness and intelligence, his skill with his carver's tools, and especially the way he set her heart to racing whenever he simply looked at her. Colleen loved David so much that she was just like one of those desperate heroines from one of Lady Ash's romantic novels. Those women were silly creatures, all of them—but damn it, Colleen understood their odd impulses now.

"I know he feels the same for you," Celeste said, sounding more resigned than angry. "And my son has a keen sense of the future. This all might be for some good reason. Although I can't for the life of me think of what."

The future? Just the thought made Colleen's head spin. She gripped the table for support. Colleen wanted to believe Lady Fortuna had some reason for catapulting this child into the world right now, but she had a hard time trusting Fortuna because she'd visited so much *misfortune* onto the O'Neil family.

Colleen closed her eyes and visualized the reading David had done with his cards. Travel by water, temperance, and a difficult choice. Her heart sank as she contemplated those future influences in light of her pregnancy. A ship to steal them away North? Fantastic by itself. Temperance? A necessary thing for making successful plans. But Colleen's impatience in that buckboard, the decision that instigated this whole business, had thrown temperance clear out of a moving carriage. Now, she and David had a very difficult choice to make, specifically how to get the hell out of Louisiana without getting sold. And they didn't have nearly enough time to make those plans.

For a moment, Colleen wanted to curse the child for all the trouble it brought. But no. That wasn't right. She breathed deeply and touched her stomach. She couldn't blame or wish away that defenseless creature, the tangible proof of her and David's love. "I don't know what to do," Colleen said.

"How far along are you?" Celeste asked as she filled a bucket with water.

Colleen rose to help Celeste. "I reckon about two months."

"No, you sit right there," Celeste insisted. She knelt on the floor and began to clean up Colleen's mess. "Well, you have about two more months before people will suspect. I know David's been planning something, and now he'll just have to move faster."

Only two months. Eight weeks. Fifty-six days. Thanks to the pregnancy, that paltry amount of time was all Colleen and David had to escape. A scourge of helplessness washed over her. She wished she could help him plan their escape, but orchestrating such a feat was beyond her. Never having left the New Orleans area, Colleen had no idea how to navigate, let alone evade capture, in this vast country.

As Celeste worked away, Colleen rested her head on the table. That vantage point offered her a view of the tiled floor. To occupy her anxious mind, she let her eyes stroll along with the tile's organic floral pattern, moving from one tile to the next at their leisure. The sound of the cook's measured sweeps across the floor with a scrubbing brush also lulled Colleen into a hypnotic state. As she relaxed, Colleen's nausea eased a bit, and the edges of her worries melted away. For the briefest of moments, she believed in the possibility of a happy future.

But then the atmosphere in the cookhouse grew heavier and somehow darker. The hairs on the back of Colleen's neck prickled up when she saw a human-shaped shadow inching across the tile. As the shadow heightened and crept toward her, the air in her little field of vision became more shallow and stifling. She then knew M. Le Jaune had entered the kitchen.

Colleen slowly rolled her body up, steadying her nerves to conceal any hint of her condition. She needed to cover her fear with a solid mask of deceit. David's life, her life, and certainly the child's life, depended on the Le Jaunes never finding out the truth.

When Colleen finally eased herself upright, she found M. Le Jaune looming over her. The haughty tilt of his head and disdainful curl of the lips made him resemble an entitled aristocrat straight out of Versaille, not a reprobate, unlucky gambler. "I didn't pay your passage so you could sleep in the middle of the day," he snarled. "Where the devil is Madame's tea?"

"Right on the counter, sir. I'll just get it for you," Colleen said, pushing down her hatred under the guise of an apologetic smile.

"*I'll* get you the tea." Celeste casually glided past M. Le Jaune with the bucket of soiled water. Thankfully, she'd by then finished cleaning the floor, and the lingering stench of fried escargot obscured any remaining smell of vomit. After the cook dumped the contents outside, she came back inside and set the bucket down. "Colleen's got a bit of a fever. She might need some medicine."

Monsieur's eyes widened, and he backed away toward the hallway door. "The *yellow* fever?"

"Not yellow fever. It doesn't come in the winter," Celeste assured him. "She's just got a normal one."

Colleen marveled at how easily Celeste's little injection of fear had calmed the enraged Monsieur. The cook was simply brilliant. Using Celeste as inspiration, Colleen slid back in her chair and let her arms hang at her side. She needed to make M. Le Jaune believe that she was weak from a mild fever but not sick enough to be quarantined away. "It *does* rather feel like the fevers I had growing up," she added in a pained voice.

By then, the look of alarm had vanished from Monsieur Le Jaune's face, but he still remained a healthy distance from Colleen. "We mustn't let her get too close to Madame until this fever resolves," he said. "There's the baby to think of."

Colleen held in her bitter laughter at the sheer audacity of Monsieur's words. David had once overheard M. Le Jaune confess something horrible to the boat captain who came to load the furniture. Monsieur had said that after the new baby was born, he had no more use for Madame. He had her dowry, an heir, and another child to inherit the family name should something befall Raoul. Monsieur had cursed his wife for shutting him out of her bed. Not that he showed Madame these feelings, though. Instead, M. Le Jaune behaved so obsequiously around his wife that it nauseated Colleen more than the child growing inside her.

"That's smart," Celeste said as she scooped the waterlogged chamomile flowers from the tea. "By the by, Madame needs more lavender honey from the convent. I can send Colleen to get some. The lady who makes it has medicine for a fever, too."

"And just how much will this medicine cost?" Monsieur asked.

The cook shrugged. "Nothing if we buy the honey."

At the mention of free medicine, Monsieur Le Jaune smiled, Colleen supposed because he could divert more money to his precious craps table. "Have Day drive Colleen to the convent," Monsieur said. "He's finished carving for the day and might as well do something useful with his afternoon."

"A fine idea," Celeste said. She then placed the steaming cup of tea out in front of Colleen. "Colleen, please bring the tea to Madame while I finish her food. Just don't get close to her on account of your fever."

"No need. I'll bring Madame the tea," Monsieur said. He picked up the cup and scurried from the room.

Colleen sat in awe of Celeste's masterful handling of that day's disastrous events. Somehow, for perhaps the first time in Colleen's life, the universe had aligned its planets and other spinning orbs in her favor. She now had the opportunity to tell David about her condition in the privacy of a ride to the convent. Colleen threw her arms around the older woman and thanked her for her intervention. "Thank you," Colleen said.

After releasing Colleen, Celeste returned to her frying pan and stared at the unholy mass of congealed snails and jam. "You're welcome. In return, pray to your saints that I can salvage something of this mess for Madame. But first, drink some tea to calm your stomach. Chamomile will do."

Colleen said a quick prayer that the meal could be salvaged. She then drank some chamomile tea and rinsed out her mouth before heading to the stable. It wouldn't do to see the man she loved while reeking of sickness. After chewing on a leaf mint for good measure, Colleen left the kitchen for the stable to ask David for a ride. She tiptoed into his work area, ready to share her secret. Colleen wanted to steal a glimpse of him first, though. She cherished the moments she was allowed to stare at the candid David.

Shrouded in the scents of wood and straw, he was seated at his desk and writing in a ledger. The golden light streaming in the window highlighted his handsome face, and bits of dusk and straw danced in the sunbeams like tiny fairies.

Although it was illegal, David and the other Le Jaune slaves knew how to read, write, and do figures. Celeste had received an education when she was owned by the Spanish planter. The tutor of the planter's legitimate son had given Celeste lessons in secret. She'd taught her son and M. Le Jaune's other slaves as well. M. Le Jaune knew his slaves could read, write, and calculate. He didn't stop them, either, because of his selfish practicality. Monsieur had no interest in running his business, other than by issuing orders, so he had his slaves do it in his stead. Similarly, Madame didn't concern herself with the practicalities of running a household, so Celeste and Beatrice, the housekeeper, handled all such obligations.

David was so engrossed in his work that he hadn't noticed Colleen standing in the doorway. With an impish grin on her face, she cleared her throat. David's attention snapped to Colleen. His warm smile, as well as the beaming light in his eyes, nearly made her heart burst. David jumped up from the chair and ran to the door, stopping just a foot away from Colleen. They couldn't touch one another without ensuring they were alone. In that foot of space between them, the tension and desire crescendoed to an unbearable level. Colleen scanned the area outside the workroom and stable. They were, indeed, alone for the time being.

Colleen threw herself into David's open arms, and he clutched her tightly to his chest. Showing their feelings so brazenly was dangerous, she knew, but emotion triumphed over reason when the heart had its own agenda.

Her sense of exhilaration shot through her just like the day at Keem Beach when she and her sister, Mary, snuck down to the shore so they could jump into the crashing waves again and again. They'd been so free. Free from the church, school, a lifetime of servitude, of societal expectations... all of it. Colleen and her sister belonged to the turquoise sea, the azure sky, the call of gulls, and the frigid water that pasted their dresses to their backs. That freedom had lasted until the whale hunters rowed their boats back to shore, shouting about their kills and staining the sea with large pools of blood. Colleen also felt free in that stable with David.

They were so close to true freedom, too. Until they escaped to Canada, Colleen and David had to contain themselves. Although their love was infinite in its capacity, they could only express it through stolen kisses, discreet glances, and hushed words of endearment. Neither of them considered giving those moments up. Not when it would make life unbearable. It was better to treasure every second they could. To Colleen, any-thing else was sinful. She nuzzled closer to David. The feeling of his heart pulsing against her face brought her peace, and she wondered if he already knew her secret.

Colleen didn't have to wait long for an answer. David pulled back slightly, and his eyes twinkled with mischief. "She'll be the best of us," he said.

Colleen's knees almost buckled. He knew! He knew *every-thing*, and if he was smiling in that tense moment, she reck-oned he knew the future, also. Surely that meant they'd escape. She briefly left his embrace to make sure they were still alone. When she confirmed that blessed fact, Colleen kissed David firmly on the lips. Under the right circumstances and with the best of lies, they could explain away a hug as simple human comfort. But never a kiss. She indulged her impulses for a few seconds before surrendering to reason, that tedious virtue that commanded her to step back until there was a respectable amount of distance between them. "Your ma says we have to escape within two months," she said. "Luckily, she's convinced Monsieur you need to drive me to the convent to get more honey. And medicine."

"Medicine?" David asked.

"Yes, medicine." Colleen leaned back against the doorframe. "Your brilliant mother convinced the bastard I'm sick because of a fever."

"She's damned smart, indeed," David said, chuckling. "We should go, then. For your *fever*."

Colleen held out her arm so David could escort her to the wagon, and he moved to link his arm with hers. Then suddenly, he pulled away as if she'd scalded him with her touch.

"Why did you—?" Colleen asked. She burned with indig-nity from his rejection. But then, she remembered they hadn't checked outside the stable for a few seconds. A fraction of a sec-ond was all it took for someone to discover them. They needed to be extra cautious, so Colleen trailed behind David until they reached the buckboard. Only then, on the wagon seat, did she risk getting close to him. Colleen didn't broach the question she'd been dying to ask until the horse had carried them safely beyond Etoile, with only the wind to witness their secrets. "How are we going to escape? We don't have much time."

David did his best to steer the wagon around a large puddle, but the wagon wheel still flung water onto Colleen's pink skirt, making the wet parts almost red. "The Underground Railroad," he replied. "The problem is, I don't know how to find a conductor without raising suspicions."

Colleen gasped. "There's a railroad that runs underground? All the way to Canada?"

"What?" David turned to her, confusion written on his face as if she'd sprung three heads. With his eyes off the road, the horse veered left. David pulled the reins and took a few moments to steer the wagon back on track. He then stole a glance at Colleen, his eyes crinkled with amusement. "The Underground Railroad isn't an actual railroad. Just a network of people who help slaves escape to freedom."

Colleen smoothed her hands on her skirt. She *knew* that a deep blush was probably spreading across her face, décolletage, and damn near her entire body. A railroad that went under the soil? What nonsense. "I see," she said. "Now that I think about it, an underground railroad like that's impossible."

"Impossible *now*," David replied in a cryptic voice.

Colleen appreciated David's knowledge of the future most times. He'd intuited the sex of their unborn baby, for example. That little revelation hadn't surprised her, not from a man who regularly spoke with spirits and read the future in a deck of cards. But his knowledge of inventions yet to be imagined surprised her. Colleen should have felt relieved, but instead, a chill crept into the marrow of her bones. She wondered if David was hiding something from her. "And our escape?" she asked, her voice tentative. "Is there anything I should know?"

As David stiffened beside her, Colleen knew her instincts were right. He did know something unpleasant lurked in their future. "That we have a difficult time ahead of us, especially with a baby on the way," he said. "We should focus on finding a conductor."

"We should," Colleen replied. She stroked David's arm discreetly under her wrap, a garment which, she'd discovered, helped conceal a great many things.

As they sat together in silence, Colleen's mind drifted back to the convent. Could the nuns help? She had her doubts. The itinerant priest who came to Etoile once per month told the slaves that the Bible endorsed slavery. She reckoned not all holy men felt that way, for many Catholic priests back in Ireland fought against their English oppressors from the pulpit. These same priests would perhaps condemn slavery in the Americas. But some of the clergy in New Orleans, and even the church itself, received endowments from local slaveholders. They couldn't afford to alienate these rich benefactors. Colleen and David needed help from someone who'd be sympathetic to their plight, an immensely difficult task in New Orleans. Someone not acclimated to slavery.

Not acclimated—

A face appeared right before Colleen's eyes; it was that of Jeanne herself. Colleen's mood lifted instantly. The beekeeper had offered her refuge at the convent and had said she understood Colleen's plight. Jeanne would find a conductor if she could. At the same time, Colleen didn't want to bring her friend legal trouble. She would also have to disclose the reason for this urgent escape, namely the baby.

Although Jeanne hated slavery, Colleen didn't know how the beekeeper felt about relations outside of marriage, something forbidden by the church. Of course, because of Lord Ashington, Colleen wasn't as pure as the Virgin Mary. Her former employer had forced himself on Colleen, though. She'd been a *very* willing participant in her activities with David. Even if Jeanne judged Colleen's wantonness, however, Colleen doubted the woman would tell anyone and risk David's life. Colleen had to trust Jeanne. That was, if David felt they should. Colleen took a deep breath for courage. "Jeanne might be able to help us find a conductor."

David turned to her, narrowing his eyes before cracking a smile. "That's not a bad idea," he said. "And to think Madame sent us right her way."

"Fancy Madame being good for something," Colleen said.

And with that, they burst into laughter and indulged in silliness until Colleen's side ached. Somehow, David maintained his faculties enough to avoid careening into the well-dressed ladies and gentlemen promenading along the street.

Not that Colleen would've minded if the wagon crashed into the stuffy couples, who reminded her of the Le Jaunes. It would've amused her greatly to see them scream like exotic birds evading a predator. Colleen imagined beasts with long fangs drawing blood from the stuffy prey, their fine clothes stained a beautiful deep crimson. The rest of the way to the convent, she entertained herself with these depraved fantasies.

This vengeance-infused daydream captivated her so completely that before she knew it, David pulled up to the convent's door. In front of that holy place, Colleen felt chagrined. The people on the street hadn't done her wrong, M. Le Jaune had. To purify her conscience, Colleen crossed herself as she hopped out of the wagon.

"Good luck," David said. The sun shone behind his hat like a halo, making Colleen damn near swoon on the street from the heavenly sight before her.

Colleen didn't have time to faint, though. Instead, she thanked David and purged her mind of everything but her mission before rapping her knuckles on the cloister door. She shouldn't fear Jeanne, a faithful friend. To calm her nerves, Colleen breathed in the lavender-scented breeze that wafted over the stone walls.

Soon, Jeanne opened the door. Beneath her broad hat, the beekeeper's face was flushed and glowing with perspiration. "I've been expecting you. You need more honey, oui?"

"I do." Colleen followed Jeanne into the privacy of the cloister. "But that's not the only reason for my visit."

Jeanne knelt in front of one of the lavender plants, which she'd coaxed out of rows of pebbles in the garden, and stroked the flowers. She'd once told Colleen that lavender grew in cooler, drier climates than New Orleans, usually during the summer months. But under Jeanne's care, the flowers bloomed all year round. "The bees said as much," Jeanne said. She craned her head and looked up at Colleen. "Are you with child?"

At Jeanne's frank question, Colleen took a step back. It appeared the bees had told Jeanne the truth. "Yes," Colleen mumbled. "David's."

Instead of condemning Colleen, Jeanne rose and embraced her. "You must get away, and soon!"

"Within two months," Colleen whispered into her friend's shoulder.

Jeanne squeezed Colleen tightly before releasing her and ushering her into the privacy of the covered arcade, close to where Jeanne had placed the honey jars. In that shady corner of the cloister, and with the drone of the bees to obscure their words, Jeanne and Colleen had extra privacy. "I will talk to Father Pierre, our new priest, who comes from the Boston diocese," the beekeeper said.

"A priest? Are you sure that's wise?" Colleen asked.

"I am," Jeanne said. She lowered her voice. "He's spoken with me about working with the abolitionists, and his grandmother was a slave when she was alive. The church does not know this, though."

Colleen brought her fingers to her lips, promising to keep Father Pierre's secret just as Jeanne was keeping hers and David's. Colleen's tension slowly dissipated. She stared at the monolithic stone walls of the cloister and felt their permanence, their *strength*, somehow infusing those same characteristics into her skeleton.

Compared to the ones in Ireland, this convent wasn't all that old. This building would stand for hundreds, or even thousands, of years. Colleen knew her friendship with Jeanne would endure likewise. With such a faithful ally, perhaps Colleen and David had a chance of success after all. Her eyes welled up with happy tears. "Thank you. How can I ever repay you?"

"Love each other," her friend replied, taking Colleen's hand. "And let Father Pierre marry you. David is waiting outside, non?"

Colleen's eyes flooded with tears. "He is. Do you mean to have us married now?" She looked down at her dress, the same one she'd worn for the disembarkation in New Orleans. Only now, the dress had a day's worth of perspiration, and perhaps the faint odor of sickness, lodged in the fabric. Her hair was likely also disheveled from her vomiting spree in the kitchen. What a sorry state for a day to marry the love of her life! *No. Don't indulge in pity right now*, she thought.

She recalled the story her ma had told about her own wedding day, which immediately lifted Colleen's mood. Maureen Gallagher had worn her Sunday dress on her wedding to Seamus O'Neil. A frayed hem marred the dress, but Seamus hadn't cared a whit. His eyes had radiated joy when they rested on Maureen, who herself was smitten with the man. Seamus had loved her despite the stain of witchcraft that haunted her family or Maureen's chance of an early death from the disease that had killed her mother. At the heart of things, Colleen's parents had truly loved one another, and that was all that mattered.

Colleen took a breath and steadied her nerves. David didn't care about her disheveled appearance. And for her part? This day would count as the happiest of her life, even though Father Pierre couldn't marry her and David in the legal sense. Louisiana's laws prohibited different races from marrying one another. Even if that weren't the case, as a slave, David couldn't marry without M. Le Jaune's consent, which would never happen. But as long as she and David were married in the eyes of God, the union would be sacred. Unbreakable where it mattered.

Jeanne released Colleen's hand. "If Father Pierre is not occupied, it would be best he marry you now, while you are here," she said. "He should have time before the Vespers. I will go get him."

"I'll go get David," Colleen said.

"No, Father Pierre and I will bring him here," Jeanne said. She paused, her lips curling into a mischievous smile. "The nuns you fear so much adore the good Father. They won't question David's presence inside their sanctum if he's escorted by a priest."

Despite her solemn circumstances, Colleen giggled at the thought of Christ's brides fawning over the priest. Jeanne was wise to have Father Pierre escort David inside a place that rarely, if at all, had male visitors who hadn't taken vows of celibacy.

After Jeanne left the cloister, Colleen sank onto a bench under the arcade. Her stomach flipped, so she leaned back against the wall and exhaled a slow breath. The chamomile was wearing off. Because she didn't want to pollute this tranquil space, she closed her eyes and inhaled the sweet breeze that drifted down the arcade. She ignored her body's discomfort and focused on keeping her breaths even, which she hoped would calm the nausea. After a few minutes of stillness, Colleen's efforts bore fruit, thank St. Brigid. She opened her eyes just in time to see Jeanne and the man she supposed was Father Pierre walk in through the cloister door that opened to the street. The priest had hair the color of night and kind brown eyes. Following behind Father Pierre, David gave Colleen a loving look that told Colleen he knew of their impending nuptials.

Colleen stood to greet the man who'd defy the law to marry her and David. "Thank you for this blessing," she whispered when the priest was close enough to hear.

Father Pierre nodded almost imperceptibly. "It is my pleasure to do the work of God. Jeanne has informed me of the..." He paused, his glance flitting to Colleen's abdomen. He continued, "urgency of the situation."

"There is an urgency at that," Colleen admitted. Her cheeks burned.

David reached out to take Colleen's hand, but he froze and

tucked his hands behind his back. Colleen supposed this was on account of any nuns who might wander into the cloister. "Where will you marry us?" he asked the priest.

Father Pierre pointed to a door at the end of the arcade. "In that room, which Jeanne uses to store the honey she packs for shipment. Many of the Sisters here know of my abolitionist sympathies, but we best perform this sacrament for God's eyes only."

"This is correct," Jeanne agreed. "And if anyone asks why we brought David into the room, I shall say I needed his help to move boxes. I alone go into the storage room."

Jeanne unlocked the storage room, and Colleen followed her friend. Father Pierre ushered David in, too. As Jeanne lit a candle on the wall sconce, Colleen scanned the room, counting perhaps fifty wooden crates. She hadn't realized how much honey Jeanne collected from the bees. The room smelled of damp stone and wood, scents that reminded Colleen of David's woodshop. The storage room wasn't a proper church, but it was on convent grounds. And when had she ever bothered with propriety? The room had privacy, and that was all that mattered. A single window opened onto the cloister, so a few rays of light beamed into the room.

Father Pierre stood in front of the window and motioned for Colleen and David to stand a few feet in front of him, in a spot near the wall and away from the window. Jeanne cracked a smile and stood to the priest's right.

"Take your beloved's hand," Father Pierre told David. David obeyed, and Colleen relished the warmth of her future husband's hand. The priest smiled in approval, his eyes darting from Colleen to David. "Because of this country's unjust laws, we don't have the time for a full mass with this wedding. But in the eyes of God, your desire and commitment are what solidifies your union."

David squeezed Colleen's hand. "And that is what's important."

"I concur," Colleen added.

"Then, with Jeanne and God as our witnesses, I shall join you in the eyes of God, a union no man can tear asunder."

Tears pricked the corners of Colleen's eyes. She interlaced her fingers tightly with David's, feeling each of his beautiful bones beneath the skin she loved to caress with her fingers, her tongue, and if she was feeling overly romantic, her soul. She cleared her throat. "Let's."

Father Pierre's eyes settled on David. "David, do you take Colleen to be your lawfully wedded wife in the eyes of God? To have and to hold her, from this day forward, for better, for worse, for richer, for poorer, in sickness and in health, until death do you part?"

David turned to face Colleen and gathered her other hand in his, holding her fast. "I do. But not even death will part us. I take Colleen O'Neil as mine for eternity."

Colleen wanted to bawl like an unruly baby then, but she stifled the sobs threatening to erupt and blinked away her tears. She looked into David's hazel eyes and studied the flecks of brown and green that danced in the candlelight and sun, the illumination of day and night. She could stay lost in her husband's eyes forever, in a place where M. Le Jaune could never find them.

Father Pierre quickly brought her back to the storage room and the makeshift wedding. "Do you, Colleen O'Neil, take David to be your lawfully wedded husband in the eyes of God? To have and to hold him, from this day forward, for better, for worse, for richer, for poorer, in sickness and in health, for all of eternity?"

Colleen smiled at the priest's use of David's words *for eternity* instead of *to death do us part*. She would be like Isolde, the unfortunate princess who loved her beloved clear into the afterlife. "I do," Colleen said. For the first time in her life, her voice held true conviction. She was so concentrated on the love pouring from David's eyes that Colleen barely registered Jeanne's sobs.

"Then, I declare you husband and wife," Father Pierre said, clearing his throat. "For eternity."

CHAPTER ELEVEN:
JUSTICE

When the Justice card appears, you should know that the universe will eventually balance all wrongs. However, you must be accountable for your actions. For assistance, seek the Irish god Lugh, who helps with music, poetry, the crafting of weaponry, healing, and justice. These are contradictory skills on the surface, but all life is bound together with strong threads of silk. Just think about how beautiful poetic justice is.

Selene

*October 30, 1860, Bourbon
Street, New Orleans*

Windows of thick glass muffled the sounds of the waves crashing on stone and the whistle of the North Atlantic wind. Celeste, Patrice, and I were in a small apartment over a store in a seaside town that overlooked a harbor. A solid granite breakwater protected this harbor, and quaint fishermen's shacks lined the little cove. Beyond the granite boundary, the sea churned furiously while the wind gusts sent snow swirling through the air. Ice clung to lobster traps and encased fisherman's floats with a new shell of glass. The outside world was cold, but all of us were snug in our little home, bundled in warm clothing and surrounded by the golden light from the fire. Then, as Patrice drew close to kiss me, I frantically scanned the room for Maman. If she didn't already know my secret, this kiss would expose the truth of Patrice's and my relationship. Maman wasn't there, though.

And then the crash of glass jolted me upright from that warm apartment in the land of ice and snow to my drafty home in New Orleans. Covered in a thin layer of sweat, I jumped out of bed and scurried through the apartment, furiously searching for an intruder. There wasn't any broken glass scattered on the floor or a prowler ransacking my few belongings. In the main room, I only found a dead fire, the lingering taste of fear in my mouth, and the sound of shattering glass rattling in my mind's periphery. Nothing could quash that uncanny sound, though, not even the din of Bourbon Street.

I plopped onto the settee and stared at the hearth. What did the dream mean? From the granite breakwater and the wintery scene, I surmised that the village was in New England. But why hadn't Maman been there? I'd never leave her in New Orleans, and she wouldn't give up her mission, meaning the dream couldn't be my future, literally speaking.

Shivering in my shift, I grabbed my father's cards and spread them face down before the dead fire in the hearth. I first drew the King of Pentacles, which meant I had the wisdom to intuit what I needed from the dream. The king stared back at me in the waxing morning light. He sat on a throne and held a long sword securely in his hand. No one could doubt his courage, strength, or that he ruled his domain wisely and with an appropriate measure of discipline. I needed his power to fulfill my destiny, so I envisioned myself sitting on the king's stately throne and embodying his prowess. I vowed to find out what had sabotaged my parents' plans.

After a few minutes of concentration, my muscles seemed to strengthen. My mind became clearer. Strangest of all, my heart sheathed itself in an invincible armor. I opened my eyes and slid the card back into the deck, resolved to find out the specific details of Maman's plans, lest we work at cross purposes.

I pondered the significance of the breaking glass until Mrs. Shelley's cook knocked lightly on the door. She did that to let me know she'd left my breakfast outside the door. I dressed quickly and nibbled on fresh, aromatic bread between sips of café au lait.

As I held the coffee cup, I realized it would crash with a heavy sound if I dropped it. Whatever had broken in my dream was similarly clunky, not something like a champagne flute, which would make a lighter shattering sound upon breaking. No, the sound in my dream was more like a bottle hitting the floor.

Like one of Maman's laudanum bottles.

A blob of moist bread stuck in my throat like wet mortar, choking off my air. I chugged the coffee to clear the lump of food. Maman was in danger. My hands trembling, I clanked the cup on the table just before it slipped from my clammy grip and tripped down the stairs leading to the street. As I pushed out the door, the birds scattered aloft.

"Selene, is anything the matter? Where are you running to?" asked Mrs. Shelley as she hovered in the threshold of her front door.

I seethed because her questions were delaying me from helping Maman. In Raoul's employ, Mrs. Shelley had morphed from a benevolent landlady into a female leader of the Spanish Inquisition.

When I was very young, I'd often begged the spirits to make Maman take interest in my daily life, even if that meant she'd end up annoying me to no end. I'd prefer she bother me than be absent when she chased the mystical dragons that lived in her heavy glass bottles. Mrs. Shelley wasn't my maman, though, only a spy swathed in a scratchy petticoat.

Although she certainly didn't deserve an explanation as to why I needed to run to Marigny, I still needed to provide one lest I anger Raoul. "I fear my maman is ill," I replied, my voice tight. "And Monsieur Raoul's given me permission to visit her."

To her credit, Mrs. Shelley flushed with shame. "I'll have

Samuel drive you. He's already got the wagon hitched up for a trip to the mercantile."

Considering I might need to fetch Maman a doctor, I very much appreciated the offer of the wagon. "Thank you," I said. "That would be lovely."

Not five minutes later, I was seated next to Samuel in Mrs. Shelley's wagon, which reminded me of the one my father used to drive my mother around. The city sped by. Although New Orleans glittered with magic and diverse culture, I saw the truth of the place, too. The city had cracks that spread at a snail's pace and lizard carcasses baking in the sun.

Maman had gladly flirted with Death for many years in this city. I couldn't bear to watch her destroy herself. I tried to distract myself from that fear by creating stories in my mind about the people we passed on the road. When the wagon sped by a stern-faced governess who was chastising a young woman, I wondered if this budding girl had recently been plucked from the arms of a forbidden lover. Most likely, she'd done something far less indecorous, like talking back or eating with the wrong fork. People accused girls of her class of serious crimes for the most minute of offenses.

Although the drive to Maman's house didn't take long, for it was only about a mile away from my apartment, the wagon in front of us crawled along. Samuel hadn't said a word. I worried I'd angered him because my detour would delay his other duties. However, as the French section of New Orleans gave way to the cottages of Marigny, Samuel finally spoke. "Now that I'm taking you to your mother's, I can tell Mrs. Shelley that's where you really went," he said. "Mr. Raoul thinks you've got a gentleman lover."

"Well, Mr. Raoul is wrong," I said, keeping my voice even, though Samuel's soft warning had sent my stomach straight to my throat. I knew Raoul had tasked Mrs. Shelley with spying on me, of course, but hearing he suspected I had a lover alarmed me. Because I did—just not in the way Raoul thought. I didn't want to put Patrice at risk if Raoul was increasing his scrutiny.

"Oh, I know," Samuel said with a twinkle in his eye. "You've got one of the *lady* variety."

Well, then. I now had evidence of Samuel's keen perception. He brought Patrice to visit often, but he'd evidently sussed out our true feelings. My cheeks burned as I studied my hands, tracing my eyes over the veins that threatened to pop out of my skin. To cover the callouses I'd developed from cleaning my house since I could hold a scrub brush, Raoul had bought me an assortment of kid and lace gloves, but I'd forgotten them that morning in my haste to leave. My skin felt as exposed as my deepest secret was at that moment.

"Best guard your feelings better," Samuel continued. His tone had shifted from lighthearted to serious. "Men like those Le Jaunes can be dangerous."

Samuel's words harrowed me to the bone. I'd been too careless. "Thank you, Samuel," I replied. "I'll be *much* more careful."

And with that promise, we said not another word. I focused my energies on how to deal with whatever I discovered at Maman's. We finally reached her cottage a few minutes later, and Samuel offered to wait in case we needed to get a doctor. I jumped from the wagon, sprinting to the door.

Death himself lingered in the morning shadows. I threw open the door and crossed the ratty threshold, only to find the house quiet instead of filled with the sounds of Maman cooking breakfast or the clink of her laudanum bottle against her teacup. Only the cooing of mourning doves in the back garden broke the silence.

I scrambled to Maman's bedroom and found her lying prone on top of her quilt. A field of glass shards, which glittered menacingly in the red morning sunlight, surrounded the bed. My dream had been right. As I raced across the floor, jagged pieces of the broken laudanum bottles crunched beneath my boots. Time slowed on that trip to Maman's bed, almost as if I were suspended in molasses. My heart pounded in my throat. When I finally grabbed her wrist, though, I felt her heart pulsing under her clammy skin.

She was *alive*, just intoxicated out of her mind. I should have felt relief, but instead, my mind replayed almost every morning of my childhood. Little girls didn't deserve such responsibility.

Those memories pressed on my heart, draining it of its last ounce of sympathy for Maman. I wanted to slam my fist against the wall to wake her. To make a hole in that crumbling plaster and destroy this prison she'd willingly confined herself to.

But no. I was the dutiful daughter. The adult in the room. Daughters shouldn't hate their mothers, and I didn't want mine to die, but I couldn't hold in my anger any longer. "Maman!" I hissed as I shook her shoulder. "Wake up!"

Her brow wrinkled in sleep-laden confusion. "Selene? What are you doing here?"

What was I doing here? Attempting to save her life, quite simply. Not that she cared a whit.

Satisfied Maman would live for now, I threw open the curtains and window. Light cascaded onto her face. She needed *something* to clear the murky atmosphere, which reeked of M. Le Jaune's perspiration. However, my efforts to brighten up the space proved futile. People usually associate sunshine with happiness. With cheery, balmy days made for picnics and merriment. But not me. Not then. That particular morning's sun illuminated the tarnished brass bed Monsieur had purchased for his and Maman's conjugal activities. The natural light also showed the true grayness of her skin and sunken cheeks. She usually covered up the evidence of the laudanum sickness with the expensive French powder M. Le Jaune bought her.

"Another bottle? Why?" I demanded even though I knew the answer. From the few times I'd taken laudanum for medicinal purposes, I remembered its euphoric effects, how it warmed the body and dissolved away worries and pain. Maman's life with M. Le Jaune was unbearable. Why else would she consume enough laudanum to supply an apothecary for an entire year?

Maman eased herself up and screwed her eyes shut against the sunshine. "Never mind that. Be a good daughter, and make me some coffee."

Gritting my teeth, I trudged to the pantry, a little nook in the dining room. I then went out to the tiny, detached kitchen near the garden to prepare some coffee. She'd be more cogent after some coffee and food. After I swept up the glass, I left her alone to dress and told Samuel that she didn't need a doctor. He continued on to do his errands for the day, and I commenced with my mission.

I first brewed coffee, adding a generous heap of sugar to her cup. Maman always craved sugar after a laudanum binge. Thankfully, she also had some bread and cheese in the larder. Because some sun and fresh air would also do her good, I arranged the makeshift feast outside on a table so we could eat under the tree. I even set the sugar container beside her cup in case she wanted more, so determined was I to make her receptive to my desire for details about her plans.

I sipped my coffee, and Maman eventually drifted into the garden. She wore a dress and wrap and, strangely, also held a book in the crook of her arm. "Bless you, Dear," Maman said as she grabbed her cup and rested the book on the table. A look of absolute pleasure crossed her face as she drank the brew. "And you remembered to sweeten it. How perfect."

"Please eat something, too." I looked down at the book, which was called *The Spolia of Ancient Rome*. When had she acquired an interest in architecture from the age of Classical Antiquity? Only the saints knew. "I have questions, and I expect answers."

Maman scowled at the food I'd artfully arranged just for her. "I might eat later, *perhaps*. But I may answer some of your questions."

I'd lost the food battle but hadn't given up on the war. To draw peace from conflict, opponents often make concessions. This maxim held true for Roman emperors, simple vendors, and daughters trying harder than diamond miners to extract valuable information from their Mamans. My own combativeness had set her terms for engagement. For the moment, I had no choice but to accept them. I thus launched into my questions, hopeful she'd answer them. "What went wrong with your and Papa's plan to escape? Did Monsieur Le Jaune stop you and kill Papa?"

Maman swirled her coffee with a spoon, staring into the whirlpool she created. "Those are difficult questions. So many things went wrong; so many stubborn opinions collided. I can't blame Monsieur Le Jaune for everything."

"Fine, then," I said. I slammed down my coffee cup and ripped apart a piece of the bread. She neither blamed nor acquitted Monsieur for Papa's death. She also hadn't revealed anything useful about the failed escape plan. "If you can't tell me that, at least explain how you and Tante Jeanne plan to free Monsieur's slaves."

A mysterious smile played across Maman's lips as she added more sugar to her coffee. "What do you think Jeanne's been doing with the money for your lessons? Certainly not spending it. She brings the convent so much money through her honey, it covers her expenses and more. The convent lets her keep a percentage of the honey profits. She's built up a tidy sum, more than enough to buy every one of his slaves. Including you."

I dropped the piece of tattered bread on the plate and stared at Maman. She was far craftier than I'd given her credit for. Not to mention the new respect I had for Tante Jeanne, who'd saved money from nearly eighteen years of lessons for this great purpose. "How will you get him to sell them to either of you, though?" I asked.

"A priest named Father Pierre has agreed to be our purchasing agent. Not that it matters," Maman replied, pouting as she bit off a corner of bread. "M. Le Jaune won't sell unless he's bankrupt."

"The same Father Pierre who married you and Papa? The one who was going to help you escape?" I asked, leaning forward in my seat.

Maman's eyes snapped up to meet mine. "You know about Father Pierre?"

"Yes," I said. I looked away as I said the next words. "Papa showed me."

Maman didn't reply. She took more delicate bites of the food, and I didn't dare interrupt her despite my thirst for information. When she'd finished half the piece, she drained her coffee cup. "Maurice is a degenerate gambler, so he'll bankrupt himself eventually, but we're running out of time."

"Because of Raoul?" I asked.

"Exactly," she said. "Soon, he'll have expectations from you. I forbid it. You need to go with Jeanne."

"I can't leave you here alone," I said, even though the mere thought of entertaining Raoul made me understand Maman's laudanum use. I couldn't abandon her, yet I couldn't submit to Raoul. Maman's plan couldn't move forward unless M. Le Jaune bankrupted himself. We had to find a way to make that happen before Raoul demanded I fulfill his expectations. How to accomplish that grand feat? I had no influence over Monsieur and only a tenuous amount of control over Raoul.

Raoul.

He liked to gamble just like his father. I sat up straighter in my chair and stared at Maman as my role in her plan crystallized. I could use Raoul's love for gambling to force M. Le Jaune to the bargaining table with Father Pierre. I gathered Maman's free hand in mine, careful not to crush her delicate bones. "*Raoul* is the key. I can help."

Maman shrugged me away. "The boy likes his gambling palaces, but he's not nearly as reckless as his father. You should go with Jeanne."

"I can't go with Jeanne," I said. Still, Maman had raised a valid point. The elder Le Jaune lost money with careless abandon. And while Raoul's eyes held a maniacal glimmer when he recounted his exploits at the gambling tables, he always stopped gambling when he lost the money he arrived with. He just needed a little push over the precipice to ruin. M. Le Jaune would have to settle Raoul's debts. I doubted Monsieur had the capital to do so, which meant he might sell his slaves to Father Pierre.

Closing my eyes, I tried to gather energy from the world as Marie had taught me. The withering blades of grass in the courtyard were on their way to death, so I extracted a bit of strength from them for courage. I could use Raoul for Maman's and my ends. I *could* do it. Provided, of course, that I could dispel his suspicions about me having a lover. I opened my eyes and took another sip of coffee. "Marie will help me use Raoul," I explained. "He's going to marry Vivienne, and then Monsieur will have access to the poor girl's dowry. We need to bankrupt him first."

"Raoul can't *ever* know you're working against him," my mother cautioned. She looked into her coffee cup and spooned in five helpings of sugar, mixing it with the coffee dregs at the bottom of the cup. "And ask Marie for an impotence potion to keep you safe from that horrible boy."

"Whatever Marie thinks is best," I replied. My teeth ached as Maman brought spoonful after spoonful of coffee-diluted sugar to her mouth.

"She's wise," Maman agreed.

My mother had given me information, but I still had myriad of questions. I took a deep breath and hoped the copious amounts of coffee and sugar Maman had consumed would make her amenable to more questions. "What went wrong with your and Papa's plan?" I asked.

Maman set her sugar-crusted spoon on the table and gazed at the shadowy edge of the garden, a place full of withered, winding brambles. She'd long ago stopped tending to the rosebushes, so the only living plants were the live oak tree and scattered weeds that poked up through the cracked brick pavers.

Like me, she found the aesthetics of decaying civilization beautiful, I think because it reminded her of Papa's death. She cherished her mourning because it kept her close to him. At that moment, though, Maman radiated absolute loathing for the dead garden. I wondered if she was staring down a monster only visible to her, one only she could name. Was it M. Le Jaune? Madame? Some other phantom I'd never met? Eventually, Maman turned back to me. "Your grandmother, Celeste, got sick right before the escape. We couldn't abandon her, and then, everything went to hell."

I didn't dare ask what this hell consisted of, not unless I wanted to usher Maman right to a fresh bottle of laudanum. If I was lucky, she'd stay sober until this afternoon. Perhaps she'd even eat more bread before that tempting liquid murdered her remaining appetite. "I understand," I said. "No more laudanum today, please."

Maman narrowed her eyes at me. "I'll tend to my own affairs," she said in a voice sharp enough to cut glass.

In addition to craving sugar, after her laudanum wore off, Maman usually became an irritable monster. I'd won part of this war by extracting information from her, but on the laudanum front, I'd lost. "Then, promise me you'll eat more," I begged. "You're as pale as Death."

I braced for more tongue lashing, but instead, Maman burst into laughter, which damn near shattered my heart. I would've preferred anger to this lunacy. Her fit continued for a minute, until a gust of wind blew over the garden wall and Maman's cheeks turned red from the cold. She stopped laughing and dried her tears. "Oh, St. Brigid, please grant me that," she said.

"Grant you what? Death?" I asked.

Maman gave me a sad smile. "You know I've been praying for it since your father died," she replied. "But I promise I'll eat. I have a mission to accomplish, after all. As do you."

Opponents in war have to accept their small victories, so I made an uneasy truce with Maman's death wish. I knew she prayed to join Papa, and she probably didn't feel her life had any value except for her mission to free M. Le Jaune's slaves.

Tante Jeanne would have helped Maman escape with me years ago, most likely, if my mother would have allowed it. Maman had stayed here, though. She'd sacrificed her body and mind for almost two decades for the good of others. Determined to do my part and force Raoul to the gambling table, I stood and kissed Maman on the head. "Goodbye. I'm off to see Marie."

Maman picked up *The Spolia of Ancient Rome* and cracked open the book gently. "Be a dear and ask Marie if there's any way I can see David. I miss him terribly."

"*I* can bring Papa here," I said. I should have done just that as soon as I'd gotten the power to do so. "We'll see him together."

Maman shook her head. "No, thank you. He and I need to have a private conversation."

And with that, my mother delivered another blow. Despite the ground I'd gained, she still held her secrets close. If she'd allow it, I'd summon Papa and leave them alone. She didn't trust me not to eavesdrop on their conversation, however. I only hoped those secrets wouldn't follow her to the grave. Maman and I had nothing more to say, so I left her alone with her laudanum bottles and breakfast.

Bitterness poisoned my heart. *Better anger than devastation*, I thought to myself. As I walked briskly to Marie's home on Rue St. Ann, the bustle of the streets distracted me from my woes. The sounds of shopkeepers setting up their wares and horses clopping on the street filled the air with the songs of hope. The therapeutic effects of physical exercise calmed my anger, too, by the time I reached Marie's home.

I knocked on the door, expecting Marie to open it. However, an elderly woman with dark tan skin greeted me instead. "Are you here to see Marie?" she asked. She had a kind voice and warm eyes.

"Yes, I'm one of her apprentices," I replied.

The woman smiled and pointed down the hallway toward the altar room. "She's giving my mistress some *beauty advice*."

I suppressed a giggle at her emphasis on beauty advice. Although well-versed in the sciences of beauty, Marie was a Voodoo queen through and through. Many clients, however, couldn't admit they came to her for such services. Marie solved this dilemma by branding herself as a fashion and beauty expert. Any lady could, consequently, visit her without reproach. Many women used this ruse to visit because the wealthy and poor alike suffered from love troubles. "I'll see if Marie needs help," I said.

"My mistress needs all the help she can get," the woman said, her voice grave.

Suffice it to say, that comment piqued my interest. I walked toward the altar room and tried to identify the energy coming from behind the door. After focusing my energy as Marie had taught me, I felt waves of desolation with a dash of fervent hope. Marie's customer loved someone desperately, but an obstacle blocked her path.

When I opened the door, I found Marie and a young woman seated at the table, where Marie had placed a collection of dried rose petals, jasmine, and lavender. A solitary candle sat in the center of these plants, telling me Marie had blessed them. When Marie's client heard me enter, she startled and looked at me, her pale brown eyes opened wide. This young woman had a kind face and chestnut-colored hair. From her immaculately tailored silk dress, pearl necklace, and lace gloves, I deduced she belonged to the highest echelon of society.

Marie patted the young woman's hand. "Mademoiselle Devereaux, this is my protégé, Selene, a woman of discretion."

"It's a pleasure to meet you," I said.

"Likewise." The young woman blushed furiously as she stood and inclined her head respectfully to Marie. "Thank you, again, for the advice."

Marie picked up some dried plants from the table and secured them in a small package. "My instructions are inside."

"Goodbye," Mademoiselle Devereaux said as she fled the altar room, leaving a hefty dose of French perfume in her wake.

"Love spell?" I asked.

"The young lady wants to marry her old beau, someone she truly loves," Marie said as she swept up the remainder of the herbs from the table. "Her father forced her to accept another man's proposal. The wedding's not far off, so she wants help stopping it."

I felt a rush of sympathy for Mademoiselle Devereaux. Although rich, she had little control over her life. "Bon chance to her."

"Indeed," Marie said. She sighed and pointed to the chair. "I offered to cast the spell for her, but she refused to give me the name of her heart's desire *or* the man she wants to avoid wedding. I'm working on softening her father's heart. She's determined to do the rest on her own."

"Why? Is she afraid either the man she's being forced to marry, or her true love, will find out?" I asked as I sat at the table. It seemed foolish for Mademoiselle Devereaux to withhold information from Marie, who offered her clients absolute discretion. If the young lady wanted to keep some information private, though, Marie wouldn't force the issue.

"Perhaps." Marie snuffed out a candle she'd used for Mademoiselle Devereaux's spell with her fingers, not even flinching as she touched the flame. Mischief glinted in her eyes. "Now, you need Raoul to ruin himself at the gambling table before he makes demands from you?"

Marie's knowledge of my situation stunned me even though it shouldn't have. She likely knew the rest of Maman's plan, purchasing agent and all. "I do," I replied. I relaxed back in the chair. "My mother joked you should give me a spell to make him impotent."

Marie walked over to a cabinet and retrieved a small purple glass vial. "Not now. An impotent man can be dangerous. His embarrassment could turn into anger at the object that failed him. No, Raoul must think he's conquered you."

"How do I get him to think that?" I asked.

"Give him an elixir that will make him fall asleep and forget," Marie said. She handed me the vial. "In the morning, tell him he was a marvelous lover. He won't disagree because of his pride. Add a few drops of blood on the sheets, and he'll no longer worry you have another gentleman lover."

I rolled the smooth glass vial in my hand, admiring how the sunlight made it glow like an extravagant stone. It was certainly a precious object to me, for it held my salvation, a protection against what Maman endured at the hand of M. Le Jaune.

Objects. Things without a will of their own that exist solely to be exploited by their owners. That's what Maman and I were to men such as Raoul and his father. I needed to invert that paradigm and deceive Raoul into trusting me. Objects lack agency, so they pose no threat. "How much do I use? And when?"

Marie locked eyes with me, drawing my full attention. "He'll ask to see you two evenings from now. Put nine drops of elixir in his drink. You'll have an hour before he collapses. Make sure he's in bed when this happens, and then place some blood on your sheets. As for the rest, the loas are working on your behalf. You'll know what to do next when the time is right."

"I'll do my best," I promised, grasping the vial firmly. Marie wanted me to trust myself and have patience, just like Papa said. "Is there anything else I should do?"

"The morning after Raoul's visit, return here for Fete Ghede. It's a festival to honor Baron, Brigitte, and all of their followers." Marie smiled coyly as she imparted the next words. "And Patrice is coming. It's beyond time you attended celebrations with the living as well as the dead."

Marie's announcement shot a jolt of lightning up my spine. I would be seeing Patrice! And joining an assortment of jolly spirits, as well as a crowd of boisterous people who saw the world as I did. All were compelling reasons to attend this gala for the dead. "I'll certainly come," I assured Marie.

Instead of replying, my mentor stared at her altar, her lips moving in silent whispers. I stayed still in case she was speaking with the spirits. After a minute or so, Marie nodded and returned her attention to me. "I also want to do a lave tet ceremony on you during the festival."

"Lave tet? Like a baptism?" I asked. Patrice had undergone the ritual a few years ago, during which point she'd learned of her patron loa. During the three-day ceremony, Marie had also washed away Patrice's negativity and doubt with water. Literally speaking, a lave tet was a washing of the head.

Marie nodded. "Yes. Only, because of your circumstances, we will do the whole ceremony at once. Raoul Le Jaune will grow suspicious if you are with me for three days."

"You are wise, Marie," I agreed. "You are wise." My horrible patron tolerated my visits with Marie because he thought I sought beauty advice and information about my father's heritage. I could attend Fete Ghede with Patrice under those auspices, but I doubted his tolerance would extend to a multiday ceremony. I had to be very careful considering the deception I planned on enacting during our upcoming dinner.

CHAPTER TWELVE:
THE HANGED MAN

When you see the Hanged Man in a reading, don't be too frightened by the alarming imagery. You aren't doomed to the noose, but instead, must surrender to the inevitable and put your plans on hold. Take this time to learn from the world around you. You may need to adopt a new perspective to move forward. Do not struggle.

Selene

November 1st, 1860, Bourbon Street, New Orleans

I studied my reflection in the gargantuan brass candelabras Raoul had purchased for the dining room table. They dwarfed the delicate china he'd bought in a set of two. Unless mistresses had visible places in society, and thus more daring patrons, they needed but a few place settings. "The food is excellent," I said politely after I swallowed a bite of coq au vin. "Mrs. Shelley has outdone herself."

Raoul attempted a wink, but this action looked more like he had a mosquito trapped under his eyelid. "Something special on the night of your deflowering."

The Night of Your Deflowering. I nearly choked on my wine at his title for this evening, which suited a medieval play featuring helpless ladies and lustful knights much better than my plans. How was I supposed to react? Not coy, certainly, when Raoul might still suspect I had a lover—a notion I needed to oust once and for all. Instead, I forced a chaste blush to my cheeks. "In... indeed."

"I'm sorry. That was crude of me," Raoul said, an apologetic expression replacing his lustful one. "Would you like some more wine? It'll help you relax."

My contribution to this evening's feast was an excellent Bordeaux. I'd coated the inside of Raoul's glass with precisely nine drops of Marie's elixir before he arrived. To keep him from becoming suspicious, I poured wine for both of us from the same bottle as he watched. I had been gently sipping on my drink all evening, making sure I kept a clear head. With all the work ahead of me, it wouldn't do for me to pass out as well. "No, thank you. Too much wine makes me feel ill, and I want to savor this evening with my wits about me," I said, lifting my glass for a toast. "To us."

"To us and a night of magic," Raoul said as he raised his glass. The candlelight added flecks of gold to the red wine.

A night of magic? How apropos. I sipped my wine and watched in satisfaction as Raoul drained his glass. Marie had said the potion would take full effect an hour after consumption. I had to direct the night's events carefully. If Raoul dragged me to bed too early, he'd have the chance to conquer me as he intended. We couldn't wait too long, though. If Raoul fainted before he reached the bed, I wouldn't be able to lift him, so I slowed my bites and prepared to gauge Raoul's political views.

A *tiny* part of me felt guilty about forcing him to gamble away his family's money. I had noble goals, but what if there was the slightest chance Raoul would sell me and his father's slaves of his own volition? I had to offer him the opportunity. "Raoul, may I ask you something?"

"Of course," he said.

I wet my mouth with another sip of wine. As long as I asked for a trifle, like a dress or moderately expensive piece of jewelry,

Raoul would happily grant my wish. I desired freedom for myself and his father's slaves, though. Raoul would need to question his sense of entitlement to grant me that. I couldn't ask Raoul to convince his father to sell me and the other Le Jaune slaves to Maman's purchasing agent directly. Instead, I needed to gauge Raoul's feelings, or plant the idea in his mind without revealing my hand. I thus chose a topic close to most men's hearts. Not love, but war, for I'd heard murmurs in the street of a conflict between the North and South on the horizon. "How likely is a war with the North?" I asked. I then dropped my eyes to the plate and cut a small piece of chicken.

All evening, the gentle clink of forks and knives against the china plates set the rhythm of the meal. But after I asked that loaded question, Raoul's fork clanged loudly against his plate as he dropped it. "Why do you ask?" he demanded. "Are you hoping for that Northern scum to reach here? That abolition nonsense?"

His severe reaction told me all I needed to know about his sympathies. Or lack thereof. Raoul feared I wanted my freedom, and for my plan to work, I needed to disabuse him of that notion. "*Hope* the Northerners come?" I crossed my arms in front of my chest and willed the color to drain from my face. "They'd *hurt* me. What if the fighting reaches New Orleans?"

"You have nothing to fear, mon fleur," Raoul said. The harsh angles of his expression softened. "If those godless Yankees somehow make it to New Orleans, we'll push them all the way to Canada. The war'll be over within a month."

"Thank *goodness*," I said. For good measure, I let my hands tremble as I sliced into my chicken. The knife glided through that tender, wine-drenched flesh as smoothly as a knife does butter. I no longer felt guilty about deceiving Raoul. He'd made his feelings as plain as day.

Over the next half an hour, we finished our coq au vin. I ate slowly, just like a proper lady, and asked Raoul questions about poker and other games he played at his favorite gambling palace. His eyes flashed with delight as he explained the twists and turns of his dance with Lady Fortuna. I understood only half of what he said, but my feigned interest drove him mad with pleasure. Dessert also presented an opportunity for delay. I took nimble bites of my delicate pastry and simply let Raoul ramble on. As his words became slower and his gaze less focused, I wondered when to urge him to the bedroom.

The timing had to be *precise.*

Suddenly, something pulled my eyes to the fireplace, where I saw Baron crack a smile in the burning logs. I next heard the swish of Maman Brigitte's skirts. My spirit friends wanted me to act. "Let's adjourn to the bedroom," I said in Brigitte's voice. I curled my lips into a coy smile just like she would do if she wanted to seduce a man.

"Most certainly," Raoul said. He didn't comment on my new sultry persona, either because he was too inebriated, or his lust had taken control of his better senses. He stood but teetered, clinging to the table for support. "This wine is powerful."

Afraid he'd collapse on the floor, I jumped up from my seat and linked my arm with his. "Let me escort you."

It took all my strength and feats of balance to guide my unsteady patron to the bed, whereupon he plopped down so hard that the springs creaked and groaned. "Come here, my flower," he sang as he patted the space next to him.

I eased onto the bed but kept my leg muscles contracted, ready to jump away from Raoul if necessary. Thankfully, he'd be dead to the world before he could complete his nasty agenda.

I avoided cringing as Raoul's hands fumbled on the buttons at the back of my dress. I'd planned my wardrobe for this evening with great care, deciding against a corset since I'd need help getting it off. If Raoul fell asleep before he could remove it, my cunning plan wouldn't work. He'd never believe he *deflowered* me while I was still confined in that satin and whalebone prison.

Although Mrs. Shelley had buttoned the back of my dress earlier in the evening, I could undo the buttons myself with some skilled contortions on my part if needed. The stars aligned in my favor, though. Raoul managed to undo the last

THE GARDEN OF STONE HOUSES

button. The cool night air tickled my back, and I turned around to see Raoul's chest rising and falling with deep, regular breaths.

"Are you awake?" I jostled his shoulder, but he didn't flinch. I breathed a sigh of relief and prayed he'd sleep until daybreak.

A rush of triumph warmed me as I removed Raoul's clothes. I arranged his jacket, pants, shirt, silk brocade vest, and cravat into a beautiful mess on the floor to create a look of disarray and passion. I next cajoled his body under the blankets. It required effort and well-placed leverage on my part, but I finally succeeded.

For the final bit of theater, I poured the entire vial of chicken blood Marie had given me onto my side of the bed. I'd convulsed in horror when my father showed me his blood-soaked body in the vision, but the crimson liquid racing across my white bedsheet struck me as beautiful. I changed into my shift as the blood dried, happy Raoul couldn't see me naked. Finally, I got under the blankets and lay beside my catatonic patron. My plan worked, courtesy of Marie and the spirits.

Even though my eyes burned with exhaustion, sleep refused to come. The oil lamp next to the bed flickered and cast shadows against the wall. I closed my eyes and imagined I was on the far-off island of Bali, where puppeteers created dramas with shadow puppets. Shadows of princes, peasants, and artisans danced in front of my eyes. My heart slowed as I tried to calm my racing thoughts. Soon, the vision of the shadow dancers shifted, and I found myself soaring above a mist-shrouded field. Small ants ran furiously across the grassy expanse. Curious, I decided to descend, and as I got close, I realized the mist was smoke from cannon fire, and the ants were not insects, but soldiers.

War. The powder keg would explode as soon as something lit that eager fuse. I watched the soldiers charge, shoot, and die. The group of men wearing blue uniforms gained ground steadily as the conflict progressed. My dream instincts told me the Northern troops wore blue and that they'd emerge victorious. And then, a soldier wearing a gray uniform caught my attention as he collapsed onto the wilted grass. I drifted over to him until I could see his face.

It was Raoul. His lifeless eyes stared at the sky, and blood soaked his uniform. Not rivulets of blood like the tributaries of the Mississippi River, but a great swathe of it. He breathed not a wisp of air.

I felt a flutter of sympathy for him as I would for any doomed person. What could I do when he woke, though? Even if Raoul believed I saw visions of the future, he'd refuse to sell his father's slaves. Raoul would also fight in the war according to his own inclinations.

As I drifted toward the quiet darkness of deep sleep, a place beyond visions, a piece of me took pleasure in the suffering M. Le Jaune would feel at the loss of his heir. I quickly squelched that feeling. Hoping for Raoul's death qualified as revenge, not justice. I let apathy comfort me in my last moments of consciousness on the night of my alleged "deflowering."

Dawn's pink light woke me as it crept along the wall opposite the bed. When I first opened my eyes, a sense of uneasiness, a feeling of alien energy in the room, quickened my heart. I heard someone, or some*thing*, breathing beside me. I bolted upright and looked to my side, only to see Raoul, who was snoring lightly. He was alive, unlike on the battlefield in my vision. I pushed back the covers and got out of bed, and the floor squeaked as I stepped on a loose floorboard.

Raoul stirred. He sat up and rubbed his eyes before looking at me. "Selene? What happened last night?"

There it was. The question I needed to answer exactly right. A cold sweat broke out on my skin, making me tremble in the cool morning air. I begged the spirits he couldn't distinguish between chicken blood and human blood. "You conquered me," I replied, furrowing my brows into a look of confusion. "You've forgotten?"

"Of course not," Raoul said in a flustered tone. He looked around the room and saw his clothes on the floor. Raoul then drew back the blankets on my side of the bed. A lewd smile spread across his face when he saw the red stain. "I must confess, I was worried you resisted me so long because you had a lover," he said.

I let out a little gasp. "What?"

"Men are silly, jealous creatures, you see." Raoul then jumped out of bed, an action that made his strange organ sway with his body's momentum, almost like a lamprey swinging on a fishline. I'd been so preoccupied last evening with maneuvering Raoul under the blankets that I hadn't paid attention to his naked body. How strange he looked unclothed. I much preferred my delicate Patrice's body.

Raoul took me in his arms, crushing me against his chest. Unfortunately, because of our respective heights, this also smashed his member against my stomach. When he pulled back, a few interminable seconds later, Raoul yanked my hand to his lips and delivered a wet kiss. "And how did you enjoy your conquering?"

His tight grip on my hand and expectant stare told me all I needed to know. I had to flatter the man. My fate, as well as that of Maman's plan, depended upon Raoul believing I wanted nothing more in the world than him. I needed to transform my pure loathing into believable desire, which was to be a herculean feat. I looked back into his eyes, thought of Patrice, and told Raoul a truth of sorts. "It exceeded my expectations," I said.

Raoul released my hand. "I hope I didn't hurt you."

I discreetly ran my wet hand on the back of my shift, wiping off Raoul's spit. Little did he know, he'd provided me with an excuse to avoid engaging in amorous activities for a little while. "I'm sore, but my mother said that's to be expected."

"She's prepared you in other matters, too, I hope," Raoul said.

Other matters? Raoul's meaning evaded me until I put myself into a mistress's mindset. He wanted confirmation I wouldn't get pregnant. Of that, he needn't have worried one iota. "Maman gave me a special tea," I said.

Raoul sighed with relief. "I expected as much. Your mother's managed to avoid it with my father, thank heavens."

Yes, thank all the saints, all the spirits, and every god and goddess under the sun and moon above. A cold draft blasted through the nooks and crannies of the woodwork, so I went and retrieved my robe, wondering what to say next. While I wanted to rush to Marie's and help her prepare for Fete Ghede, it would be indecorous to throw Raoul out right after my supposed deflowering. My stomach rumbled just then. "I'll have Mrs. Shelley prepare us some breakfast," I said.

"That sounds lovely," Raoul agreed, eyeing me hungrily. "But only after I feast my eyes on you one more time."

Should recently deflowered women be coy or innocent? Perhaps a combination of both. I dropped my robe and shift, avoiding his eyes as a demure girl would but also turning full circle so he could see every bit of me. I performed a precarious dance of innocence and seductiveness. The whole while, Raoul stared at me as an alligator does a rabbit.

As his eyes roamed over my body, I waited in the cold morning air for his stare to break. Finally, Raoul noticed my trembling limbs. He picked up my robe and draped it over my shoulder. "I'll have you when you recover, mon fleur. Get me some breakfast while I dress," Raoul said. Then, his expression soured. "Best get the day going. I have to meet with Vivienne today. *Wedding* plans."

I threw on a day dress and, when out of Raoul's sight, wiped the taste of him from my lips. Poor Vivienne. I certainly didn't envy her future. And what lay ahead for me? Would the same potion keep me safe again, or would Raoul grow suspicious? I didn't know. I'd have to trust Marie.

To my relief, Raoul ate quickly. I did, too. To endure those final minutes with him, I thought about the Fete Ghede, Patrice, Marie, and a garden of dead souls who were, by all accounts, often more pleasant than the living.

***

November 2, 1860, Congo

Square, New Orleans

C andle lights flickered and danced like exploding galaxies throughout Congo Square, a large, open space not far from Marie's home. This place bordered the French section of the city and uncultivated swampland. Perhaps a hundred people moved to the beat of the drums. The music fused with Papa's blood, which coursed through my veins, possessing my heart to go thump, thump, thump in time with the beat. Most people dressed in white, purple, and black, the colors sacred to the Ghede. As they danced, the celebrants looked like torrents of spinning white clouds with accents of sunsets and thunderstorms.

Patrice and I stood on the perimeter of the square, watching the dancing. Every so often, we looked into one another's eyes and knew beyond all doubt the universe had forged us from the same bit of flesh. I lost track of time as I squeezed Patrice's hand. The combined heat from our bodies sizzled in the night air. "Thank you for bringing me here," I said. Indeed, I was grateful. My love had also given me a white dress to wear in honor of my lave tet so I didn't have to use Raoul's blood money.

"Watch Marie," Patrice urged me. She pointed to the center of the square, where Marie sat upon a stool. My mentor wore a white dress as well as a dark purple sash and tignon. "She's about to be mounted."

My eyes widened in curiosity. I knew that when the loas possessed a person, it was called mounting, but I'd never before witnessed the event. *Possession* conjured up negative visions of demons inhabiting some poor soul, but the loas were benevolent spirits. I thought about how Maman Brigitte had inspired me to speak in a sultry voice at the right moment during my dinner with Raoul. "I know it's nothing to fear, but losing control still scares me," I said.

"Don't worry, mon amour," Patrice said, drawing me close. "The loas will *always* protect those they inhabit."

Patrice's words relaxed me. I needn't fear the unknown. The man next to Marie began drumming harder, and I watched in awe as Marie's dignified face became more regal when Maman Brigitte took over. Marie jumped off the stool and launched into a languid dance, swaying her hips exactly as I'd seen Brigitte do. For that reason, I knew Brigitte, not Marie, directed the movements of Marie's body.

Next, a man holding a large bottle of rum approached Marie. From his confident movements and the way he gazed adoringly at Marie, I surmised that Baron Samedi possessed this man. "Hot peppers have been soaking in that rum for a month," Patrice explained. "It's a test of true possession. No human could tolerate the heat of that drink."

A month? Simply imagining that rum's bite caused my mouth to burn, but Marie snatched the bottle from the man Baron Samedi inhabited and took a large swig, swallowing the fiery liquid with nothing but the look of pleasure on her face. Marie, or rather, Maman Brigitte, then locked her eyes onto mine. "Selene O'Neil! Approach!" she called above the drums.

My heart pounding in my chest, I stepped forward, and the crowd parted. I slowly walked toward Brigitte to the beat of the drums. Why had she called me forth in front of so large an audience? I didn't fear her, but I worried I'd fail her. When I finally reached Brigitte, I curtseyed, just as I'd done when she sashayed in through my window when I was a wisp of a girl at only six-years-old. "Yes, Maman Brigitte?"

Maman Brigitte whispered something to Baron Samedi, and he winked at me. "Congratulations, Selene O'Neil." He then promptly ushered the rest of her entourage toward the crowd. The men and women who'd stood next to Brigitte toasted with more rum before joining the reverie.

"It's time for the lave tet ceremony," Brigitte said.

"In the square?" I asked, scanning the dancers, who seemed absorbed in the merriment.

"No, we will go to my home, where you will also accept me as your met tet, if you wish," she whispered so only Patrice and I could hear her. "Doing so will give you the strength for what lies ahead."

My heart began to race. Marie's eyes emanated Maman Brigitte's knowledge of mysteries beyond my understanding. I was fortunate the loa had given me the choice to formalize our relationship. I certainly needed strength, as well as all the help the universe offered, for the grand task my parents had put before me.

Still, I had to ensure that I accepted the offer in good faith. Marie had once explained that a met tet was the loa who ruled someone's head. For a Voodoo practitioner, a met tet functioned as a guardian angel, patron saint, mentor, and intermediary with the spirit world. Practitioners offered special devotions to their met tets in exchange for patronage. This relationship was sacred, not one a Voodooist should take lightly. What if I failed Maman Brigitte somehow? Would she and Baron Samedi abandon me? That dreadful thought struck me senseless. I didn't want to risk my relationship with the spirits I'd known since childhood. I looked at Patrice. "What if I fail?" I asked. "Will the spirits hate me?"

Patrice looped her arm in mine. "They will not. Don't be afraid of devoting yourself to someone you love."

As usual, my lover was the voice of reason. I shouldn't be afraid to enter a covenant with someone dear to me. I trusted my heart to Patrice, and I could do the same with a dear spirit I'd known since childhood. I swallowed the lump in my throat. "I'd be grateful."

Brigitte's eyes gleamed with approval. "Then, follow Marie," the loa said.

Follow Marie? Was the loa leaving me? I watched as the sultry expression on Marie Laveau's face became more solemn. "Marie?" I asked.

"Yes, child, it's me," Marie replied. "My possession is over, but Maman Brigitte will return for you tonight."

Patrice and I trailed behind Marie, who led us to her home on Rue St. Ann while the party continued on under Baron Samedi's patronage. My love and I followed the Voodoo queen into the altar room. Marie stoked the fireplace, lit some candles, pulled a chair into the center of the room, and instructed me to sit.

To keep my nervousness at bay, I eased onto the chair and focused on Patrice, who was working as an assistant for the ceremony. My love gathered sacred herbs and added them to a bowl of water at Marie's request. The scents of lavender and calendula flowers tickled my nose, but I couldn't identify the other herbs. Patrice told me that mambos and houngans had their own secret combinations of herbs used for the ceremonial washing. Marie struck some incense and stood in front of me. "Selene O'Neil, do you consent to having me wash away all that holds back your heart and soul?"

"I do," I replied.

Patrice handed the bowl of water to Marie, who walked behind me. "Then, close your eyes," the Voodoo queen commanded.

I suspected Marie would pour the contents of the bowl over my head. After all, a lave tet ceremony was literally a washing of the head, but I didn't know what to expect beyond that. I obeyed my mentor and closed my eyes. A few seconds later, a slow trickle of water hit my head and washed down my face. I noticed only physical sensations from the water at first. That was, until Marie started chanting in Creole, the language she used to speak with the loas.

Suddenly, my heart cracked open. It felt like my heart shattered, most certainly. A fragment of pain emerged. Then, the floodgates of my soul opened. All of the anger and frustration at Maman and her laudanum binges that I'd imprisoned in my heart exploded out in a flood of tears. I cried. I cried for my parents, who'd been cheated of a life together on Earth. I cried for myself as a young girl, a child forced to parent her mother.

My tears soon transformed into cries of rage. I yelled strings of nonsense as my fury at M. Le Jaune and Raoul poured out of my soul. During all of this, Patrice stayed close to the fire and refreshed the incense as needed. The storm inside me raged on, but by the time the candles burned halfway down, my heart started to calm. Soon, a wave of peace came over me, and my need to scream ceased. I quieted. Then, the telltale rustle of Maman Brigitte's skirts alerted me to her presence. I next saw her materialize in front of the fireplace, her eyes aglow. "Will you accept me as your met tet, child?" she asked.

I was happy the spirit appeared to me in her traditional form instead of possessing Marie, because that was familiar—comforting during a vulnerable time. This old spirit had called me home. I'd have a *home*, a notion that warmed me like a lump of precious coal on a frigid day. I, the daughter of a laudanum-addicted mistress and a slave, had a *place* in the world. I'd never felt such belonging before. Even with my spirit friends, my family, and Patrice, part of me had always felt separate from the greater world, but that was to be no longer. This wasn't just a "more formal entry" into magic, but also into a relationship I needed so very much. "I do," I said with all the conviction my soul had to offer.

CHAPTER THIRTEEN:
DEATH

The Death card is as frightening as the sound of a banshee's wail echoing off the green hills and ancient cairns of Ireland. The banshee foretells death. Some say this creature appears as a beautiful young woman, and others believe she's a wizened crone. Whatever her appearance, she's of the fairy world. If you hear a keening sound, pray it's just an odd bird.

Colleen

January 20, 1842, Etoile, New Orleans

"**W**ould you hand me the saw?" Colleen's husband asked, pointing to the wall of tools behind her. *Husband* was such a beautiful word, even if Colleen could only sing it under the cover of night. Colleen watched David covetously as he studied the large, flat piece of wood, running his hands across its edges like Michelangelo would with a virgin piece of marble. David could coax a masterpiece from any piece of wood. As Colleen handed him the tool, she had to restrain herself from stroking his hand. "Of course, dear one," she whispered.

"Thank you, my love," he whispered back, a hint of a smile on his lips.

Those precious tokens of affection didn't satisfy David and Colleen, so they cherished the gestures when they could. Colleen awoke every morning and began contriving excuses to spend time with her husband. She frequently asked Madame Le Jaune if she wanted some fresh herbs from the stable, or even better, something from the city.

It was Madame's desire for a cradle that gave Colleen the perfect excuse to loiter in David's workshop. As one of the most talented carvers in Louisiana, he was the perfect candidate to create an exquisite cradle for the newest Le Jaune. Colleen had also convinced Madame she'd help David because she knew about Europe's en vogue designs in furniture. Colleen, therefore, had permission to spend part of her day in David's woodshop. Given David's talent, she knew he'd create a beautiful cradle, a thought that consumed her with melancholy and rage. He should've been carving something for their own child, not the Le Jaune babe. "What design will you carve on it?" Colleen asked, her throat tightening.

David traced the lines of the wood with his hands. "A fleur-de-lis."

"The symbol of French royalty? But *of course,*" Colleen said in an affected French accent before erupting into laughter. "Perhaps next, Madame will put a powdered wig on the poor bébé."

David joined in the laughter. Soon, plumes of mist curled from their mouths as their hot breaths hit the cold afternoon air, twisting together like a pair of dancing dragons. They kept laughing until a crow's hollow, mournful cry rustled through the drooping boughs of the live oak tree. David stiffened. "Those birds are warning us about something."

"Let's not dwell on that," Colleen said. She tried to banish the chill that ran up her spine. She knew nature sometimes foretold the sinister. After all, a menacing wind had whistled outside Ashington Manor the night before Lord Ashington had assaulted her. Colleen couldn't bear to give credence to bad omens, though, so she changed the subject. "Any news on Monsieur's furniture shipment?"

Furniture shipment was their code phrase for Father Pierre's ingenious escape plan. In one week, Monsieur Le Jaune's main furniture buyer would pick up a large shipment at Etoile's dock. All the furniture carvers would be required to transport furniture from the workshop to the dock and load it onto the boat. Well, all the carvers save for David, who would feign a minor injury right before he had to help at the dock. Monsieur wouldn't want David to injure himself further when his intricate creations brought M. Le Jaune most of his money. Colleen and David hoped Monsieur would order him to rest while the other slaves loaded the furniture. David, Celeste, and Colleen would then walk a mile down the riverbank, where a small boat would pick them up and bring them to the convent. Father Pierre had scheduled a load of honey to depart from the convent at the same time as Monsieur's furniture shipment would leave the dock. Hidden among the shipment of honey, the three escapees would travel to an Underground Railroad station. Colleen loved the plan for its simplicity.

Before he answered Colleen's question about the furniture shipment, David checked to see if anyone lurked outside his workshop. "We should consult the cards," he said when he saw they were alone. "Something has me rattled."

"Are you sure? What if it's bad news?" Colleen touched his arm for the briefest second, a risky move on her part. He'd once told her that knowing the future takes courage, but right then, Colleen didn't feel brave. Until she'd met David, life had taught her one unforgiving lesson after the next. David was her first true gift—someone she couldn't imagine living without.

"I'm sure," David replied, stroking her face gently. "We need to know what's ahead."

Colleen gave him a weak smile and took a seat at his worktable. If he believed they needed to consult the cards, then consult the cards they would. She chastised herself for her lack of faith as David retrieved the cards from their hiding place in his living quarters. He soon returned. After he ensured once again they had privacy, David shuffled the deck, rested the pile on his worktable, and turned over the first card.

And then all the color drained from his face.

Materially speaking, David's tarot cards had little weight to them. Their pictures and symbolic meanings, however, wielded the power to destroy her and David's future in a single blow. Her heart racing, Colleen followed David's panicked gaze to the card that had alarmed him so much. At first, her eyes landed on the number thirteen, which someone had painted at the bottom of the card. Colleen frowned and wondered what the fuss was about.

Then, as her eyes traveled up the card, she saw *it.* The thing that inspired such fear. An old woman set dead center in the card. The crone's mouth hung open in a silent, bloodcurdling scream that was frozen in time. Colleen could almost hear the wail of a banshee, the spirit that foretold death through her wails. A shiver wracked her body. She gingerly placed the card back on the deck, hoping not to offend the creature. "Does it mean death?" she asked in a wary voice.

"That's the card's name." David swallowed the lump in his throat. "But it usually just means a profound change of some type."

He hadn't said the card's name aloud, and Colleen vowed not to repeat the word lest she empower it. She felt as if she were teetering at the edge of a high cliff, staring at jagged rocks and crashing waves below.

Her only consolation was that the card also pointed to a big change. Or, she hoped, the death of someone *not* dear to her. Let Monsieur Le Jaune perish. Or Madame. Or whoever. Anyone but her, David, or their child. Perhaps that wish would damn her to Hell, but Colleen didn't care at that moment. Determined to bring up David's mood, she pointed to the deck. "Draw another card," she said. "No need for the long face until we know for sure."

"You're right," David admitted. "I'm just terrified. I have too much to lose."

Colleen reached forward to take his hand, but something

stopped her. Instead, she rested her hand on the table and tried to comfort David with words. "Have faith."

"Have faith in what?" a voice asked from behind her.

Colleen spun around and saw Monsieur Le Jaune standing in the frame of the door that led outside. Because he'd neglected to wear a colorful cravat or vest, Monsieur's black suit made him look more like an undertaker than a gentleman factory owner. She thanked the saints she'd obeyed the instincts that had stopped her from touching David. Colleen worked to control her breathing. She knew they had but a few seconds to salvage the situation, so she focused all her energy on keeping her voice bright and casual. "I was telling Day to have faith that the furniture shipment will be profitable," she said.

M. Le Jaune strode over to the table and glared down at David's deck of cards. "Fortune telling? That's witchcraft."

"It's my fault. Colleen's a good Catholic," David quickly added, lowering his head. That demeaning gesture made Colleen want to slap Monsieur Le Jaune right there and then. "I wanted to see if I could do something else to bring you more money on this shipment. I thought it couldn't hurt to ask."

Avarice flickered in M. Le Jaune's eyes. He seemed ready to pounce on the bait David had laid. But then, Monsieur's jaw tightened, and he took a step toward Colleen. He stopped, but he was still close enough for her to smell the brandy wafting off of him. "There's no time for that now," M. Le Jaune said. "Madame's having bad pains. She needs a doctor."

Death. Was the banshee stalking the poor unborn babe? Colleen cursed herself. She pulled her wrap tighter around her to protect her child. David nodded and stood. "I'll hitch up the wagon and get the doctor," he said with measured calm.

"Right now," Monsieur commanded, turning to Colleen. "You. Come help me with Madame."

"I'll just grab some chamomile first to calm her nerves," Colleen said. She hoped Monsieur agreed because she wanted a few moments of privacy with David before they went on their respective missions.

"Be quick about it," M. Le Jaune said before leaving the stable as if the Devil himself were chewing at his heels.

With Monsieur gone, David quickly gathered his cards and thrust them into Colleen's hands. "Hide these somewhere safe. He'll burn them otherwise."

Colleen slipped the cards into her pocket, feeling uneasy about being responsible for so precious a gift. She then held her husband's gaze. For a fleeting moment, there was nothing else in the world but them. No slavery and no threat of death, simply a lifetime of love frozen into a second. One of the hurricanes she'd heard about could smash Etoile into a mess of sticks and dust, but she and David would still hold fast and safe because they were together.

Colleen broke the gaze all too soon. They didn't have time to waste. David grabbed a bundle of chamomile for Colleen and then rigged up the wagon.

On the way to the kitchen, as she crunched over the winter grass, Colleen remembered that her ma had pains with her last baby, the one who'd died because it came too early. The chamomile would help calm Madame, but it wouldn't keep a premature child alive. And as much as Colleen would prefer the Le Jaune babe die instead of someone precious to her, she wouldn't wish death on an innocent creature. That was, unless the universe required a sacrifice to keep Colleen's dear ones safe. She'd rather Madame's baby die than her own. Colleen knew those were devilish thoughts, so she vowed to help Madame as best she could for penance.

After giving Celeste the chamomile to brew into a tea, Colleen ran to her bedroom, desperately searching for a safe hiding place for David's cards. Under her mattress? No, anyone could find them there. In her trunk? Not the best idea. All someone would have to do is rummage through her clothes. After frantically surveying the room once more, Colleen's eyes drifted to the trunk. It was where she'd stowed her ratty carpetbag. She scurried to the trunk and pulled out the carpetbag. The old thing had a rip in the liner. Colleen placed the cards in the space between the liner and the bag, intent on sewing the rip later for extra protection. With the cards as safe as she could make them, Colleen left for Madame's boudoir. She ran downstairs from the attic and through the second floor hallways until an overwhelming feeling of dread forced her to a hard stop right outside Madame's door.

Colleen didn't have the gift of foresight like David, but she sensed Death had infiltrated Madame's quarters. The plaintive wail of a banshee pierced through the door, confirming Colleen's fears. She worked to twist the doorknob, but her sweaty palms slipped on the faceted glass. After a few seconds, though, Colleen managed to find her grip and opened the door. She found a world of competing light and shadow inside. Madame had likely ordered the heavy drapes drawn over the windows, so the only light in the room came from the fire blazing in the hearth and a scattering of oil lamps.

Mme. Le Jaune lay on the bed, which hid her body in darkness. Her sweaty face, though, glistened in the firelight. Madame twitched in agony, and Beatrice, the housekeeper, sat at her side. Beatrice wiped Madame's head with a wet rag, soothing her with shushing noises. As Colleen drew in a breath for courage, the tangy scent of sweat assaulted her nostrils. She plowed through the room's chaos until she reached Madame's bedside.

In the midst of his wife's suffering, Monsieur Le Jaune stood close to the fireplace, drumming his fingers along the mantel with one hand and clutching a drink with the other. His cut crystal glass reflected firelight as he sipped its contents, which made the drink look like a cocktail of blood and liquid gold. *He's like an alchemist from Hell*, Colleen thought. "You're finally here," he said. "Her pains are getting worse. Day left to get the doctor?"

"He was hitching up the wagon when I left," Colleen replied.

M. Le Jaune watched his moaning wife. Colleen thought she saw him frown with concern, but she wasn't sure. After all, his face naturally rested in a sneer. If anything, he worried for the unborn child and not Madame, who he regularly slandered. Monsieur drained his glass and set it on the mantel with a thud.

"I'll make sure Day left," he said. And with that, Monsieur vanished in a trail of brandy fumes.

Madame cried out again, so Colleen banished thoughts of M. Le Jaune. She sat next to his wife, opposite Beatrice. "What can I do, Mum?" Colleen asked.

"Make the pain stop," Madame begged, her eyes glazed over.

"Day's gone for the doctor," Colleen said. She squeezed Mme. Le Jaune's hand in what she hoped was a comforting gesture. Then, smelling copper, Colleen looked down at the bed and cringed as she saw a deep red stain eating its way across her mistress's pink blanket. She caught Beatrice's eye. "How long has she been bleeding?" Colleen asked in a hushed voice.

"Nearly a quarter of an hour," the housekeeper said.

"Does this mean I'm losing the baby?" Madame whined. Her fingers clenched at the blanket as a wave of pain struck. "I didn't bleed this early with Raoul."

"I'm sure the babe is fine," Colleen said with forced cheer. She prayed for Madame and the little one, but if either of those deaths satiated the banshee on David's card, Colleen also prayed the creature would take them instead of her loved ones. At the same time, Colleen pushed away the specter of death that haunted the house. She couldn't devote any energy to that phantom. Not in her condition.

Another wave of pain seized Mme. Le Jaune, who crushed the bones of Colleen's hands. Colleen grimaced and breathed deeply against the pain. The contraction continued for the next minutes, and Madame's screams reverberated through the room.

Colleen and Beatrice exchanged panicked glances. They had no respite from that noise. Just as Madame's pain waned, Celeste entered the room, a steaming cup of tea in her hand. "Chamomile tea with a hefty dose of laudanum," she told Colleen. "Have her drink it, and I'll go wait for the doctor."

After giving Celeste a look of profound gratitude, Colleen offered the cup to Madame. "Have some laudanum, Mum, and you'll feel better soon."

Thanks to the Blessed Virgin and the damned host of saints, at the mention of laudanum, Mme. Le Jaune released Colleen's hand. Madame slowly sat up and took a small sip. Then another, and yet another.

Time slowed for Colleen, who focused on getting her mistress to drink the mixture in its entirety, the only relief she'd get until the doctor arrived. Gradually, Colleen's efforts bore fruit. The tension on Madame's face eased, and she relaxed back against the mountain of pillows Beatrice had arranged. The immediate crisis had been averted.

Colleen was tempted to fetch Madame some fresh clothes. In her sweat and blood-drenched nightgown, Mme. Le Jaune looked like she'd fought a legion of demons in Hell and lost the battle. Madame could do with something less gruesome for when her husband returned, but Colleen couldn't bear to interrupt her mistress's calm state. Instead, Colleen and Beatrice enjoyed their brief respite while they awaited the doctor, praying all the while the laudanum kept Madame's misery at bay.

Before long, men's voices echoed down the corridor outside Madame's room. The voices got louder as they neared, and soon, a dapper man with a leather bag in his hand stormed into the room. From his purposeful walk, Colleen deduced he was the doctor. He set his bag down on Madame's bed and pulled out a collection of instruments more appropriate for a medieval dungeon than a lady's boudoir. "I'm Dr. Timkins," the man said in a brusque voice, barely glancing at Colleen and Beatrice. "Have either one of you delivered a baby?"

"I have," Beatrice said, which made Colleen sigh with relief. Although Colleen had seen her ma give birth to five children, the local midwife had done the difficult work.

"Good," Dr. Timkins said. He turned to Colleen. "Get some rags. The cook's already boiling some water. We need both as quickly as possible."

Colleen nodded and rushed out of the room, nearly bumping into Monsieur, who had planted himself right outside his wife's door, thereby blocking Colleen's passage down the hall. "B-bitch," he slurred as he teetered forward. "Yer a bitch for not givin' me what I'm due."

As a cloud of brandy hit her face, Colleen realized he was dead drunk. He hadn't reappeared at his wife's side, and Colleen had assumed he'd gone with David to get the doctor. But no. Supporting his wife or fetching medical help was the thing a kind man would do. Instead, Monsieur had likely remained at Etoile, drinking the entire damned time. The miserable man disgusted her. His wife needed him, but in this state, he'd only get in the doctor's way.

Colleen took a deep breath to calm her wits. She shouldn't agitate the man further. She had the rags to get. "Monsieur, please let me pass," Colleen said. "The doctor needs some boiled water and rags to save Madame's life."

M. Le Jaune stared at his wife's door, his bleary eyes seething with what looked like hatred. "Let 'er die. But I need the baby. A spare heir."

Let her die, let her die, let her die. That cold-blooded refrain rang in Colleen's head. She wanted to condemn him right there but stopped herself. *She* had also willed Madame or the babe dead to satiate the banshee. Was she as terrible as Monsieur? Remorse flooded Colleen as she cursed herself for her profane wishes. She had to make amends for those evil thoughts. "The boiled water and rags are for the baby, too," Colleen added in a soft voice. She had no earthly idea how a bunch of torn, ratty clothing would help the child, but it seemed like the right thing to say under the circumstances.

"Rags for the baby," M. Le Jaune repeated. He mulled over that bit of information for a moment. And although he did step aside so Colleen had room to pass, the leer never left his face.

Some people were silly when drunk, others catatonic. But Monsieur? He was nothing so pleasant. He was simply a mean drunk, and mean drunks were the most dangerous kind.

Before Monsieur could instigate more trouble, Colleen hurtled down the corridor and outside to the cookhouse, where she found both Celeste and David. What a blessing on that miserable day.

The cook had already set a large pot of water to boil, and David was helping Madame's cause by tearing old sheets into rags. The doctor likely told David what was needed before he left the buggy. Colleen moved as close as she dared to her husband, an action which prompted David to quickly move a healthy distance away.

"Monsieur was blind drunk when I brought the doc back. He told me to stay away from you," David said.

Celeste checked the water's temperature on the stove. "He's lost his mind," she said. "Both of you need to be careful until the furniture shipment next week. Don't even speak. I'll pass on your messages to one another."

Colleen was about to promise Celeste she'd do just that when a crow cawed loudly right outside the cookhouse, causing David to flinch. The crow shouldn't unnerve him so. Not unless he was keeping a horrible secret from her.

Colleen dropped the sheet and wiped her trembling, clammy hands against her skirt. She couldn't allow herself to entertain the thought that Death stalked her and her loved ones. Not if she wanted to stay sane.

But Death whispered and hissed near her ears, baiting her. Colleen knew that phantom never truly disappeared. It lived on the crowded street corner and in dank, moldy sanitariums. It hovered around broken carts and carriages, waiting eagerly to strike. Death was a funny thing. It was a curse for those who love the world, but also a welcome respite from the world's pain. And pain in the world... there was plenty.

Colleen thought back to her ma, who'd endured unimaginable pain in the end. Had she prayed for the Angel of Death to take her? Colleen understood the logic of surrendering to the inevitable, but looking to her side and seeing David, Colleen knew she couldn't give up as her mother had. Not when she had so much to live for.

When the wind whistled outside or the crow cawed, she told herself that was a screeching banshee heralding in the death of the unborn Le Jaune. Or even Madame. Not *her* child, and certainly not David. Colleen couldn't permit herself to believe anything other than that.

CHAPTER FOURTEEN: TEMPERANCE

The Temperance card indicates you should strive for balance, which necessitates moderation in all things. Take the middle path. Too much water causes one to drown, but people quickly die without it. There are times for action and inaction, and overall, they should drive one down the path to success. Victory, rest, victory, rest. The cycle continues forever.

Selene

November 7, 1860, Bourbon Street, New Orleans

A few days after the lave tet, I sat cuddled up to Patrice on my settee and watched the autumn leaves blow by on the wings of the wind. I now saw things I previously couldn't. In certain drapes of Spanish moss, I saw the dead in flowing dresses. My eyes also sometimes recognized the sparkling energy in storms, as well as fairies and nature spirits that inhabited rocks, streams, and plants.

People often achieve new clarity after they complete proverbial trials by fire. The lave tet wasn't anything as extreme as walking over hot coals, but it did emotionally exhaust me. The ceremony also allowed me to awaken into the next phase of development.

After Marie washed away my grief, and I accepted Maman Brigitte as my met tet, I spent the day relaxing in Marie's altar room as many loas came to speak with me. I met Erzulie Freda, a beautiful spirit who loved gold jewelry and the finest champagne. La Sirene, a loa who looked like a mermaid, also appeared in one of Marie's mirrors. In addition, my dear Papa Alegba came to visit. He was an old man who laughed with nearly every breath. I expressed my thanks for all the times he'd opened the door to the spirit world for me. The lave tet made me comfortable with serving these loas. Still, Maman Brigitte was my met tet, the loa who, quite literally, owned my head. I wasn't a slave to Maman Brigitte, though. After all, I'd consciously devoted myself to her. She was, in essence, a patron saint and guardian angel wrapped in one benevolent package. Maman Brigitte would protect and guide me and in turn, I would honor her first among the other loas. I'd previously considered Maman Brigitte and Baron Samedi as cherished friends, and now we had a more formal relationship.

In addition to a stronger connection with the loas, the lave tet brought me more confidence. How I could convince Raoul to gamble away his future remained unclear, but if I trusted my instincts, my timing would coincide with that of the loas. *Hopefully.*

Perhaps most important of all, I gained perspective from the ceremony. In this great world with its millions of people, I was but a speck. While the loas might bring me opportunities, I had no right to demand a perfect life because I served them.

Patrice adjusted her position on the settee, and my eyes flitted from the window back to her. My love was happily immersed in *The Elements of Astronomy* by John H. Wilkins. She most appreciated the book's tables and charts. The diagrams of constellations and planetary movements sometimes reminded me of the vèvès, or symbols, we used to summon the loas. The spirits had their own vèvès, which Marie had taught me to create using cornmeal.

Patrice was so focused on the book's pages that it felt like a great sin to bother her. I tried to focus on my book. *For the improvements of Ages have had but little influence on the essential laws of man's existence as our skeletons, probably, are not to be distinguished from those of our ancestors,* said Henry David Thoreau, a writer I greatly enjoyed. (When I could concentrate, that was.)

Unfortunately, that afternoon, my rambling thoughts kept ripping me away from the tranquil shores of Walden Pond and to my present circumstances. Or, more specifically, Raoul.

Between the wedding preparations and lessons from Vivienne's father about how to run a plantation, Raoul had little opportunity to stalk my bed. For that, I thanked the spirits profusely. He dropped by briefly some afternoons but left soon after, claiming his business and familial obligations exhausted him.

I didn't doubt it. Although Raoul scoffed at the idea of hard work, he did exactly what Vivienne's father told him to. Raoul didn't dare ruin his family's financial prospects by being lazy. A pity.

My life would be easier if Raoul sabotaged his upcoming wedding, thereby blocking M. Le Jaune's access to Vivienne's dowry. The faster the Le Jaunes were destroyed, the better. But *no*. Raoul also behaved himself because he believed he'd one day run Vivienne's father's plantation. Little did he know, though, that the South's defeat in the upcoming war would demolish those dreams. Even if Raoul survived the conflict, the abolition of slavery would eradicate the planter class' wealth, a notion that brought me so much joy I beamed. Oppressors like that deserved their future misfortunes.

Right after my dream of Raoul's death on the battlefield, I had tried to persuade Maman to abandon her plans and leave New Orleans with me and Tante Jeanne. She didn't have to sacrifice herself anymore if Monsieur Le Jaune's slaves would soon be free. Admittedly, I didn't know when the war would happen, but the dead Raoul in my dream hadn't appeared much older than present-day Raoul. I'd told Maman that war wasn't more than a few years hence, but she maintained her course. *I believe you, Selene, but I still made a vow to free his slaves myself,* she'd told me. *It's a promise I hold sacred.*

I couldn't argue with Maman about the sanctity of her vows. I had promises to keep, too. Maman drowned herself in laudanum to cope, but I had a better antidote to misery. *Patrice.* To keep me from growing lonely in his absence, Raoul had encouraged Patrice to keep me company at night. He assumed we were simply bosom friends, and dear friends of the same sex would naturally sleep together if there was only one bed to be had. We did, however, confine our carnal activities to the night, when Raoul wouldn't make a surprise visit.

Raoul's absence did present a problem, though. I had fewer chances to urge him to the gambling tables, leaving me tangled in a web of inertia. Not that I preferred hurtling forward in Raoul's company. I needed to thwart his advances with a new weapon because he'd likely grow suspicious if I used Marie's elixir again. Thinking of Raoul in that fashion made me shudder, which jerked Patrice out of her book. "What's wrong? Did a mosquito bite you?" she asked.

"An insect called Raoulus horriblis did," I confessed. "I'm afraid of what to do when Marie's potion doesn't work."

Patrice stiffened and rested her book on her lap. "Chérie, you'll simply find a way to bankrupt his father without submitting to him. Promise me again you won't sacrifice yourself for your maman's plans."

My love looked radiant in the late afternoon light as the orange hues of the sun warmed her beautiful dark skin. Her eyes held the sun's fierceness. "I promise," I replied. "Marie said bedding Raoul wouldn't be necessary."

Patrice relaxed against the settee. "Then, do not worry. Trust in the spirits. We'll just go away before something bad happens."

At first, Patrice's vow to abandon New Orleans for the chilly North, the place in my dream, filled me with warmth. But then a coldness wormed its way into my heart. Despite that dream's cozy feeling, I remembered Maman's absence. She wouldn't leave this city until she succeeded in freeing all of M. Le Jaune's slaves. I wouldn't abandon my mother, but I also couldn't submit to Raoul. All my competing promises made my head throb. Just when I thought I'd succumb to all that stress, Patrice stroked my arm. My eyes darted to her face, where her worried frown told me not to borrow trouble. "You'll truly come with me when I leave?" I asked. Patrice had told me she would, but I wanted to be sure. Part of me worried she'd end up missing her parents and New Orleans too much.

"Why would I stay here without you?" Patrice asked as she inched closer to me. "You are my life, and I'm yours."

And there it was. Our devotion was again sealed with that promise. I didn't care that society or the Catholic church deemed Patrice's and my love evil. She was my lover—my knight and my damsel.

On the settee, I decided to play a consummate damsel. I leaned against her, snuggling into her bosom and inhaled her scent, something that instantly comforted me. Patrice, in turn, stroked my hair and kissed my head. My body stirred for her, and this craving had but one remedy. "Let's adjourn to the bedroom," I whispered into her ear.

"What of Raoul?" Patrice asked, breaking our embrace. "It's late afternoon. He still might come. We could hear him come through the door from here on the settee, but not the bedroom."

I considered Patrice's words. Ever since Samuel warned me to take care with Patrice, we hadn't touched or gazed too fondly at one another unless we were alone, and it was late in the day. My lover was a voice of reason. Normally, I paid voices of reason their proper due, but that day, something lustful took over. "We'll lock the bedroom door. If Raoul comes, we'll simply say locking the door was an accident and that we needed an afternoon nap."

Then, before she could reply, I yanked Patrice toward me for a kiss. She gasped and nearly pulled back, but then nibbled back on my lips with equal force. Pull, push, pull, push. Did I act the knight as I pulled her by the hand into the bedroom? It didn't matter.

That evening, we alternated between the roles of vanquisher and willing victim as we saw fit. It was as if the stars above guided our actions, and we willingly gave ourselves over to these divine impulses.

To be safe, we locked the door and remained quiet so we could simply pretend to be sleeping if Raoul came. But I heard no sign of Raoul outside the little enclave I shared with Patrice that night. As I lie next to her, long after she'd fallen asleep, thoughts of the past vexed my mind.

A crow cawed right outside the bedroom window, reminding me of the visions Papa had shown me. I still needed to see what, specifically, had derailed their plans and how my father had died. Because I'd had a lave tet, I believed I could process the truth without exploding. Quietly sliding out of bed, I prepared to summon my father so he could tell me the final installment of his story here on Earth.

***

Colleen

January 22nd, 1842, Etoile, New Orleans

A cold front descended upon New Orleans, glazing the world with a crispy layer of frost. The slaves wrapped themselves in blankets because they had no choice but to go about their regular work in the chill. Madame, however, had installed herself on her chaise lounge near the fireplace in her boudoir, where she hibernated under layers of quilts and stared blankly at the flames dancing in the hearth.

Colleen didn't blame her one bit. As much as her mistress annoyed her, Colleen felt terrible about the Le Jaune baby's still-birth. And that wasn't the worst news by far. Dr. Timkins had informed Madame she couldn't have more children. That news had driven Mme. Le Jaune to her bed with only Colleen and Celeste to comfort her. Monsieur offered no solace, for he treated his wife as coldly as the winter winds that blew through the mansion's nooks and crannies. Etoile used to have an air of luxury, but after Madame's loss, the house was as foreboding as a mausoleum.

Holding a cup of chamomile tea that was generously laced with laudanum, Colleen gently tapped on Madame's door. "Mum? I have your tea."

"At last. I've been waiting for an eternity," Mme. Le Jaune said. Her voice was weak, but it had an underlying bite to it, a hint of acrimony.

I was busy making you this damned tea, Colleen thought. But then, she remembered why Madame mourned. A heavy dose of guilt settled on Colleen's heart. She'd sacrificed the Le Jaune babe to the banshee after all. Colleen banished that thought and pushed open the door.

Immediately, a cloud of anger hit Colleen. She stepped across the threshold and waited in the preternatural darkness for her eyes to adjust to the dim light. When she could walk, Colleen tiptoed across the floor until she reached Mme. Le Jaune, who was secured under her layers of quilts. "Here you go, Mum." Colleen rested the teacup on her mistress's nightstand. She also discreetly turned the knob up on the oil lamp. It wouldn't do to have Madame spill the tea for want of light.

As Madame sat up and grabbed the tea, the lamplight illuminated her pained expression. Her matted hair hung in disarray over her shoulders, and patches of red marred her skin. Before her loss, Mme. Le Jaune had ordered Colleen to dress and coif her to perfection. Colleen resisted frowning when she noticed Mme. Le Jaune's slovenly condition, though. By necessity, lady's maids handled their mistresses in all states, including when they were drunk, mourning a husband's affair, or even engaging in a dalliance of their own. A competent maid also knew when to speak and when to remain quiet. Right then, Colleen didn't have enough insight into what Madame would prefer, so she did the wise thing and bit her tongue.

"Why didn't you just bring me the doctor's bottle?" Madame asked Colleen in an accusatory tone between sips. "*That's* what I asked for."

Because you might down the whole thing, Colleen thought. Dr. Timkins had left plenty of laudanum to soothe Madame's melancholy, but Colleen and Celeste decided to keep it out of the poor woman's reach. Colleen wouldn't admit it to her mistress, though. No, she blamed the doctor. "The doctor says it's to stay in the kitchen," Colleen added.

Scowling, Madame swallowed the remainder of the tea. "What does my *husband* say about the matter?"

"I couldn't say, Mum," Colleen replied, hoping Mme. Le Jaune believed that lie. Colleen was hiding a big secret from her mistress. Monsieur had wanted the medicine to stay within his wife's grasp. When he'd found out Amelie couldn't bear more children, he'd wished her dead, especially since she didn't want to share her bed for activities that wouldn't produce children.

"First, he wastes my dowry like an imbecile. And then he neglects me?" Madame wailed. With an unexpected burst of vigor, she threw the teacup on the floor. It thankfully landed on her Persian carpet, which cushioned the blow. She stared at the spilled laudanum and dissolved into a flurry of tears.

Despite Madame's faults, she had legitimate grievances against Monsieur. Colleen took a seat on the chaise and rubbed Madame's back. "Oh, Mum," Colleen gently soothed.

"Don't touch me!" Mme. Le Jaune pushed Colleen away with such force that she rolled off the bed and tumbled onto the floor. "I see how he looks at you."

Realizing a cloud of anger had settled over her, Colleen slowly stood and backed away from her mistress as if she were a wounded tiger. Colleen knew the futility of denying the truth. Madame might be aloof and spoiled, but she had her womanly intuitions. "Nothing's happened," Colleen said in a calm voice.

"Yet," Madame replied. She fluffed her pillows and reclined against them.

"Nothing will *ever* happen," Colleen said. She backed up another step. "I never encouraged him and never will."

Madame's eyes glowed with animosity. "That doesn't matter. He was tempted by you, and that's enough. You've got a witch in you."

"But, Mum... you don't even want him in your bed," Colleen said. Indeed, Madame had devised all sorts of plans to keep her husband from her room. Why did Mme. Le Jaune care where her husband's eyes wandered? Perhaps she didn't want any scandals he caused to taint her. Or, more likely, Amelie fretted her husband sought other women because she wasn't attractive enough to hold his interest.

"Be that as it may, I deserve his devotion," Madame said. Her face settled into an unnatural smile. "My husband always gets what he wants. I'll enjoy seeing you suffer when he gets this."

Madame's happiness struck Colleen as bizarre until she remembered that Lady Ashington had reacted the same way when she found out about her husband's advances on Colleen. Neither woman particularly liked their conjugal duties, yet they blamed Colleen for their husbands' infidelities. Perhaps the way these women were raised to think about marriage had poisoned their thinking. On the other hand, maybe Lady Ash and Mme. Le Jaune just needed someone to blame for their misery, and Colleen was the closest target. The true blame rested with Lord Ashington and Monsieur Le Jaune. Their wives, however, failed to see that truth. In that dark, stifling room, Colleen felt hatred toward her mistresses. She'd resorted to begging Lady Ashington for a favor, but Colleen wasn't about to give Mme. Le Jaune the same pleasure. Colleen straightened her spine. "That won't happen."

Madame glared at Colleen, pointing to the teacup on the

floor. "Get me another cup of tea. Add plenty of the doctor's medicine."

"Right away," Colleen said, grateful for a reason to leave the boudoir. She was tempted to bring Mme. Le Jaune the whole bottle but decided against the idea. Colleen didn't need to add another death to her conscience. Instead, she'd keep the laudanum in her pocket, ready to dispense the amount recommended by the doctor.

"And, Colleen," Madame added. "As soon as I find another lady's maid, I'll have you working in the garden or cleaning the house. You're still indentured and owe us another three and a half years of service."

"Whatever you say, Mum," Colleen replied as she opened the door.

"Remember, my husband gets what he wants!" Mme. Le Jaune called behind her.

In the safety of the hallway, Colleen smirked. She had no doubt Monsieur was accustomed to having his way. But this time, he wouldn't get it. Colleen, David, and Celeste would vanish before M. Le Jaune had his chance. *Not on your life*, Colleen thought.

CHAPTER FIFTEEN: THE DEVIL

When the Devil card appears, be aware of sinister people. Alternatively, the card calls you to question your own negative habits. Sometimes, we're our own worst enemies. Make sure you don't become trapped in your own devices. You must break free to defeat your adversaries.

Colleen

January 28, 1842, Etoile, New Orleans

We all bring a little darkness into the world, Colleen thought as she wrung the water from the cloth in her hand into a basin. No one lived a sinless life. Those who sinned brought evil into the world and, therefore, deserved blame for their actions. But what about illnesses, which had no malice? Colleen couldn't blame a miasma for the destruction it wrought, even though she desperately needed to. Mayhem slithered into Colleen's life on the day she, Celeste, and David intended to leave.

At daybreak, Celeste mentioned she felt cold even though she was working in the winter kitchen right by the fire, leading her to believe she had a slight fever. The mild discomfort didn't alarm the cook, so she kept right on working. As the day progressed, she developed a cough that started small but soon crescendoed into a hoarse bark that people could hear throughout the house. Finally, when Celeste started shivering violently, she took to bed.

Colleen tried to keep her fears at bay. What would they do? Postpone the escape for a few days? Try to bring the sick cook along, assuming she could travel? David had wanted to get the doctor, during which time he planned on stopping at the convent to inform Father Pierre of Celeste's illness, but Monsieur had refused to permit David to leave Etoile. Instead, M. Le Jaune ordered David to finish carving a nightstand for the shipment that night, and then supervise the loading of the furniture onto the boat. That left the escape plan in tatters.

Colleen couldn't leave Etoile without a driver, and more to the point, she couldn't abandon Celeste. Colleen was torn between caring for the cook and the equally pressing need of coordinating new plans with David. "You should have some tea and a bit of laudanum for the cough," Colleen told Celeste as she bathed the cook's brow with a cool rag. Colleen had taken some of Madame's medicine and put it in a vial she used to hold chamomile extract. She replaced the missing volume of laudanum in Madame's bottle with water. She desperately hoped that the medicine and a strong brew would heal Celeste enough to travel soon.

"Not too much laudanum," Celeste croaked.

"Just a pinch," Colleen said. She fixed a strong cup of tea and added a few drops of the stolen medicine before sliding the vial back into her dress pocket. After the beverage cooled enough to drink, Colleen held the cup to Celeste's lips.

Monsieur Le Jaune had crowded most of his slaves into two primitive cabins near the furniture factory, but Celeste, David, Beatrice, and Rachel each had their own quarters. For this, Colleen was grateful. Celeste's private nook was in the outbuilding used as the summer kitchen, which meant she had access to a fireplace to keep her warm. Colleen also appreciated that she had some much-needed privacy with Celeste. "Do you think you'll be well enough to travel?" Colleen asked.

"No. You and David have to go." Celeste reached out from under her blankets and grabbed Colleen's arm. "The boat'll be here in an hour or two."

Colleen wanted to do just that, but she knew David wouldn't abandon his mother. And Colleen certainly wouldn't leave without her husband. She gently pried the cook's hands from her arm. "We'll simply go when you're better," Colleen said. "Everything will be fine. You'll see."

Although she'd intended her words to calm Celeste, Colleen knew she'd failed when sorrow flooded the sick woman's glassy eyes. "You have to convince David to go," Celeste groaned as she shifted positions. "If you can't, you'll have to go alone. His and the baby's lives are at stake."

Leave David here? I'd never do such a thing! Colleen opened her mouth to protest, but a crow cawed, interrupting her train of thought. She loathed those birds now. *It's an omen*, she thought. *A terrible omen of things to come.* Colleen fought the lump in her throat. Her only hope was to convince David to leave with her. "David's stubborn," she said. "It'll be like getting a mountain to budge."

"Then, start pushing," the cook said before erupting into a coughing fit.

Colleen doubted she had the strength to fight David's bull-headedness, but she promised Celeste she'd try. The dead winter grass crunched beneath Colleen's feet as she headed to David's workshop. From the storeroom, she heard the tense shouts of the slaves, who were loading furniture into wagons and staging the rest for transport.

Soon, they'd have to roll those wagons to Etoile's docks. Colleen didn't have much time. If, by some grand miracle of the universe David consented to leave, he'd have to fake his injury soon. Monsieur Le Jaune would, hopefully, take command of the furniture operation himself. Colleen and David could then escape downriver.

The scents of chamomile and hay greeted Colleen as she

stepped inside the workroom. David smoothed a small night-stand with a lathe. "Hello," Colleen said.

"How's my mother feeling?" David asked. His face was hope-ful, which made it all the more difficult to tell him the truth.

"Still poorly," Colleen admitted. Her heart raced as she said the next words, knowing David would resist. "Your mother thinks our part of the furniture shipment should continue as planned. She'll reschedule hers when she's feeling better."

David's expression darkened. He walked to a table and plopped the lathe on it with a hollow thud. "*Your* part has to stay on schedule."

Damn it. Colleen had anticipated David's response, of course, but hearing him order her to leave without him sent her heart careening into a pit of despair. She needed to throw herself into her husband's arms and convince him to leave with her. She stepped forward ever so slightly but stopped when David shook his head. The cavernous space between them amounted to ten feet, but it felt insurmountable. Colleen couldn't bear an-other moment as a time thief, someone forced to steal seconds, minutes, and rarely, hours with her beloved. She remembered Celeste's command and prepared to nudge the mountain into compliance. "Furniture should stay together," she countered, meeting David's eyes.

David ran to the door and checked their surroundings. Satis-fied they were alone, he gripped her firmly by the shoulders. "Go to the rendezvous point. My mother and I will join you in a week or so. I *promise.*"

"No!" Colleen shook away his hands. She hadn't moved the damned mountain a bit, so she had to try another tactic. Plead-ing. Negotiation. Cruelty. *Whatever it took* to convince her hus-band to abandon his mother. Even if David resented Colleen for manipulating him, she'd live with his anger. "I'm not going without you."

"If you stay, Monsieur will find out about the baby and kill me," David said. His eyes burned with desperate anger, and Col-leen knew a battle waged in his soul. He emphasized the next words with such force they became etched on Colleen's soul. "And you'll be responsible for my death."

You'll be responsible for my death. Those ruthless words wounded Colleen more than a knife ever could. She knew David didn't truly mean them, not when he struggled to hold back tears.

She heard a crash, probably from the factory and workroom adjacent to the stable building, but she pushed that disturbance from her mind. She needed to find *something* to convince her stubborn husband to leave Etoile. Perhaps he'd listen to reason, if not her anger. "I'm putting your life at risk if I *leave.* Monsieur is suspicious," Colleen insisted. Then, an idea struck her. It wasn't the best of plans, but the words spilled out of her in a torrent of desperate hope. "We'll convince Monsieur to let us take your mother to the convent. He disagreed before, but we'll just remind him how wonderful a cook she is—how expensive replacing her would be. Then, we'll all leave on the Underground Railroad from the convent. *Together.*"

"And then Monsieur would suspect the convent and send the slave catchers there," David said. "Father Pierre saves many lives. No, you have to go meet the boat now."

No. *Never!* Somehow, in her world of ceaseless grief, Colleen had finally found the person who made life worth living. She'd never give him up.

At a pragmatic level, Colleen knew they could probably escape separately, but she couldn't risk letting him go. She'd follow him anywhere, for better or worse, just as she'd promised in her marriage vows. Invoking all of St. Brigid's strength, Colleen crossed her hands across her chest and stared down her husband. "You've always said we have to live with our choices. This is mine. I'd rather die than be separated from you."

A gust of wind blew through the workroom, sending a tornado of straw across the room as the tension built between them. David closed his eyes and rubbed his temples as Colleen awaited his response. She stretched her stiff fingers. If David refused to get on the boat with her, she'd stay. After ten more seconds, which felt to Colleen like an eternity of slow ticks on a grandfather clock, David opened his eyes. Colleen saw resignation and sadness instead of hope. "I relent. We'll get on the boat together."

Colleen's worries vanished as the clenching on her heart eased. She ran up to David and threw her arms around him, burying her head against his chest. His heart beat strong inside his warm body, and everything felt right with the world once again. "I love you," she said.

Suddenly, David pushed Colleen away so hard she almost fell on the workroom floor. *What in heaven is wrong with him?* She spun around to see what had startled her husband. And then she saw it.

Colleen had always wondered if some people, right before their deaths, saw the Devil staring them down. She had her answer. Yes, they did. In the doorway of David's workshop stood M. Le Jaune. "I knew you were nothing more than an Irish slut," Monsieur snarled at Colleen, his face contorted with fury and, strangely, vindication. He then turned his vitriol on David. "You think you can defile what's mine? Not on your life."

Not on your life. Colleen had thought those words in defiance to Madame and her predictions. Now, Monsieur taunted her with those same words. Colleen tried to silence her racing thoughts. She needed to act—to intervene and redirect Monsieur's wrath onto her. Holding her hands in front of her to placate the man, Colleen approached him. "You're mistaken," she said. "I simply hugged the man for agreeing to carve me a trunk. We Europeans are more demonstrative. As you saw, Day pushed me away."

"Yes, that's right," David added. "I pushed her away."

Monsieur Le Jaune worked his jaw as he mulled over Colleen's excuse. He kept looking back and forth between her and David, keeping them both in suspense. Despite the chill running through her bones, Colleen didn't dare waver from that precious lie. Finally, he cracked a menacing smile. "So be it. I'll take you now since it won't matter to either of you."

Out of the corner of her eye, Colleen saw David tense. *Don't move*, she begged him silently. She knew he could read her mind at times. Colleen needed him to listen then. *You can bear anything if you deaden yourself inside. The unpleasantness won't last forever*, Ma had once told her. Granted, her mother had dispensed that advice with chores in mind, but it applied to Colleen's current situation, too. All she had to do was endure Monsieur for a little while, and then she and David could all escape at some other time when they wouldn't fall under suspicion. Colleen took a deep breath and nodded to M. Le Jaune. "So be it."

At Colleen's words, M. Le Jaune's face hardened with triumph. He reminded her of a military commander who'd just conquered a civilization. Her heart in her throat, Colleen inched toward Monsieur, resolved to get through the upcoming torture as quickly as possible. The next moment sped by because she had no time to react, but simultaneously, seemed to drag on for an eternity. Those events would remain seared in her mind and heart forever.

Monsieur grabbed Colleen's arm so hard she gasped, a short-sighted move on his part since she'd consented to his perverted wants.

That single action had precipitated the end of everything Colleen held dear.

In response to M. Le Jaune startling Colleen, David sprung toward Monsieur, yelling something that got drowned out by the rushing panic in her ears. Before Colleen could protect her husband, Monsieur pushed her to the ground. He then swiftly pulled something from his breast pocket and pointed it at David. Colleen recognized the object in M. Le Jaune's hand.

A gun. A pearl-handled pistol that gleamed with its owner's hatred. Colleen let out a heartbreaking scream, which was drowned out by a gunshot that reverberated through the stable, her skeleton, and her entire future.

A crimson peony of blood bloomed across David's shirt, and he sank to the ground, mumbling what Colleen thought was *keep her safe* before coming to rest on the straw, his dead eyes screwed open in shock. Colleen couldn't hear anything over the sound of her screams, a hoarse keening that could rival a banshee's. Her anguish, her complete disbelief that she'd landed herself in this hell, was so great that she didn't react when Monsieur hit her right temple with the gun before throwing it down near David's body.

Colleen's vision blurred. M. Le Jaune then pinned her to the floor and jerked her skirt upward, exposing her legs to the cold air. "Careful. Baby," she said, her voice coming out as a harsh whisper.

"I don't give a damn," Monsieur said as he plunged into Colleen.

Feeling split in two, Colleen immediately deadened herself. It took no effort at all. From that point on, she was a dead woman who could somehow also walk, talk, and go through the motions of survival without really living. She closed her eyes and inhaled the smell of fresh hay and her husband's blood, the last precious memory she'd have of his life force. She vowed to carry that scent with her for the rest of her mandatory days on earth. Then the world vanished in a blanket of night.

***

Selene

November 7, 1860, Bourbon Street, New Orleans

Every choice we make has a risk attached. Sometimes, it is a minimal one, and other times, great. Talking back to Monsieur Le Jaune when I was seven was perhaps the first true risk I took, after which point Maman set me straight with her wooden spoon.

The next big risk came when I asked Patrice to sneak away with me to the garden of stone houses the day after I'd first met her at her family's mercantile. I couldn't help but fret as I wondered if she felt the same as I. What if she thought me debased? Patrice hadn't explicitly said she returned my affection, but her little glances and implicit gazes gave me enough courage to try. We'd kissed in the city of the dead, first tentatively and with the sweetest of reservations. As we grew to know one another, our mutual passion took over, and we'd knotted our bodies together. Only spirits and ghosts witnessed what society considered unholy, and they kept our secret well.

Passion, if one isn't careful, can take hold of the senses, so Patrice and I minimized risks as best we could. Her parents and my maman thought us simply the closest of friends. Our passion remained contained, burning brightly behind the safety of walled gardens of the dead and, only just recently, inside Raoul's apartment.

When passion rages out of control, however, it can destroy people just like anger does. Anger sometimes appears as a slow burn, much like kindling made from slightly damp wood. This tempered type of fury is easy to control because it doesn't rush forth and blind the senses. But anger can also manifest as a violent storm that drowns out all reason.

When I finally witnessed my father's death, I immediately understood why he'd waited to show me the truth. I longed to destroy my apartment furniture after that vision. I also fantasized about plunging a knife, a shimmering steel blade powerful enough to sever bone, into M. Le Jaune's chest. My heart sang with joy as I heard his sternum crack and saw blood soak his suit. Had I been in M. Le Jaune's vicinity, I would have drawn an ocean of blood in a campaign of beautiful vengeance.

Thankfully, or unfortunately, I was instead perched on the edge of the settee in the sitting room. Patrice slept in my bed, and my father's ghost watched as I struggled to contain my emotions. A scream lurked in my throat, ready to claw out of me. But my anguished cries would awaken Patrice or cause Mrs. Shelley to burst into the room, a cast iron pan in hand. Instead of yelling, I clasped my wine glass so tightly it shattered. I made nary a sound as the shards pierced my skin. I simply watched, transfixed, as my blood mixed with red wine, the fusion of these liquids dripping in red rivulets down my hand and arm.

"I understand you want to kill him," Papa said. He stood near the fireplace, resting his ghostly shoulder against the mantel as if he had a body.

"That's an understatement," I replied. I ran to the dining room table and grabbed a napkin to staunch the blood dripping down my hand. What the devil was I supposed to do with this information? The answers I'd sought brought me only despair and confusion.

Feeling dizzy from anger, I didn't trust myself to remain upright, so I returned to the settee and awaited my father's explanation. Not only had M. Le Jaune murdered my father, but he'd also violated my mother right on Papa's blood. Little wonder she resorted to downing bottles of laudanum to get through life. I'd do likewise if the same happened to Patrice. "How could you let Maman be with that man after what he did?" I asked, my eyes begging for an answer that made sense.

Papa sat next to me. "Your mother thinks she's responsible for my death, so she chose to punish herself and avenge me. I only let her know, in my own way, I don't blame her for choosing that path. I want you to choose better than she did, though."

I nodded, my head heavy with the burden of new knowledge. Maman obeyed her inclinations despite my desperate interventions. I couldn't force her to do anything. I could only control my actions, and Papa wanted me to make the right choice. Should I stab Monsieur, as my instincts told me, or help Maman fulfill her mission?

I calmed my racing thoughts and considered my options. If I killed M. Le Jaune, then Raoul would inherit the slaves. At least until he died in the upcoming war. And I would probably end up in prison or hiding from the law, neither of which would do Celeste and the others any good. Only the spirits knew what would happen to Maman.

Although I noticed the bleeding on my hand had slowed, I tightened the napkin around it. "I won't kill him," I said. "But I want to make him suffer."

"Remember, you want justice," Papa cautioned. "Let that guide your actions as you help your maman."

I noticed how my father had deliberately chosen the word *justice* instead of revenge. Certainly, freeing all of M. Le Jaune's slaves qualified as justice for the suffering he'd visited on many. Maman and I planned to realize this goal by getting Monsieur to bankrupt himself through his son. We couldn't force the Le Jaune men to do something they didn't want to do, though. Maman and I would harness their natural inclinations. That said, Monsieur would probably wish for death instead of living under reduced circumstances. Whatever M. Le Jaune suffered, I wouldn't shed a tear. "How do I get Raoul to the gambling table?" I asked.

"Don't surrender so quickly," Papa said. "*Think.*"

I closed my eyes and thought about how to make Raoul reckless. Alone with my father's ghost on that velvety cool night, I realized he guided me from the spirit world because he lacked that chance in the flesh. Perhaps good parents didn't simply *give* children the answers they needed, but rather fostered their ability to find the answers themselves.

When concentrating hard on my goal, I remembered Marie had said that angry people act carelessly. It followed that I needed to make Raoul angry. A plan started forming in my mind as I thought of Raoul's possessiveness toward me. He'd become furious if he caught me with another man, or even Patrice in an act of carnality.

Still, that plan made me uneasy. Monsieur Le Jaune had murdered my father and violated my mother when he felt betrayed. I didn't trust Raoul not to direct that anger toward me or Patrice. I couldn't risk her life for Maman's plans. I had to make Raoul angry enough to be reckless with his fortune but not angry enough to hurt me.

After a few seconds, the name *Vivienne* appeared before me. Yes. That was it. Vivienne had to come upon me with Raoul. Hopefully, he'd direct his frustration at losing Vivienne, and thereby her dowry, to the gambling table. I opened my eyes and looked at Papa with excitement. "I'll cast a spell to make his fiancée, Vivienne, find us together. The magic will use his energy against him."

Papa smiled proudly. "Exactly, mon petit. The best forms of justice happen when you help people manifest the destiny they've chosen for themselves."

My father was very wise. He'd given me the push I needed to think for myself. I had a revelation that night. To execute a plan of that magnitude, I needed Marie. She was the master clocksmith who understood all the moving parts that whirled around me. "I'll ask Marie for help. Is there anything else I should do?" I asked.

"Comfort your maman," Papa replied. His eyes held a deep sadness. "Seeing her suffering tortures me. She didn't know this, but a few days before M. Le Jaune shot me, I had a dream that he killed *her* with that same gun. That's why I tried so hard to get her to leave."

I gasped. My father's visions had shown me the world from Maman's point of view, not his. "Wait. *Maman* was supposed to die? That's what the cards were telling you?"

Papa nodded gravely. "Yes. I couldn't permit that."

"Why didn't you leave with her immediately, then?" I asked. "You two would've had time to escape if you hadn't argued."

"I was afraid Monsieur would kill your grandmother instead," Papa replied. "I had to see if your maman would leave without me first. When she refused, I relented."

I let out a long breath, my shoulders sagging. The events leading up to my father's murder swirled in my head as I tried to make sense of the tragedy. Papa feared his wife would die, so he tried to get her to leave without him. Maman, of course, refused to abandon her husband. Left with no other choice, my father gave into her demands, an action that might have condemned Celeste to die had events played out differently. My mother hadn't known the nightmare that lurked in her immediate future when she threw herself into Papa's arms.

Could my parents have done anything different in the next second, when M. Le Jaune discovered my parents in a compromising position? Monsieur had ruined everything. Nothing satisfied him, not even my mother's willingness to let him rape her on the stable floor. That bastard had grabbed her. My father jumped forward to protect the woman he loved. And then? Monsieur shot Papa.

I gritted my teeth and looked at the ceiling. Why didn't the universe intervene and halt that tragic cascade of events? I wanted to cry then, but I couldn't scrounge up the tears. "Is that why you lunged at Monsieur Le Jaune?" I asked, even though I knew the answer. "You thought he was going to kill Maman?"

"It is," he admitted. Papa touched my shoulder. "Are you ready to see what comes next?"

"Yes," I lied. I didn't have the fortitude for more tragedy. Not one bit.

CHAPTER SIXTEEN:
THE TOWER

When the Tower card appears, think of the Morrigan, the Celtic triple goddess associated with war, ruin, and fate. Sometimes, she manifests as a crow. The Morrigan is often the harbinger of something undesirable. However, her appearance also encourages warriors to act courageously in the face of danger, making her a positive goddess, too. The Morrigan and the Tower card both signify times of blood. Disasters may come, but recovery is possible if you have courage and foresight.

Colleen

January 28, 1842, Etoile

C olleen was lying next to David on Keem Beach. His body and the day's warm sun made her glow as brightly as a star. But then, a garish ray of light penetrated through her eyelids, intruding into their peaceful little niche on the beach. Next, Colleen noticed how the world smelled of copper, almost like a munitions factory instead of the beach's normal sea air. Something was peculiar. Wrong.

Colleen twitched when something pricked her bare legs, an action that sent pain shooting through her head and pelvis. Her legs were cold. David's body no longer warmed her.

David. Where was he? As Death's icy fingers inched up her body, Colleen desperately clung to those precious seconds in dreamland, when anything in the world was possible. Anything broken could be fixed before waking up. Any dead person could resurrect.

Dead, dead, dead. That word did flips in Colleen's throbbing skull until she was conscious enough to understand it. Something bad had happened. The coppery smell was blood. David's blood. David was dead.

Please, no! she thought. *Let it have all been a dream.* Colleen gingerly sat up and steadied herself against the pain. It took a few minutes for the hammering in her skull to cease. Colleen reluctantly opened her eyes, only to see a world saturated with blood unfurl before her. David's blood. But no body.

A searing white ray of agony slammed into Colleen, drowning her physical aches until they were but whimpers. She never realized until then how excruciating pure heartbreak could be. Her grief radiated from her heart, her muscles, and every bone in her body. Colleen begged for death, but her lungs continued to breathe. An eternity later, that torment sharpened to a knife's edge, which Colleen pushed into her fractured heart. She then realized she was just as dead as David... only she could still walk, speak, and most importantly, exact revenge. Colleen would use the knife in her heart to stab the life out of Maurice Le Jaune.

At least he hadn't taken the child. Or had he?

Colleen grabbed her stomach. The baby quickened, which sent a jolt of devastation through her. With the baby still alive, Colleen couldn't give up and join David in the afterlife. She'd have to remain on this godforsaken Earth and raise their child.

After that child grew up, though, Colleen didn't want to live. How could she? She had killed David with her stubbornness and stupidity. All the things she could have done to change her horrible circumstances ran through Colleen's mind. If she hadn't thrown herself at David, Monsieur wouldn't have become suspicious. David would also be alive if she'd just *gotten on the damn boat* in the first place. Maybe, too, the universe wouldn't have taken David away if Colleen hadn't offered up the unborn Le Jaune babe to the banshee.

If, if, if. How she wished she could manifest any of those *ifs.* But Colleen's selfishness and impetuousness had killed her husband. She'd lost him forever. *No!* she thought. *Not forever. Just until my physical body dies. My mind and heart have gone with him already.*

Eternal sleep, a warm velvet darkness in which she'd see David again, tempted Colleen. It would be so easy. She could just walk into the river and let the languid waters lull her to sleep and usher her to David. She fumbled in her pocket and found the laudanum vial still there. Colleen held the glass vial in front of her. It sparkled like a jewel, a beautiful jewel that offered an escape from her pain.

Then the baby moved again. No. She couldn't do it. David would be angry, and the church taught that people were damned to Hell for committing that horrible sin. Colleen couldn't risk losing David forever, and she had to protect the child, as he'd said.

Colleen then remembered the tale of Tristan and Isolde, one of her mother's bedtime stories. Tristan and Isolde were star-crossed lovers who ended up dying under tragic circumstances, but their love endured death. The trees growing from their respective graves intertwined their branches. After the lovers died, they were reunited in the afterlife. Tristan and Isolde wasn't the most pleasant of stories to tell a babe trying to nod off, but the story held a poignant lesson.

Colleen closed her eyes and breathed in the scent of her husband's blood. She'd see him again one day. She'd just have to endure this brief life on Earth until her natural death. And then, perhaps because she'd just remembered her mother's stories, a thought comforted Colleen. Ma had died early, like most women in her family. Colleen prayed to her saint she'd have a similar fate. Unlike her bargain with the banshee, Colleen would offer the universe something in exchange. Not a mere trifle, either. No, Colleen would perform a selfless act to earn her ma's fate.

Saint Brigid, she prayed in a low whisper. *Take me into Heaven as soon as you can. Ma died early just as her ma, and her ma before that. It's my destiny, regardless. In return, I'll free not only Celeste but all of M. Le Jaune's slaves. All I ask for in return is the gift of an early death.*

Colleen didn't hear the saint speak aloud, but a wave of peace washed over her, assuring her the wish would come true. To fulfill her part of the bargain, Colleen would have to remain in New Orleans and use all her energy to deceive M. Le Jaune.

Madame would order Colleen to scrub the house from top to bottom and work in the garden. Colleen would endure it all until she somehow freed Monsieur's slaves. Then, Jeanne could take the child so Colleen could die in peace. This plan had potential unless Monsieur tried to force Colleen to give the child up for adoption. Most likely, Colleen would simply have time added to her indenture if her work suffered when carrying the child. She'd endure it all to see David as quickly as the universe permitted.

Colleen laughed with delirium when she remembered how the busybodies in her Irish village believed God cursed the women in her family with early deaths for their witch's blood. But this *curse*, this precious curse, would allow Colleen to join her husband in the afterlife all the quicker.

So long as her child wasn't in danger, she would do whatever it took to free Monsieur's slaves. In that promise, Colleen found the strength to stand, warily at first. She used her pain to cement her resolve for what came next—the unpleasant task of telling Celeste what had happened. If the cook didn't already know, that was. The summer kitchen wasn't far from where M. Le Jaune had murdered David in a flash of gunpowder. Surely, Celeste had heard the horrible crack of the pistol.

Colleen used a table to help her stand. Her head pounded, so she took a small swallow of laudanum. Just enough to take the edge off the pain. She needed to see David's body and say a proper goodbye.

Colleen scanned the workshop. Sunlight streamed in the window, illuminating the nightstand he'd been working on. She walked up to it and stroked the scroll pattern David had started carving just before his death. She then noticed a small piece of uncarved wood on the back. He hadn't even finished.

Finding only torment in the workshop, Colleen moved to David's tiny sleeping quarters, which were no more than the size of a closet. His body wasn't there, either. The small room felt cavernous in his absence. She lay down on his small bed and savored his remaining essence, the faint scent of lemons and wood. As her lips spread into a blissful smile, something told Colleen to look under the thin mattress. She obeyed this instinct and slipped her hand under the mattress, where she discovered an envelope with her name written on the front. Her curiosity piqued, Colleen sat up and opened it. Her hands shook as she read the final message from her husband.

My Love,

I hope you never read this. If you do, it means I'm dead. I've been having conflicting dreams as of late. In some, Monsieur shoots you with a gun. In others, you and our daughter starve to death in Ireland. And yet in others, M. Le Jaune kills my mother or me. I don't know what to do anymore. Every action paralyzes me with fear. Please forgive me if I'm the one who's dead. That means I've left you alone in this harsh world.

Whatever you do, don't go back to Ireland. Many will soon die there. With all my heart, I want you to go North with our daughter and live a peaceful life. Another dream told me you won't do that, though. In that dream, you made a promise to St. Brigid because you need to avenge my death and overcome your feelings of guilt. I say you have no guilt to bear, and there's no need to avenge me. But I know from the dream that you're stubborn. Whatever you decide to do, I forgive you and will love you always. I'll be watching you every moment and will be there to greet you when you reach the other side.

Colleen's eyes flooded with tears as she tucked the letter into her pocket. She would keep the letter close to her heart every day of her life. What a burden David had carried in his final days! He'd seen many possible futures in dreams but didn't know how to react. He'd even known about her promise to St. Brigid.

A bit of warmth glowed in Colleen's heart. She didn't think it was the laudanum. No, David's words gave her hope. He said he'd be waiting for her on the other side. Not only that, but he'd stay with her as she navigated this hell on earth.

Colleen looked around the room and wondered if he was there now. Perhaps she just couldn't see him because of the confines of her earthly body. She closed her eyes and took a deep breath. After a few seconds, the edges of her consciousness detected David's presence, a few molecules of his soul that the universe saw fit to grant her. Colleen let his presence wash over her before opening her eyes. She could endure her sentence of time on this Earth for the promise of an eternity with her husband. Colleen took one final look around her husband's room, searing each detail into her heart, mind, and soul. When she needed to, she'd imagine herself back there.

Colleen headed back into the workroom, intent on searching Etoile so she could see David's body one last time. Only, instead, she found a red-faced, disheveled Monsieur standing in the doorway that led outside from the workroom, barring her way out. A dart of fear shot through her veins. *Dead women have no fear*, she reminded herself. With that affirmation, the fear died. She straightened her spine and smoothed her skirt.

"Because of you, my best worker's dead," he muttered.

Colleen clenched her fists until her nails dug into her skin. The bastard only cared about the money he'd miss out on, not that he'd murdered a living, breathing human being whom Colleen loved more than anything in the world. Still, she didn't argue. David's death was her fault, after all.

A sudden fit of dizziness hit Colleen then, either from the laudanum or when Monsieur hit her with the gun. Her brother, Colum, once got a blow to the head from a hoe. He'd felt out of sorts and dizzy for a week. Colleen grasped a support beam and tried to focus. She needed a sharp mind for what was ahead, and she'd stupidly had some laudanum. "I'd like to see his body," she said.

"He's long gone," M. Le Jaune said, snickering. "I fed him to the gators."

Gators. The last time she'd heard that word, David had said it. Colleen looked down so Monsieur wouldn't see the pain in her eyes. Maybe it was for the best, though. If she saw David's body, she didn't know if she'd have the strength to avoid a lethal dose of laudanum. Colleen noticed something on the ground that gave her comfort—the blood-soaked straw at her feet. A tiny piece of her husband remained, and she'd find a way to grab that straw. Colleen looked at her husband's killer and braced herself for the long drag of misery she knew awaited her. "What are you going to do now?" she asked.

"The great unanswered question." M. Le Jaune straightened his cravat and took a few steps toward Colleen. "You still owe us years of service, yet my wife no longer wants you as a lady's maid." He paused, leaving Colleen in suspense. From the smug look on his face, Colleen gathered he was enjoying himself immensely. "I could tell the sheriff you killed Day. Damaged my property. You'd hang."

"I'd welcome it," Colleen replied. She angled her chin up. Indeed, for a few moments, the noose beckoned her more than earning her revenge. She could join David immediately. Just as Colleen was about to tell Monsieur to call the damned sheriff, the baby stirred, which melted her frozen heart enough for her to think. "But is there an alternative?"

Monsieur Le Jaune looked her directly in the eyes as he unleashed his next words. "I'll make you my mistress. I have access to a little cottage in Marigny that would suit that purpose well."

Dead women might not be afraid, but they could still experience anger and hatred. As Colleen pushed her fury back into her heart for later use, she wondered if she could endure being M. Le Jaune's mistress. David said he'd forgive whatever path she chose. Death at the noose tempted Colleen again, but deep in her heart, she knew she couldn't give up just yet. David had ordered her to take care of their daughter, so she choked down her disgust and consoled herself with the fact that as M. Le Jaune's mistress, she'd be close enough to ruin him. "Fine," she said.

"Very well then," Monsieur said. Chuckling, he drew a piece of paper and a fountain pen from his pocket and unfolded it. "Sign this. You'll need to extend your indenture to compensate me."

"How many years?" Colleen asked. Not that it mattered. She had her mission and a grand exit to Heaven after. Colleen took the paper and studied it. The French words swirled about the page in an array of chaos. Although she should have asked for the contract in English, she didn't want to get sent to the sheriff, not with the child on the way. Colleen walked over to David's desk and dipped his quill in the inkpot. She scratched her name on a line at the bottom of the page, presumably where she ought to sign. Colleen then deposited the paper in M. Le Jaune's waiting hand.

Monsieur smiled. "I take it your French is still poor?"

"And what of it?" Colleen asked. Her head throbbed, so she touched her temple where M. Le Jaune had struck her. She'd likely end up with a large bruise. "I'm not a lady's maid any-more. Madame won't care if I speak French or not."

"You've just sold me your unborn child as compensation for Day's death," Monsieur spat out. He marched toward her, stop-ping only a few inches from her face. "I own it, and I'll sell it if you displease me."

Colleen covered her abdomen with her hands as the edges of her vision became dark. No! She couldn't have done something so stupid. Instead of protecting the babe, she'd given it over to the monster who had killed David. She thought of the glass vial of laudanum in her pocket. If she smashed it, could the broken glass cut Monsieur's throat? He deserved to bleed out on the floor. If not that, the jagged vial could certainly pierce the spongy tissue of his eyeball. Even if she just maimed him, Col-leen would delight in hurting M. Le Jaune.

Don't kill him, a ghostly voice whispered in her ear. *You'll hang, and our baby will die before it can breathe.* A pang of agony spread through her chest. David was with her. He didn't want her to hurt Monsieur, so Colleen used all her strength to keep her hand from her pocket. She wouldn't give her husband's murderer the satisfaction of seeing her cower, either.

She had to be strong. Colleen simply had to add her child to the roster of slaves she needed to free. In the meantime, she'd wear a mask of obedience. But every second of every minute, Colleen would devote her energy to destroying M. Le Jaune. She wouldn't only make sure she freed his slaves, but she'd also make sure he ended up bankrupt and miserable. When M. Le Jaune's life became a hell he couldn't escape, Colleen would laugh in his face. Only *then* would she permit herself to die. This plan would work. She could do it. Monsieur, though ruthless, wasn't very astute, as evidenced by the fact he'd just killed David.

The other slaves would make him money, but not nearly what David had brought in. Colleen drew comfort from the fact that Monsieur loved the gambling tables. Madame's dowry couldn't last forever. Oh, yes, Colleen would bide her time until she could hasten Monsieur along to his eventual end. "I'll be your mistress, but I'll keep the child," she said with more conviction than she felt. "The child should also be educated by a lady named Jeanne. If you don't agree, then hang me. I'll welcome death."

M. Le Jaune's lips curled into a triumphant smile. "I'll educate the brat so long as I get a return on my investment. If it's a girl, Raoul can have her when she's old enough. A girl with a bit of learning will hold my son's interest. If the brat's a boy, he'll do my bookkeeping or make himself useful."

Colleen gave him a curt nod even though she'd never let her daughter become Raoul's plaything. Jeanne would certainly take the child to safety before that happened. Still, Colleen wondered why Monsieur didn't just kill her outright. It made no sense for him to keep her on. "Why do you want me for a mistress?" she asked, searching his face for an answer. "I have a child on the way. Surely, there are other women more suited to you."

"You're right that I need a mistress. Amelie is useless on that count, especially now that she's barren." M. Le Jaune smirked, much like the jack-o-lanterns the people back home used to carve at Samhain to keep the evil spirits away. Only, he was the evil spirit, not its deterrent. "Day took what was rightfully mine. I'm taking it back. Preserving a man's reputation is worth any price."

Well, so is revenge, Colleen thought. Hate cascaded through Colleen's dead limbs, brain, and heart, its strong current enough to fuel her revenge for decades if need be. But she needed to do a few things before indulging in her anger. "I'd like a moment alone here before I pack my things," she said. Then, Colleen remembered the unfinished piece of furniture now sitting in David's workshop. "And I'd like to take the nightstand he was working on. For the child."

"So long as it stays in the brat's room. Otherwise, I'll burn it," M. Le Jaune warned. "And remember, I expect you to behave. If not, I sell the child."

Monsieur had intended those words to frighten Colleen, but dead women couldn't be afraid. She'd behave herself, oh yes. With enough laudanum and the fire of vengeance to sustain her, she could do anything. "I understand."

"You need to move into the cottage today. People shouldn't see you looking so... mussed," Monsieur said, scowling, as he noticed the blood on Colleen's dress. "A slave will load the furniture into the wagon while you pack. Take the back stairs up to the attic so no one sees you." M. Le Jaune then left her alone to mourn her husband.

Mussed in my husband's blood, Colleen thought. She knelt on the ground near David's life force and closed her eyes, repeating her vows to her husband and St. Brigid. In lieu of a body to mourn, Colleen scooped up some straw and secured it in her pocket. Then, she stood and left without another word, determined to also take David's cards with her so she'd have something to give their daughter.

Colleen trudged across the barren yard and toward the summer kitchen, the periphery of her vision blurring slightly. She stopped and steadied herself. No matter how much Colleen craved oblivion, she didn't have the luxury of fainting away again. She had to face Celeste. At first, Colleen had feared the cook's anger, but now she welcomed it. If Colleen could absorb any of Celeste's suffering, she would. She deserved to carry that burden.

Colleen scanned the yard, looking for activity, but only the crows cawed overhead as the trees rustled in the wind. She took a deep breath. The smell of swampland—of rotting leaves and stagnant water—invaded her nostrils. She then heard the soft whispers of ghosts layered into the wind. People had died here, haunting the land with their suffering. The grounds of Etoile were surely cursed. Colleen had the feeling David would leave with her, though. His ghost wouldn't suffer with the others in this place. Not unless he was comforting his mother from beyond.

Celeste. Colleen's heart exploded with pain. She focused her attention back on the summer cottage, which lay only a few yards in front of her. Each step forward felt heavy, as if she were dragging the weight of the world behind her. Her dead heart picked up its pace as she stepped into the summer kitchen, a blast of heat from the roaring fire stealing her breath. She prayed Celeste already knew the truth. Colleen could bear the cook's anger, but not her initial heartbreak upon hearing of David's murder.

After they adjusted to the early evening darkness, Colleen's eyes rested on Celeste, who sat at the table. Beatrice, the housekeeper, sat at the cook's side. The fire reflected off the unspent tears in Beatrice's eyes, but Celeste's glowed with a fury all their own. Colleen had confirmation that David's mother knew of his demise, then. "It was all your fault," the cook said, her voice strangely flat. "You killed him."

A brief flash of pain cascaded through Colleen, only to be replaced with calm acceptance. And resolve. "I know it," Colleen replied. She didn't dare deny her culpability in David's death. True, M. Le Jaune had fired the gun, but she all but loaded the ammunition herself.

The cook glanced at Beatrice and nodded to the door. "Leave us for a minute."

"Are you sure?" the housekeeper asked, casting a wary eye at Colleen.

"I am at that," Celeste insisted. She squeezed Beatrice's hand. "Don't worry. I won't kill her. There's been enough blood spilled here today."

Colleen stiffened as Beatrice passed her on the way outside. She could feel the housekeeper's anger rolling off her in waves, a feeling that struck Colleen to her core. "I'm so sorry..." Colleen said.

"No—" Celeste interrupted, her jaw trembling. Colleen took a step back to give the cook, who looked like she'd explode any second, some space. Celeste swallowed and then continued, "I don't want to hear your apologies. I told you to *be careful!* I had to watch as the furniture carvers dragged David's body into the wagon and carted him off. To the *swamp,* I was told."

As tears pricked her eyes, Colleen nodded, eyes downcast. She then turned around to make sure she and the cook had privacy. She scanned the grounds outside the summer kitchen, finding no one about, not even Beatrice. Colleen slowly approached the table and kept her voice soft. "I'm going to ruin that devil. I *promise* you. He tricked me... so he now owns David's child. But I won't rest until I wreck the bastard and what's left of his fortune. Not only that, but I'll free *every single one* of his slaves.".

When Colleen mentioned that the baby now belonged to M. Le Jaune, a flash of concern replaced the steely look of anger in Celeste's eyes. "You must send that poor girl to Jeanne! Keep her away from here. And that devil."

"I'll send her with Jeanne before Monsieur has the chance to hurt or sell her. I'll keep her safe, no matter what it costs me," Colleen promised. Just then, the hint of a vision struck her. She saw Celeste, Jeanne, a young woman with David's eyes, and another young lady gathered around a table in front of a hearth. The merry group was in a house near a winter sea. Colleen didn't see herself in that vision, which made her internally sigh with relief. It meant that one day, her daughter and Celeste would be free. And Colleen would be with David in the afterlife. She didn't want Celeste to have to wait for her freedom, though. Colleen added, "Jeanne could take you away now, too."

Celeste's features hardened. "Only after I see you redeem yourself by destroying that bastard."

Colleen offered the cook a sad smile. She only hoped her mission wouldn't take too long. She craved her reward with every fiber of her being that Monsieur hadn't killed.

***

Selene

November 10, 1860, 152 Rue St. Ann, French section, New Orleans

At the table in front of Marie's fireplace, I whisked together laudanum, quinine, licorice powder, and Bordeaux in a bowl, hoping the strong wine would disguise the taste of the other ingredients. The poison my maman used to endure M. Le Jaune now served as my weapon. Just a pinch would do. I didn't want to hurt Raoul, simply limit his masculine prowess. Marie said this concoction would kill Raoul's libido and make him amenable to selling me to Maman's purchasing agent.

Marie didn't want Raoul to turn his anger and frustration on me, though. For that reason, she developed a second phase of the plan, where Marie and I would craft a spell to bring Raoul's fiancée to my door. We hoped that when Vivienne found Raoul and me together, her father would allow her to cancel the wedding. Ideally, the loss of Vivienne's dowry would drive Raoul to the gambling tables with enough anger to fuel extreme carelessness. Marie and I wanted him furious enough to jettison his common sense.

She cautioned me, however, to remain calm at all times. For inspiration on that front, I looked to my maman, who contained and focused her rage as needed. Witnessing the aftermath of my father's death gave me a precious window into her psyche. I'd previously thought of her as selfish and aloof, but I now viewed her as self-sacrificing and calculating. Because of her example, I learned how to measure out my anger into palatable, manageable doses. *Palatable portions.* That's how Raoul would have to drink his potion. As I looked into the bowl, I saw that the bloodred wine still had clumps of licorice powder in it. That wouldn't do at all, so I beat the mixture with more ferocity.

"I appreciate everything you've done for Maman and me," I said to Marie as she joined me at the table.

Marie rested her hand on mine. "Just as your maman is grateful you've helped her get her heart's desire."

I stopped mixing my potion and set the bowl on the table, frowning. Maman's heart's desire? From the visions my father had shown me, I knew she wished for death more than someone thirsted for water in a vast desert.

Wait. Did that mean?

I wanted the answer to be no, but as Marie stroked my back in a soothing motion, I couldn't deny the truth. I hadn't made the connections in the vision because I'd blinded myself. But in Marie's altar room, I cracked open that terrifying door and saw Death behind it.

Thankfully, Marie caught me and steered me to a chair. Tears pooled in my eyes as *everything* about Maman's empty bottles, transparent complexion, and fatigue made sense. She did not drink copious amounts of laudanum just to endure M. Le Jaune.

No, the drug also soothed the terrible pain her family curse inflicted upon her. She was dying of a tumor, to her great delight. Marie drew me close, and I took a moment to lament Maman. Strangely, though, my reservoir of sadness emptied quickly. I then felt joy, so strange an emotion under those circumstances. Maman *deserved* to be with Papa. She wanted to die so badly, and now that I was old enough to take care of myself, I couldn't hold her back from her destiny. I'd miss her, though. Terribly.

"When your mother soon dies, you'll see her just as you see your father", Marie said, reading my thoughts. "Now, let's focus on getting Vivienne to visit you at the right time. Three days from now should do."

CHAPTER SEVENTEEN: THE STAR

Destruction sweeps away false delusions. After the tragedies associated with the Tower card, the Star brings renewal. A new beginning. If this card appears in a reading, know that your life will become blessed once again, especially if you have hope and open your heart to the universe's possibilities.

Colleen

January 30, 1842, Faubourg Marigny

I n architecture, spolia are objects, such as statues or columns, that are confiscated as spoils of war or as a result of conquest. Spolia are also, generally speaking, building materials that are reused for a new purpose, Colleen read in the book about Roman architecture she'd stolen from M. Le Jaune's library. After collecting her scant belongings and stuffing them into her carpetbag, she'd found refuge from Madame among Monsieur's vast book collection. M. Le Jaune's ancestors had probably acquired the books since Maurice Le Jaune didn't care a whit about the printed word.

As Madame Le Jaune's screeches filled the mansion, Colleen felt the sudden compulsion to slide one of Monsieur's books into her small carpetbag. She hadn't even read the title until he'd left her alone in the Marigny cottage. How fitting that Colleen had taken a volume about *spolia*, for both the purloined book and Colleen qualified as such.

Just like a repurposed column, M. Le Jaune had commandeered a battered Colleen for his own ends. The cottage she now lived in also qualified as a type of spolia, at least symbolically. Instead of ownership, Monsieur won the rights to the cottage's use in the course of his inglorious gambling career. That simply meant M. Le Jaune couldn't sell the place and profit. Still, moving Colleen to the cottage cost Monsieur little, only some money for basic necessities. The only furniture he'd bought was a bed, on which Colleen would have to endure all manner of torment.

The child's room would be a small refuge, though. Colleen had placed David's nightstand in that little room. In that cherished piece of furniture, she'd secured his cards and the straw. She didn't worry about the Le Jaune bastard finding them. He avoided that room. David's last remaining artifacts would be safe there. Other than those mementos, Colleen had only David's ominous letter as a material connection to her dead husband. Well, save for the child.

Colleen shifted on the bed and winced as pain shot through her pelvis. At least the baby still lived. Colleen had thus far kept one promise to her husband. Although only early afternoon, Colleen's eyes felt heavy, meaning sleep called to her.

David and St. Brigid came to Colleen in her dreams. When awake, Colleen perceived a gaping hole in her world, the absence of the other half of her being. She saw people cross the road and conduct their regular business. Ships arrived on schedule. Birds congregated in trees as usual. Few people perceived David's absence as more than an inconvenience. But those who did miss him walked with their hearts dragging in their feet. Colleen could barely breathe as the weight of her grief pressed down on her chest and damn near crushed her sternum into dust. Nevertheless, she resolved to put one foot in front of the other, trampling on the dead grass and dusty road. Her anger would fuel her breaths in the waking world until she left it. Colleen stretched on the bed, closed her eyes, and smiled, eager to see her husband in the dreaming world.

Before Colleen could descend into slumber's warm embrace, however, a sharp rapping on the front door jarred her wide awake. Groaning, she hauled herself upright and tried to blink the blurriness from her eyes. Colleen knew the unwelcome caller wasn't M. Le Jaune. That monster wouldn't do her the courtesy of knocking. He'd simply barge right in and demand what he thought he owned. The knock came again, this time more urgently, so Colleen gritted her teeth and walked toward the person who'd ripped her away from her dreams. "What is it?" she yelled as she threw open the door, only to see Jeanne standing there.

"I'm so sorry," Jeanne said, her eyes mirroring Colleen's grief. Jeanne slammed the door behind her and gathered Colleen into her arms.

In her friend's safe embrace, Colleen finally broke down, mourning David like she would not allow herself to do in front of his murderer. They spent a few moments like that, and when she'd spent her grief, Colleen led Jeanne into the parlor and pointed to the worn, stained settee. "I'll fetch you some tea," Colleen said. Jeanne opened her mouth to protest, but Colleen shushed her. "I need to do something. Let me get us some tea."

Jeanne nodded, and afternoon sunlight flickered on her tear-stained cheeks. "I understand."

Colleen went through the motions of a living person, boiling water over the hearth and steeping tea in chipped cups. She soon returned to the parlor and found Jeanne's eyes roaming over the room's worn furniture and dingy walls. The beekeeper, evidently, knew of David's murder. Colleen handed Jeanne a cup. "How did you know to find me here?"

"When you didn't come to the rendezvous point, I brought some honey to Etoile hoping to find out what went wrong," Jeanne replied, blinking away fresh tears. "That evil man told me he'd killed David and made you his mistress. That he'd installed you here. Why did he do it?"

Colleen, who used to be called *wife* by the world's most splendid man, recoiled when Jeanne said *mistress*. The word tasted of ashes in her dead mouth. She'd made an unholy bargain to keep her daughter safe and get revenge for David. Although M. Le Jaune had agreed to pay Jeanne for the child's lessons, Colleen wondered why he'd told the beekeeper where to find her. It was a kindness she didn't think Monsieur would grant her. Not that Colleen particularly cared. She cared very little about anything anymore. Except revenge. She met Jeanne's eyes. "He spouted off some nonsense about preserving his honor. He killed a man for that."

"Honor!" Jeanne slammed her teacup down on the dilapidated coffee table, shattering it. Shards of ceramic and drops of tea rained down on both women. Colleen didn't mind the spontaneous shower or when debris struck her cheek, yet Jeanne still gave her an apologetic look. "Have I ever told you why I hide from the world?" the beekeeper asked as she swept pieces of the broken teacup from her skirt.

Colleen shook her head. She'd wondered about Jeanne's past, but she didn't want to pry. "No."

"I was once in love with my dear Philippe," Jeanne said. A faint pink blush had settled on her cheeks. She stood up and walked to the window, her skirts dancing in a whirlwind of purple calico. Colleen stayed quiet. She knew the story must take a tragic turn, or else Jeanne and her Philippe would be married. Jeanne took in a few breaths. She continued, her voice quieter but harder. "My family didn't approve."

"Why not?" Colleen asked. Her mind wandered back to the convent, when Jeanne had first guessed Colleen's feelings for David. Jeanne had said she understood Colleen's situation.

Jeanne returned to the settee. Her normally soft features had hardened, making her face look as if someone had carved it from stone. "Philippe was a free man, a photographer. But his mother had been a slave."

"Oh, Jeanne," Colleen said as clarity dawned on her. She

understood why Jeanne had embraced Colleen and David's relationship so readily. Why she had offered to help them escape. What had happened to Philippe, though? Colleen daren't ask in case answering that question would force Jeanne to relive untold horrors. Instead, Colleen did the best thing she could. Let Jeanne speak at her own pace.

"One day, my brother challenged Philippe to a duel," Jeanne said. Her eyes became distant and heavy with longing. "I begged Philippe to run away with me, but he met my brother under the dueling oak. Shots rang out, and Philippe lost."

Philippe lost. Two words that had changed Jeanne's life forever. Colleen's heart broke for her friend. "I'm so sorry," Colleen said, hoping those insufficient words brought her friend comfort.

"I left my family," Jeanne said. She wiped the tears from her cheeks. "And I never visited them again until today, when I asked my mother to invite Madame Le Jaune to her next ball. I used that favor to learn your address from Monsieur."

"I see," Colleen replied. Now, Jeanne's sudden appearance made sense. Madame Le Jaune craved status, and an invitation to a ball at Jeanne's family home would soothe Madame's ire at losing her lady's maid. "And you are reconciled with your family?"

Jeanne shook her head. "Non. My mother hates Amelie Le Jaune, but she'll consider it her penance for what happened to my Philippe. She didn't want Etienne, my brother, to kill him. I'll stay at the convent. The abbess lets me live there in exchange for my work. You and the child could, too. I'll ask the convent to pay off your indenture. Or we can have Father Pierre make other arrangements. It won't bring David back, but you'll have some peace."

Jeanne's offer briefly tempted Colleen. For a moment, that was. Colleen's life would be easier without M. Le Jaune. She couldn't accept Jeanne's proposal, though. Colleen needed the guarantee of an early death. She'd likely inherit her family's curse regardless, but she couldn't bear more time on Earth than necessary. David had taught her that love drove people beyond reason. So did grief. "Thank you, Jeanne, but I can't," Colleen said. She searched for the words to relay the bad news. "Monsieur owns the child. He tricked me into signing her over to him as compensation for David's death."

Jeanne's eyes opened wide in horror. "Mon Dieu! We *must* get you away now. I'll have Father Pierre make the arrangements. For Celeste, too, the poor woman."

"Thank you, but not now." Colleen gave Jeanne a sad smile. "Celeste wants to see Monsieur Le Jaune pay. For my part, I made a bargain with St. Brigid that I'd free all Monsieur's slaves to avenge David's death," she said. With nothing else to do but plan revenge, Colleen had spent every torturous waking moment planning and scheming. "Father Pierre can't smuggle everyone away. When the Le Jaune bastard notices people disappearing, he'll lock them up."

"How do you plan on doing this?" Jeanne asked.

Colleen leaned forward, her eyes burning. "I'll save the pittance Monsieur gives me for household expenses and find someone to buy his slaves when he bankrupts himself," she said. The plan emerged so easily from Colleen's lips when she ignored all the complications with her mission. "The person who buys them will manumit them."

"But that will take years," Jeanne protested. "Think of the *child*."

"If the child's ever in danger, I'll send her away with you," Colleen assured her.

"So, David's told you the child's a girl?" Jeanne asked. Her voice had a ring of false cheer, but the change of subject abated some of the tension in the room.

Colleen nodded, almost choking up when she remembered how happy her husband had been when imparting that news. "He did."

"I'll keep her safe," Jeanne promised. She took Colleen's hand. "You mentioned a bargain with St. Brigid? What do you earn from it?"

Colleen hesitated, debating how much of the truth her friend could endure. At that point in the afternoon, the sun streamed in through the parlor window and illuminated the friends' interlocked fingers with a beautiful mixture of gold and crimson light. Colleen had no living allies aside from Jeanne. The beekeeper gave Colleen devotion, and Colleen owed Jeanne the truth. "I died with David," Colleen said. She took a deep breath, the caws of crows and the wind's whistling filling the air. "And as a reward for freeing all Monsieur's slaves, I asked St. Brigid for my family curse, which to me is a blessing. An early death. From a tumor."

Jeanne drew back, her beautiful face aghast. "I understand your grief, but are you sure you want this?"

"More sure than I've ever been of anything," Colleen replied.

Jeanne released Colleen's hand. The beekeeper pulled a handkerchief from her reticule and dabbed her eyes. "Then, let me help," Jeanne said. "Monsieur Le Jaune told me he'll pay me to teach the child. We will save this money toward buying his slaves. I'll also make sure the girl learns everything I can teach her. Knowledge is a weapon."

"The saints know women need to fill their quivers," Colleen said. She felt genuine hope for the first time since David's death because of Jeanne's friendship. That companionship, as well as the coming baby, would sustain Colleen until she earned her rightful death. "Thank you, Jeanne."

"How else can I help, mon ami?" Jeanne asked.

What else could I possibly dare ask her for when she's already done so much? Colleen wondered. Then, she remembered the straw she'd hidden in David's nightstand. Monsieur had dumped David's body into the swamp, like trash or carrion, and Colleen wanted the last remnants of her husband to rest in a proper tomb. "I have some straw with David's blood on it," she said. "Is there a tomb in the convent cemetery you could add the straw to? I want David to rest with someone worthy of him. And if possible, I'd like you to add my remains to that same tomb when my reward comes."

Colleen's request made perfect sense in New Orleans. Because the water table was so high, the dead needed to rest above ground. The living kept dying, one generation after another, but the real estate in the cemetery didn't increase with it. As a result, the dead often shared tombs.

"I will, and you can visit him there, on hallowed ground," Jeanne said. "I'll make sure you join him there, too."

Husband and wife in life, and husband and wife after death, Colleen thought. Just as things should be.

***

Selene

November 13, 1860, Bourbon Street, New Orleans

"How'd you hurt yourself?" Raoul asked. He gently took my hand and stared at the bandage Patrice had tied over the injury I'd gotten from crushing the wine glass.

Because I watched your father murder mine right before he raped my mother, I thought. Maman Brigitte helped me with many skills, such as the ability to hide hatred under a coquettish demeanor. I gave Raoul a nonchalant smile as I extricated my hand from his. "It was a silly accident I had while visiting Maman," I said. "It won't interfere with tonight's plans."

"I'm happy to hear that," Raoul said. His eyes burned with lust as he pulled out a chair for me at the table, where Mrs. Shelley had laid out a feast. "You look ravishing in that new dress."

"I bought it with you in mind," I replied. The crimson silk gown, which hugged my figure beautifully, had a shroud of black

229

hanging over the skirt. Raoul had given me money to purchase something special for the evening. I did just that, but not in the way he'd intended. To Raoul, red meant seduction and the deflowering that occurred only in his imagination. Red meant something quite different to me, though, considering the tragic events that had brought me to this night. I wore red to signify my father's blood and my intentions to bring him justice.

Marie and I had meticulously planned the evening's other *accoutrements*, too. The food before us included roasted quail, herb-crusted red potatoes, and some sweet yams, a meal I'd asked Mrs. Shelley to have prepared for us. And, of course, Marie and I had made a special Bordeaux, the pièce de résistance of the night. I'd poured wine for both of us before he arrived. Mine, however, lacked the adulterants I'd added to his. To avoid making Raoul suspicious, I decided to give my landlady the credit for the food and drink. "Mrs. Shelley was so kind. While I dressed, she set out the food and poured the wine so it could breathe. She wanted everything tonight to be *perfect*."

Raoul raised his glass of wine and flashed me a seductive look. "To us, and to a special evening."

"Indeed," I said, reciprocating his toast. I sipped my wine and watched the candlelight dance in my crystal goblet. Fire attracted me at an elemental level, for it both nourished life and destroyed, depending on the dose. Just like poison, magic potions, and my burning need for justice.

In preparation for this special evening, Marie led me to her altar, where we focused our energy on a small poppet with the name *Vivienne* written across its chest. We had Papa Alegba open the gate and then called through Erzulie Dantor, a spirit who helps heal betrayals. Marie and I asked this great loa to show Vivienne a vision of her fiancé in my arms. Ideally, Vivienne would then obey her instincts and come to my apartment to confront Raoul.

I didn't feel bad about using Vivienne as an instrument of justice. This spell would liberate her from Raoul, whose family would drain her fortune just like they had Madame Le Jaune's if given the chance.

During the spell, Dantor's fury swirled through the air. I didn't know *how* the loa would execute this plan, but it didn't matter. At the center of all spellwork was simple trust in the spirits, God, and that fate would manifest itself. I hoped that this spell would free Maman, myself, and M. Le Jaune's slaves, as well as enact justice on my father's behalf.

Before helping with the spell, Maric tested me to make sure I understood the difference between justice and revenge. She used my mother as an example. Maman wanted to make Monsieur pay for my father's death so badly that she'd blinded herself to other options of freeing M. Le Jaune's slaves. Tante Jeanne would have found a way to free everyone.

Maman wanted to see Monsieur bankrupt and miserable, though. I did, too, but not at the expense of the larger goal. Because of her fixation on seeing M. Le Jaune ruined, Maman had suffered as his mistress for almost two decades. Marie told me my mother would have died young despite her bargain with her saint. She could have had a peaceful life with me until her death, but she'd rejected that idea.

I believed Marie's assessment of Maman's choices and motivations, but from the visions Papa showed me, I knew Maman's grief consumed her so completely that she needed the guarantee of an early death. She also felt responsible for Papa dying and wanted to punish herself with years of suffering. I wanted to avenge Papa just as much as Maman did, but I refused to sacrifice my well-being or let anger consume me.

"Is this wine mulled?" Raoul asked after he took another sip of wine. He swirled the liquid, frowning in confusion. "It tastes... bold."

"Mulled with spices to warm us on this cold evening," I said, resting my glass on the table so he wouldn't see my trembling hand. I needed to distract him. "Try the quail. It's delicious."

Raoul complied, and his face melted with pleasure. "So tender. And not too gamey."

"I'm so glad you approve." I sampled the bird and had to agree with Raoul's assessment. The quail tasted delicious, as did the savory potatoes. As Raoul demolished his food, I nibbled on my portion and tried to set the right pace for the evening. I also needed to force the bastard to drink more wine without noticing the additions to it. How to accomplish this formidable task? Well, if Monsieur Le Jaune was any indication, men drank to excess when feeling inadequate or frustrated. Nothing vexed Raoul more than his impending nuptials, so I held up my glass for another toast. "Vivienne's father is so generous to *finally* give you a free evening."

Raoul slammed his fork down on the table. "He demands all my time to teach me about plantation management! How hard could it possibly be?"

Although I imagined running a large estate was complex and time-consuming, not to mention cruel if it depended on slaves, I forced a sympathetic smile to my face. "You poor dear."

"Thanks to my father's failures at the craps table, I don't have a choice," Raoul grumbled. He then took a long sip of wine and settled his eyes on my décolletage. "But that's why I have you. I can keep you right in my breast pocket, tucked away forever."

An eternity with Raoul... What a nauseating thought. So I wouldn't vomit all over the bones of my non-gamey bird carcass, I let Maman Brigitte speak for me. "I'm not the only thing that needs tucking away tonight."

Brigitte's naughty words almost made Raoul choke on his quail. In one long swallow, he downed most of his Bordeaux to clear the detritus from his throat. The wine flowed into Raoul like my father's blood had flooded onto the stable floor. Before long, the potion would affect Raoul. About fifteen more minutes according to the clock on the mantel.

"Not that I'm bothered by the vixen who's suddenly emerged, but where did you learn to speak like that?" he asked.

"Why, my maman, of course," my voice replied. For the evening to go as planned, Marie told me to entice Raoul and then put on the mask of an ingénue. She believed my capricious words would keep me safe from Raoul's ire. My dear Maman was the perfect source for saucy words, for Raoul thought of her simply as a well-dressed whore. Not that he would say aloud anything so déclassé, of course.

With the hint of a lecherous smile on his lips, Raoul cleared his throat again. "Well, let's finish our dinner and then retire to the settee."

His eager voice and confident demeanor gave me faith he was in the proper mindset for the evening's events. I ate slowly, like a proper lady, controlling the pace of the meal. At the proper time, I'd maneuver Raoul to the settee. Where Vivienne would come upon us.

Raoul wouldn't be able to perform in the way he expected, thanks to Marie's potion. As for Vivienne's timing lining up with my own, I left that up to the spirits. I had to trust in the loas and focus on my role in the night's drama.

After another five or so minutes of resoundingly loud tick-tocks from the clock on the mantel, just as Raoul swallowed his last piece of potato, I heard my father whisper, *Now, Selene.*

My heart fluttering with nerves, I dabbed my lips with my napkin. "Shall we adjourn to the settee?" I asked, a coy smile on my lips.

"Yes, let's." Raoul jumped up so quickly he almost toppled his chair.

Although Raoul had a raconteur's heart instead of a gentleman's, I let him escort me to the settee for the sake of that evening's drama. A sheltered young girl would find Raoul dashing based solely on his superficial characteristics. But what lies beneath the skin—such as the heart, mind, and soul—all surface in their own time. And Raoul's intangible parts were rotten.

He sat far too close to me on the settee, but at least my swirly mass of a crinoline kept him off my lap for a moment. Then, however, Raoul pulled me toward him with such force that my head slammed into his brocade vest. Anchored tightly against his chest, I smelled tobacco, bourbon, and sweat. Nothing too offensive. But certainly nothing appealing. I glanced longingly at my apartment door, which I'd left unlocked to permit Raoul's fiancée easy entrance. *Please come soon, Vivienne.*

Raoul tilted my head up for a kiss and pressed his quail-scented lips to my mouth. I couldn't very well kick him away, so I kept my lips screwed together tightly. Suddenly, he pushed me away and looked down at his lap. I followed his gaze and saw no evidence of his lust, meaning Marie's potion had taken effect. "What's wrong?" I asked.

"Nothing at all," Raoul insisted.

Before I could reply, Raoul pulled me close and all but devoured my neck with his urgent kisses. If Marie's plan worked, his desperation would soon transform into outrage. I only hoped Vivienne appeared before he focused his anger on me. The soft sound of the door creaking open told me the universe had answered my prayers. So absorbed was Raoul in rising to the occasion that he didn't hear the door. I twisted my head away from Raoul's torso so I could see the door and, hopefully, Vivienne. Instead of a person, I saw a monumental pink cloud of a skirt bumble in through the door. And when I finally saw the wearer of that skirt, I wondered if my eyes had failed me.

Vivienne, Raoul's poor fiancée, was none other than Mademoiselle Deveraux, the woman I'd met at Marie's home when she'd purchased a love potion! My mind spun at this turn of events. Raoul had called Vivienne "plain" during our first meeting, but Mademoiselle Deveraux was quite pretty.

I wondered why Raoul had wanted a mistress at all until I remembered something Maman had told me long ago. High society wives, unlike mistresses, had to behave chastely even as they fulfilled their marital duties, something men didn't find very exciting. Even more infuriating for women, men like Raoul expected their wives to accept mistresses and less formalized dalliances alike.

I suspected Raoul had vastly underestimated Vivienne, though. She'd already rebelled against her family's expectations by enlisting Marie's help. Vivienne wanted to marry the man she loved, not Raoul. These two facts would make my night all the easier. When her eyes rested on Raoul and me, Vivienne's eyes flickered with what looked like elation and recognition. Did she remember me from Marie's? In any case, she now had an excuse to break her engagement to Raoul. "Raoul!" she yelled.

Raoul pushed me to the floor and jumped off the settee. "Wh-what are you doing here, chérie?" he asked as the color drained from his face. "I hope you didn't walk the streets alone!"

An older woman, Madame Deveraux, I presumed, stepped out from behind Vivienne's elephantine hoop skirt and glared at Raoul. "My *daughter's propriety* shouldn't concern you," she said, her voice icy enough to freeze the Mississippi River. Her eyes then settled on me. "As for why we're here, Vivi had a dream of you with this *whore*."

Raoul stepped forward, attempting to block the Deverauxs' view of me. "Surely, you know this is common enough." He let out a flustered sigh and shifted his attention from Vivienne to her mother. "It doesn't change my love for Vivienne."

"Clearly, you have no love for me," Vivienne replied, before dissolving into tears worthy of a prima actress. She then grabbed a handkerchief from her reticule and covered her face, perfecting the portrait of a distraught fiancée.

"Love for her substantial dowry, more likely," Vivienne's mother added, her voice heavy with righteous indignation. "Vivi's papa and I knew your father's a degenerate gambler and whoremonger, but we hoped the apple fell far from the tree in this case. I now see that aristocratic lineage has nothing to do with nobility."

If Raoul had any sense, he would have apologized and begged Vivienne for forgiveness. Not that it would have done him any good, considering Vivienne's desire to sabotage her engagement to Raoul. But no, Raoul straightened his posture and tried to smooth the wrinkles on his jacket. "Despite my father's obvious failures, I am nothing like him," he insisted. "I believe I should speak with your father."

"Papa's in the carriage outside. He'll challenge you to a duel if he sees you," Vivienne said. Earlier, I supposed that she'd contrived her emotions for dramatic effect. Now, though, her eyes burned with true indignation. "I'm formally canceling the wedding on my behalf. Papa will agree once he learns of what I've seen."

Then, with her head held high, Vivienne spun around and marched out the door. Her mother followed behind her with great purpose in her stride. After witnessing that glorious scene, I wondered if my spellwork had helped Vivienne or if hers had helped me. Perhaps both of us ended up working in tandem to right the universe. Not that I could show my joy in front of Raoul. A palpable tension filled the room as he nervously paced back and forth. I daren't breathe for fear he'd turn his anger on me. Thankfully, Brigitte took control of the situation. "I'm sorry," she whispered. My mind chattered, *Sorry your father murdered mine. Sorry my mother suffered for years. Not sorry this day brings me vindication.*

At first, Raoul ignored my apology. His eyes shot daggers at the door. "Everything will turn out right in the end," he finally said, nodding slowly, as if to convince himself of this truth. "Vivienne is simply upset and needs time to calm herself. Don't worry your pretty little head, Selene. I'll have you both."

And with that overly optimistic assurance, Raoul gave me a quick peck on the cheek and left. The tendrils of his seething anger lingered behind, and I delighted in those tidbits of fury. Hopefully, his anger would drive him to the gambling den, where he'd surrender to drink, desperation, and complete abandon. That night's events had worked in my favor thus far. I prayed that the rest of Raoul's decisions would ultimately end up freeing me, Maman, and the rest of Monsieur Le Jaune's slaves. That was the sweetest revenge I could conjure up in my expectant heart.

CHAPTER EIGHTEEN: THE MOON

The Moon card symbolizes intuition and women's mysteries. When this card appears, you should think with your heart instead of your mind. Emotions and dreams govern the time of the moon and the world of magic. Your intuition will allow you to discern pretense from reality. Although dreams and imagination have their place, you must also dispense with false illusions. The moon signifies a time for womanly magic. Do not be surprised if men cannot understand it.

Colleen

March 1, 1842, Faubourg Treme

Colleen pulled her shawl tight around her to protect her child from the cold as she walked to Du Bois Mercantile. She looked up at the sky and willed the sun to set faster. She wanted to sleep. When Colleen envisioned David in Heaven, she pictured him floating above the clouds. Her version of Heaven, though, contained a moon-spun sky instead of one drenched in sun. David glowed a beautiful luminescent blue under this moon.

When Colleen wanted to be close to her husband, she stood beneath the moon in the garden outside her prison of a cottage and spoke to him. She felt closest to David in her dreams and under the night sky.

Thankfully, Monsieur Le Jaune only visited her three or four times per week. Colleen spent her free time with Jeanne, doing errands, or most preferably, sleeping so she could be with David. On the nights she tossed and turned on the creaking bed because of the pregnancy, Colleen downed laudanum to usher her to sleep. She daren't drink the liquid more than a few times per week—not when Jeanne warned her she could grow to depend on it. For that reason, Colleen appreciated distractions, such as sewing a new dress to accommodate her growing unborn child and trips to Du Bois Mercantile.

The cold wind at her back, Colleen pushed open the mercantile door and stepped inside. She let down her guard when she saw Madame Du Bois standing behind the counter. Unlike other shop owners who gossiped in hushed tones when Colleen entered their sanctified premises, Mme. Du Bois was a genuinely kind person. She also was expecting her first child. A girl, she'd once told Colleen. "Hello," Colleen said to Madame Du Bois as she approached the counter.

Mme. Du Bois gave Colleen a sad smile. "How lovely to see you. What can I do for you today?"

"I'd like a bolt of calico, please," Colleen said.

"On account of the baby?" the shop owner asked.

Colleen nodded. Her and David's baby. *David.* Colleen slammed the tiny rift in her heart shut. She couldn't bear the pain right now.

The smile on the shopkeeper's face died, and she went to the storeroom, leaving Colleen alone with her morbid thoughts. Colleen closed her eyes and inhaled the room's scent. She detected wood, like David's workshop. Fresh linen. Coffee. Tobacco. Various other sundries. Another deep breath, and her muscles relaxed. She felt David's ghostly fingertips brush her hand, and when she let her mind sink deeper into the daytime fantasy, snowflakes danced across her cheek as the scent of the sea tickled her nose.

Then the vision appeared before her. She and David walked

along a beach in the winter, yet neither was cold. They moved toward a golden light that flickered ahead on the beach. Was it a lantern? Colleen and David, arms linked, sprinted through that light toward the snow. As Colleen neared the light, she saw it was, indeed, a lantern. A person was standing next to it, too.

Just then, the crinkling of paper yanked Colleen out of her daydream. Her eyes flew open, and a weight of sadness settled on her heart. Madame Du Bois was wrapping her fabric in paper. "How are you feeling?" the shop owner asked Colleen.

"Like I'm dead," Colleen replied. She looked up at the sky through the window. "And like eternity's *just* out of my reach."

Her face awash in sorrow, Mme. Du Bois handed Colleen her package. "You should talk to Marie Laveau. She's here today, back in the storeroom, reading cards for people," the shop-keeper said.

The mention of Marie Laveau jerked Colleen out of her mental wanderings. David's mentor had been named Marie Laveau. Could it be the same woman? Colleen hoped so. David had respected his mentor immensely and had often spoken of her powers. He hadn't taught Colleen how to read his cards, so if she wanted to know the future, Marie seemed like the logical person to tell her. Colleen slipped her right hand into her pocket to count the remainder of her blood money from M. Le Jaune. "What's Marie's fee?" she asked.

"There's no fee; you're David's wife," Mme. Du Bois said.

At the mention of her husband's name, Colleen's breath caught in her throat. This Marie Laveau was, indeed, David's mentor. "I'd love to speak with her," Colleen said.

"Excellent." The shop owner waved Colleen to the back of the store. "Please, follow me."

Her package in hand, Colleen followed the store owner into a back room, where she found a stunning woman sitting at a small table, a deck of cards before her. In addition to her physical beauty, Marie had a magnetism that captured Colleen's attention so completely that she didn't notice when Mme. Du Bois left the room.

"Colleen, please sit," Marie said, gesturing to the empty chair across from her. "David has some messages for you."

Colleen's vision blurred as she sat down. She now had confirmation that David was out there in the universe, accessible to her in places other than dreams. A joy she hadn't felt since before David died filled the holes in her heart. Knowing this bliss was temporary, she cherished it and broke into almost giddy laughter. "And here I thought I'd only be getting fabric today," she said in a choked voice as she brushed away her tears. "What does David say?"

Marie pulled her tarot cards out of a silk pouch and shuffled them. "First, he says to name your daughter Selene," she said. "It means moon."

"Selene," Colleen repeated. The name had a beautiful ring to it, and it was appropriate, given that she liked talking to David under the night sky. "I like the name. It's feminine but also strong."

"He also wants you to know your daughter will be different from others," Marie said. She stopped shuffling and met Colleen's eyes. "She'll love another woman in the same way you love your David."

Love another woman? Colleen was puzzled for a moment because she hadn't ever heard of such a thing. In her tiny Irish village, people tended to conform or hide. But when Colleen thought about it, Marie's revelation didn't bother her a whit. Love, not convention, determined what was good or not. She and David loved one another and, despite this country's laws, their love was holy and beautiful. So would be their daughter's love, Colleen hoped. "Love is love," she said.

"That it is," Marie agreed as she laid three cards face down. Colleen's heart clenched when she noticed Marie's cards had the same purple and gold background as David's. The Voodoo queen shifted her focus from the cards to Colleen. "David also wants me to read your future. He thinks it will comfort you."

Colleen's heart pounded in her head as she stared at the cards, remembering the times she and David had consulted the tarot when planning their escape. The cards hadn't saved them because of Colleen's stubbornness. *A difficult choice to make*, the tricky card had said.

Colleen had made the wrong choice because she couldn't muster up the mental fortitude to be without her husband. If she had simply gotten on the boat as David and Celeste had ordered her to, Monsieur Le Jaune wouldn't have found Colleen and David together. Most importantly, David would still be alive.

She tried to shake away her guilt. She had to focus on the future, on her plans and earning her death. All Marie had to do was flip them over, and Colleen's future would be laid bare, either dashing her hopes or giving her solace. "I want to hear everything David and the cards have to say. For example, will I keep my promise to my saint?"

Marie turned over one card and smiled, tapping the image of two trees, their branches intertwined. "You will," the Voodoo queen said. "This card represents The Lovers."

"Just like Tristan and Isolde," Colleen said as she stared at the interlocked branches. She remembered the story of the star-crossed lovers who met with tragedy in life but were together in death, Tristan and Isolde. David and Colleen. She let out a contented sigh. She'd see David again. All she had to do was free all of M. Le Jaune's slaves and endure the horrible man's touch. At thoughts of her husband's murderer, Colleen's mood sobered. "Does David forgive me for what I'm doing?" she asked.

"He forgives you anything," Marie assured her. She turned over another card, which featured a queen sitting on the throne. "This is the Empress. Your husband wants you to let Jeanne free Monsieur Le Jaune's slaves while you take the child and go North, somewhere safe where you can enjoy your years with Selene. You'll get your early death regardless."

Colleen drew in a deep breath. David's letter had said the same thing. "But he knows I won't?" she asked with a wry laugh.

Marie chuckled. "That's right. He knows you're stubborn." She turned over the final card, where Colleen saw angels playing trumpets. Marie studied the card until a crow cawed outside. "This is the Judgment card. Since you're bent on this course, strive for justice, not revenge," she said, looking back at Colleen. "You also don't need to punish yourself."

She didn't need to punish herself? Images of David collapsing to the floor and his blood staining the straw spun before her mind's eye. No, Colleen *needed* to endure years of pain, or else she couldn't live with the guilt. She simply had to stay the course and free M. Le Jaune's slaves. She hoped that was justice, not revenge. "I can't do that," she told Marie. "It's my fault he died."

"It's *not* your fault," Marie said, her voice firm.

"On that, we'll have to disagree," Colleen replied. Not even David's or a Voodoo queen's assurances could alleviate her guilt. Her eyes settled on the trio of cards. "The Judgment card means I have to judge myself, too."

Marie gave Colleen an encouraging pat on the hand and pointed to the final card. "We're our own harshest judge. The Judgment card also means your husband's murderer will damn himself, too, though. Work for the greater good, and you'll bring your husband justice."

And see Maurice Le Jaune broken and destroyed, Colleen added for her own pleasure. She envisioned the man's horrible end until Marie cleared her throat and tapped the third card again. Colleen would struggle to keep the bitterness in her heart from consuming her entirely, but she'd focus on her ultimate goal— freeing the people under Monsieur Le Jaune's subjugation and joining her husband in eternity. "Will God object if I toast to that day with the champagne I buy with that murderer's money?"

"He will not object," Marie said as she gathered her cards into a pile.

Colleen didn't want to leave the storeroom, but her reading had come to an end. She had a distinct feeling Marie Laveau would remain an important figure in her life, even if behind the scenes. "I can't thank you enough. Do you have any parting advice?" Colleen asked.

"Trust your Saint Brigid. Also, you mustn't give M. Le Jaune reason to suspect you're working against him," Marie cautioned.

"I won't," Colleen promised as she stood. She remembered how much Monsieur hated David's cards and what they represented. She'd have to be canny. At least planning gave her something to do while she endured the rest of her time here on Earth.

***

Selene

November 13, 1860, Bourbon Street, New Orleans

Ghosts have the enviable ability to travel anywhere in the world and see what needs to be seen. Such a gift would have enabled me to follow Raoul to the gambling tables after he stormed out of my apartment, reeking of entitlement and hubris.

Thankfully, though, Marie taught me an equally valuable skill called astral projection. Before the evening Vivienne canceled her wedding in a brilliant dramatic performance, I'd only been able to project in Marie's presence. But as with many things in life, if needs must, we learn to fly on our own. I had to see if Raoul did, indeed, head to his favorite gambling palace after leaving my apartment, so I willed myself to project into the astral world without my mentor's help. I first lay down on my bed. I'd placed the nightstand my father had carved next to the bed because it brought me comfort, and now, perhaps strength. Next, I began the process of relaxing my body. I started with my toes and slowly worked my way up to my head. When my body sank into the mattress with the weight of a rain-drenched horse blanket, I focused my mind.

There's a misconception about traveling in the astral realm, namely that the spirit leaves the body. That's not true at all. The body simply falls asleep while the mind stays awake. Astral projectors therefore go on an inward journey, not one outside of themselves.

The mind has all it needs to see beyond the physical realm when it focuses deeply on someplace special, so I chose to enter the astral world via Ireland instead of New Orleans. Because Maman had described Keem Beach on Achill Island in such vivid detail over the years, I thought of that stretch of pale shore and turquoise sea. Soon, blue lights swirled around me. My body began to vibrate. As the minutes passed, the intensity of the vibrations increased. Pressure continued to build in my chest, pressing on my ribs, until finally, I shot above the beach with a great pop, almost like a cork from a champagne bottle. I then found myself hovering above the blue-green water of Keem Bay.

The beach looked exactly like Maman described it. Selkies danced in the waves below, and their merriment tempted me. Although I wanted to frolic in the waves with them, I couldn't let otherworldly creatures waylay me. I had a mission to complete.

As I flew toward New Orleans under a sky carpeted with blue and white pinpricks of starlight, I was careful not to think of my physical body, lest I get pulled out of the astral world. The journey from Ireland to Louisiana had taken Maman months by ship. But in mere seconds, I traversed the Atlantic Ocean in the astral world. I knew I'd reached the outskirts of New Orleans when the stars transformed into the French section's gaslights, which flickered like golden fireflies on a sizzling summer's evening.

I whispered Raoul's name and drifted where the astral wind decided to carry me until I reached a two-story building with an intricate gallery made from wrought iron. The metal flickered with gold flame thanks to the gas lanterns, and men of all ages walked in and out of the front entrance. Some of the men had women on their arms. With their intricate costumes and rouged faces, these ladies of the night oozed seduction and the promise of victory at the gambling tables.

I wondered if my astral body wore clothes, so I looked down. How *perfect*. I wore the crimson costume from that night. *Blood for blood.* Only, Raoul or anyone else wouldn't shed blood on Papa's behalf. Instead, Papa and the spirits would help Maman and Tante Jeanne *free* human beings. To me, that meant we sought justice, not revenge.

Dazzled by the lights and gaiety, I glided into the gambling palace, invisible to everyone. Women in off-the-shoulder dresses and plunging décolletages poured champagne liberally into sparkling cut-glass stemware. Although a cold wind blustered through the night sky, the inside of the gambling palace steamed with the hopes and dreams of frenetic gamblers. I scanned this lively cavern of sin for my quarry. I whispered Raoul's name again, and the astral world whooshed me across the room until I found myself suspended above one of the small café tables that surrounded the gambling area.

To infect everyone with the aura of chance, the proprietors of this establishment had wisely positioned their dining area near the gambling activity. I focused my attention on the café table under me. My astral heart raced as I saw M. Le Jaune and Raoul at the table, listlessly slouching in their chairs and sulking. They were far too morose for a night of gambling. Unless their luck had soured, of course. *Please, please, let their fortunes have plummeted to hell*, I begged the astral creatures around me.

Suddenly, Monsieur Le Jaune rose out of his stupor and waved over one of the minimally dressed waitresses. He waited to speak until she had deposited new glasses of champagne in front of him and Raoul. "*What* was Vivienne doing there?" M. Le Jaune asked his son. "Surely, you weren't stupid enough to tell her about the apartment or Selene!"

My eyes drifted to Raoul. Despite his father's acrid remarks, the younger Le Jaune was mesmerized by the dealer at a nearby table. The dealer swished cards through his nimble hands with marvelous skill. Raoul's potential futures, such as ending up as a rich planter, being forced to live a pauper's life, or ending up dead on a battlefield, moved elusively through that dealer's hands. Little did Raoul anticipate he'd end up a dead soldier in a few years or so. "Of course not! I didn't tell her about Selene or the apartment," he eventually replied, slamming his glass of champagne down so hard that a gentleman at a nearby table frowned in disapproval. "Vivienne said she knew where to find me because of a vision. That makes no sense."

"Witch—" M. Le Jaune began, only to have the waitress interrupt him. She placed two small plates of duck a l'orange in front of him. Raoul and M. Le Jaune's eyes flickered with distress at the sight of the duck carcass.

If my astral body could smell, I knew I'd detect fear, and a strange combination of sweat and nervousness, emanating from him. How perfect. I wanted him off-kilter and oblivious to the machinations the spirit world had set in motion to ruin him. He waited until the waitress was out of earshot to continue. "Selene's witchcraft is responsible for this catastrophe."

Witch. Yes, from both sides of my ancestry. I hoped, though, that the label wouldn't bring me the wrong kind of trouble. I wanted Raoul to sell me to Maman's agent, not drown me in the Mississippi River or dispose of me in a remote bayou as M. Le Jaune had done with my father. Those morbid thoughts made my astral form shiver. If events turned against me, I'd have to fly back to my body at a moment's notice.

Laughing dismissively, Raoul sliced into his food with gusto. "Selene? A witch? You're drunk, Papa."

"Don't be flippant," M. Le Jaune mumbled into his champagne. "I might very well be drunk, but you don't know her history. Her father was a Voodoo-worshipper."

"*If* that's true, why did you select her for me?" Raoul asked as he took a bite of duck.

Monsieur drained his glass and scoffed. "Because we already own her, of course. Mrs. Shelley gets furniture to sell or use as she sees fit instead of cash for Selene's room and board. All that little witch costs is a bit of pocket money. Finding someone else for you would cost me money we don't have."

With a hint of concern etched on his face, Raoul took small bites of his meal. Monsieur hadn't provided any damning evidence, but I could sense Raoul's affection for me evaporate as he digested his father's words. I understood why. The potion I'd given him earlier had snuffed out his masculine desires, and it was easier to blame that failure on witchcraft.

My heart rejoiced when the waitress handed Raoul and his father fresh glasses of champagne. The more alcohol, the better, especially since the duck would inhibit some of the alcohol's effects on Raoul. I hoped the small amount of laudanum in the potion would augment his drunkenness. And as for Monsieur Le Jaune? He only stared vacantly at his untouched food. When I saw a hint of nausea lurking behind his glassy eyes, I knew he'd soon be completely inebriated. What a beautiful thing.

After finishing about half of his duck, Raoul rested his fork beside his plate. "Papa, how do you know Selene's father was a Voodoo worshipper, or whatever you called him?"

"It's obvious. He snuck around to see Marie Laveau, the Voodoo queen," M. Le Jaune replied.

"Selene visits Marie Laveau," Raoul said, anger hardening his gray eyes. "She said to learn about beauty and her heritage, which I didn't think much of at the time. I don't trust her."

M. Le Jaune's lips curled into a smile. "Then I'll sell her. Vivienne will surely take you back if she knows Selene is gone."

"I suppose I'll have to beg Vivienne for forgiveness, too," Raoul said. He leaned back in his chair and released a dramatic sigh. "If that doesn't work, a well-placed threat to spread rumors should encourage Vivienne to comply."

Contrary to what Raoul thought, Vivienne would never take him back. She had too much sense and loved someone else. Also, after witnessing Madame Devereaux's disgust when she saw Raoul and me on the settee, I knew Vivienne's family would fight against any well-placed rumors. M. Le Jaune must have thought so, too, because he rolled his eyes to high heaven. "Good God, boy," Monsieur said. "Vivienne's father won't provide the dowry if you coerce her to the altar. No, you must beg forgiveness and woo her, gift her some jewelry. Your mother will sacrifice something to preserve this wedding."

"No. Madame Devereaux will say I'm just after the dowry if we give Vivienne one of Maman's castoffs," Raoul insisted. He paused for a moment, the golden light from the gaslights flickering in his eyes. "We have to convince them all I love Vivienne, and an expensive gift will do just that. We'll use some of the profit from the furniture shipment we're sending out tomorrow. You expect a tidy sum, correct?"

Instead of answering his son's question, Monsieur summoned the closest waitress with a wave of the hand. "Take my food away and bring me a bourbon," he commanded while staring at the chasm between her bosoms. Monsieur's uneaten meal in hand, the waitress darted away.

"What is it you're not telling me?" Raoul asked, rapping his fingers on the table.

When his father didn't speak, the younger Le Jaune resumed eating, a worried look in his eyes. Soon, the waitress returned with Monsieur's bourbon and set it down in front of the elder Le Jaune before scurrying away. Monsieur slowly turned the beveled glass of amber liquid around in his hand, watching the patterns the gaslight chandelier cast on the crimson tablecloth.

Shameful secrets make themselves known no matter how hard the secret holder wishes to conceal them, and I loved watching Monsieur's obvious discomfort as he struggled to keep some dreadful secret hidden. After looking from his son to his drink, Monsieur downed the bourbon in one mouth-puckering swallow. "The entire profit from the furniture shipment must go to keep Etoile. I took out a loan against it," he admitted, clearing his throat with a hoarse cough.

I smiled as this secret burst forth from the lips of my father's murderer. The Le Jaune finances were much worse than I thought, which made *my* fortunes all the better, especially considering the amount of alcohol Raoul and his father had so far consumed.

At his father's news, Raoul's mouth dropped open, and a piece of semi-masticated duck fell on the table with an unceremonious plop. I loved the palpable discomfort between the two men. They simply needed the tiniest shove over the precipice toward their glorious ruin, something the spirits would have to do.

Just then, a mysterious stranger arrived at the table. My instincts told me that this gentleman with dark hair and flaming green eyes was working on the spirits' behalf. In his tight suit and silk cravat, this man cut a dashing figure. He also reeked of money, or at least the illusion of it.

The stranger slid into an empty seat next to Raoul. "I'm Philippe Le Roux of the Seven Oaks plantation," he said in a jovial voice. "I couldn't help but overhear your conversation. I'd like to sponsor your next game."

Those words sent a pulse of fear through me. With a sponsor, Raoul's luck could turn in his favor—quite a bad thing for me and Maman. I chased away those negative thoughts and hovered over M. Le Roux's shoulder, trying to gauge his purpose. He had a red aura around him. I'd never seen such a thing in the astral world. Was Philippe an angry person? Someone out for his own revenge?

I focused my energy as Marie had taught me. On the surface, Philippe appeared happy-go-lucky, but when I pierced deeper, I detected an agenda. An agenda that involved the Le Jaune men. Curious, I drifted back over the table, eager to see how the night progressed.

At Philippe's offer, Raoul blushed and threw his napkin over the food that had fallen from his mouth. "Are you quite serious?" he asked.

"I see my offer's shocked you," Philippe replied, offering Raoul an apologetic smile.

"It certainly has," Monsieur Le Jaune said. He swayed in his chair. "Why the sudden generosity?"

Philippe reached into his vest pocket to retrieve a mother

of pearl cigarette case. He languidly drew out a cigar. "You deserve an explanation," he said as he lit his cigar. Philippe paused to enjoy the first few puffs and blew out two pungent rings of smoke. "Games of chance bring me a thrill, and I sympathize with the young monsieur's engagement woes. My own heart's desire left me for another man. Thank God, I eventually won her back, but the pain of her absence drove me to dens of vice such as this. But that's neither here nor there. Accept my offer or reject it as you will."

"But Monsieur, what's your price?" Raoul leaned forward and stared at M. Le Roux, trying to probe the man's intentions with his inebriated eyes.

"There is, of course, a price," Philippe conceded with a quick nod. "I require the initial stake back plus half of your winnings after that."

"But what if I lose?" Raoul asked.

M. Le Roux tapped his cigar in an ashtray, and an ember sizzled on the ash pile for a second before dying. "Then you must pay me back with the proceeds of this furniture shipment you spoke of."

Yes. My astral heart soared. Philippe *wanted* Raoul to lose. I could sense it from the sardonic edge in Philippe's voice. As Raoul's eyes opened wider for a moment, I saw an eagerness burning deep inside. Temptation is a powerful lure. That I knew from how much effort it took me not to stab M. Le Jaune for his crimes.

Speaking of Monsieur, Raoul looked to his father for guidance but found he'd collapsed back in his chair, his eyes half-open and unfocused. "I don't know if I should risk it," Raoul said, frowning.

"The choice is yours, but there's something else you must consider," Philippe said.

"Such as?" Raoul asked.

"You must woo your intended with a new necklace not only to demonstrate your *affections*," M. Le Roux began. He paused to clear his throat. "But also to hide your family's financial woes.

The young woman's father won't want to hand over her dowry."

To my delight, Raoul held out his hand. "I accept your offer, sir."

"Splendid," Philippe replied, shaking Raoul's proffered hand. "Let's adjourn to the craps table. You've done poorly at cards, it seems, so let's try something different."

Philippe and Raoul each threw an arm under M. Le Jaune, who mumbled and let himself be carted off without protest. Whatever secret Philippe had concealed, Raoul and his father hadn't detected an inkling of it.

Courtesy of the night's many intoxicants, Raoul and his father remained ignorant of an obvious solution to their problems. Selling me would have brought them enough money to buy Vivienne a necklace. Had they pursued that line of thought to its logical end, they wouldn't have needed to accept M. Le Roux's risky offer. For the myriad of reasons the Le Jaunes remained blinded, I thanked the spirits and saints alike.

CHAPTER NINETEEN: THE SUN

The Sun card symbolizes bliss and warmth. When this orb appears in a reading, you can expect happiness and radiance. Let your inner child rejoice at the abundance around you, for you have no more reason for sorrow.

Selene

November 13, 1860, the Astral World

What brings joy to some can bring misery to others. The beginning of my happiness arrived under such ominous terms. Then again, those who suffered for my benefit did so because they earned it with their own hands. Beautiful Justice appeared on that night as soon as Raoul and Philippe Le Roux reached the craps table.

Time in the astral plane moved too quickly for my taste. I wanted to fully enjoy the Le Jaunes's suffering, something Marie had cautioned me against.

Like everything else in an elegant gambling den, the craps table sparkled as the large glass chandeliers fragmented the golden light from the gas lanterns onto the table's surface. The whole atmosphere prickled with excitement. You could see vibrant women, perfumed to high heaven and with gay, taut smiles on their faces surrounding the tables. The women's eyes were sparkling with the expectation of gratuities.

One woman in particular aided Maman's and my cause. She wore a low-cut red silk dress, a color that perfectly complemented her red hair, rouged cheeks, and crimson lips. Her gown reminded me of my dress. We were physical and astral counterparts, working together in perfect harmony.

As Raoul extended his arm over the table to throw the dice, this mysterious woman snuggled up to his right side. "Do you need luck, Monsieur?" she asked.

"And just what will it cost me?" Raoul asked, nudging her away. The tension in his voice confirmed his disappointment with this evening's progress. Not that I needed such proof. He lost game after game, which ballooned his debt to M. Le Roux. For some reason, Philippe kept staking Raoul.

Because he was passed out drunk at a table about fifty feet from the craps area, Monsieur Le Jaune didn't know his son was gambling away the furniture shipment's profits. Raoul had also downed more liquor courtesy of M. Le Roux. After two bourbons, which nerves had compelled him to consume in under half an hour, Raoul had to clutch the edge of the table for support.

The young woman pouted. "Cost you? If I bring you luck and you wish to reward me, then do so. If not, I'll still have spent the night with a handsome man."

"Ah," Raoul said. With inebriated eyes, he appraised the beautiful woman. I hoped she would bring Raoul the opposite of luck if he let her try. My instincts told me this woman had targeted Raoul for some reason. Why risk her evening's gratuities on him out of all the men in the gambling palace? I knew not. I could only watch the night's events unfold from my astral perch. After a few seconds, Raoul gave her a gallant bow. Or at least a drunken impression of one. "I'm Raoul Le Jaune. At your service."

The woman held out her hand. "Brydie."

"Enchante, Brydie," Raoul said as he kissed her hand.

"So, how is it you propose to bring him luck?" Philippe asked Brydie. "You see, I'm staking the fellow's venture."

"I can blow on the dice," Brydie suggested.

"A wonderful idea." M. Le Roux nestled some coins in her dainty hands. "But first, get bourbons for the three of us. We'll toast this next roll."

"Should we?" Raoul asked. During the entire exchange with Brydie, he'd kept one hand firmly anchored to the table for support.

M. Le Roux slapped Raoul on the back. "Liquid courage, my friend."

Liquid ruin was more like it. At least, that was what I hoped. Brydie soon returned with three generous glasses of bourbon on a tray. On Philippe's cue, all three compatriots clinked their glasses. And while Philippe and Brydie took but a sip, Raoul hurled the liquor down his throat and rested his glass on the edge of the table with an ambitious thump. He tried to concentrate on the confusing array of numbers and colors before him, but his perplexed expression told me he'd failed on that front.

As someone who didn't understand craps, I fared no better at deciphering the game's rules. I watched with bated breath as Raoul threw down the dice at Brydie's urging. From Raoul's plaintive cries after each roll, I knew he was losing. He couldn't wrench himself away from the table despite these losses. In fact, from his optimistic cheer before each role, he appeared to expect a different result each time.

Raoul's calamitous trajectory served my ends nicely, but I still wondered why gamblers threw caution to the wind as they did. I once asked Maman how M. Le Jaune managed to lose so much money gambling. Maman had laughed for a long minute before explaining that many gambling palaces rigged the games in their favor and kept their patrons playing with the promise of riches, the lure of beautiful women, and of course, copious amounts of alcohol. Raoul's experience that night confirmed that gambling palaces manipulated their patrons well. At the same time, with his silver tongue and seemingly limitless resources, Philippe Le Roux was the main force who ushered Raoul toward insolvency.

I no longer doubted Philippe had ulterior motives. He was either a sadistic opportunist or someone with a personal vendetta against the Le Jaune family. Perhaps both. I watched, enthralled, as Philippe took a puff on his cigar, and the hungry ring of flame consumed yet more of the tobacco leaves. He slowly reduced the expensive cigar to ash and smoke with each breath.

I didn't know how much it would cost for Maman's agent to purchase all of the Le Jaune slaves, or if M. Le Jaune was ruined enough to sell them, but we were on a steady path toward that end goal. I cheered Philippe on with all my astral might.

"How much do you want to bet on this round?" M. Le Roux asked Raoul, as if the entire Le Jaune future didn't rest on this throw of the dice. "You owe me two thousand dollars so far."

"Good God!" Raoul faltered and clung with dear life to the table's edge.

Philippe hid his smirk as he steadied Raoul. "Lady Fortuna has been unkind."

Raoul stole a glance at his father, who remained slouched in his chair and snoring. For a moment, I thought Raoul might faint dead away. His face had lost all its color, including its respectable alcoholic flush. But then, Raoul straightened his spine and adjusted his wrinkled cravat. He must've found a hidden well of determination. "Let me wager another thousand," Raoul said. "That should be enough to right my course."

"But of course." M. Le Roux gave Raoul a hearty smile and then waved his hand to get the attention of the person in charge of the table, called the *boxman*, as I'd learned from watching the game. "Please extend my friend another thousand dollars' worth of credit," Philippe said. "You may add it to my tab."

At first, the boxman stared at Philippe as if he'd lost his mind, but when M. Le Roux didn't waver, the boxman shrugged and looked to Raoul. "Do you wish for this credit, Monsieur?"

"I have no choice," Raoul said, his eyes roaming over the table where his fate was splayed out before him as an unintelligible mess of numbers and probabilities. Perhaps his current debt to Philippe would compel M. Le Jaune to sell us to Maman's agent, but the more indebted Raoul was, the better. That's why I did a happy spin in the air when Raoul gave the boxman a nod. "So, yes. I accept Monsieur Le Roux's stake."

Brydie linked her pale arm with Raoul's. "Mon amour, perhaps you should try something different this roll. What is it the Romans used to say? Carpe diem?"

"Carpe diem, indeed!" Raoul boomed, pulling Brydie close. Somehow, he appeared more alert. The spirits only knew the source of this sudden burst of energy. Raoul snapped his fingers until the boxman met his eyes. "Let's simplify this game," Raoul said. "If these dice add up to an even number, I win a thousand dollars. If they total an odd, I lose another thousand. What say you?"

Both Brydie's and M. Le Roux's eyes sparkled at this suggestion, but the boxman remained impassive. "A thousand at once? If you're sure."

"I am sure," Raoul insisted. His words were slightly slurred. He leaned forward, eyes fixed on the boxman. "Will you do it, or do I need to go find your *superiors*?"

Raoul's emphasis on the word superiors earned him a stony glare from the dealer, who thrust the dice into Raoul's hand. "No need, *sir*. I have full authority to run this table as I see fit."

"How daring!" Brydie hopped up and down like a rabbit, clapping her hands. "Let me blow on them!"

Raoul nodded and held the dice out for Brydie. She gave them a delicate blow, christening them with her intentions. Raoul concentrated on the table so fully that deep furrows appeared on his brow. And then, he cast the dice to the night's fickle embrace. I held my astral breath as those two cubes of fate swirled about again and again. They'd determine not only my future but also Raoul's. The dice eventually settled, as all things do, and I strained to see the numbers of dots on each. My astral stomach lurched from the suspense.

One die read three, and the other read four.

Seven in total.

An odd number.

The reactions of the people at the table varied considerably. The boxman looked smug, Brydie excited, and M. Le Roux, triumphant. And, finally, my astral eyes settled Raoul's face, where I saw pronounced horror. "C-can, can we roll again? Double the wager?" he begged Philippe.

"Lady Luck's been indifferent despite your attempts to woo her," Philippe said as he slapped Raoul on the back. "I doubt your father's furniture shipment will earn more than three thousand dollars, so this is the end of our fun."

Brydie hid a smile as she rested her hand on Raoul's. "We should wake your father."

"But he'll kill me," Raoul protested, shaking her away as if she'd scalded him.

"Considering you're his only heir, I very much doubt it," Philippe quipped. He handed Brydie some coins. "Mademoiselle, please get the Le Jaunes some strong coffee. They should be sober for what comes next."

For what comes next. *Justice!* Delicious, beautiful, mouthwatering justice for Papa. M. Le Roux dragged a paralyzed Raoul to the small table where M. Le Jaune still snored away in blissful ignorance.

I gloated as the talented Brydie, while holding two cups of coffee, jostled M. Le Jaune with her hip to awaken him. The man who had murdered my father frowned and slowly opened his eyes as Brydie rested a cup in front of him. He struggled to sit up straight in the chair. But after managing to get himself erect, M. Le Jaune carefully sipped his coffee while Brydie offered Raoul a cup, too.

This mysterious woman then left the Le Jaunes to their fate, and when out of their view, Philippe handed Brydie a small purse. She then pocketed this gift and slipped away with a knowing gleam in her eye. What a surprising evening. Brydie had worked with Philippe to sabotage Raoul.

Brydie. Brydie was another name for Brigid. I froze in the astral ether. Had my dear Maman Brigitte made an appearance? I believed she did. I'd honor her for it later. At the moment, though, more pressing matters needed my attention.

Under the diamond firelight of the chandeliers, I witnessed the two Le Jaune fiends grapple with reality. Monsieur stayed quiet at first, allowing the caffeine to gradually restore his senses. He probably suspected Raoul had lost a great deal. And Raoul? From his somber expression, I gathered he hoped the earth would swallow him up.

"How much did you lose?" M. Le Jaune asked when he finally finished his coffee. "A hundred dollars? Two?"

From his ambitiously low guess, I reckoned M. Le Jaune had lost consciousness soon after Philippe started backing Raoul's losses. I couldn't wait for that murderer to learn the truth. Raoul simply stared at the craps table, prompting M. Le Jaune to wince. "*Three* hundred?" Monsieur asked, his voice numb.

Raoul took another sip of coffee, but his trembling hand sent drops of coffee splattering onto the red tablecloth. At his son's evasive behavior, M. Le Jaune's pained expression morphed into an alarmed one. "Raoul? For the love of God! How much?"

"Three thousand dollars," M. Le Roux replied. His handsome features curled into a smug smile. "Your furniture shipment should cover a small portion of your son's debt. Although you're lacking in cash, you have collateral to sell, I assume?"

M. Le Jaune's eyes flooded with desperation as he processed Philippe's news. When my father's murderer understood the full implications of this news, his grief would *slightly* approach the level of my maman's when she saw her husband murdered.

Although Marie cautioned me against relishing this moment too much, I couldn't help myself. Monsieur Le Jaune's future now only contained ashes. His despair brought me such joy. He had no way out from the prison he had erected for himself, unlike Maman, whom Death would soon release from her misery.

After she lost Papa, Maman had felt agony with every breath. She hadn't truly enjoyed the taste of food, the scent of a spring rain, or, although it pained me to admit, even my company. She navigated her way through life as a walking corpse while her mind and heart lived in the afterlife. I hoped she knew about the night's events. If not, I would witness everything so I could tell her in person.

At Philippe's news, M. Le Jaune's face became the color of a newly minted cadaver. "Tell me he's not serious, Raoul," M. Le Jaune begged.

Beautiful tears, ones that avenged my parents, poured down Raoul's cheeks. "I'm sorry."

"You're *sorry*?" M. Le Jaune bolted up from his chair and towered over his son. "We're ruined! I'll have to extend the loan on Etoile until more furniture is ready and sell your mother's last jewelry to cover this debt. You have to get Vivienne to take you back by any means necessary."

"Yes, Papa," Raoul said, nodding fiercely.

At the mention of Vivienne, M. Le Roux's smile grew even wider. "That won't be happening, Monsieur."

"Raoul will get the stupid girl back," M. Le Jaune shot back as he plopped down on his chair. "We'll extend our loan on the estate, use the furniture shipment's profits to pay you, and sell a slave or two to cover the rest of Raoul's debt and buy Vivienne a necklace. It's what we should've done instead of falling for your poisoned offer."

"You misunderstand." Philippe relaxed in his chair, pulled out another cigar, and lit it. "Vivienne is engaged to *me*."

If astral beings could be gobsmacked, I certainly was. So, *that* was Philippe's motivation for staking Raoul to the point of destitution. From the expressions that erupted on Raoul and M. Le Jaune's faces, one would expect that a unicorn had descended right into the gambling palace, perhaps with a banshee mounted on its back. Raoul's jaw dropped. "What?" he asked.

"Vivienne is my fiancée," Philippe repeated. "*Once again.*"

While Raoul continued to look perplexed, understanding dawned on M. Le Jaune. "So, *you're* the one," he said.

"Exactement," M. Le Roux replied. He took a puff of his cigar and blew a ring of smoke at Raoul. "I was engaged to Vivienne until your father convinced Monsieur Devereaux to break our engagement in favor of your proposal. But immediately after your *indiscretion*, Vivienne convinced her father to let her marry me."

"Considering the size of her dowry, of course, you sabotaged Raoul," M. Le Jaune said, his voice dripping with contempt.

"Raoul sabotaged himself. If he'd have won, I would have honored my part of the bargain." Philippe tapped the ash from his cigar into an ashtray and sent Monsieur a glare icy enough to freeze Lake Pontchartrain clear to the bottom. "As for my motives, I love Vivienne and would cherish her even if she were penniless. She deserves justice for what your family put her through."

Philippe's love for Vivienne brought me joy. But then, I remembered the war clouds on the horizon.

Curious about their future, I glided down and rested my hand on Philippe's shoulder. The astral world then brought me to a townhome in the city. I floated inside and found a family of four seated around a table. At the head of the table sat Philippe, and across from him, Vivienne. They both looked to be about ten years older than in present day. Vivienne dressed well, but not ostentatiously, and she gazed across the table at her husband with absolute love. Two girls sat between them on opposite sides of the table. The family radiated genuine love. Satisfied, I thought of the gambling palace so my astral body could see what happened next in the Le Jaune saga.

"For what we put Vivienne through? I would have treated her well had she married me," Raoul said.

"I doubt that very much," M. Le Roux said. He stood and looked back and forth between Raoul and M. Le Jaune. "I assume you'll fulfill your obligations. It would be a shame if you didn't."

Shame. A word steeped with so much meaning. On one hand, if Raoul didn't pay his debt, he would taint his family name with more dishonor than his father had already earned for it. But *shame* had more sinister connotations, too.

I recalled Tante Jeanne's story of her fiancé, also named

Philippe. Tante's brother had challenged her fiancé to a duel, and Tante's love had died. I didn't know if Philippe even planned to meet Raoul under the Dueling Oaks, perhaps the city's most notorious site for settling gentlemanly grievances. However, both Raoul and his father understood the implied threat, and considering how disinclined Raoul was toward work and deliberate practice, I doubted he excelled at either swords or pistols. Philippe Le Roux had trapped Raoul and M. Le Jaune.

"You'll get what you're owed," Raoul said. His words held bravado, but his slumped shoulders told me otherwise. "I'm a gentleman, after all."

"We'll bring you the proceeds from the shipment tomorrow evening," M. Le Jaune added through gritted teeth. His eyes burned with intense hatred, much like they had before he murdered my father. Only now, he was the powerless one.

"I'll come to Etoile tomorrow evening myself and save you the trouble," Philippe gave M. Le Jaune a condescending wink. "Lest you gamble it away."

And with that, Philippe Le Roux spun around and left a pair of devastated Le Jaunes in his wake. Despite this night's blissful turn of events, I still wasn't sure if M. Le Jaune would be forced to sell all of his slaves, not when he could potentially extend the loan on Etoile and pay some of Raoul's debt with the furniture shipment. Had he mortgaged all of Etoile or just part of it? I didn't know.

I silenced my doubts and trusted in the spirits, a frustratingly passive endeavor at times. Thankfully, I didn't need to wait long for reassurance that the loa still worked on my behalf. M. Le Jaune and Raoul immediately ordered another few rounds of drinks, a stupid thing considering that alcohol had contributed to their ruinous evening. I watched with pleasure as they downed drink after drink. Then, at around three in the morning, and while still quite inebriated, the Le Jaune men hired a carriage to bring them back to Etoile.

Although M. Le Jaune surely had many condemnations to hurl at Raoul, the alcohol kept him quiet and gave Raoul a much-needed reprieve. But this temporary period of amnesty couldn't last forever. Before the driver fully stopped the carriage in front of the mansion, Raoul eagerly leaped out, almost landing flat on his face. "I'll fix this, Papa. I *promise*," he muttered as he steadied himself against the carriage.

M. Le Jaune stumbled out of the carriage and swung his arm over Raoul's shoulder for support. "Damn right, you will. Now, let's go check the furniture. We need to calculate how much of your debt it will cover."

"I'm tired," Raoul whined.

Monsieur grabbed his son's arm, somehow managing to propel their combined mass steadily toward the storage building. "You can sleep *after* you help me tally the profits."

"I don't even know how to do that," Raoul mumbled. Still, despite these words of protest, my patron let his father all but drag him along.

When they eventually reached the building, M. Le Jaune fumbled with the lock. "Damn it to hell. I can't see. Raoul, do you have a match?"

"What gentleman wouldn't?" Raoul asked. He reached into his breast pocket and fumbled for some matches. He succeeded despite his clumsy movements and handed the matches to his father.

"Good, good," M. Le Jaune said. He struck the match and saw a lantern hanging near the door. After some more unsteady sleight of hand, he managed to light the lantern, which he handed to Raoul as he retrieved the key to the lock. "Here's a lesson, my boy. Always secure your valuables, whether they be furniture, money, or women."

"Always secure your valuables," Raoul repeated.

When his son stumbled a bit, Monsieur snatched the lantern away from Raoul. "Follow me. *Carefully*."

With the firelight to guide them, both men stepped inside the storage building and looked around, their eyes wide as if they were seeing Ali Baba's cave of treasure. To be fair, the cache of furniture was their last bulwark against complete ruin.

The lantern light reflected off something in the corner. I peered closer and thought I saw Baron's glasses and my father's ghost in the shadows. My heart in my throat, I wanted to fly over to them and chatter about the night's events. But something stopped me. They were here for a reason, one that became evident in the next second.

M. Le Jaune tripped and lurched forward, dropping the lantern. The glass shattered, and sparks spread across the straw-covered floor. My eyes darted to the corner. Baron and my father were gone. They had done what they came to do.

With surprising coordination, Raoul then leaped forward, grabbed his father's jacket, and dragged him outside. Straw burns, and varnish helps such kindling combust. The physical fire that mercilessly consumed every stick of furniture in M. Le Jaune's storage shed matched my soul's burning need for justice.

As Raoul and Maurice Le Jaune watched their last remaining hopes go up in flames and smoke, I realized my father's murderer would have no choice but to sell all his slaves. I had my reward. My *justice*. Finally satiated on that front, I thought of my physical body so I could prepare for what was ahead.

CHAPTER TWENTY: JUDGMENT

At the time of the second coming, trumpets will sound, and balance will be restored to the cosmos. Those who await their just rewards will rejoice. When the Judgment card appears in a reading, you should take stock of your life, make amends to those you've wronged, and leave the past behind. Only in transcending our limitations can we move on to the next stage of being.

Selene

November 14, 1860, Etoile, New Orleans

P eople do many things under the pink and yellow skies of daybreak, such as trudging home after a night of gambling, heading off to a long workday, and shaking off the last embers of sleep. To that list, I could add offering up slaves to settle a family's gambling debts.

That was how I ended up seated in a carriage next to an anxious Raoul Le Jaune and headed somewhere mysterious before the crack of dawn. We rode in silence, save for the percussive canter of the horses' hooves thumping on the street.

"Where are we off to so early?" I asked, even though I already knew he'd picked me up at the apartment so his father could sell me, along with the family's other slaves. I still had to play the part of an ignorant girl so Raoul wouldn't grow suspicious of my role in his devastating night of gambling. He already believed I was a witch.

"We're going to Etoile first," Raoul said, shifting uncomfortably next to me. "And as I said, the rest is a surprise."

I touched his hand and continued with my pretense. "How thrilling."

Raoul kept silent. He'd said very little since he'd stormed into the apartment less than an hour ago and ordered me to pack for a spontaneous trip. I'd expected him, of course.

The transition between worlds had been sudden, so in one moment I'd been happily watching my conflagration of justice, and in the next, I'd found myself curled up in bed. Wasting not a second, I'd changed into a fresh calico dress, retrieved my father's cards, and asked Samuel to drive me to Tante Jeanne.

I felt guilty for rapping on the convent's garden door before dawn, but a kind nun named Sister Catherine assured me that everyone had already awoken for early morning prayers. She brought me directly to Tante Jeanne's room, a secluded space near where she kept her bees. To my surprise, I found my aunt awake and counting coins at her desk.

"The bees told me that Raoul and Monsieur's furniture got destroyed and that they lost a lot of money gambling," Tante said in response to my astonished face. "How much?"

I eyed the large pile of coins, hoping she had enough to cover Raoul's debt. "They lost three thousand dollars to a Monsieur Philippe Le Roux."

Tante Jeanne did a quick count of the coins. "Perfect. We'll have some left."

"You got that much from my *lessons*?" I asked.

My aunt laughed softly. "There were many years of lessons, Selene. Like the wise son from the Bible who invested his father's talents in secure ventures, I have done the same."

"Thank you." In addition to a beekeeper of good repute and teacher, my prodigious Tante was a financial maven. I threw my arms around her, almost jostling the piles of coins she'd expertly stacked on the desk. I released her and tried to calculate how much the coins were worth. "Do you think Monsieur will sell everyone for that amount?"

"He will if he wants to keep Raoul alive, and he has no alternative. People die under the Dueling Oaks," Tante Jeanne replied. She looked out her small window at the cloister, her face pinched with sorrow as she likely recalled the death of her beloved.

I didn't have time to waste, so I gave Papa's cards to my dear Tante for safekeeping. She then instructed me to go back to the apartment and wait for Raoul or Monsieur Le Jaune while she gave the money to Father Pierre.

From what I understood, Tante Jeanne planned to send her purchasing agent, Father Pierre, to Monsieur Le Jaune's mansion before daybreak, lest Monsieur rush everyone to the slave market to raise quick funds. Most importantly, Tante Jeanne had told me to act devastated when I found out I'd be sold so I wouldn't implicate myself in the catastrophe that befell the Le Jaunes. Because of Tante Jeanne's wise advice, I'd kept a mask of distress tucked in my little carpetbag, ready to pull out when needed.

As the night surrendered more of its darkness, the carriage ground to a halt in front of Etoile. Raoul jumped out first and held out a damp hand for me. Thankfully, my lace gloves protected me from his sweat.

Acorns crunched beneath my feet like fragile bones as I stepped out of the carriage. Only a few hours had passed since M. Le Jaune's storage building had burned to the ground, so woodsmoke hung on the crisp air and danced with the tendrils of mist that rose from the dewy grass.

Raoul escorted me to the front steps of the portico, where Celeste and nine other people, who I presumed to be M. Le Jaune's other slaves, stood. From their stiff postures, one would expect they planned on receiving Queen Victoria. Either that, or they were simply too terrified to move a muscle. I wanted to greet Celeste with a warm hug, but instead, I knit my brows together. "Is this the surprise you spoke of?" I asked Raoul.

Raoul turned away, and Monsieur Le Jaune emerged from Etoile's main door. "We're selling you all," he said, inching close enough for me to smell the stale alcohol on his breath. "If you make trouble, I'll throw your mother out on the street today. But if you behave, I'll give her a month to find other arrangements."

I didn't have to fake my look of disgust as I pretended to contemplate the offer. "I'll behave," I said.

"Good," my father's murderer said. "Go stand with the others." He then gazed onto Etoile's grand front lawn, his face set in a resigned expression. How long could Monsieur keep Etoile before his creditors called in the loan? Unless a miracle happened and he stopped gambling away every cent that made its way into his grubby fingers, the family was doomed.

Hoping Maman's purchasing agent would soon arrive, I joined Celeste under the portico. I winked at my grandmother when I felt sure Monsieur Le Jaune couldn't see.

"Child, this is a serious matter!" Celeste chided quietly, taking my hand.

"Don't worry," I whispered back softer than a bee's buzz. "Papa's plans are coming to fruition."

Celeste's grip on my hand tightened, and when I stole a glance at her, I saw tears pricking in her eyes. Dare I say she felt hope? She and I had the sound of early morning birds and the beautiful smell of burnt furniture to reassure us of a better future.

That morning, the rising sun painted the sky with luminous pinks, reds, and oranges while the last bits of darkness silhouetted Etoile's live oak trees against that fiery canvas. Despite last night's wondrous events, my heart quickened. I prayed Tante Jeanne had enough time to enact her plans. What if M. Le Jaune sold us to someone other than Father Pierre?

Have faith, I reminded my anxious brain. *You've seen evidence that the spirits are working in your favor, so trust in them.*

And then, as if to answer my prayers, a wagon turned onto

Etoile's semicircular avenue. That buggy stood out as a black shadow against the pink dawn. I held my breath as I struggled to identify the shadowy driver. I prayed with all my might that it was Father Pierre. During the long seconds it took for the wagon to crawl toward the portico, this person remained shrouded in the morning's remaining shadows.

Some people cower when afraid, but others become defiant. My grandmother must have felt bold that day. "Who the devil did you sell us to this early?" she asked Monsieur.

"Quiet," Monsieur said, glaring at Celeste. "I'm giving you to the bastard who cheated us, not sending you to the slave market, although he might do just that."

Philippe? We were going with Philippe, not Father Pierre. Something had gone wrong with Tante Jeanne's plan. M. Le Jaune must have contacted Philippe and told him about the fire, offering us up instead of charred furniture to fulfill Raoul's debt. Had Father Pierre even spoken with Philippe? I had no idea. My mind spun as I wondered how to convince Philippe to sell us to Father Pierre. A planter didn't need artisans, after all.

Finally, the wagon came close enough for me to see the driver. Sure enough, none other than Philippe Le Roux drove the wagon. Damn it all to Perdition. He halted the wagon in front of the mansion. "*Whooaa there,*" he told the horses, his voice piercing through the nervous silence.

"Is this part of the plan?" Celeste whispered to me.

"All will be well." I squeezed her hand and prayed I hadn't just lied to her. At the very worst, we'd end up captives of M. Le Roux or some other bastard until the upcoming war freed us. We'd then carefully bide our time. Maman's long years of effort would be in vain, but we couldn't help that.

"A pity about the fire," M. Le Roux taunted as he jumped out of the wagon.

Monsieur Le Jaune cleared his throat. "As I said at your place, I have eleven slaves. The eight men are skilled artisans. If you don't want to sell furniture, they'll work in the fields or drive your buggy. And the two older women can cook and clean house," he said, pointing to my grandmother, and Beatrice, the housekeeper I recognized from my father's visions.

Philippe stopped in front of each of us, assessing our potential with his stare. When he reached me, he stopped. "What does this one do? I hope something useful, or you're still in my debt."

Even poisonous seeds will grow if given time and an environment toxic enough to nourish them. The dirty seed M. Le Jaune had planted in Raoul's heart last night had finally sprouted in all its glory. Raoul's face darkened just like a thundercloud rolling in off the Gulf of Mexico. "She's the whore that *your* bitch, Vivienne, saw me with."

Confronting Philippe thus was hardly the smartest thing Raoul could have done in his position. At least I wasn't that stupid or destructive. But what if Philippe punished me? He didn't know of my role in helping his and Vivienne's cause.

To calm my worries, I breathed deeply and focused on a large oak tree in the garden. And then, I saw something amazing in the Spanish moss as the morning breeze rifled through it. My father's ghost. He gave me an encouraging smile, a gesture that slowed my racing heart.

What I saw next froze my blood. Maman materialized out of the ether and linked her arm with his. She could astral project? I hadn't known. Then again, she had witch's blood flowing through her veins. Tante Jeanne must've told Maman about the plan, after which point my mother had decided to watch the proceedings from the astral world. She deserved to see what her years of sacrifice had yielded. I couldn't wait to see her in person after this ordeal was complete so we could talk without the burden of her troubles.

I nudged Celeste and nodded toward my parents. I knew my grandmother saw them when her face lit up like the rising sun. From his position under the tree, my father whispered, "You'll all soon be free." Some benevolent magic was afoot, and I needed to let it work.

"For the love of God, Raoul, be quiet!" M. Le Jaune cried before turning to Philippe. "Have her extract the dye from your damn indigo plants or sell her to a whorehouse. Your choice."

I bristled at the word *whorehouse*. Not on Philippe's life would that happen. I leveled my gaze with his, hoping he'd understand my intent. Oddly, though, I saw a humorous twinkle in his eyes. "What's your name?" he asked.

I stole a glance at my parents standing near the oak tree. Papa nodded. Apparently, he wanted me to play along with M. Le Roux's odd game. "Selene," I replied.

"Will you take her and cancel Raoul's debt?" M. Le Jaune asked.

Philippe scanned the crowd in front of him as if debating the offer, drawing out Monsieur's agony. Finally, he nodded. "We have a bargain as soon as you give me their papers."

It's strange that something as insignificant as paper can serve as legal currency for the totality of a human life—from its blood, bone, and spirit, to the entire compilation of its loves and heartaches. *Paper* had the power to determine one's very right to live and breathe.

I held my breath as our ownership papers, which M. Le Jaune had at the ready in a dossier, went into Philippe's hands. In exchange, Philippe handed M. Le Jaune a receipt that absolved Raoul of his debts. Just like that, pieces of paper light enough for a breeze to carry away transformed the very trajectories of our lives.

"I have a good feeling," Celeste said under her breath.

I did as well. For reassurance, I looked at the tree where my parents hovered. They smiled once more before dissolving in the morning air. The spirit world, in the form of gods, goddesses, loas, angels, spirits, and saints, guided everyone who sought aid. We were so close to freedom—an eventuality that I could taste on my tongue and hear from the spirits whistling through the trees.

However, true freedom required an unburdened heart and the propensity to let go. Was I ready to let go of the hate I had for M. Le Jaune? I closed my eyes, and a wave of peace settled over my anger-choked heart. When I exhaled my breath, I concentrated on releasing my hatred. My grief then evaporated with the morning dew. Without that burden of hate, I opened my eyes. Somehow, the world seemed brighter.

Philippe yanked down the back gate of the freight wagon. "Climb in."

As much as I'd enjoyed seeing M. Le Jaune fume during his exchange with Philippe, my stomach heaved at Philippe's command. M. Le Roux had brought a freight wagon to haul us to our next destination, much like potatoes, cotton, or his precious indigo. He was a slave owner, someone who didn't see us as human beings with hopes and dreams.

I didn't begrudge him a future with Vivienne, but I had no sympathy for the fact that he'd likely lose a fortune by the end of the war. My feelings about M. Le Roux were complicated to say the least. I had no other choice but to trust the spirits that the day would turn out well, though.

One of the artisans climbed into the wagon first and held out his hands for the others. When it was my turn, I clasped his hand and leaped into the wagon, eager to leave Etoile and my family's legacy of trauma behind forever.

Everyone crammed together on the wagon's floor, not daring to speak that close to M. Le Jaune's ears. We plodded along. And when the wagon finally reached Etoile's exit, I braved one last look at that horrible place. The morning sun rose behind Raoul, casting a red halo around his head. His eyes had remained fixed on the wagon ever since it pulled away. Even though I couldn't see the hate stifling his vision, I knew it lingered deep in his soul. He blamed everything on me and Vivienne. He likely wouldn't develop any self-awareness before he met his fate on the battlefield. *Good riddance*, I thought, turning away from Etoile forever.

The man to my right shook his head in resignation. "Another place, another pile of horseshit," he said in a low voice.

Before this remark, Philippe had been concentrating on the road ahead, likely relishing his triumph over the Le Jaunes. After the word *horseshit*, though, he shot a glance over his shoulder. "What's your name, friend?"

"Anson," the man replied, his voice wary.

"Well, Anson, it's not the regular horseshit this time," M. Le Roux said. "Believe it or not at your own pleasure, but I'm selling you to a priest who plans to manumit you."

Anson frowned, but my nervous heart welcomed the rush of relief. Tante's plan had worked. "Jeanne found you?" I asked.

Philippe tipped his hat. "A beekeeper who lived at a convent and a priest sure did," he said. "They came to my door right after that Le Jaune bastard left. Offered to buy you after I picked you up. I was more than happy to oblige."

How Tante Jeanne had known to go to Philippe's home at the moment she did, I had no idea. Probably the spirits or her bees. "I'm glad of that," I told him.

"Jeanne also told me Vivienne found you with Raoul, and that's what allowed her to break the engagement. I'm in your debt for that alone." Philippe hesitated, as if considering his next words. "And this might sound peculiar, but I also think you had a role in last night's events. Vivi told me she knew to go to your apartment because of a dream."

Philippe left that implication hanging in the air. I debated how much of the truth to tell him, weighing the consequences of a full confession as the horse cantered along. He'd already promised he'd sell us to Father Pierre, so I figured he deserved an honest answer. Still, I didn't want to implicate Vivienne's workings with Marie in case she wanted that to remain secret. Women deserved to keep their special workings private. "I saw what happened last night in a *dream*," I said. "I prayed Vivienne would come to my apartment so she could find me with Raoul. I knew he planned on using her for her dowry."

"Well, your prayers must've sent Vivi that dream," Philippe said, chuckling softly. "I've never been much for praying, but I had a dream that told me to go to the same gambling palace as the Le Jaunes and to pay that girl Brydie for her help. A man named David with eyes like yours told me I'd get Vivi back if I listened."

Celeste, who sat on my left, gripped my arm tightly as my

breath caught in my throat. Papa had saved us. He'd worked with the spirits to sort through the chaos of human intentions and actions, somehow leading to our salvation. I leaned back against the side of the wagon, grateful for the spirits' help. Anson nudged me. "I don't understand. Why is this priest going to free us?" he asked.

"David and Colleen arranged it," my grandmother said. She leaned closer to me. "Selene's their daughter. Her parents worked from beyond the grave to help us, and now they're finally together."

Celeste's words cut me to the bone. *They're finally together.* Maman hadn't been astral projecting. She was *dead.* I let out a choked cry, and Celeste pulled me to her as the horse ferried us swiftly through a world of sweetgrass and morning cicadas.

I needed a sign, any sign at all, that things would be fine. And then the spirits brought me that particular comfort. When we turned a bend in the road, the muddy Mississippi River came into view, glowing in the creeping dawn like a sinuous golden ribbon.

My parents once had the chance to escape along that river until a man, now a ruined man, killed Papa and dumped his body in a swamp. Thankfully, his spirit wasn't forced to wander that haunted bayou with other ghosts. Instead, he and Maman found a blessed place in the afterlife. My mother deserved her reward after she had endured M. Le Jaune all those years.

Based on how happy she looked standing next to Papa at the oak tree, I knew that keeping her bound to this earthly plane would be selfish. Tears tracked down my cheeks as I remembered how she looked more alive as a ghost than when she'd breathed on this Earth.

My heart thumped like a hummingbird's wings. The sound of the horse's hooves striking the pavement filled up the space in my soul. As the wagon sped through the early morning streets of New Orleans on the way to the convent, I tried to commit to memory every last detail of this city. I'd miss its secluded court-yard and walled cemeteries, as well as the smells of early frost and coffee hanging on the breeze. But I didn't mind leaving behind the scents of animal dung or old vegetables rotting in the gutter.

Eager for any distraction from my grief over Maman's death, I let the pastel homes, starchy palmettos, and graceful live oaks subsume me until we reached the convent. The ride didn't take long. When Philippe stopped the wagon, I hopped out and knocked on the garden door. Tante Jeanne threw the door open. Her face, which was laced with heartbreak, confirmed what I already knew. "You'll see your maman again with your father in the garden of stone houses," Tante Jeanne said as she took me in her arms.

CHAPTER TWENTY-ONE: THE WORLD

When this card appears, you've completed this phase of your journey. Bask in the joy of your fulfillment, and take the time to savor your victory. Although change is inevitable, you should pause and enjoy the rest you've earned.

Selene

January 15, 1861, Gloucester, MA

The war drums of the future pounded in my ears as I walked down Main Street, a basket of gifts dangling on my right arm and a lantern in my left hand. I rested the basket and light on the ground so I could pull my cloak tighter around my body. That gesture was a small comfort against the wind blowing in from the North Atlantic.

However, I believe small comforts are still worthy of the name despite their diminutive size. I could have hired a carriage to take me from our new mercantile to the beach, but it was only a mile away. I relished the journey on such a magical night.

Snowy air swirled around me like a tornado, yet part of the sky remained clear. The bright rising moon also made the snow-flakes glow blue like fairy lights. Picking up my basket and lantern once again, I descended the hill, my path also illuminated by gas lights. The town's homes and shops danced down the hill all the way to the shore and docks. Even in the chill, I marveled at the bare beauty of the winter vista unfolding before me. We were lucky to have settled here.

The four of us arrived in Gloucester not long ago with select possessions and enough funds to purchase a small store with an apartment above it. To my surprise, Philippe Le Roux simply handed us all over to Tante Jeanne and told her to divide her money among everyone equally, so that we could begin new lives. I hadn't anticipated that action one iota. Perhaps Philippe had heard the war drums, too, and wanted to bolster his luck with good works before chaos descended on the South.

That night had also yielded another surprise. Tante Jeanne had been with Maman as she drew her last breath, and Maman had told her to visit M. Le Roux instead of having Father Pierre go to Etoile. That's why Philippe arrived at Etoile instead of Father Pierre. My mother had learned this from Papa in a dream. The universe was like an intricate clock. When things ran smoothly, they ran smoothly indeed.

Fate turned out well for all of M. Le Jaune's former slaves. Most of them used their share of the money to start new lives in Ohio, New York, or faraway Canada. Anywhere they felt safe.

As for Tante Jeanne, Celeste, Patrice, and me, we combined our funds to buy our little mercantile and apartment. The four of us formed a unique quartet, and we each contributed to our little household. Patrice ran the mercantile and gave lessons in mathematics. She also worked as a bookkeeper for the seamstress next door and was writing a book on the stars. Celeste baked delicious goods to sell at the store, and Tante Jeanne and I gave lessons to the town's children in subjects other than mathematics. All in all, we had a simple, yet happy, existence. More importantly, our home felt safe and cozy in the firelight during the cold Massachusetts nights. Patrice's parents would soon join us, too. They also heard the war drums and planned on leaving Louisiana as soon as they sold their property.

Because New Orleans was so dangerous for us all, Father

Pierre and Tante Jeanne orchestrated almost immediate transportation out of the city. We took a steamboat north on the Mississippi River all the way from New Orleans to Pittsburgh, a trip that took just over two weeks. Although we meandered along the river pleasantly, I didn't truly relax until disembarking in Pittsburgh. Black clouds of coal dust tinged the air in that industrial city and barreled into our lungs. But, thankfully, we soon rode a train to Boston and then hired a wagon to drive us to Gloucester. Why this particular town? Tante Jeanne read about this store, which had been advertised for sale in a Boston paper. It looked just like the one in my dream.

As Good Harbor Beach came into view, the low-hanging yellow moon shone like a gold coin over the water, and near the shoreline, branches of bare trees crisscrossed the sky. I chose the beach because Maman and Papa had dreamed of visiting one together while they lived. M. Le Jaune had robbed them of that simple dream.

After my mother died, Tante Jeanne had placed her in the same tomb that held the straw with Papa's blood on it. They were together in death, just like Tristan and Isolde. I wasn't sure if two interlocked plants grew from in front of my parents' shared tomb. It didn't matter, though. Not when they would now have eternity together.

The sound of waves crashing on the rocky perimeter of the beach roared louder as I neared the sea. I crossed the snow-laced sand until I found a place to set down the basket and lantern. As snowflakes accumulated on my boots, I pulled out the gifts for the loas and asked the winter wind to bring my parents. I saw movement down at the other end of the beach a few minutes later. They then drifted out of the night, happy and vibrant amid the swirling snowflakes.

In this whaling and fishing town, the sea held many tales of woe, of sailors lost and women pacing their widow's walks until they wore grooves in the floorboards. But not on that beach at that moment. I saw only joy radiating from my parents' eyes, their hands intertwined like the branches from Tristan and Isolde's graves.

"Are you in a happy place?" I asked, my throat tight. I already knew the answer, but those of us left on Earth needed confirmation from the dead.

"We are, mon petit," Papa said.

Maman looked up at him, her ghostly eyes burning with far more life in death than they ever had before. "He's right, Selene. Are *you* happy?"

"Of course," I smiled. Why wouldn't I be happy? I was free, and Patrice was with me, as she should be. From the visions my father sent me, I found out that Maman already knew about my love for Patrice, and that she supported me fully in that endeavor.

"Enjoy this time and relax," my father said. "There are some more challenges ahead—if you want to take them."

I frowned in that snowy, moon-filled darkness. "Challenges?"

"Help with the war effort. But only if you want to," Maman replied.

Although I'd had enough excitement and drama to last a lifetime, others still lived in bondage. Would I want to get involved in the conflict between the North and South? I wondered what I could possibly *do*. My parents, who'd both been waiting for my response, gave me reassuring smiles. "Don't think about it now," Papa said. "There'll be time enough for that later."

I was far too weary to launch myself into another conflict at the moment, so I heeded my father's advice and let my worries and fears drift away with the ocean tides. I'd have time to think about the future down the road. My parents hadn't had the luxury of simply spending time with one another as they deemed fit, and I wouldn't allow that to happen with Patrice. I'd appreciate the gifts I'd been given properly. When the time came, I would entertain the idea of a more exciting, and perhaps dangerous, path. I looked to my parents and smiled, knowing I'd have their guidance from beyond the grave when needed. Ever since Maman Brigitte and Baron Samedi drifted in through my bedroom window all those years ago, I'd never been truly alone.

ACKNOWLEDGEMENT

I owe a great debt to Lisa Jordan and Erik Evans at Chandra Press. You both believed in this project, and I thank you so much for your magical tweaks-of-all-sorts throughout the process. In addition, I send tons of appreciation to my beta-readers, Halo Scot and A.C. Merkel. Thank you, also, A. Craig for the awesome Louisiana feedback. Thank you, all!

ABOUT THE AUTHOR

Anya Pavelle

Anya Pavelle was born in Massachusetts but eventually settled
in Florida, where she currently
lives with her husband and dog.
She's a trained art historian
who sees the quiet beauty in nature, art, and literature. Anya
has been imagining new worlds
since she was six years old and
like many morbidly curious
people, she's obsessed with dys-
topian literature. The Moon
Hunters is her first foray into science fiction. She's currently
working on the sequel and also plans on writing a prequel. In
addition to writing, Anya loves traveling the world, SCUBA div-
ing, relaxing with her friends and family, and finally, curling up
with a new book and a glass of wine on a moon-lit humid night.

BOOKS BY THIS AUTHOR

The Moon Hunters

For fans of The Hunger Games, Divergent, and The Gender Game comes a captivating new story like no other.

The Pestilence sweeps the globe with terrifying speed. A group of survivors finds an island sanctuary.

Three generations later, no one has heard from the outside world in years. The old radio only crackles with static. The Pestilence either finished its job or the world tore itself apart.

In the Village of Lehom, Leilani has been called to court as a Virtue by the King. Going to court means losing her independence and self-respect. Unfortunately, she doesn't have a choice.

Leilani decides to take a stand; the King be damned. She plans a daring escape and sets in motion a series of events that will shake the foundation of her village and the island to its core.

Made in the USA
Monee, IL
09 February 2021